Rave reviews for Fiona Buckley and *Queen's Ransom*

"Now is a nice time for Tudor fans to light a flambeau, reach for some sweetmeats, and curl up with *Queen's Ransom*."
—*USA Today*

"Buckley's amusingly modern characters mesh successfully with the well-researched plot."
—*Publishers Weekly*

"Quick pacing, a sympathetic and modern heroine, and political intrigue make this sixteenth-century mystery series as complicated and charming as an Elizabethan knot garden."
—*The Tampa Tribune*

"An excellent historical."
—*Library Journal*

"Ursula is the essence of iron cloaked in velvet—a heroine to reckon with."
—*Kirkus Reviews*

QUEEN'S RANSOM

A Mystery at Queen Elizabeth I's Court
Featuring Ursula Blanchard

Fiona Buckley

POCKET BOOKS
New York London Toronto Sydney

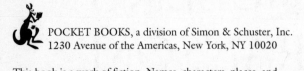 POCKET BOOKS, a division of Simon & Schuster, Inc.
1230 Avenue of the Americas, New York, NY 10020

This Pocket Books trade paperback edition May 2008

For information about special discounts for bulk purchases,
please contact Simon & Schuster Special Sales @ 1-800-456-6798
or business@simonandschuster.com.

Manufactured in the United States of America

10 9 8 7 6 5 4 3 2 1

Library of Congress Cataloging-in-Publication Data is available.

ISBN-13: 978-0-7434-8909-6
ISBN-10:   0-7434-8909-8

For Dalip

QUEEN'S
RANSOM

CHAPTER 1

Treasured Memories

Sir Robin Dudley, Master of the Queen's Horse, had broad
shoulders and swarthy good looks, a dashing taste in doublets,
and a great deal of personal charm. I was a young woman of
only twenty-seven and I ought to have found him attractive.

Instead, I detested him.

He wasn't a kindly man, for one thing, and I appreciated
kindness. The uncle and aunt who saw to most of my upbring-
ing had so conspicuously lacked it.

And for another thing, Dudley came of a family so fiercely
ambitious that his father and one of his brothers had lost their
heads for plotting against their sovereign, and Robin once
came near to plotting against her himself.

Queen Elizabeth knew this perfectly well, but remarkable
individual though she was, in this respect she was the one who
was conventional, while I was not. Dudley's masculine beauty
entranced her and at twenty-eight, not much older than I was
myself, she was not yet hard enough to have that handsome
head and that muscular set of shoulders separated by the executioner's ax. She and Robin were not lovers, but he was still
her favorite.

There were those who looked on her liking for him with a
sentimental eye; for instance, Sir Henry Sidney, who had married Dudley's sister. Well, Sidney had the virtue of kindness

but in him it sometimes went too far. As Sir William Cecil, the Secretary of State, once said to me in a private fit of exasperation, Sidney was too sweet-natured for his own good and every now and then his intelligence drowned in the sweetness like a wasp in a jam pot. "On this business of the queen and Dudley," Sir William said furiously, "Sidney is a simpleton."

The majority of the council members were not simpletons and they were anxious. My immunity to Robin's attractions was useful to them. For although I was outwardly just a Lady of the Presence Chamber, I also took a wage from Cecil for (among other tasks) keeping an eye on Sir Robin Dudley and reading his correspondence whenever I got the chance. As a way of earning a living, it sometimes hurt my finer feelings, but somebody had to do it, for Elizabeth's sake.

I should be honest, though. I owe Robin something. In 1560, eighteen months after Elizabeth took the throne, I came to her court as a widow with next to no money. My husband was dead of the smallpox, and I had a small daughter to rear. I entered the risky but remunerative world of spying through an errand that Dudley asked me to do, and because of that, I was thereafter able to pay for the clothes and education that would give my little Meg a chance in the world.

Then, in 1562, quite by chance, and without ever knowing it, he could be said to have saved a life that was dear to me. But for Dudley and his ambitious skulduggery, there would have been no royal inspection of the Tower treasury that March, and the result could well have been tragedy.

Elizabeth was no fool. She had forgiven Dudley for his scheming, but it had disturbed her deeply, all the same. What Dudley had done was to tell the Spanish ambassador that he wanted to marry the queen, but feared this would be such an unpopular move that there might be a rising. If so, would Philip of Spain oblige the lovebirds with an army, if in return they promised to bring England back to the Catholic Church?

We learned, much later, that good-hearted Sir Henry Sidney, anxious for his queen's happiness, had actually encouraged Dudley in this lunacy. It was the Spanish ambassador, Bishop de Quadra, who refused to take it seriously. It came to nothing. But it was not forgotten.

Sometimes, walking with her ladies, Elizabeth was more candid than she was even with her councillors, perhaps because we were women like herself. On that afternoon near the end of February, when she was strolling in the garden of Greenwich with me and Lady Katherine Knollys, she suddenly spoke of the matter. "My father would have had Robin's head for it," she said frankly. She rubbed a hand across her brow. Elizabeth was occasionally subject to violent headaches, and she had woken with one that morning. It had only just subsided. I sympathized, for I was sometimes a victim of the same malady. "But I was loath to lose my sweet Robin," she said, and then sighed.

I had never told Elizabeth what I thought of her sweet Robin but she knew, all the same. There was still a line between her golden-brown eyes, left there by the pain of the headache, but she gave me a challenging look.

"He is devoted to me," she said, "and devotion can make fools even of strong men. He will not be so foolish again, nor will Sidney. Though Sidney meant no harm; he was only trying to help, however misguidedly. Whereas Robin—is ambitious."

Ambition could have much the same effect as devotion. Dudley was probably drawn to her as much by her royal power and the dream of sharing it, as by her slender, enigmatic person. Elizabeth, I thought, probably knew that, too.

Sir Henry came into the garden at that moment, as though Elizabeth had conjured him up by mentioning his name. She raised a hand in greeting and he stepped across the grass to join us, a neatly made man, not tall, but athletic in his movements. He had red-brown hair and a tidily trimmed auburn beard, and a liking for russet-colored clothes, which went with his coloring. He made his bow with grace, sweeping his tall hat from his head.

"Ma'am. Are you recovered, then? I heard that this morning you were unwell."

"I was. But yes, I am better now. I have been worried, however."

"Indeed? Can I help at all, ma'am?"

"Perhaps," said Elizabeth, but walked on for a while in silence, her long skirt, blue silk with little yellow fleur-de-lis embroidered on it, swishing gently on the scythed grass. Sir Henry fell in on one side of her while Lady Katherine and I walked on the other. Lady Katherine was there because she was Elizabeth's cousin and one of her closest friends and I was there because I was soon to leave the court for a while and Elizabeth said she would claim the company of her dear Ursula while she could.

A chilly wind blew up and died away before Elizabeth at length said: "I am worried because of that sorry business last year when Robin thought of asking Spain to further his matrimonial aspirations by force of arms."

Sir Henry went slightly pink with embarrassment.

"I much regret what he did," she said, "not least because he may have planted a seed that could one day grow. It has been much on my mind. De Quadra did not respond this time but nevertheless, would it not be wise to find a way of making sure that Spain thinks of England as a place too strong ever to attack?"

"There could never be any harm in showing England to

be a strong and well-ordered realm," Sidney said carefully.

"Or a solvent one," said Elizabeth. "But we need subtlety. A parade of men and weapons could impress, but it's too obvious. De Quadra must not think we fear his master. We want a graceful hint, perhaps disguised as a pleasant occasion."

We were being invited to offer ideas. "A state banquet?" suggested Lady Katherine. "With costly entertainments and perfumed candles, and a full array of gold plate?"

"The good bishop has attended several of those already," said Elizabeth dryly. "On one occasion, I actually saw him weighing a gold dish in his hand, obviously wondering how pure the metal was. I half-expected him to wrap it in a napkin and steal it away to be assayed. Well, I have heard that Philip of Spain has had some of his gold plate melted down to keep himself out of debt . . ."

"Really?" said Sir Henry. "The council has not been told of that."

"It was a rumor," said Elizabeth. "Hearsay. But I suspect it's true, all the same. My own position is happier than Philip's and my gold plate is all it should be. Yet a sovereign could keep gold plate for show and still have an empty treasury . . ."

"But, ma'am," said Sidney, "your treasury is surely far from empty."

"That is true," said Elizabeth. "But De Quadra hasn't seen it." There was a pause, while we walked another ten yards. Then she observed in pensive tones: "A well-filled treasury is a sign that a ruler can pay and equip an army. Display the treasury, and one would not need to parade the army. Yes. I will speak to my Lord Treasurer tomorrow."

It was to be an informal royal inspection of the treasury in the Tower of London. The queen would be accompanied by Sir

Robin Dudley, by his brother-in-law Sir Henry Sidney, by her favorite ladies, including Lady Katherine and myself, and by selected guests such as the French and Spanish ambassadors. There was to be no ceremony.

This meant in practice that Sir William Paulet, the treasurer, and Sir Richard Sackville, the undertreasurer, and a horde of minions spent days in advance in the Wardrobe Tower where the bulk of the treasure was housed, lining shelves with black velvet, burnishing choice items with soft cloths, arranging them on stands that would display them to advantage, and laying strips of blue carpet to provide Elizabeth with a pathway around the display.

It also meant that within the Tower enclosure, the informal escort for the royal party consisted of the lieutenant of the Tower, the gentleman porter, three yeomen warders, Sir William Paulet, Sir Richard Sackville, two gentlemen from each of their households, and two trumpeters, who went ahead to announce the queen's approach. There were a couple of page boys in attendance, too, to run errands, hold doors, and pick up anything that was dropped, and the whole business had been carefully rehearsed half a dozen times over the previous morning.

Rehearsal was needed, though, because the occasion was unusual. Having once been imprisoned in the Tower, Elizabeth disliked the place and rarely visited it, splendid though it was, and is. It would be better named the Towers, plural, for it contains any number of them. There's the White Tower, which is the keep in the middle; there are towers dotted all around the huge encircling walls and over the gatehouse; and there's the Wardrobe Tower, standing alone at the southeast corner of the keep. After a brief pause to take wine in the lieutenant's lodgings, and a side excursion, as it were, to inspect the queen's jewel house and admire her regalia and her personal gold and silver plate, we set about the serious business of the day, which began with the gold and silver bullion ingots in the basement of the Wardrobe Tower.

"Please take care on the steps, ma'am. They're steep," Paulet said anxiously. Paulet himself was elderly and had rheumatic joints. He didn't come down with us. Sackville, however, though middle-aged himself, was fitter and acted as guide. Flambeaux in wall sconces lit the way as we descended. Dudley, just behind the queen, kept a hand under her elbow. Sidney stepped down lissomely, but the French ambassador almost tripped, and muttered a Gallic oath under his breath, while short, dapper De Quadra murmured a warning to his colleague that the stairs were worn in the middle. The flambeaux threw misshapen shadows, which glided over the stone of the walls, and although the staircase was dry, there was a river smell about the place. It was cold.

I didn't like it any more than Elizabeth did. It reminded me too much of an earlier visit I had made to the Tower to see a condemned man. My work could send men to their deaths, and sometimes accusing faces appeared in my dreams. In some ways, I, too, needed to be harder than I was.

We crowded into a torch-lit underground vault where ingots of precious metal were stacked like firewood along one wall. Elizabeth, oh so casually, asked Sackville what the total estimated value of the ingots came to, and then repeated the answer in Spanish and French for the benefit of the two ambassadors, apparently out of courtesy but in reality to make sure they'd got it right.

Listening to this piece of dulcet political maneuvering, I thought, once again, how weary I was of intrigue and how glad I was that I would soon be on my way to France, free for a while to keep my nose out of other people's business. Indeed, I seemed lately to have lost my skill in investigation. I would gladly have left the court forever, except that I needed the money for my darling Meg. And if disenchantment with intrigue wasn't my only reason for going, well, the other was foolish and I wouldn't confess it, even to myself.

We climbed back to the daylight and up some more steps, easier ones this time, into a chamber where sunshine streamed through tall, slender windows to sparkle on the treasures so carefully arranged there. This was better. We moved along the azure carpet, marveling at spectacular sets of gold and silver plate, silver spoons with exquisite chasing, salts and candlesticks, gemmed boxes and figurines, ceremonial arms and armor . . .

Elizabeth had beckoned the ambassadors to her side and without any prompting from Paulet or Sackville was artlessly telling them the history of this and that, dropping in further references to the extraordinary value of the items.

"In an emergency, they would be sold or melted down, of course, but as you saw, our stores of bullion should make that unnecessary. We can keep these works of art and thereby honor the skill of the craftsmen . . ."

Dudley had drifted away from the queen and was talking to one of Sackville's gentlemen, commenting on a recent court scandal. "The girl was a perfect fool. There she was, as pregnant as a waxing moon, with no proof of her marriage because the so-called husband was abroad; she'd lost the document he gave her that acknowledged her as his wife; she didn't know the name of the clergyman who married them, and the only witness died last year . . ."

"I know who he means." Sir Henry Sidney had moved to my side. "Personally, I pity her. A silly girl—but she was deep in love and I daresay she believed that she was married."

"I know who she is, too," I said. "And I pity her as well, even though I don't like her very much."

But Dudley clearly had no sympathy for her at all. As I said, unlike his brother-in-law, he was not kindly.

And because the girl who was so obviously not an object of his concern had once figured importantly in one of the intrigues that were so much a part of my life, the thought of her was like that descent into the treasury basement, bringing back insistent memories that I didn't want.

Once, I had had an alternative to this life of intrigue. The smallpox had killed Meg's father, my first husband, Gerald Blanchard, but I had married again. I had been in love and it should have been a good match, but a matter of conscience had forced us to part. Nowadays, I used my former married name, that of Mistress Blanchard, and I kept Matthew's wedding ring in my jewel box and wore instead the one Gerald had given me.

And that was that, I said to myself fiercely. I had made my choice. I was a wantwit even to think about Matthew these days. My life was here at court and although I was about to go away for a while, I knew I must return in due course and go on with my work and be grateful that I had it. Be content with that, Ursula.

"And here," said Paulet, leading the way to the next array of exhibits, "we have ceremonial weapons and mail. This corselet, heavily embossed, and inlaid with a pattern of enamel and gilding, is of German manufacture—it was made in Nuremberg, to be precise—and this one . . ."

The shelves and tables on this side were set out with ornamental breastplates and helmets, swords and curved Oriental scimitars, their hilts and scabbards all sparkling with gems. Sir Henry and I found ourselves in the company of Sir Richard

Sackville. He was stiff in manner, and had an affected habit of using turns of phrase left over from the last century, but I liked him. He did not know of my work for Cecil and the queen (few people did; not even Sir Henry, who was so high in Elizabeth's confidence), but both he and Paulet knew quite a lot about my background, for they knew the man for whom Gerald had formerly worked.

"Since good Bishop de Quadra is among us," Sackville murmured, "we thought it wisest not to enlarge upon the means by which some of these objects came hence. But that corselet there may interest you, Mistress Blanchard." He pointed to the expensively adorned affair from Nuremberg. "Made in Germany it may have been, but it was ordered for the armory of the Spanish administration in Antwerp. It's one of two thousand corselets taken from thence by divers tricks and strategems, and brought across to England."

"Where are the rest of the two thousand?" inquired Sir Henry with interest.

"We shall see them as the last part of this visit," Sackville said. "Weapons of all kinds and a great store of gunpowder were also taken from that same Netherlands armory and brought hither, and they and the other corselets lie in the vaults beneath the White Tower. There was not room enough for them here." He smiled at me. "Mistress Blanchard may well know more of how they were brought out of the Netherlands than even I or Sir William Paulet."

"Really?" said Sir Henry. "I knew you had lived in Antwerp, Mistress Blanchard. Gerald Blanchard was in the service of Sir Thomas Gresham at the time, was he not? But surely you didn't spend your time there stealing gunpowder and corselets."

"I didn't steal them myself," I said. "But Gerald did."

Gerald and I had lived in Antwerp for nearly a year, as part of Sir Thomas Gresham's entourage. Gresham was a financier employed by Elizabeth to improve her credit and raise loans for her abroad. He had interpreted this brief somewhat liberally.

"Gerald helped Gresham to—er—obtain weapons and armor and other valuables from the Netherlands and get them to England," I said. "Not always—not even usually—with their owners' knowledge or consent." No, we had better not let De Quadra realize where they came from.

"You must have had an exciting time in Antwerp," said Sir Henry, amused.

He was quite right. Gerald's work had included finding people who could be bribed or blackmailed into lending keys and forging requisitions in order to get valuables—ingots, plate, armor, all manner of things—out of storage. Sometimes, Gerald took temporary charge of the filched goods. More than once, we had had consignments hidden under the bed in our lodgings, awaiting a ship or a better hiding place until a suitable ship was in port. It had indeed been exciting.

I glanced around the display. The queen was now examining a sword with a spectacular hilt, encrusted with cabochon emeralds and rubies, and the French ambassador, in conversation with the lieutenant, had strolled back across the room to look once more at the gold and silver plate. With Sackville and Sir Henry still at my side, I followed them, wanting a second look myself. Sackville had jolted my memory. Yes, of course. That fine set of gold plate was one I had seen before. Gerald had taken me to see it aboard the ship that was to carry it illicitly away from Antwerp. And just before the smallpox struck, there had been another splendid consignment . . . I scanned the table and moved along it. But none of those items seemed to be on view.

"That isn't all the plate from Antwerp, is it?" I asked. "I take it that the rest is stored somewhere, like the corselets?"

"Oh no. We keep all the plate together, here," Sackville said. "It is so very beauteous. As you see, we have had stands made on which to set it out. Why do you ask?"

It had been two years ago. That particular consignment had rested, briefly, in our lodgings while Gerald checked it over. I had helped him, writing down a list of items as he dictated them, before he and the manservant we had then took them away to be stowed, not under anyone's bed, not that time, but under the floor of a rented warehouse. The rent had been paid for five years in advance and the agreement contained a clause forbidding the owner to enter the property until those years were up.

I could still hear Gerald's voice in my head, dictating that list. As a child, I had shared my cousins' tutor, and he had made a great point of training his pupils' memories. I could re-cite verse by the furlong, and carry a shopping list of thirty or more items in my head with ease, after hearing them told over just once. I could remember almost word for word what Gerald had said, and besides, I had seen most of the items myself.

Slowly, as near as I could, I repeated the inventory.

"Item, one full set of gold plate, value approximately ten thousand pounds, including twenty-four drinking goblets, marked with the badge of a noble Spanish house, set in cabochon rubies and emeralds.

"Item, a golden salt, two feet high, shaped as a square castle tower, with a salt container under each turret and spice drawers below. Decorated with the same badge, set in rubies. Value approximately twelve thousand pounds.

"Item, a silver salt, with a fluted pattern and a chased pattern of birds and leaves around the rim. There is a hinged lid in the likeness of a scallop shell, beneath which are four salt containers that may be lifted out. Value approximately three thousand pounds.

"Item, sundry small costly ornaments, total value approximately seven hundred pounds.

"They're not here," I said. "But they were among the things which Gresham, well, sequestered, with my husband's help. Was some of the treasure from the Netherlands broken up—or melted down? Or sold?"

"One would hope not. Such exquisite artifacts should never be destroyed." Sir Henry was quite shocked.

Sackville, however, was nonplussed. "Mistress Blan-chard, I have never seen the items you describe, nor found them on any list. When were they sent to England? On what ship?"

"Gerald was arranging for a ship at the time when he fell ill," I said. "Come to think of it . . ."

His illness had struck suddenly and from the moment when I first knew what it was, I had thought of nothing except him and Meg and how best to care for them. I had had smallpox as a child, without my complexion being much harmed, but I would take no risks with Meg. In frantic haste, I had arranged other lodgings for her and her nurse; and, thank God, neither of them caught it. I myself had stayed with Gerald, to nurse him and worry about him and at last to grieve for him. From then until now I had not thought, even once, about that hidden treasure. I hadn't even thought about it when I transferred Gerald's keys from his key ring to my own and noticed, vaguely, that the warehouse key, a distinctive affair in ornamental ironwork, was with them. I had meant to return it, but in the exhaustion and preoccupation of bereavement, I forgot. I was in England when I noticed the key again, and then trying to return it seemed like pointless effort.

It was only a key, after all. No one reminded me that it might unlock a treasure. Our manservant, John Wilton, had probably assumed that all arrangements for transporting the valuables were in hand. At least he had never mentioned it to me and I could not now ask him, for he, too, was dead.

The key was still on my ring; a souvenir of past happiness and nothing more.

"Come to think of it," I said again, "I doubt if those items ever left Antwerp. I expect they're still there."

I knew precisely where, too. When Gerald first rented the warehouse, he had shown it to me, and shown me the hiding place under the boards of the ground floor where, he hoped, not just one but a succession of consignments would rest. The first consignment had been the last, but I knew he had got it safely as far as the warehouse. It must still be where he hid it.

Well, it could stay there as far as I was concerned. I wanted no part of it. It was just another symbol of the intrigue of which I was growing so tired that even though France was now a country on the edge of civil war, and even though March was a terrible month for voyaging, I was prepared to travel there on family business just to get away for a while from plots and politics.

And to pass, perhaps, within a few miles of where Matthew de la Roche, my current husband, was probably living. Back it came, my longing for him, persistent and absurd.

I pushed it away. I would not try to see him and I didn't imagine he would want to see me. Matthew was gone forever and the sooner I accepted that the better.

CHAPTER 2

Jeweled Manacles

I returned to Greenwich with the queen, by river, and found my two servants busy packing for our journey.

Fran and Roger Brockley were a married couple, although they hadn't married until they had joined my service, and I still called Fran by her maiden name of Dale. They were in their forties, both of them—a solid and reliable pair, though Dale did have a tendency to grumble and I had never been able to stop Brockley from hinting that my way of earning a living was unsuitable for a lady and he wished I would settle down to a more becoming (and safer) way of life.

At least, if not precisely safe, the journey for which we were preparing was quite private. It was an errand of mercy, connected with my first husband's family. This was Blanchard business.

Gerald and I had married against the wishes of our respective families and when I was first widowed, and applied for financial help to his father, I was coldly refused. But that was before I joined the court and rose in the favor of the queen. My former father-in-law, Luke Blanchard, somehow got to hear that his son's despised widow was prinking around the court in expensive damask dresses, had been seen in friendly conversation with Elizabeth, was on visiting terms with the Secretary of State and his wife, and that Meg, my daughter, was being fostered by a family who were friends of the Cecils. At that, his attitude abruptly changed.

The next thing I knew was that he and Ambrose, Gerald's older brother, were presenting themselves at court, dressed in their best doublets, asking to see me, and, in a piquant reversal of the previous state of affairs, appealing for my assistance.

"We feel," said Luke Blanchard, as persuasively as a man can who is six feet tall with an arrogant aquiline profile, is austerely dressed in black velvet, and has glacial blue eyes and a voice so deep that he sounds portentous even when he is only remarking on the weather, "that although France is a perilous place just now, someone like yourself, my dear Ursula, highly regarded by our queen, could visit it with a degree of safety. Your presence in my party would amount to protection for me."

I never thought the day would come when I would hear Gerald's father call me his dear Ursula. I gazed at him in astonishment.

"A well-equipped escort and the countenance of Queen Elizabeth, who is maintaining normal diplomatic relations with the court of France, should work wonders," Ambrose agreed. His tawny doublet and hose were more attractive than Luke's black velvet, but physically he was just a younger version of his father and his attempt at an ingratiating smile met with only limited success.

Gerald had been short and dark and friendly, and had told me that he resembled his long-dead mother. I was sure that this was true. Certainly he was nothing like his father or his brother. Gerald was also in the habit of coming to the point. These two seemed to prefer rigmaroles. I had been allowed to see them in a private room, and to offer refreshments. I poured wine for them and cut the preamble short by saying: "But what do you want to go to France for, precisely?"

It was simple enough. Luke Blanchard's mother had been the sole heiress of her father's Sussex manor of Beechtrees, and she had married a Frenchman. "That was when the name Blanchard came into the family, as no doubt you know," Luke said. "Before that, the name was Fitzhubert."

Luke had had a sister who married back into France, taking as husband a distant cousin, another Blanchard. He had died young, leaving his wife to bring up their daughter, Helene, and now his wife had died as well.

"Under my sister's will," my father-in-law said, "I am appointed as Helene's guardian. She is about sixteen. She is with her father's relatives at the moment, perfectly respectable people, and I would be happy to leave her there but for the state of affairs in France. Civil war between the Catholics and the Huguenots could break out at any moment."

"Quite," I said, amused. As one of the queen's ladies, often present when she received messengers and ambassadors, I knew more about the shaky state of law and order in France than he did.

"Helene," said Luke Blanchard, "is living at a place called the Château Douceaix—the name is said to mean Sweet Waters—which is not far from Le Mans. Not that it matters where she is; if trouble breaks out, all France could be equally dangerous. As a responsible guardian, I am bound to feel concerned. I wish to fetch her home. But I think she should have the company of a gentlewoman on the way—and I am very nervous about the risk to myself . . ."

His voice trailed off at this point. Then, shamefacedly, he said: "I'm not so young anymore. Ambrose is willing to go, of course . . ."

"Yes, I am," said Ambrose, quite pugnaciously.

". . . but I have lost one son and I can't spare the one I have left." It was the only reference he had so far made to Gerald. There was the faintest note of accusation in his voice, as though marriage to me had somehow made Gerald vulnerable to smallpox. But he went on without pausing.

"Also, I am the one who is Helene's guardian. And you, Ambrose, have a wife and young children. I prefer you to stay in England. If we can get Helene safely out, I have a good marriage in view for her. Now, Ursula, will you, if you can obtain permission, come with me to fetch her? I don't think the danger will be nearly as great if you are there."

I didn't like either Luke or Ambrose very much but it would get me away from the court, and carry me to France, and it was true that for me, a member of Elizabeth's household, the risk would be much reduced. And so I decided to set out for France in March, equinoctial gales notwithstanding, and help my father-in-law, even though he had no shadow of a right to expect it.

I had hoped to come back from the Tower to find all the packing done, but although, when I entered my quarters, Brockley was on his knees beside a hamper, grunting with effort as he tightened the straps, the lid of the biggest hamper was still open and the contents were in confusion because Dale had just pulled a gown out of it and was busy erasing creases with a damp cloth and a hot iron.

"Dale, what on earth are you doing? That rose damask was packed yesterday!"

"There's word that you're to go to the queen after she's supped. I expect she wants to say a formal good-bye," Dale said. "Just let me finish this, and then sit you down, and I'll put your hair right. That wind on the river's pulled half of it out of your cap. Then I'll get you dressed for an audience."

"Dale, I've been with the queen all afternoon. She never mentioned this."

"Well, those were the orders, ma'am. It was Mistress Ashley told me."

Kat Ashley was the queen's principal lady, though she hadn't come with us to the Tower. If the orders came from her, then there was no mistake. "Very well," I said.

I worried, though, as Dale got me ready. What if Elizabeth had changed her mind and decided to forbid me to go? In due course, a page came to fetch me and I followed him to Elizabeth's study. Evening had fallen and the room was lit by lamps and candles, plenty of them, for Elizabeth, though in many ways careful about expense, would not stint on light when she wanted to read. She had more respect for her eyesight. She was reading now, seated at her desk, with Sir Thomas More's *Utopia,* that fanciful description of an ideal state, open in front of her. When the page brought me in, she said: "Welcome, Ursula," but she finished the paragraph she was studying and a few seconds passed before she looked up.

For a moment, therefore, I stood by the door, looking at her bent head, with the delicately curved profile outlined against the paneled wall beyond. The candlelight glinted on the silver threads in her loose cream gown, on the rings that encircled her slender fingers, and on the crimped waves of light red hair in front of her pearl-edged cap. She had grown older, even in the two years that I had known her. A crown is a heavy weight. But one thing was unchanged, and that was the curious mingling of power and fragility that was essentially Elizabeth, like a snowflake made of steel.

I was a little afraid of her, like nearly everyone else at the court, but I had affection for her, too, and I knew that she had affection for me. Not just because of the secret work I did for her, although that perhaps was part of it, but also because,

long ago, my mother had served her mother, poor Anne Boleyn, who had been beheaded.

She slipped a marker into her book and turned, signing to
me to move to where she could see me clearly. "Come in,
Ursula. I will not keep you long. You leave early tomorrow, I
believe?"

She hadn't called me here to withdraw her permission, then.
I made my curtsy and said: "Yes, ma'am. We set out for South-
ampton at first light. We shall be quite a large party. Master
Blanchard is taking five manservants with him."

"He's nervous?" Elizabeth said.

"Yes, ma'am. He has worried over how many men he should
take. He said that too many would attract attention and look
provocative, but to travel with too few felt unsafe. In the end,
he settled on five."

"He will have eight," Elizabeth said crisply. "Cecil is pro-
viding you with an additional escort of three of his own men,
wearing his livery. They will present themselves in the morning
and will ride with you to Southampton."

"Three of Cecil's men?" I said. "Master Blanchard will
surely be pleased. But . . . is there any particular reason?"

"Oh yes. Ursula, do you know what a white night is?"

"Yes, ma'am." Seeing her now, at close quarters, I noticed
what she had managed to conceal during our visit to the Tower:
how very tired she looked. "A white night," I said, "is a night
without sleep, no matter how you may long for rest."

"Yes. You sound as though you speak from experience,"
Elizabeth said. "Last night, I had no sleep. I have just received
news that has made me very anxious. We have, I think, dem-
onstrated to De Quadra that England is not to be trifled with
but Spain is not the only cloud on the horizon. France is in an
alarming condition. In Normandy, at a place called Vassy, there

has been a massacre. Five hundred Protestants at worship—in France they call them Lutherans or Huguenots—were recently attacked by Catholic forces. The news reached us yesterday. About forty people were butchered. Civil war has come several steps closer. I was wakeful last night, Ursula, because I was wondering if I should let you go to France. I would forbid it, except that there is an extra errand I wish you to carry out for me—an important one—and this dreadful news makes it more important than ever. But it will keep you in France for at least an extra week, since it involves traveling on to Paris before you return home. Both Cecil and I felt that his men should go with you as an added safeguard—just in case."

There was silence. This was the very last thing I had expected. As the seconds slid by, I realized how very badly I needed to escape, for a while, from the tasks set me by Elizabeth and Cecil. Above all, I wanted to recover from certain changes that the work had wrought in me. I had relished it once and part of me still did. But I could not forget the day I had tricked my way into a prisoner's cell and given him a phial of yew poison, so that he could evade the disemboweling knife.

In effect, I had put him in that cell, had thrown him to the executioner. I had saved him as best I could. But brewing the poison and passing it to him, looking into eyes that were staring at death because of me—all this had warped something in me. Sometimes, when I visited my daughter at her foster parents' home, and held her in my arms, I feared she might sense something amiss with me and recoil; I even feared that I might in some way corrupt her innocence.

I believed that I had failed in my last task because something in me had simply turned away from my work. I would—I must—get over it. But I needed time to heal myself. Now, escape seemed impossible.

"If you will undertake this," Elizabeth said, "you will be doing me a great service."

I said what I was expected to say. With Elizabeth, one had little choice. "Of course I will serve you in any way I can, ma'am." Though I couldn't forbear to add dryly: "Although I am not always successful."

I was referring to my failure. As well as watching Dudley, I had been told to keep an eye on Lady Catherine Grey (another of Elizabeth's cousins but nothing at all like the wise and kindly Katherine Knollys). Catherine Grey had been acting oddly—turning up in places where she shouldn't have been, and failing to arrive at places where she was expected. I had prowled after her for months, in vain, until she solved the mystery herself by confessing to a secret marriage and a pregnancy. She was the foolish girl at whom Dudley had been laughing, in the Tower. But foolish or not, she had managed to deceive me.

"If you mean my silly alley cat of a cousin," said Elizabeth, who didn't mince her words when annoyed and had been very annoyed indeed by Catherine, "I regard that matter as insignificant. This is very different. I don't wish you to find anything out, but only to deliver a message. I hardly need to describe the situation in France to you, Ursula. I did hope, you know, that after the Catholic government ceased its persecution of heretics, peace would prevail. Now I fear that it will not. Both factions have leaders from the great houses of France. The Huguenot leader is the prince of Condé, who is distantly related to the royal family. But I hear from Ambassador Throckmorton that the regent and queen mother, Catherine, is doing all she can to bring about a settlement. I wish to tell her that I am willing to help in any mediation between the two sides, but I want to tell her privately, as it were. Some maneuvers have more chance of success if they remain in the shadows. For one thing, other people have less chance of interfering."

A square wooden box lay by her right hand. Opening it, she took out a sealed cylinder of parchment and held it out to me. "This is a letter to Queen Catherine. When you and Master Blanchard have taken charge of his ward, I wish you to go on to Paris and place it—personally, Ursula—in the hands of the queen mother."

I took the cylinder doubtfully. It bore the superscription *Catherine of France,* written in Elizabeth's own fine Tudor hand. She had beautiful handwriting, and it was said to be a characteristic of all the Tudors. "Will I be able to get an audience with her?"

"I've made sure of that, naturally." From the box, she took out a further cylinder of parchment. "This is a letter of introduction to smooth your way. Take it!" I accepted it with resignation. It bore a similar superscription to the first, but with the word *Introduction* in smaller letters below the name of Catherine. "Now, listen," said Elizabeth. "There are those who might not like this errand of yours. Let us hope they never learn of it! My private letter to Queen Catherine, you must therefore keep secret. But this letter of introduction, bearing my seal, will give you, effectively, the status of a royal messenger and together with the extra armed men, should give you good protection."

"Does Master Blanchard know about all this?" I asked.

For the first time, Elizabeth smiled. "Of course. He will have to go with you to Paris. Cecil has told him. But Cecil has also assured him that your party now has complete diplomatic immunity and has pointed out that a visit to Paris, to the court, would be instructive for his young ward. Any inquisitive outsider can be led to believe that you are going to Paris purely to present my compliments at the French court. Cecil's escort have already been told that, though they understand that importance is attached to it. Master Blanchard accepted all this quite willingly. He raised no objections."

I was sure he hadn't. People did not raise objections to the queen's orders, at least, not unless they were Robin Dudley or Cecil, or some equally privileged associate, and even they knew when to stop arguing.

Nor could I raise objections now. Yet I could not quite hide my reluctance. As Elizabeth gave me the second letter, she saw it. She overcame it by opening my fingers and folding them over the parchment. For a frightful moment, I felt as though her fingers were a set of highly expensive, gem-studded manacles.

"I know, Ursula. You want to escape from intrigue for a while, do you not?" I had never said so but Elizabeth had a disconcerting way sometimes of reading one's mind. "England needs Protestant friends," she said. "There are too many Catholic powers in Europe. I need the French Huguenots to survive and if a war breaks out over there, I fear for them. I said that both sides can field armies, but the Catholic army could well prove the stronger. I have something else for you."

For the third time, she dipped into the box, and brought out a small object, which she held out on her palm. "This is one more safeguard. Take it; wear it if it will fit. If you show it at the French court, you will have the right, at once, to a private audience with any member of the royal house. It is a quiet little reciprocal arrangement that I have with them. Agents, ambassadors, messengers from both countries, have sometimes found it useful."

It was a gold signet ring, heavy. The flat signet face was engraved with a lion regardant, surrounded by tiny fleur-de-lis. I tried it on and found that it fitted the long finger of my right hand very well.

"I have done all I can for your safety and that of your companions," Elizabeth said. "I may say that although the idea of sending the letter with you was originally Cecil's, I am asking you to do this as a personal favor to me."

But she had left me no choice, of course. However subtle the coercion, it was there.

"Sleep well," said Elizabeth kindly, as I curtsied, and kissed those slender, jeweled, perfectly manicured fingers or gyves. "You need your rest, with a journey in the morning."

I went slowly back to my quarters. I had a small room of my own, a consideration that had caused some jealousy among the other ladies, especially those senior to me, for in many royal residences they had to share rooms or even beds. But my privilege was maintained in all the residences so that I would have no difficulty in talking to my servants in private. I needed to talk to them now. Brockley and Dale were still there, waiting for me, wondering what my summons to the queen had portended, and there was no thought in my mind of concealing my new task from them. I trusted them and had often needed their help.

Briefly, I explained what the queen had asked me to do and why, and described the safeguards she had given me. "Although," I said soothingly, "there is no war as yet, and the persecution of heretics has ceased."

It was Brockley who put his finger, instantly, on the flaw in all this. "If the danger is so slight, madam," he said, "do you really need extra armed men and the right of instant access to an audience with one of the French government?"

I sat down on the edge of my bed. "I don't know, Brockley.

I hope that the queen is just—making doubly certain of our safety. It's true that there are those—I fancy on both sides— who might not like my errand, should they ever come to hear of it. We ought to be discreet."

"That goes without saying," Brockley remarked. "But I don't care for this, just the same." Brockley had blue-gray eyes, very steady, and a high, polished forehead with a dusting of light gold freckles. Normally, his dignified countenance was inexpressive. Now, however, worried lines had appeared on them. "France is on the edge of war between Papists and Protestants," he said. "And to a Papist we'd be heretics. They're not being hounded now, so you tell us, but if war starts, anything could happen. That could change."

He was obviously uneasy and so was Dale. Dale was quite a handsome woman, except for a few pockmarks from a childhood attack of smallpox but usually they were not very noticeable. I knew that when her face looked as it did now, with the pockmarks standing out so clearly, she was nervous.

I knew what they feared. I had never witnessed a burning but the aunt and uncle who brought me up had once forced me to listen to an account of one. I do mean forced. I had been prevented from either running out of the room or blocking my ears while the details of what they had seen and heard and smelled were relentlessly described. It had left on my mind a scar so terrible that years later, it was the reason why I had parted from Matthew. He wished to bring back the Catholic religion to England. But if that ever happened, then the burning of heretics would return with it. It was my horror of that which, in the end, had come between us.

"As an official messenger," I said, "I should be safe enough and so should you. I agree that we must be discreet about what we believe as well as about my errand. Dale, I know how you dislike Papists, but in France, you must watch your tongue."

"Of course I will, ma'am," said Dale, slightly affronted.

I hoped so but Dale was an essentially simple being whose remarks were apt to reflect her thoughts. Well, I could rely on Brockley to back me up.

Brockley, however, was still worried. "From what you've told us, Master Blanchard has chosen a very long route to this place, Douceaix. I wonder the queen hasn't asked him to change it. Quickest is safest as a rule."

"Master Blanchard wants to travel through country where Huguenot influence is strong," I said. "He hasn't been asked to think again, apparently."

I had felt puzzled by it, too, but I hadn't commented for I had my own reasons—albeit absurd ones—for favoring his choice.

Most people, when traveling to Paris, sailed from one of the southeast ports, or perhaps from the Thames, crossed the Channel, and then either went overland from Calais, or traveled down the coast and up the Seine. But Master Blanchard meant to take ship from Southampton, go south and sail up the Loire. It would take two days to reach Southampton and even with fair winds, about four days to reach the Loire. We would disembark at Nantes, nearly forty miles up the river, and then ride northeast for a hundred miles or so to reach Douceaix, where we would collect Helene. The Huguenot influence, which Luke Blanchard seemed to think would be a safeguard, was strong in the area between the Loire and Douceaix. Now, however, we would have to ride on for a further hundred and thirty miles or thereabouts to Paris.

"Well," I said, "at least I shan't look much like a royal courier and perhaps that's better than looking too official. Couriers usually do assume that quickest is safest, as you put it,

Brockley. Listen, both of you. I am not forcing you to come with me, not if you are uneasy."

But they shook their heads. "No, madam," said Brockley. "We shall go where you go, as always. Now, you had better get your rest. May my wife join me tonight? She'll be back in good time to help you rise."

"Yes, by all means," I said.

They had regular nights to be together and this wasn't one of them. But they occasionally made a special request. I thought little of it at the time. Indeed, when I look back, I see that I was in a state of blissful ignorance about a great many things. Some of them directly concerned me; others were never meant to concern me but did so quite by accident.

It was possibly that same night in early March that in a hostelry in Marseilles, in the south of France, an intrepid and resolute but by most people's standards slightly crazy merchant adventurer named Anthony Jenkinson was disturbed in the night by would-be assassins. He and the two men with him woke up in time and it was the assassins who lost their lives. On a table by the bed, he left sufficient money to pay the innkeeper's bill and then he and his companions fled stealthily from the inn by climbing out the window and down the creeper that clung to the wall outside. They also left two unknown corpses of Mediterranean appearance in the wide bed for the innkeeper to find in the morning.

The meeting that had put the assassins on Master Jenkinson's track must have been held much earlier, perhaps late the previous year. We never knew for sure, nor did we know exactly where it was held. But it probably took place in Istanbul. Quite a number of men must have been present, some of them Venetian and some Turkish. I can visualize them seated around a table in some well-appointed room with windows designed to protect the occupants from the sun rather than let it in. But this must have been winter and the weather could well have been quite cold. If any of the windows gave a view of the Bosporus, the gleam of the water could have been steely rather than bright. I have never seen the Bosporus but my cousins' tutor was a traveled man and rather good at geography. He had been to Istanbul, and had described it.

I can visualize, too, the men who sat at that table: their olive complexions and their dark eyes; some lively, some unfathomable, all intelligent. Some would have worn robes and some would have been in dignified gowns or doublets; most would have had rings on their hands and jeweled brooches in their turbans and hats. I can hear their voices: grave, courteous, formal, speaking—what? Greek, very likely. The tutor had once said it was a commonly spoken language in the area.

Venice and Istanbul—different cultures, but both based on Mediterranean ports with much coming and going between them over the centuries. The representatives of the two cities had much in common. They might have different religions but they were all men of commerce. They were a consortium of Venetian and Turkish merchants, working together to get the best profit possible out of goods passing from the East to the West. They considered themselves sober, practical businessmen. I have no doubt that in general they were responsible husbands and fathers, respectful sons to their parents, probably well loved by their families.

I feel sure that if you were to stumble in the street and fall down on the cobbles in front of them, they would help you to your feet, inquiring solicitously if you were hurt, and might even beckon a servant from their entourage to escort you safely to your home.

If you threatened their profits, they'd kill you.

Lightheartedness wasn't one of their most noticeable traits but, nevertheless, I think that to some extent they shared Anthony Jenkinson's sense that to be a merchant is to be an adventurer, for their name was imaginative.

Translated into English, the title they gave themselves was the Levantine Lions.

CHAPTER 3

An Aversion to Cheese

Elizabeth's errand changed my feelings about the forthcoming journey and next morning, as we prepared to set out, my spirits were low.

Today, I knew, the queen would be receiving a visit from the Spanish ambassador, who would be rowed from his house in Whitehall in the official Greenwich barge with the red satin awning and comfortable cabin. She would receive him in audience, with her ladies and courtiers in attendance, and later on, they would all go to watch a tilting contest. I wished I were going to watch it, too.

I had other regrets, as well. Dale and Brockley came to me early, Dale to help me dress and Brockley to take the hampers downstairs. I saw that both of them were heavy-eyed, the mark of a couple who have had a night of conjugal passion. It annoyed me. I was married, too, but the privilege of conjugal passion was out of my reach. Before I was dressed for departure, I had managed to snap at poor Dale twice, out of sheer envy.

The last thing I did before we left was to stow the queen's two letters safely out of sight, but on my person. I was as usual wearing a kirtle and an open overgown and like all my overgowns, this one had a capacious pocket stitched inside it. Here, I was in the habit of carrying a purse of money, a small sheathed dagger, and a set of lock picks. I left what I thought of as the tools of my trade behind when entering the presence of the queen—one does not come into the vicinity of royalty carrying weapons and lock picks—but I was rarely parted from them otherwise. I had them with me now, and the two letters with Elizabeth's signature joined them in their hidden pocket.

Luke Blanchard knew about the letters. But I remember wondering what on earth he would say if he knew what company they were keeping. Thinking about it gave me just a little amusement on that cold, depressing morning.

My former father-in-law was not short of a penny or two. He had done more than just buy passages for us; he had chartered the whole ship, which meant that he could dictate the route. The *Chaffinch* was not one of the big merchantmen, but a trim craft, about ninety feet long, painted in shiny green and built for passengers and cargo alike. Her interior belied her pretty looks, though. The cabins were tiny and Master Simon Ross, her hearty, weather-beaten owner and captain, was not one to miss a chance of trading. His hold was packed full of merchandise. This included bales of good wool cloth and, unfortunately, well-ripened cheeses. Belowdecks, the whole ship reeked of them.

"I regret the discomfort," said Master Blanchard's deep voice from my threshold. He ducked his head in at my cabin door and stood there, sniffing the air with distaste. "You are a good sailor, I trust?"

"Reasonably so, I think," I said. "I've crossed the North Sea twice. But neither ship had an atmosphere quite as exhilarating as this."

"I have complained, but in vain. Captain Ross," said Master Blanchard, "is a difficult man." I had heard the altercation.

Blanchard had tried to domineer, and Captain Ross had refused to be impressed. It wasn't surprising. Ross could hardly be expected to unload half his cargo and throw it into the harbor. "Let us pray for fair weather," Blanchard said. "A combination of cheese and rough seas won't be agreeable. I would not have traveled in March from choice."

I had known Luke Blanchard most of my life, for the Blanchards lived only ten miles from my own family, the Faldenes, and the two households were well acquainted. But as a girl, I was rather afraid of the tall man with the cold face and the bass voice. Later, when he broke off all relations with his Gerald because of our marriage, and then rejected his own granddaughter, fear had been augmented by sheer dislike. Now, I began to see that beneath it all was a timid streak. Cecil had undoubtedly recognized it. Cecil's light blue eyes, with the permanent worry line between them, missed very little. No wonder he had let Blanchard have his way about the route. Pressed to travel by a route he thought wasn't safe, my father-in-law might even have defied the queen, abandoned his ward, and refused to go, or—more likely—had a diplomatic illness so that he couldn't.

"The ship seems seaworthy," I said reassuringly.

At least we would have beds. The crew and most of our men had to make do with hammocks, but the little cabins each had two quite comfortable bunks in them. I was to share my cabin with Dale, and Blanchard's personal man, Harvey, would occupy the second bunk in his. Captain Ross had the biggest cabin to himself, and the last and smallest, which was empty as yet, would if all went well, be used by Helene on the return journey. The *Chaffinch* would wait three weeks in Nantes for us, though she would sail without us if we hadn't reappeared by then, or sent any message.

There was a small saloon, and an inconvenient galley on deck, with a built-in brick fireplace. When welcoming us aboard, Captain Ross, clearly none too enthusiastic about having women aboard, had said that the food might not be what delicate ladies were accustomed to. But it shouldn't be a long voyage, he added. The wind was in the right quarter for it, and brisk. We should be warned that if the sea did get rough, cooking would be impossible and food would be cold. Dale and I had said that we quite understood.

I sniffed the air, like Blanchard, and wondered whether I would have much appetite anyway.

I didn't. It was an awful voyage. The sick headaches to which I was prone were usually due to worry or doubt, and I suppose I might well have had one anyway as the ship drew away from England. I had said good-bye to my daughter at her foster home near Hampton two days before that visit to the Tower treasury, and she had cried at parting. I had urged her to take heart, saying that I wouldn't be away for long—that I was often at court and not able to visit her for weeks together and this would seem no different. But now as the sea widened between us, I realized that it was different. For the next few weeks we would be in different countries. It mattered, and I minded. The rough weather which seized us before we were two hours on our way made disaster certain for me. I lay for three days in my bunk, clutching my temples and a basin alternately, and fervently wishing I were dead.

Oddly enough, Dale did not succumb. She was terrified by the heaving waves that marched greenly past our porthole and spattered it with foam, and by the scream of the wind in the rigging, but she wasn't sick. Brockley was, however, and so was Master Blanchard, and so, in varying degrees, were all the eight men of our escort.

On the two-day ride to Southampton, constantly changing horses in order to keep up a steady pace, I had got to know the escort, both Blanchard's men and those Cecil had sent. They were all respectful, but Blanchard's five were inclined to be distant. Their leader William Harvey, who acted as Blanchard's personal servant, was of an age with his master and had been with Blanchard since before my marriage. I could see that to him, I was still the penniless wench who had run off with Gerald, stealing him from the better-dowered bride, who, incidentally, was my cousin Mary. I rather thought that he had passed on this attitude to most of the others. The redheaded Searle, whose Christian name I never learned, was very cold toward me, while Tom Clarkson and Hugh Arnold, though quiet-spoken and courteous when they had to speak to me, noticeably did so as little as possible.

The pleasantest of the five was the youngest, a curly-haired fellow named Mark Sweetapple. When in health, he had a robust appetite for his food, and a friendly smile, which did come my way now and then. Perhaps having a surname like that sweetened one's nature, too, I thought.

Cecil's three were all amiable, however, clearly regarding me as their charge. Their leader, John Ryder, middle-aged and brindle-bearded, had served as a captain in King Henry's army during the war in France in 1544. Brockley had also fought in France and said that although he hadn't served under Ryder, he was sure he remembered him, and they found that they recalled some of the same events, including one particularly unpleasant forced march in a downpour, when the supply wagons failed to catch up with them at nightfall. They had had to camp out in a wood, and make do with a few provisions carried on baggage mules, and some food commandeered from a small and indignant hamlet.

"We all thought the French would come creeping to cut our throats in the night and I'm not sure I'd have blamed them," I heard Brockley say once.

For some extraordinary reason the memory made them laugh. But it acted as a bond, which was a good thing.

The other two men from Cecil's household were a pair of brothers called Dick and Walter Dodd. They were stolid and reliable, very alike to look at, since both were sandy-haired, blue-eyed, and stocky, but Dick was about ten years older than his brother. As a result, Dick preferred the company of Ryder and Brockley, while Walter sought out young Sweetapple. Again, it seemed a good thing, creating bonds between the two groups of men.

But on the ship, old and young, Cecil's men or Blanchard's, they groaned in unison. It wasn't until the *Chaffinch* entered the mouth of the Loire that they—and I—at last staggered wanly up on deck.

"I believed I was going to die," Luke Blanchard told me, when we went to the saloon to take our first square meal. "I commended my soul to God a dozen times over. I am amazed to find myself still on earth. You are pale, Ursula. You have been as ill as I have, I imagine."

I knew what I looked like. I had a hand mirror with me and I had glanced in it before emerging from my cabin. My hair was dark and although my eyes were actually hazel, they often looked dark as well, especially if I was unwell.

Just now, they resembled black pits. The nausea and the racking headache had let go of me, but they had left me with a complexion that was nearer green than white, and I felt as shaky as though I had had fever for a month.

However, the ship had anchored for a while in the mouth of the river, and someone had gone ashore for fresh bread. When it was brought aboard, it smelled wonderful. "I'll be better when I've eaten," I said. "So will you be, I'm sure."

The bread was served with the meal, and it was all that its aroma promised. The hot meat stew that was the main dish was good, too. Blanchard ate little, but the rest of us made up for the meals we had missed. I felt strength going into me after only a couple of mouthfuls. Mark Sweetapple didn't so much spoon stew into his mouth as shovel it in, and Dale ate with such enthusiasm that Captain Ross noticed, and grinned. "Seems the ship's food suits the ladies after all," he said. "You ought to eat up, too, Master Blanchard. You need it."

"My belly muscles ache from retching," Blanchard complained.

"Ah well. Maybe we'll have a good voyage home," Ross said. "I'll most likely have wine in the hold on the way back. Maybe you won't mind that as much as the cheese, Master Blanchard."

"I wouldn't mind anything as much as the cheese," said Master Blanchard pallidly.

We reached Nantes late the next day and slept on board overnight. In the morning, Ryder and Brockley went ashore to arrange for the hire of horses and pack mules. We dined on board, early and quickly, and disembarked shortly after noon to begin our land journey.

As for the first time in my life I stepped onto the soil of France, I turned dizzy and almost fell. Mark Sweetapple was beside me and took my arm to steady me. "This is what comes of sea travel, Mistress Blanchard. You'll get your land legs back in a moment."

I thanked him, and managed a smile. I knew that the dizziness had had nothing to do with sea legs or land legs. I had

had a shock. It had come home to me, as I stood on the quay, gazing back at the quietly flowing Loire, just how strong my second, hidden reason for wishing to make this journey had been, how strong and how misguided.

I had told myself that I needed to rest from my work; that because I had stood face-to-face with a man about to die because of me and handed him a phial of poison to make his passing easier, I might have become warped, a source of contamination for Meg. I had pretended to myself that this was why I wanted to leave her, and England, for a while.

The truth was that I had decided to say yes to Luke Blanchard the moment he told me the route he wanted to take. The moment he uttered that magical word, *Loire.*

I looked again at the river and experienced an almost physical tug from upstream. Somewhere up there was the place where my estranged husband Matthew lived, or at least, I supposed he did. In these uneasy days, he might well be in Paris, but his house, the Château Blanchepierre, was on the Loire.

I would never see Blanchepierre now, still less become its mistress. I knew that well enough. But I had come on this journey mainly for the bittersweet pleasure of being for a little while in the same country as Matthew, of being on the banks of the river beside which he lived.

Of all the foolish, sentimental, utterly ridiculous things to do. I knew I still loved him, of course. That, it seemed, was something I could not tear out of me. But Matthew had plotted to bring back to England the terror of the heresy hunt, and among his associates was a man whom I regarded as a human nightmare. Dr. Ignatius Wilkins did not know what pity meant. Last year, Matthew had fled to France only just in time to save his life. I rejoiced in his escape, but his fellow conspirator Wilkins had fled with him. I was sorry that Wilkins had escaped, and sorrier still that Matthew was prepared to accept such a man as his friend.

And yet, like a lovelorn milkmaid, I had come to France, simply in the hope of passing, secretly, near the place where Matthew might be. Oh my God, Ursula, I said to myself; what a fool you are.

But I said nothing aloud. As far as I was aware, Luke Blanchard knew nothing of Matthew de la Roche or my second marriage, and I did not want him to know. I had been saddled with an errand for the queen and I must help my father-in-law bring his ward Helene out of France. I had better put my mind to these things. I shook the dizziness out of me, mounted my horse and turned my face to the northeast, toward Douceaix and ultimately, Paris.

We had been three hours on the road when we found the bodies. The track passed a small grove of trees on the edge of some fields, and corpses were hanging from the boughs. We smelled them before we saw them. We halted to look, aware at once that this was not judicial business; these were not felons dangling from an official gibbet. We rode on warily. We came to a small hamlet that had once had a church. It was nothing now but a burnt-out ruin. The villagers were sullen and afraid, but from them we learned what we had already guessed and feared.

The killings in Vassy had borne the expected fruit. These were revenge attacks. If civil war had not yet begun officially, it was perilously close. We went on for a little way, but once outside the village, we reined in by mutual consent to confer.

"Do we go on?" I asked Blanchard. "Or give up our journey and return at once to the *Chaffinch?*"

As I spoke, I fingered my skirt surreptitiously, feeling the queen's letters. I had accepted the task of delivering them, and

I knew I must carry it out if I could. I caught John Ryder's eye, and he said: "Sir William Cecil gave us to understand that Mistress Blanchard has an errand to Paris on behalf of Queen Elizabeth, and to Paris, therefore, she must go. But that need not compel you to go on, Master Blanchard."

"I am still not feeling well," Blanchard said, "and I wish to God we were all safe back in England. But I'm responsible for Helene, and we are, after all, English travelers, with documents that should protect us. I think we had better continue."

Dale sighed, but I nodded. "We've come so far already that it would seem absurd to turn back. But we should make haste, and waste no time," I said.

Once more, we rode on. We tried to hurry, but Master Blanchard really did seem ill at ease and we were relieved, presently, to come across an undisturbed hamlet where there was an inn. Here, however, my father-in-law made the mistake of announcing us too loudly, as though we were royalty and any French innkeeper ought to prostrate himself before Master Luke Blanchard and Mistress Ursula Blanchard and their entourage, and the landlord, bristling, at first said he had no room for so large a party. After some wrangling, however, he fitted us in by billeting Mark Sweetapple and the Dodd brothers in the village. He even found a decent-sized bedchamber for Blanchard, who went to bed at once.

The inn itself was reasonably comfortable, but when we set out next morning, Sweetapple and the Dodds said that their overnight accommodations had been squalid. The Dodds had slept on a dirt floor beside a fire trench, amid a horde of children, and with nothing but a piece of sacking between them and the couple who were their parents.

"We could hear everything those two did," Walter said. "Everything! As if they hadn't got enough children already."

We all gazed at him with interest. He had the fair skin that goes with sandy hair, and this now turned pink. "It was embarrassing," he said defensively.

"The poor don't have many pleasures," Ryder said dryly. "The seigneurs and the Church tax these French peasants until the pips fly out of them. Don't grudge them their amusements."

Sweetapple had slept on straw, in the half-loft of another uncomfortable and dirty house, and been given an unsatisfying breakfast of pease pottage and rye bread, a major sin as far as he was concerned.

"I was born on a farm and we treated our pigs better," he said roundly.

"Now that," said Ryder, "is an exaggeration for sure."

"No, it isn't," said Sweetapple crossly.

Blanchard said he still felt unwell, but could ride and wished to do so. For my part, I was relieved to set off again. The sun shone warmly, and we saw fields and meadows, green with lush grass and young corn. One could sense that this was a much bigger country than England. I looked at the dense trees in a belt of forest, and knew that no English woodland would be so deep, and that this French one might even harbor wolves.

It was the time of year when stags shed their antlers and Brockley, catching sight of an antler by the roadside, dismounted to pick it up. It had eight points, which meant that the stag that had dropped it would have carried sixteen points altogether. "I worked for a gentleman once who was knowledgeable about deer," Brockley said to me. "You hardly ever get a sixteen-pointer in England, but here it's quite common. Plenty of big, fat deer in these woods, it seems."

"And the seigneurs eat all the venison," said Walter Dodd.

"The peasants get pease pottage, evidently." He grinned at Mark Sweetapple.

"Plain folk don't eat venison in England, either. When did you last taste deer steak?" inquired Ryder.

"We don't need it," said Sweetapple. "My parents have chickens and geese and they kill a pig every year. There's always ham and bacon in the house, and we can take rabbits on our own farm. These folk hardly seem to have meat at all."

He was right. With every mile we traveled, I grew more and more conscious of the poverty in the villages and on the small farmsteads. The people who came to their cottage doors or straightened up from their tasks in field or garden to watch us pass were thin for the most part, and poorly clad as well, many of them barefoot.

By contrast, we were all well fleshed and well dressed. Even Dale, who always looked eccentric on horseback because she felt safer astride, and wore breeches, still had good-quality clothes and polished boots. My dignified side-saddle and my russet riding dress with the dark green felt hat and matching cloak; Master Blanchard's severe but costly black velvet, with gold embroidery and a collar of cream voile; the stout buff jackets and gleaming helmets of the men, including Brockley, made us look like aristocrats compared to the people of the villages. Some of them stared, and not in a friendly way, and some of the women hurried their children indoors when they saw us coming.

We saw more signs of violence as we rode on, as well. I commented on them to Luke Blanchard. I couldn't like him, for I couldn't forget his unkindness to me in the past. But I had agreed, for my own reasons, to come on this journey with him and the least I could do was be polite. That meant making conversation from time to time.

"The people look as if they envy us and our clothes and horses," I said, "but they're very frightened, too. Did you see how those women ran indoors at the sight of us? And though we've seen corn growing, I doubt if these people eat much of the bread. I fancy the seigneurs are selling the grain away to buy arms and pay soldiers."

Blanchard, who being a tall man had hired a tall horse, looked down at me from his saddle.

"You are a surprise to me, Ursula," he said unexpectedly. "One would not expect a young woman to be so sharp. You are right, of course. I wish this journey were safely over." He pulled a pained face and put his hand to his stomach. "But my belly still hurts me. We'd better find another inn soon and put up until tomorrow. It will waste time but I don't think I can ride on much farther just now."

We found an inn, in a prosperous small town, named St. Marc after the massive Norman church on one side of its market square. The roofs of an abbey were visible behind the church, as well.

There was a sense of tension in St. Marc, as there was everywhere. We saw groups of people gathered here and there and talking with much sad shaking of heads and some excited nodding. But on the whole business here seemed to be going on much as usual. Smoke trickled from the chimneys of the red-tiled houses and cottages, and from the nosebag spillings and broken bits of this and that in the square in front of the church, a market had recently been held there.

The inn, on the opposite side of the square, was red-tiled like the other buildings and quite big, with trestle tables and benches on a forecourt, an arched courtyard entrance and a sprightly inn sign, on which a prancing horse was painted in yellow. It was still only afternoon, well before the time when wayfarers begin to arrive at inns in search of shelter. Le Cheval d'Or, we thought, could surely take us in.

But to my irritation, Blanchard once more adopted his policy of announcing us as loudly as though we were the most important people who had ever entered its portals, and once more, the innkeeper bristled. Harvey joined in, hectoring in very bad French, which did nothing to help. Jean Charpentier, proprietor of Le Cheval d'Or, didn't match his sprightly signboard. He was no cheerful, rubicund host, but a lean and disillusioned individual with a grimy shirt under his sleeveless jerkin, and a sour face. He looked as though he enjoyed refusing people, particularly loudmouthed Anglaises.

Ryder tried to propitiate him, but as Ryder's French was even worse than Harvey's, this merely added confusion to irritation. The only other person in the party who could speak the tongue was myself. I had learned French with my cousins and improved it when I was married to Gerald, who had excellent French, as all the Blanchards did, and had encouraged me to study it. I cleared my throat and intervened, with an attempt at coaxing.

This finally had results. Charpentier eventually agreed that although he was very full, he could just squeeze us in, but some of the men would have to bed down in his barn. "It's dry and there's plenty of straw, so there'll be nothing off the bill, I'm warning you," he added.

The Dodds and Sweetapple said it would probably be better than their billets last night. "Could hardly be worse," said Mark with feeling.

The innkeeper's insistence that he was full seemed odd, however. The hostelry was very quiet and Brockley, bringing hampers in from the stableyard, reported that the stable was half empty. Blanchard, unwell or not, was irritated enough by our discouraging reception to raise the matter with Charpentier when at last we had dismounted and were indoors. "I don't understand it," he said. "It's early in the day and the inn is large. You've got attic rooms and two floors besides, and wings stretching back. How can you be full? It isn't market day."

"No, seigneur." Charpentier did not sound amiable. "Market day was yesterday. You are Anglaises," he observed, "which no doubt means heretic. Well, I will tell you for nothing that I am a good son of Holy Church, and heresy is a grief to me, and this whole district is infested with Huguenots. I'd cut all their throats if I had my way. But it means that men and arms are on the move and it brings in business. By tonight, I will have a young seigneur here, bound for Paris with a dozen retainers, and a prelate of some standing with ten more, also making for Paris. They are taking their men to swell the government's forces. Both sent word ahead and their rooms are bespoken. I also have a Netherlander merchant staying, with two companions, while he does some business in the district. Some men will do business even when the clouds are raining blood." Charpentier shrugged. "He, too, is a Protestant, but his money is good as yours is, I trust. By nightfall, my hostelry will be full enough. Are you answered?"

Any normality in St. Marc was clearly fragile. The religious divisions of France were seething under the surface, ready to burst out at any moment. Charpentier quite evidently bracketed all Protestants with cockroaches.

Beside me, despite my warnings before we left Greenwich, Dale muttered something indignant about Papists. Charpentier heard and apparently understood. He shot her an unfriendly glance. Blanchard eyed her repressively before saying:

"Well, it is an answer, though in England, innkeepers address their clients more respectfully. As it happens, I am on my way to visit Catholic relatives at Douceaix, near Le Mans. There is no need to regard me as an enemy. Now, kindly show me to my chamber, and if I could have some warm water or milk, I would be pleased. I have an upset stomach."

The innkeeper's expression suggested that this was just one more transgression, almost as bad as heresy. But he led us upstairs and showed us a couple of rooms, not large, but clean. Harvey hurried his master into his chamber, wondering aloud if the village had an apothecary. Dale and I took the second room, which was just across a square lobby. "A couple of your men can sleep in the lobby but only two," said Charpentier. "It's the barn for the rest."

Brockley fetched my hampers up, arriving in time to hear me taking Dale to task for her remarks about Papists.

"The mistress is right, Fran. While we're in France, we'd better keep our opinions to ourselves. But the sooner we go home and get out of this country, the better. Which means getting on with our journey, if we can. Madam, have you any idea what's wrong with Master Blanchard? He should be over the seasickness by now. The rest of us are. I hope he's not sick in some other way."

"So do I," I said earnestly. "Master Blanchard falling ill in a French inn with a hostile innkeeper in the middle of an insurrection—what more do we need?"

We had dined along the way in a fashion, on bread and meat brought from the first inn. But fresh air and riding make one hungry, and Dale began to grumble that it was a long time until supper. "And if there's one thing I can't abide, ma'am, it's a grumbling stomach."

"I'm getting tired of other people's stomachs," I said. "My own was trouble enough on the boat. Now it's yours and Master Blanchard's. Well, you can go down and see if the kitchen can provide anything to eat. No doubt we could all do with it, the men included. Anything will do except cheese. I don't think I ever want to eat cheese again."

"But, ma'am, I can't talk French."

I was tired. I was no longer ill, but the voyage had drained strength out of me and the queen's letters in my hidden pocket felt like an almost physical weight. In addition, the atmosphere of France oppressed me. Now, it seemed, I must take on the task of looking after my servants, instead of being looked after by them.

But perhaps, Dale being Dale, it might be better if she didn't talk to the local population too much.

"Oh, very well," I said. "I'll go."

CHAPTER 4

The Hooded Man

Dale sighed with relief at not having to ask for food in sign language. Brockley offered to come with me, but I saw no need for an escort inside the inn. "I'm only going to the kitchen, Brockley."

I left them unpacking the hampers, and hurried downstairs. I followed the smell of cooking along a stone passage to the kitchen where I found the landlord giving orders to a greasy youth in a leather apron, and a hefty woman with thick black hair in a knot on the back of her head and arms as massive as though she had spent her life shoeing horses. "Master Charpentier?" I said mildly from the doorway.

He turned to me, frowning. "I've sent Master Blanchard's hot milk up to him. There's soup and bread if the rest of you are hungry, and the wine of St. Marc is good."

"Thank you. That's what I came to ask about. Most of us do want something to eat and drink. Where . . . ?"

"Weather's warm. I'll have it put on the tables out in front."

"Would you? It will be most welcome, believe me." I was trying to placate this difficult man, but I wasn't having much success. Which was a pity, because there was something else I wanted to ask him.

Huguenot influence might be strong in this part of France

but St. Marc did not feel Huguenot, and Jean Charpentier certainly was not. Also, we had not yet traveled so very far from the Loire. Both of these things had been simmering together in my mind since we reached the inn. I had no idea how well known my husband Matthew was in his own country, but the owner of a château was usually known over a sizable area, and in the present troubles, he and Charpentier were on the same side. It was worth trying.

"In England," I said, standing my ground, "I was for a while acquainted with a visitor from this part of the world. He's back in France now. I wonder if you've heard of him? His name is Matthew de la Roche."

I had no shadow of right to ask after Matthew, but I couldn't help myself. It was unbearable to be so near, and not even inquire. The result, however, was shattering. The greasy youth and the black-haired woman froze, mouths open, and Charpentier first stared into my face with furious brown eyes, and then grabbed my arm and shoved me up against the wall. Close by was a table with cabbages and carrots on it, and also a sharp little knife. To my utter disbelief, he snatched it up and held it to my throat.

"Who are you?"

"What are you doing? Master Charpentier, please! I'm Mistress Blanchard, from England!"

"What are you doing in France?"

"I'm traveling with my . . . my father-in-law." I was stuttering with fright. "He has a ward in France, a young girl. He wants to take her to England, away from the war. She's been orphaned. He wanted her to have a woman to travel with. We're on our way to fetch her from the relatives she's with now, at Douceaix, near Le Mans. That's all. Please, Master Charpentier!"

His left hand was crushing the muscles of my upper arm painfully, but the vegetable knife was more terrifying. Peering down my nose at it, I could see that it was very sharp indeed. I was carrying my dagger but I knew that I had no chance of reaching it and getting it out of its sheath quickly enough to help me. I wished I had let Brockley come with me. In future (assuming I had a future), I wouldn't stir a step without him.

Charpentier put his head close to mine, breathing garlic into my face. "Why are you asking after De la Roche?"

"I met him when he came to England. I was asking if you knew of him! I wanted to ask if he was well! That's all!"

"Is it? Is it? We have had English spies before, asking after De la Roche."

"I'm not a spy! Oh, really, Master Charpentier! This is ridiculous! Do I look like a spy?"

"How do I know what a spy looks like? If I were sending out spies, I would see that they seemed innocent! As innocent as you, traveling with your father-in-law, who seeks only to take a young girl out of the path of a war!"

"You're making a mistake," I gasped. "We're on our way to visit a Catholic household. Do you intend to murder me here in your kitchen?"

"It is not murder to dispose of a spy."

I drew breath to scream for Brockley but the black-haired woman (I never found out whether she was Charpentier's cook or his wife, and didn't care, either) had moved closer to me and as I opened my mouth, she clapped a powerful palm over it, silencing me. "No noise, my lady. Shall we take her outside, Jean?"

I aimed a kick at Master Charpentier's shins and brought up my spare hand to wrench at the woman's wrist. I might as well have attacked a couple of trees. The pair of them were impervious. I don't know what would have happened next if there had not, just then, been a merciful interruption. There was the sound of men and horses and a voice from the front of the building calling for the innkeeper. Assured, booted feet came ringing along the stone passage, and a young, cool French voice said: "Charpentier? Where in the devil's name are you? We're earlier than we thought to be but it's the first time since I've known you that you haven't come out at a run at the sound of fifteen horses and four pack mules! *Mon Dieu!* What is going on here? Who is this girl?"

"She's English and she's asking after Matthew de la Roche," said Charpentier over his shoulder.

This, apparently, was sufficient explanation. I twisted about and tried to speak and the elegant young man who had appeared in the doorway said: "Never before have I arrived at a hostelry to find the innkeeper about to cut the throat of a young woman in the kitchen. It tends to undermine confidence in the cuisine. Charpentier, I think she wants to say something. I would like to hear it."

The muffling hand was withdrawn. "I'm a completely innocent traveler from England," I said angrily. "Not long ago, in my own country, I met a visitor from France called Matthew de la Roche. I simply asked after him—I know he lives somewhere along the Loire. That's all! And then this man Charpentier attacked me and threatened to kill me!"

"A little extreme, I agree," said the stranger. He was sophisticated and of some standing, with quantities of embroidery on his dark blue doublet and the matching cloak he wore tossed over one shoulder, and gems upon his sword hilt. I was grateful for his intervention, but for all his gallantry, he didn't make me feel a great deal better.

As he came indoors, he had removed his dashing high-

crowned hat as a gentleman should and his unshadowed face
was sharp and cold. So were his eyes. They were disconcerting,
both indeterminate in color, but not a match. One of them
tended toward brown and the other toward blue, and they
held a chill that made me uneasy. He gave me the same feeling as Robin Dudley. Here was a man of whom one should be
wary.

"I call this behavior *very* extreme!" I said vehemently, and
let my voice carry, in the hope that some of my own companions would hear it. I was trembling, but now it was partly with
anger. I rounded on Charpentier. "And foolish! May I remind
you that I am traveling not only with my father-in-law but also
with an escort of eight men? If I were to vanish, do you think
that nobody would notice?"

My captors had slackened their hold and I shook myself
free of them. As I did so, the contents of my hidden pocket
bumped against my knee, and I heard, faintly, the clink of the
lock picks and the rustle of Elizabeth's letters. It was not the
moment, though, for bringing out the letter of introduction
to Queen Catherine. Elizabeth had confidence in the status
of her messengers but these people might well see her only as
a heretic queen, and the letters as somehow proof that I was
a spy. Elizabeth knew that France was dangerous, I thought
grimly, but she had no idea just how dangerous.

Anyway, I had a champion, even though he was in his way
nearly as alarming as Charpentier.

"The lady has a point," the stranger was saying. "We have
the reputation of France to consider. If Madam were to disap-
pear, her friends might take home a sorry impression of us."
He bowed to me formally. "Seigneur Gaston de Clairpont, at
your service. I regret this incident, madam, but I should say
that it is not advisable to ask after Seigneur Matthew de la

Roche, not in an English voice. I take it, Charpentier, that you did not answer her questions?"

"I only wished to hear that a former acquaintance was in good health," I expostulated.

"He is in perfectly good health, and will, I trust, remain so," said De Clairpont. "Let her go, Charpentier. I hope you are not hurt, madam?"

"Fortunately, no," I said. I was going to have a badly bruised upper arm but it wasn't worth remarking on. "I and the rest of my party," I said with emphasis to Charpentier, "will be glad to take bread and soup on the tables outside, as soon as it is ready." Then, holding my head high, I walked out. No one tried to stop me. De Clairpont bowed again as I passed. I inclined my head to him graciously. On shaking legs I made my way back along the stone passage and met the Dodds and John Ryder hurrying toward me.

"We heard your voice. You sounded alarmed," Ryder said.

"I was. I hoped someone would hear. You're a reassuring sight, all three of you. Come back upstairs and I'll explain."

We went up to my room. There, with Brockley and Dale to swell the outraged audience, I described what had happened.

"I never heard of such a thing," Dale gasped. "Innkeepers threatening their guests—attacking a lady! What sort of a country is this?"

"Charpentier had better be careful," said young Walter Dodd. "If he takes to slaughtering his guests in the kitchen, people will wonder what he puts in his casseroles."

Everyone laughed except Dale, who snapped: "That's disgusting!"

"The Seigneur de Clairpont said much the same thing," I said to her. "I just hope it impressed Charpentier!"

"This Matthew de la Roche," Ryder said. "You say he's an

acquaintance of yours. Perhaps I should tell you that we do know that he is your estranged husband. Sir William Cecil told us. I knew before, anyway. I have known Sir William since he was a boy, Mistress Blanchard. My mother was maid to his mother. I can remember clipping Sir William Cecil's ear for him once or twice, when he was a lad!" He laughed. "It was natural enough for you to ask after him. Why shouldn't you?"

"Charpentier doesn't know I'm married to Matthew. I wish now that I hadn't mentioned Matthew at all," I said. I wondered, in passing, whether, after all, Luke Blanchard knew about Matthew, too. Not that it mattered. "I shan't ask after him again," I said. "It isn't safe."

Brockley, who was fuming, said that he would go down and punch Charpentier on the jaw, but I forbade it. "We don't want to get into trouble. What we do want is to carry out our business and go home safely. The sooner we leave this detestable inn, the better."

"There's not much chance of that just now," said Dick Dodd glumly. "We have just seen Harvey. He says that Master Blanchard is very unwell, won't take anything except warm milk, and by the look of him, we're likely to be stuck here for days."

I went at once to see how Luke Blanchard was. He was lying in his bed, his proudly curved nose pointing to the ceiling and his short gray hair tousled. He looked miserable.

"I'm not at all well, Ursula," he said when I asked him how he did. "I fear it's beyond me to leave this bed."

"What are your symptoms? My mother taught me some simple remedies. Perhaps I can help."

"My stomach's been hurting ever since I was so sick on the ship," he said fretfully. "And I've no appetite. If I try to eat anything, I feel sick. Milk is all right. Charpentier says he shouldn't, because it's Lent, but he let me have some milk all the same."

I asked a few more questions. He had had loose motions, he said, but not to a violent extent and no, the stomach pain wasn't more in one place than in another. But it got worse if he moved about. He just wanted to lie still. I said I hoped he would feel better soon, and went worriedly away. "Just when we need to get on with our journey, this has to happen!" I said to Dale when I rejoined her in our room. "Well, we had better take some food ourselves."

As promised, Charpentier had set out a meal on the fore-court, and Lent notwithstanding, there was meat in the soup, and the bread was fresh and crusty. The red wine was full-bodied and there was cream cheese, so delicate and light that I found I could eat cheese after all. Mark Sweetapple positively wolfed it. We also had some kind of fruit preserve that went well with the bread. We all felt better when we had eaten.

A maidservant waited on us, but Charpentier presently emerged, behaving as though the scene in his kitchen had never happened and inquired, like any other innkeeper, if all was to our liking. I took courage and said politely that it was, and then asked if there was an apothecary in the town, as Master Blanchard was still ailing.

Charpentier said yes, there was such a one, but the shop would be shutting by now. It would open early in the morning. If Master Blanchard was no better at daybreak, I said, I would see what the apothecary could recommend.

When we went indoors after eating, we found De Clairpont in the wide entrance hall talking to another man. De Clairpont called to me.

"Mistress Blanchard, I hear that your father-in-law is ill. I am sorry. A miserable business for him, away from home, and in a troubled land. I wish him better health soon."

"Thank you," I said. I glanced at the second man, wondering who he was. He did not, somehow, go with De Clairpont. He was some years older, and did not have the air of a retainer, or even of a Frenchman. His brown doublet and hose were very well cut, in a style often seen in London. He had a plain linen collar, but his sleeves had scarlet slashings and his boots were of very good kid. He had a compact, broad-shouldered build, a rosy-brown face, a brown beard and bright dark eyes, and reminded me of an outsize robin redbreast.

He smiled, and announced in competent but heavily accented French that he was Nicolas van Weede, merchant, from Antwerp. "I, too, am a guest at this inn. I have been hearing of your unhappy experience this afternoon. It is wise, in France just now, to be most careful. You are recovered from your fright, I trust?"

"Indeed, we both hope so. A most disturbing experience for a lady," said De Clairpont.

"I am quite recovered, thank you. It was all a misunderstanding," I said carefully.

I went on my way. Dale had lingered, waiting for me. "Who would those gentlemen be, ma'am?" she asked. "Do you know them? How do you know who to trust, in this nest of Papists?"

"Dale!" I snapped warningly, pushing her ahead of me up the stairs, and when we reached my room, I shut the door after us and once again gave her a piece of my mind. "One more remark like that and you'll regret it, Dale. I've never raised a hand to you but how many more times must I warn you?"

"Oh, ma'am, I'm sorry. I'm sorry!" I had never spoken to Dale quite so harshly before and now her eyes filled with tears.

But France was a perilous place and for Dale's sake as well as my own, I had to make my point.

"Never mind about being sorry; just watch your tongue, do you hear? Either De Clairpont or Van Weede could have overheard you and it just won't do, Dale. I suspect that Van Weede may speak English. De Clairpont's obviously educated and may understand it, too. Keep your opinions to yourself while we're in France. De Clairpont rescued me from Charpentier, which entitles him to my courtesy, and Van Weede I've never met before, which means I have no reason not to be polite to him." Dale's tears were now streaming and I moderated my tone. "All right. You understand now, I think. I am grateful to De Clairpont and I quite liked the look of Van Weede, but trust doesn't come into it. De Clairpont is rather frightening, somehow, and as for Van Weede . . ."

I had lived in Antwerp with Gerald and met many Netherlander merchants. I had heard them trying to speak French, too. Sir Thomas Gresham had a cosmopolitan household in which people were forever trying to communicate with one another in languages not their own. Netherland merchants didn't dress or speak like Van Weede. At a guess, I would have said that he was English.

"I must say I don't care for this feeling of mysteries all round," I said, after I had explained this. "I want to leave here quickly and I can only pray that Master Blanchard will be better in the morning."

He was not.

I came down to breakfast next day, to find William Harvey trying to explain to Charpentier that his master needed a physician. Because of Harvey's bad French, Charpentier couldn't understand him.

"Can I help?" I said.

Brusquely, Harvey explained. "Master Blanchard's worse," he said to me. My heart sank. But in seeking medical help, Harvey was doing the right thing. I translated for Charpentier, who, once he understood, informed me that the local apothecary whose direction he had given me the day before, was also the local physician. His name was Dr. Alain Lejeune. "And fetch him quickly," he said. "Sick guests don't do an inn any good. People wonder if it's catching, or if the food is bad."

De Clairpont had already made the point that murdered guests were even worse for an inn's reputation than sick ones. I refrained from repeating it. "I'll fetch the doctor, Harvey. It had better be me, since I speak French. Dale will come with me."

Harvey nodded brusquely, and after a pause had the grace to say: "Thank you." He even added: "Last night, you and Dale supped upstairs, to keep out of the way of the other guests. Best you do the same for breakfast now."

I took his advice. Dale and I took some food quickly and privately, and then we set out.

Lejeune lived at the other end of the main street. We had come through it to the square where the inn stood. It was a narrow, straggling affair of shops with dwellings over the top, and it was busy with rattling carts and housewives carrying baskets. We walked briskly, because the morning was cool and overcast. When I first sensed that someone was following us, I took it for my imagination.

I was alerted by a skill I didn't know I possessed. Amid the busy sound of feet on the cobbles, mine and Dale's and those of all the other people, my ears by some means picked out the one pair of footsteps behind us that kept exactly to our pace, slowing down when we stopped to let a cart turn into a yard, speeding up again when a gust of fresh wind made us quicken our steps to keep warm.

Halting abruptly in front of a bakery, half-turning to face it, I pointed out some particularly inviting pastries to Dale and from the corner of my eye I shot a glance back along the street. I caught the quick movement as someone, a man, wearing a hooded cloak with the hood up, also stopped and turned sideways to stare in at a shop.

"Come along," I said to Dale. She glanced at me questioningly, and made a half gesture at some cinnamon buns.

"I know, they're mouthwatering," I said. "But I really stopped because I thought someone was following us and I think I'm right. He's wearing a brown cloak and hood."

"What? What'll you do, ma'am? Will you speak to him?"

"No, I can't do that. Whoever it is has only to say I'm talking nonsense. I don't want an embarrassing scene in the street. But we'll cross the road. When we get to the other side, we'll go into that place selling leather goods, and I'll peep out and see if he's crossed after us."

We did this, dodging around another cart and a small boy who was busy shoveling up horse droppings, no doubt for use as garden manure. The leather shop, like most of the others, had an open front and a table jutting into the road, laden with a display of wares. These were guarded by a fat woman, seated on a chair beside them. Behind, was a cavernous room where the proprietor worked at a counter under a skylight, busy with punching and stitching. Various items including saddlery were on racks within the shop.

Dale and I plunged straight past the display table, as though to examine some saddles. Then I edged back to where I could see the road, and there he was, his face still hidden by the side of his hood, studying some silk fabrics on display next door.

I pulled Dale out to the street again. "We're just going a few yards," I said into her ear. "Then I want you to stumble and pretend you've almost lost your shoe. That'll give me a chance to swing round and I'll see if I can catch sight of his face."

"Oh, ma'am," said Dale protestingly. "I'm no good at pretending. I just can't abide it."

"Nonsense, Dale, you're wonderful at pretending. Just do as I say. Now!"

We were passing another shop with a display table, this one laden with pots and pans and other ironmongery. Dale tripped, quite artistically, and hopped on one foot, leaning on the edge of the table and grabbing at the heel of her shoe. The table rocked and I turned at once, helpfully steadying a pile of cooking pots. I was just in time to see the hooded figure melt smoothly out of sight among the leather goods.

Grabbing Dale's elbow, I hustled her back to them. With luck, I thought, our pursuer had made a mistake in taking refuge there, since he had walked into a dead end.

But there was no sign of him. There was a back door behind the workbench, and it was ajar, tapping lightly as the wind disturbed it. I made for the bench.

"Excuse me, but did someone come through here just now?"

The proprietor glanced irritatedly up from his work. "No, madam. Why should I let any member of the public through into my private yard? This is a shop. It is not a thoroughfare."

"Thank you," I said, and, once more, led Dale back toward the street. The woman in charge of the table asked us as we went by whether any of her wares interested us, and feeling that we had probably annoyed these people quite enough, I stopped and bought a pair of new riding gloves. Dale, however, had been using her eyes.

"Ma'am," she said as soon as we were back in the street, "that man with the hood *did* go in there! I saw him, too. And there was a gold coin lying by that shopkeeper's hand, as if he'd put it there for the moment while he finished his work."

"Really? I saw that the yard door was ajar, but I didn't see the coin. Well done, Dale. Oh well, if we've lost him, then he's lost us. Come along. We'd better find that physician."

CHAPTER 5

An Unseen Hand

We found Dr. Lejeune stooping over a fireplace, stirring a smelly pot. A pestle and mortar stood at his side, and the walls of his room were lined with shelves full of bottles containing powders and potions. Hanging from the ceiling were various dried herbs and roots. On the floor were several immense glass vessels containing some extraordinarily nasty objects, preserved in what looked like oil. One seemed to be a small crocodile—I had seen pictures of these reptiles and knew what they looked like—and another, most horribly, resembled a half-formed baby.

Lejeune himself was thin and somehow dusty and I doubt if he ever smiled. His face was blank when I described Luke Blanchard's symptoms, and I didn't feel much confidence in him, but he was all there was. He consented to come with us to Le Cheval d'Or, and did so, but had little to say when he got there. Blanchard was complaining miserably of pain all over his stomach and said the very thought of food was unbearable, beyond a little milk. "Even that's better mixed with water," he said wanly.

Lejeune prodded at him, peered down his throat, shrugged, and recommended a potion that he said he would send along later by his boy. I wondered what would be in it but preferred not to ask. Lejeune then demanded what I considered an exorbitant fee, and left. I looked worriedly down at my former father-in-law.

"We'll get you better," I said reassuringly, and on impulse added: "I'll make you up a potion of my own, if I can get hold of the ingredients. I've as much faith in that as in anything that doctor's likely to produce."

Harvey had tidied his master's bed and brought him fresh supplies of milk and water. Dale and I hurried out again.

I had a few basic medicines with me, including a salve for cuts and bruises and a chamomile draft in case of sick headaches, but I had nothing that might help my father-in-law. However, although I would never have called myself skilled in herbal medicine, as some women are, my mother had taught me a little and Dale had a certain amount of knowledge.

After some anxious discussion, we decided on a formula and set out once more, this time in search of a shop selling flavorings and condiments. Here, I bought root ginger, valerian, and dried marshmallow. "I don't think they'll make things worse," I said to Dale, "even if they can't cure him!"

After my last foray into the kitchen, I was nervous about going there again, but I couldn't prepare an infusion unless I did so. I took a deep breath and marched in. The black-haired woman was rolling dough while a girl I hadn't seen before beat up some kind of batter in a basin and the greasy youth was filleting fish. I cleared my throat, explained what I wanted to do, and asked for a small cooking pot and some water and permission to use a corner of the hearth. The woman regarded me with dislike but reached a long-handled pan down from a hook and passed it to me.

"You can use that and get yourself some well water. It's out at the back. But don't get in the way. Knives and spoons are hanging up over there if you want them."

Dale and I cut my ingredients small before putting them in the water, and then set about brewing up a draft. Charpentier came into the kitchen while we were there and I had to explain to him what we were about. I also had to explain to Hugh Arnold when he put his head in to say that Sweetapple and Harvey were sitting with Master Blanchard and wished to have their dinner there, and could they please have it early?

"You Anglaises make work," the black-haired woman told me when Arnold had gone. "That man Sweetapple eats as if he's been starved since he was a baby. Oh well, it will all go on the bill at the end."

I was sure it would. My father-in-law must somehow be got fit enough to leave this inn, or quite apart from the delay to the queen's correspondence, Charpentier was the type to hand us a bill that would bankrupt us.

As soon as it was ready, I asked, very politely, for the loan of a jar with a stopper and put my infusion into it. Then we went upstairs to give Master Blanchard a dose. Harvey and Sweetapple were there and Harvey at once asked suspiciously what was in the potion. When I recited the ingredients, however, Sweetapple spoke up and declared that his mother had used the same things for digestive ailments. "It'll do you no harm, sir, anyway," he said encouragingly to Blanchard.

Master Blanchard consented to try it, diluted with water. He made a face and said it tasted horrible, but he drank it down. I could only hope that it would benefit him.

Most of us dined downstairs, for last night's guests had either left or gone out and the inn was quiet once more. Dale and I went up again after the meal, but presently Harvey tapped on my door to say that a messenger had come asking for me. It turned out to be Lejeune's boy, bringing the promised medicine. It was a murky brew in a small glass bottle and it smelled appalling, far worse than my own concoction. We had paid a high consultation fee, however, and I supposed I should at least offer it to Blanchard. I found him still in bed, his face set in lines of depression. Sweetapple and Harvey and the remains of their dinner were still there. So was a lingering aroma of fish.

"You should get those used platters out of here," I said. "The smell of food may make him feel worse. Master Blanchard, this has come for you from the physician. You can try it if you will."

"I'm no better," he said dismally. "But I daresay you're trying to help me. I'll swallow this if you wish."

It was a short attempt, however. One mouthful of Lejeune's potion made him gag and clutch at his stomach muscles again. "Yours wasn't very palatable but *this!*" he said disgustedly. "I can't get it down. Take it away!"

The visit to Lejeune had been wasted. He would have to recover with the help of my homely remedies or not at all. Clicking my tongue, I fetched Dale and said that we would sit with him while the men stretched their legs and removed their dinner dishes. Sweetapple and Harvey departed, taking the used platters with them, and we stayed with Blanchard for the next couple of hours. After a time, he fell asleep. Then Arnold knocked on the door and came in to take over. "I'll bring him another dose of my potion in the evening," I said. "Perhaps by tomorrow there'll be some result."

Dale and I went back to our room. Evening was coming. The inn was quiet, but I could hear Brockley's voice in the stableyard below. I strolled over to the window to look. Brockley was down there with another of Blanchard's men, the redheaded Searle, examining the feet of one of our hired horses. My own left shoe touched something and I glanced down. Most of our things had been unpacked, but not quite everything, and a few items still remained in the hampers and saddlebags, which were all piled together in the corner next to the window. I had just kicked a saddlebag.

As I looked at it, a small cold worm moved in my guts.

I had a clear picture in my mind of how those bags and hampers had been arranged when I last glanced at them, just after dinner. Everything then had been neatly piled but now, the topmost hamper was tilting perilously, while the saddlebags, which had been compactly placed side by side, were lying apart, one of them right under the window and also under my feet.

"Dale," I said. "I think . . . I think . . . that someone has been interfering with our baggage."

We went through it together, at once, and then through the things that had been put in the cupboards and chests. Nothing was missing. Our gowns hung where Dale had put them; the case containing my few pieces of jewelry was untouched, the contents all in place.

"But someone's been at it, right enough," Dale said, horrified, staring into a cupboard. "I never folded your linen like that, ma'am, never so carelessly. All your sleeves were together, too, and here's a pair out of place on the shelf below!"

"And this book of poems," I said, examining the saddlebags, "was in the other pocket, the offside one, not in here!"

We stared at each other. Instinctively, I put a hand to my overskirt and once again felt the stiff crackle of the parchment cylinders in the hidden pocket. I turned back the edge of the skirt and drew the contents out. They were of course untouched, because they never left my person. I had put the royal letters into a little linen bag and even slept with them under my pillow. "I wonder if someone was looking for these?"

"Everyone in our party knows you're going to Paris, ma'am."

"Yes, but they're not actually supposed to know about the letter to the queen mother."

"But what if somebody does know, all the same, ma'am? And is being paid to make sure that letter doesn't get there . . . ?"

"I don't want this," I said angrily. "To think I was hoping to get away from mystery and intrigue! Well, Dale, we've just got to make sure that that letter does get to Paris safely, that's all."

Brockley had been busy with the horses and we had not yet told him of the man who had followed us. Now I sent Dale to fetch her husband, and I described to him both our strange hooded pursuer, and the way unseen fingers had searched our baggage. Tight-mouthed with anger, he said that if necessary, we would ride on to Paris without Blanchard and his men.

"The sooner we get there and get back, the better. We can manage with just Cecil's escort. Whoever's been doing these things could well be one of Blanchard's men. I only hope that Cecil's escort are all trustworthy! We can meet Master Blanchard at his ward's home afterward. That's if he gets better," Brockley added acidly, "and doesn't embarrass Charpentier by dying on the premises! Meanwhile, madam, lock your door and your window tonight."

"And once more, we'll eat supper up here this evening," I said. "We'll guard our belongings."

"I'll fetch the food up to you, madam," Brockley said.

We carried this plan out. I took my father-in-law a further dose of my herbal potion, and went to bed early, but slept very ill. Elizabeth was right to think that I, too, knew what insomnia was.

Elizabeth, though, could call on others to share her misery. Her Ladies of the Bedchamber sometimes looked exhausted, after being awakened in the small hours to read to their restless sovereign, or worse still, play chess with her. "Have you ever tried to play chess when you're half asleep?" Lady Katherine Knollys had once asked me, quite bitterly.

But I would not disturb Dale in that way. There was a bolt inside our door and following Brockley's recommendation, I shot it before Dale and I retired. I also shut the window. But it only had a latch and there was a little tree just outside. I knew, from the kind of experience that most ladies don't possess, that a thin knife blade could be slipped through the crack to lift that latch. While Dale, who was sharing my bed, slumbered at my side, I lay there, hour after hour, listening for the rustle of branches and the scratch and scrape of an intruder at that window.

There was no intruder, however. I slept in the end, for about two hours. It was nowhere near enough, of course, and I was bleary-eyed in the morning. I sent Dale to fetch cold water, splashed my face with it to wake myself up, chose a clean gown for the day, transferred the precious letters (plus dagger and lock picks) to the pocket in the fresh overskirt, and then went to knock on Master Blanchard's door, to find out if yesterday's medicines had had any effect.

"No, they haven't," William Harvey said, meeting me at the door. I went in to look at the patient, who said miserably that he was no better and no worse.

"You ought to eat. Can I ask them to send up some gruel or soup? Could you manage that?"

"A little thin soup, perhaps," said Blanchard wanly. "And

I'll take some more of your medicine if you like, but not that filthy brew the physician sent."

I fetched the soup and brought another dose of my potion. He swallowed this quite willingly, but he took only a few spoonfuls of the soup before lying disconsolately back with a shake of the head. I plodded wearily away.

I decided that we would once again eat in our room, and sent Dale to fetch breakfast. Returning with a tray, she said that although De Clairpont had left the inn, the merchant Van Weede was still there and had asked after my ailing father-in-law.

"I told him there was no good news, and he said he was sorry. It's true he speaks English but he's got a thick accent. He's a civil sort of fellow, though."

"And I'm sure he's pretending to be something he isn't," I said irritably. "What's the matter with this inn?"

We stayed in our room all morning. Brockley had advised me not to report either our hooded follower or our searched baggage to John Ryder. Ryder had been sent with me by Cecil, along with the Dodds, but: "Best think, madam, before you talk to anyone at all. We can't be quite sure even of Cecil's fellows. Better not alert the enemy until we know who the enemy is." After thinking about it, I agreed with Brockley. Were Cecil's men necessarily reliable? Bribery could reach some unexpected places. It would be best to keep silent, I decided, and wait. The foe might in some way reveal himself.

So I sat by the window and read my book of poems, and Dale busied herself with some mending. Later on, the smell of food wafted in, from which I concluded that whoever was sitting with Blanchard was having dinner in his room once again.

Then came a familiar tap on the door, and Dale opened it. Brockley stood there. His features were as impassive as ever but there was a glint in his eyes and that dignified forehead of his positively shone with righteousness.

"I think you should know, madam," he said, "that Master Blanchard, who is supposed to be too ill with stomach trouble to take anything more than thin soup or watered milk and not much of that, is sitting up in his bed, gobbling new bread and fried trout in an herb sauce, and on the table beside him is a dish of what looks like almond fritters. There's a flagon of wine there, too."

"What?"

"I was passing the kitchen door when I heard Harvey ordering dinner upstairs for himself and Sweetapple," said Brockley. "It sounded like a very good dinner for just two men, madam, even if one of them is that young gannet, Mark. So I waited until the food had been taken up, and then followed. The room has a lock but the key was on the outside of the door. I took it out and put my eye to the keyhole. It was dinner for three, not for two. That's how Master Blanchard's been kept fed all this time."

I flung my book onto the bed, swept out and across the lobby to Blanchard's room. I threw the door open without ceremony and there was my father-in-law, upright against his pillows, holding a chunk of bread and fish in one hand, while the other was just picking up a goblet full of wine.

There was shattering silence. Blanchard's face turned a give-away crimson. So did Sweetapple's. Harvey, seated opposite him at a small table by the window, regarded me with fury.

"Do you often enter the bedrooms of gentlemen without knocking, Mistress Blanchard?" he asked coldly.

I ignored him. I was light-headed with rage. I wanted to shout at Blanchard and ask him what game he thought he was playing. But caution stopped me short.

"Master Blanchard," I said, with a sweetness as deceptive as his illness. "I came to see how you were. I did have hopes of my medicine, but this is wonderful. Oh, I am so glad to see you better; I've been so anxious. You must take a turn round the inn yard this afternoon and see how strong you feel. Then, if you have a good night's sleep, perhaps we can go on with our journey tomorrow!"

Withdrawing hastily, before anyone could answer, I went back to my room, where Dale and Brockley were waiting for me.

"They know that I've found out," I said. "They must do. I put on a show, but I doubt if it deceived them."

Closing the door, I went to the window seat, where I sank down, sober now, my brief anger fading. I felt afraid, though I didn't quite know what I feared. I had the queen's letter of introduction in my pocket and her ring on my finger; I had Cecil's men to protect me. I found it hard to believe that either Ryder or the Dodds wanted to steal the royal missive. And I had Brockley. But I had always been, at heart, nervous of Luke Blanchard. Now that fear burned up like a flame.

"If I go on pretending that I just think he's got better," I said, "I fancy they'll go on pretending, too. But what does it all mean? Why should Blanchard want to delay us, and keep us here? What is he about?"

"Perhaps he's the one who's after that letter, ma'am," Dale said.

"We're nowhere near Paris yet. He's got plenty of time," I replied.

"Suppose he wants to pass it to someone here, or nearby," Brockley suggested.

"That would mean," I said slowly, "that he is in the pay of someone in France . . . it could be someone on either side, I suppose. Does Cecil suspect, I wonder? Perhaps this whole business of the letter to Queen Catherine is a trap to catch Blanchard. Well, I wish Cecil had told me, that's all. Now what am I to do?"

I had glimpsed some of the truth, but not from the right angle, and in any case none of our guesses were much help in deciding what to do next.

"I suppose," I said at last, "that there's only one thing I can do. I've been given no instructions about laying traps for Master Blanchard. I must, therefore, carry out the instructions I *was* given. I said as much to Dale yesterday and I think it still stands. I must get that letter to Paris, come what may. We leave tomorrow. With or without Master Blanchard."

We left with him, of course. He had been caught out and he knew it. After solemnly pacing around the inn yard in the afternoon and taking supper in the evening, he declared that next morning he would be quite ready to set off for Douceaix, where Helene Blanchard awaited us.

CHAPTER 6

Helene

The skies had cleared. We left St. Marc to ride through woodland full of golden dapples and the green underwater light of sunshine through young leaves. It should have been delightful. But I was worried and did little but fret.

The evening before, I had said casually to Mark Sweetapple: "Master Blanchard got over his illness very suddenly. Was he really so sick?" Once again, this produced an embarrassed flush, which was informative, but all he actually said was: "Yes, indeed, mistress. But these things do pass off suddenly sometimes. I'm sure your potion helped." Sweetapple was a good lad, but he took his master's orders. I would get no further change out of him or any of the other men. Now I was asking myself whether or not I should after all challenge Luke Blanchard directly.

But he had only to repeat what Sweetapple had said, and claim that he meant to come to me after his meal and tell me of his recovery, and then where would I be? I had let the hooded man go unchallenged for a similar reason. No; better concentrate on my errand for the queen and report the mystery to Cecil when I reached England again.

Blanchard himself made only one remark that could have been an oblique reference to the matter. As we trotted along, our horses' hooves thudding on last year's soft leaf mold, he came up beside me and remarked: "You are more of a surprise to me than ever, you know, Ursula. I begin to be highly impressed with you. I never expected that."

"Impressed?" I said. "In what way?"

But if he had had it in mind to explain or excuse his extraordinary behavior at the inn, he thought better of it. Instead, he said: "When I first learned that you had Gerald in your toils, I thought you'd seduced him in order to escape from your uncle and aunt and your life at Faldene. All I knew of you then was that your mother had been to court to serve Queen Anne Boleyn and was sent home in disgrace, pregnant by a court gallant she would not name, because she said he was married. Your grandparents, and after they were gone, your uncle and aunt, gave her a home and helped her to rear you and they went on looking after you when your mother died. But I could see for myself that you had no love for them. Frankly, I considered that you should show more gratitude and humility—"

"Uncle Herbert and Aunt Tabitha gave me a home," I said. "But they did not give me kindness. There is a saying, Master Blanchard, about the toad under the harrow. The toad knows where each tooth goes."

"You still had food and clothing and a roof—and an education. It seemed to me then that you owed them something, but instead, you ran off with my son, who should have married your cousin Mary. She would have brought him a handsome dower, whereas you brought him nothing."

"He had no need of my cousin's dower," I said. "He made his way very well in the service of Sir Thomas Gresham."

"I realize that now. I also realized, when I heard you were also making your way at court, that perhaps you were more than just—a clever little minx."

"I have never been a minx," I said. "I loved Gerald, Master Blanchard."

"Ah, well. Love." He shrugged. "What does it mean, after all? Marriage is a bargain. The man maintains the woman and gives her children, and she keeps the home and rears the babes. That is life, and it's best if there's money enough for a few comforts. What more can anyone reasonably want? But I see now that Gerald may have recognized in you a certain shrewd quality of mind that your cousin Mary lacks. A quality that could be useful to a man who hopes to climb in the world. Yes, I see. Well, well. Who would have thought it?"

"Are you apologizing to me, Master Blanchard?"

"No. My views were natural. I now see that they were mistaken, that's all. When we return to England, I must make a point of seeing my granddaughter. Perhaps you will bring her to Helene's wedding."

He had rejected Meg once and I wasn't sure that I wanted her to meet him until she was old enough to decide for herself whether she wished to know him or not. I made no direct reply, but instead, seized on the topic of Helene. "I haven't asked you yet—who is Helene to marry?"

"Ah."

I looked at him in surprise. He gave me a chilly smile.

"When I betrothed Gerald," he said, "I did it because I wanted a union with the Faldene family. There is a good deal of money there, and I never saw their preference for the old religion as a difficulty. We Blanchards have accepted the Anglican faith, but Mary would have been allowed to visit her parents at Faldene when she chose, and if she heard Mass while she was there, I would have winked at it. Well, you put an end to that. But now Helene is coming to England, and the younger Faldene son is still unmarried. Both are Catholic, and the young man is acquainted with France; indeed, he was actually in the ambassador's suite here in Paris for a time, although he has since returned home. He and Helene should have much in common. I have arranged for my ward," said Master Blanchard, "to marry Edward Faldene."

"My cousin Edward!"

"Yes. You must be about the same age. Do you remember him?"

In the interest of tact, I said: "Not very well. He was sent away when he was twelve, to finish his education in a Catholic household in Northumbria." In fact, I remembered him all too vividly. Even at twelve, he had been very like his father, my uncle Herbert, by which I mean heavily built but light on his feet, and fond of creeping up on the servants and on me, his illegitimate cousin, so that he could report us if we were doing anything to incur disapproval. He liked people to fear him. He had a cruel streak.

"The Faldenes are willing," Master Blanchard explained. "Helene has lands in France and will bring some valuable jewelry with her, too. On my side, the arrangement is highly satisfactory, because your uncle has agreed that some of Helene's dower will remain in my hands—commission, so to speak. I shall sell my share of her lands as soon as France returns to normal, and I trust to make a good profit."

No wonder, I thought, he had been so eager to get his ward out of France. If Helene were not a likely source of money, he might well have left her to take her chances in the midst of civil war. I began to be sorry for Helene.

We sighted Château Douceaix at the end of the afternoon. It reminded me a little of Faldene, which, although not a happy house, is still beautiful, standing on the side of a sheltered valley, where fields lie on the broad slopes and trees fill the lower part of the vale and thrust their ancient roots out from the banks into Faldene River, which flows along the bottom.

Douceaix had similarities. Here, too, the bottom of the vale was filled with woodland and a sparkling river flowed through it. If Helene eventually found herself living at Faldene, some of the topography would seem familiar. Perhaps it would compensate for having my cousin Edward for a husband and—God help her—Uncle Herbert and Aunt Tabitha as parents-in-law.

There were a few differences, though. The château stood on an isolated knoll rather than on the side of the valley, and the valley itself was much shallower. This was not hilly country. The slopes on either side were ripples in the land, not great waves, and the south-facing ones were planted not with wheat or barley, but with vines.

The house was older than Faldene, too, with genuine arrow slits in the towers at each end and walls topped with businesslike crenellations instead of Faldene's merely decorative ones. It also had a moat, which Faldene had not. White swans cruised there, and there was a bridge of the same pale stone as the rest of the house. It looked like Caen stone, which I knew had been used in the White Tower. At court, I had learned to recognize such things.

Harvey and Ryder galloped on ahead to announce our approach, and by the time we arrived, our hosts had gathered to greet us. In the courtyard, we were helped off our horses and welcomed as though we were beloved friends and well known at Douceaix. A tall and courtly man like a suntanned eagle, with strong wings of brown hair sweeping back from his temples, embraced Luke joyously, exclaiming in quite passable English that he was Henri Blanchard, Luke's distant cousin.

"I believe we share a great-great-grandfather. This is my

wife Marguerite." Marguerite was dark and small and dainty, gracious of smile and shrewd of eye. Her clothes mingled great elegance with great restraint. Pale green flowers embroidered on a cream kirtle and sleeves echoed the green of a plain but beautifully cut overgown; the small, spruce ruff was pure white with a hint of silver thread at the edge. If Helene had been reared in this tradition, Edward would be getting an ornamental bride.

Henri released his cousin Luke, caught sight of me, and was instantly bowing over my hand, taking me in with bright brown eyes. "And this is . . . ? My dear cousin, present me immediately to this charming lady!"

"Madame Ursula Blanchard. My daughter-in-law. She was married to my son Gerald, who alas is now dead. She will give Helene her company on the way home."

"Ah, yes. You wrote that you would find a lady for Helene. So you are a widow, Madame Blanchard? But you are so young. I am desolated for your misfortune, madam, but also charmed to have you with us. And this is your maid?" He even gave Dale a share of that appreciative smile. Henri Blanchard was one of those men who, quite simply, likes women. His smile sent a pang through me because it reminded me of Matthew's. Matthew and I had had so little time together and our last night of love had been abruptly cut short by a violent disturbance. Now, though still wedded, we were far apart. It is not easy to live between two worlds, bound by marriage and yet alone.

"My dear," Marguerite was saying to Henri in French, "should we not go inside? Our guests must be tired. They have ridden a long way and must have passed through unexpected perils. These are frightening times."

"And my father-in-law has been unwell," I said, also in

French, which produced delightedly lifted brows and another lovely smile from Henri. "We were delayed two days at an inn at St. Marc."

"But I am perfectly well now," said Blanchard firmly as we were swept up the steps and into a wide porch. "Where is Helene? I am anxious to meet her."

"She is at her devotions." Marguerite's voice was light and pretty. "Helene is punctilious in her religious observances," she said. "Never would she leave them incomplete, not even to greet her guardian. We ourselves have not known her long, for she was at school at an abbey when her mother died, and although she came to us for a while after that, she pined so much for the abbey that we sent her back—until we began to worry about the prospect of war, when we decided she should rejoin us. I think you will find her all a young girl should be. There is nothing of the hoyden in her."

I wondered if I had imagined the faint note of regret in Marguerite's tone.

We came through the porch into a great hall, adorned as such places usually are with hunting trophies. There were half a dozen pairs of antlers (none of them under sixteen points); an alarming set of boar's tusks; and the mask of a wolf, stuffed by an expert and displayed with teeth aglitter in a mouth lined with scarlet velvet. But I did not have long to stare at it, for Marguerite had taken charge of me and Dale, and was leading us toward a farther door. As we went, we were joined by an entourage of maids and manservants, bringing the baggage, and several ewers of warm water. This was a house that functioned like the workings of a perfect clock.

It was as complicated as the insides of a clock, as well. We went up some stairs and then were led through such a maze of rooms and passages that I soon lost all sense of direction. At length we climbed some more steps and at last went through a door, made of silvery oak and dramatically studded with iron, and into an enormous bedchamber, with a fan-vaulted white stone ceiling like the crypt of a church. The bed was vast and hung with turquoise velvet, and on the walls were verdure tapestries all patterned with foliage, although if you looked closely you could see stags and foxes and birds blended into the design. Tall windows looked out on the vineyards.

"I hope you will be comfortable," Marguerite was saying. "Marie"—she indicated one of the maids—"will be in a little sewing room within earshot, and will bring you down to the hall when you are ready to eat. I know the house is bewildering at first."

"Thank you," I said. I added: "Does Helene speak any English?"

"Oh yes, certainly. Her mother taught it to her when she was small. Kate was a sweet lady," Marguerite added, "though we did not know her well. My husband was as much a distant cousin to Helene's father as he is to Master Blanchard. But Helene is a credit to her parents."

She was saying the right things. But I recognized the cynical gleam in my hostess's dark eyes. "What is Helene like?" I asked frankly.

"You will see for yourself and form your own opinion." Marguerite lifted both shoulders in the fashion of her country. "She is a good girl—oh, so good. Of that there is no shadow of doubt. She will be no trouble, to you or to her guardian. She has been sorely bereaved, poor child. Although so was I, at her age. I lost both my parents in an outbreak of plague when I was only fifteen, and it was a pity," said Marguerite, without changing her calm, narrative tone, "that the man I was then betrothed to recovered from it, for I was married to him the next year and he was odious, odious. A gentleman at board but a fiend from hell in bed. He was killed out hunting two years later and I wore a thick veil at his burial, so that no one would see my thankful face. It took Henri years to court me, years to convince me that he would not think his wife was a possession to be hurt for his entertainment. So I know what suffering is. I am sorry for Helene but—"

Feet tapped and a skirt sighed on the steps up to my door. Marguerite broke off. A tall, pale girl appeared in the doorway. Her black gown was relieved only by a small white cap and her mousy hair, parted in the middle, hung in two loose loops over her temples. She had rounded shoulders, which looked like her normal way of holding herself, rather than the temporary sag of grief.

"I heard voices," she said. Her voice was high and thin. "And horses down below. I thought . . ."

"This is Helene," said Marguerite. "Come in, child. This is Madame Ursula Blanchard, daughter-in-law of your guardian, who will be your companion on your journey to England."

"Madame Blanchard," said Helene. She came forward and curtsied to me politely. "I am so happy to meet you."

She didn't look it. Her light eyes were studying me with an expression that was if anything inimical. I did my best to counter it, offering her a smile and an outstretched hand. "I am glad to meet you, too," I told her. "I hope we shall be friends."

"But naturally, madam," said Helene, still in that insubstantial, die-away tone.

Marguerite, with the faintest lift of her skillfully plucked eyebrows, signaled: "You see what I mean."

Aloud, she said: "You will wish to make each other's acquaintance. Your guardian will meet you at supper, Helene, in an hour. I will leave you now."

She withdrew, along with her little entourage of servants. The maid Marie observed that the sewing room was "just a few steps to the left, madame," bobbed, and was gone. Dale busied herself with opening our panniers. I motioned Helene to the seat in the window.

"Let us talk," I said winningly. "You speak English, I hear." I switched to English to find out. "You are—let me see—first cousin to my late husband, Gerald. Your guardian is your uncle. We are all eager to make you welcome."

Helene continued to regard me inimically. She was not a beauty. Her cheekbones were quite good, but her face was too long, especially the chin, and under the unbecoming loops of hair, her temples were pinched in. Edward Faldene wouldn't be getting such an ornamental bride after all.

"I am sure you will do your best," she said, also in English. She seemed at ease with it, although she had an accent. "My guardian wrote to me in advance. A letter reached here some weeks ago. He has told me of the marriage he has arranged for me, and I must thank him for taking such pains on my behalf."

Most of the pains incurred by Luke Blanchard had assuredly been in order to get a cut off the juicy joint that was Helene's dowry, but I had better not tell Helene that. This young girl, with her curious, guarded manner, had seen trouble enough, in losing her parents, and the brisk, sophisticated Marguerite had perhaps not been the best person to take charge of her. Whatever Marguerite had suffered in the past, I thought that she possessed the kind of personality that is toughened by adversity. Helene, perhaps, did not. I could only hope that what lay ahead for her wasn't more and worse adversity.

We were both on the window seat by now; two young women, side by side, talking, and I wished that Helene would not hold herself so stiffly. She seemed reluctant to let even our skirts come into contact. In my most friendly voice, I said: "The Faldene family, into which you are to marry, is also my own family. Faldene House, where you will live, is in some ways similar to Douceaix, and there is no lack of money."

"I am sure of it," said Helene. "I am mindful of all that is being done for me. I will be as biddable as anyone could wish."

"I hope you will be happy in England," I said.

"I think not." Helene folded her hands in her black woolen lap. "It is a heretic country. I would rather stay here. But no doubt my mother's death and this journey to England and this marriage are the will of God for me and one must accept the will of God. I have been educated, madam, at the Abbey of St. Marc, where there is a community of nuns. I would have chosen to stay there and take the veil myself had I been allowed. My mother had already nearly agreed to it. But then she died and Cousin Henri brought me here, and said that under my mother's will, which she made when my father died and had never altered, I must pass into the care of my English uncle. Now he has come to take me to England. Well, the nuns taught me that obedience is a virtue, above all in women. You, and my guardian, and my husband when I am married, can be assured of my obedience. But willingness, happiness; these I cannot command and would not if I could. I belong to the true faith, and to live where an untrue faith holds sway will for me be exile."

I was staggered, as much by the exquisite phrasing as by the uncompromising sentiments, which were those of a woman much older than sixteen.

"The Faldene family," I said, "hold by what you call the true faith. You will not be cut off from it." I tried to lighten the atmosphere. "You put your views very well, even melodiously. Do you enjoy poetry? There is a tradition of poetry in England that you may find gives you pleasure."

"There is a tradition of poetry in France that has long given me pleasure," said Helene. "No other can compare." She slipped from the seat and curtsied again. "If you will excuse me, madam, I must change my dress. My maid Jeanne awaits me. Jeanne, alas, does not wish to come to England. I shall miss her. You and I will meet at supper. We understand each other, I think. I will give you no trouble, I assure you."

She went out, closing the door after her, and Dale, who had stopped unpacking and sat back on her heels to listen to all this with wide, shocked eyes, gazed at me in wonder.

"No trouble? Biddable? Ma'am, that is trouble with a stiff neck, if I may say so."

"You may. I couldn't put it better myself. Well," I said, "Master Blanchard is her guardian, not me. I wish him—and Edward Faldene—joy of her, I must say!"

Supper was taken formally, in a gracious dining chamber adjacent to the tusked and antlered hall. The table was set in a wide window bay and was a work of art, with a great silver salt in the middle of it, which instantly brought back to my mind the spectacular salts, silver and gold, which must still lie under the floor of that warehouse in Antwerp. One day, I supposed, that floor would grow rotten and need to be replaced, or someone would drop a valuable coin or a precious ring down a crack in the floorboards and have them up to get at it, and come across a treasure trove. I wondered if I would ever hear about it.

Both Luke Blanchard and Helene were there before me and had already been introduced when I came in. I was greeted with smiles, and the rest of the family were presented to me.

Henri and Marguerite had three children, all of them neat, quiet, and charmingly well behaved, as one would expect of Marguerite's offspring. A very wizened elderly woman, who came in just after me, leaning on a stick and supported by a maid, proved to be Madame Antoinette, Henri's mother.

"*Maman,* you should eat in your chamber. It is too much for you to come to the dining room," Henri exclaimed, scolding affectionately, as the maid settled her in her chair.

"I desired to see our guests, especially the Seigneur Luke," said Madame Antoinette. "I see that although he is so distant a cousin, there is nevertheless a likeness. I am pleased. We Blanchards are a handsome family." Here, she gave my father-in-law a glance that verged on the coquettish, and briefly, I glimpsed the pretty and flirtatious Antoinette of half a century ago. She also added, with the outspokenness you often find in aging people: "Well, usually handsome," and shot a glance at Helene. Poor Helene, I thought, didn't fit into this household. Perhaps she would find her feet among the Faldenes. I had been miserable there, but Helene was very different from me.

I saw now that there was indeed a resemblance between Luke and his cousin. Luke Blanchard's aquiline profile was not unlike Henri's. Only, in Henri, it just looked strong and masculine, whereas in Luke, it seemed arrogant. I wondered what the female version would be like. Marguerite's little girls were not yet old enough to display it, and Helene certainly hadn't got it. Her nose was straight, pointed, and, alas, too long.

We had all changed our clothes. I had put on a favorite rose damask overgown, with a cream kirtle and sleeves and a fresh ruff. Luke, for once, was not in black but in dark blue slashed with crimson. Helene wore black velvet relieved by a deep violet kirtle and sleeves, and a white ruff edged in Spanish blackwork. I supposed that this represented mourning but it was so well done that it was also ornamental. I detected the hand of Marguerite in Helene's choice of dress.

The fare was Lenten, but luxurious in its own fashion: grilled pike steaks with sorrel sauce, and a fish pie, tangy with verjuice. The conversation was in French. Luke was already being avuncular toward Helene and seemed to approve of her. He and Henri had made friends, and had apparently been talking together at some length.

"I hear that your guardian actually stayed at St. Marc on the way here," Henri said to Helene. "Now, had I known he would come by that route, I would have left you in your convent and asked him to fetch you. St. Marc has stayed peaceful, so far. You could have spent a little longer with your nuns. Helene," he added to Luke and to me, "greatly misses her schoolfellows and her teachers."

"I was fetched away so suddenly," Helene said in meek tones, with her eyes on her plate. "I hadn't time to say a proper farewell to the nuns and the other girls, or to my confessor. I wish I could see them all again, just once."

"Well, we will think about it," said my father-in-law jovially. "But we hope soon to give your thoughts a new direction. Before leaving for England, we are to go to Paris, where Ursula has an errand. Ursula is a lady-in-waiting to Queen Elizabeth and has been asked to visit the French court to present her queen's compliments. We carry diplomatic protection. We shall take the opportunity to present you at the court of your own land, too, Helene."

Watching him, I wondered if he did after all have sympathy for Helene, as well as regarding her as a source of profit. Probably he had. How could one not sympathize with an orphaned girl who was about to be wrenched away from all she had ever known?

"You would like to see Paris, would you not?" I said to Helene. "I am looking forward to it myself."

I certainly was. I longed to be rid of that letter.

"May you have a safe journey," Henri said. "There will be open war soon, I fear. We are not in much danger here. Douceaix is very defensible. But these are shocking times. I have no wish to take up arms against my neighbors but I may have to, unless the trouble subsides soon. I have a younger brother who has already gone to Paris to offer his sword to the queen mother on behalf of the Catholics."

Helene raised her eyes. "I wish I could go back to St. Marc and take vows. Even if the abbey were attacked and we were all killed, I would so gladly die for the faith."

Both Henri and Marguerite looked irritated, as if they had heard all this before and found it tiresome. I opened my mouth to say: "I'm sure you wouldn't be glad when it came to the point," but Marguerite said it first, or more or less.

"You have never faced death, my dear. You don't know what it would be like. Your future has been wisely settled, Helene. If your guardian is willing for you to visit St. Marc briefly, just once more, well and good. But you should be thinking ahead, not back. Imagine it! A visit to Paris and the court! Then there will be the journey by sea, to England—that will be exciting, will it not?"

Luke caught my eye and for a moment, recalling the horrors of our recent sea voyage, we were almost at one.

"And then," Marguerite persisted, "you will have a new home, and a marriage to prepare for, and you must get to know your bridegroom. Much lies before you, Helene, and you are very young. You will be amazed how life will reach out to you and take you over."

"Yes, madame," said Helen, lowering her eyes again.

Henri made a jovial attempt to catch her interest. "The English are great travelers and traders, Helene. I admire that. At the moment, I believe there is an English merchant trying to reach a trade agreement with the Shah of Persia, so that goods from Persia can reach the West without going through middlemen in Turkey and Venice. Is that not so, Cousin Luke? If they succeed, then the English, and perhaps the French, too, will be able to buy carpets and fine brocades at much lower prices than at present. You will be able to put Persian carpets in your house without emptying your husband's purse, Helene!"

"I would never wish to empty my husband's purse," said Helene seriously. "It would be better to have bare floors and walls than to do that. I prefer simplicity, anyway. The nuns say that luxury corrupts the soul."

"Nonsense. People of position must have certain standards in the way they live, if they are to be respected by others," said Marguerite. "The nuns taught you to read and write and embroider, Helene, but you must also learn how to recognize and value household goods of quality. I am certain that Madam Ursula will be able to advise you."

"As far as Persian carpets go, all this is very premature," said Luke Blanchard dryly. "I have shares in the Muscovy Company, which is trying to set up this new agreement with the Shah, and I have some knowledge of the matter. The company sent a man called Anthony Jenkinson to Persia to negotiate last year and nothing has been heard of him since. But information has leaked out of Venice, to the effect that a group of Turkish and Venetian merchants have sworn that Jenkinson will not be allowed to get back to England. And so far, he hasn't."

"*Mon Dieu!*" Marguerite exclaimed. "One thinks of merchants as serious men of business, not engaged in plots! Surely they are not planning to murder poor Master Jenkinson?"

"There would be a lot of money at stake," I said thought-fully. "I remember hearing, last year, something about this scheme to set up direct trade with Persia. But it will take a lot of trade away from Turkey and Venice. They certainly won't like it."

Helene raised her head and gazed at me in astonishment. Marguerite smiled.

"Madame Blanchard is knowledgeable in the ways of the world, Helene, and it is in the world that you must live hence-forth. Religion is not everything. Although in these days," Marguerite added severely, "far too many people think it is. I never dreamed that here in France we would find ourselves at war over it."

Whereupon, Helene startled us with a sudden outburst.

"But of course we are at war with heretics! My confessor used to say that heresy was the wickedest thing in the world and that the souls of heretics are cast into the eternal fire. For their own sakes and for the love of God, we must fight them. If I were a man—"

"Helene, be quiet. A girl of sixteen does not speak so to her elders. I think," said Marguerite, "that Madame Blanchard requires the sorrel sauce. Kindly pass it to her."

"If Helene were a man, she would be already in Paris, along with my brother Philippe, offering her sword to the cause as well," Henri said. "However, you are not a man, Helene, nor are you likely to turn into one."

"Oh, it is all such a business." Marguerite sounded exasper-ated. "We have even had to lay in stores of weapons and food in case of a siege!"

"I, too, may have to go eventually," Henri said. "Though I am holding back for a while, hoping that peace will be restored quickly. Philippe went because he has no household to protect and we decided that it was his duty. But we are civilized people and we detest these extreme attitudes."

Helene bent her head again and made no reply. I concentrated on my food. My sympathies were veering Marguerite's way. Helene was an extremely irritating girl.

My father-in-law began to talk to Helene about England and his home, Beechtrees, where Helene would live until her marriage. There was this much meadow and that much woodland; there was a nice little brown cob for Helene to ride; Ambrose's wife was fond of hawking, with a merlin, and Helene could have one, too . . .

Helene made polite, flat responses. There was a feeling of relief when the meal ended. Dusk was coming down as we rose from the table. Marguerite announced that a fire had been lit in a west-facing gallery. "It receives the last of the daylight. There is a spinet, and I will myself entertain you with music."

The maids had withdrawn to eat separately, but came to attend us at the gallery. Marguerite was served by a pretty young woman, very elegantly dressed, but Helene's maid Jeanne was older, gaunt of build, and rather hard of feature, I thought, until I saw her smile as Helene came in. Here at least was one person who liked the girl and I was glad for Helene's sake. But Jeanne, I knew, did not want to come to England. Helene would have to part from her, too, and make do with me.

The evening had turned cool. There was a little flutter as seats were moved nearer to the hearth, and Marguerite called for candles to augment the sunset and light the music for the spinet. Henri, who had gone out briefly to take the air by the moat, came in again, glanced at me just as I had taken my seat, and scooped up a fat red cushion from a bench beside the door. He carried it over to me.

"You will surely need another cushion on that settle, madame. That oak is very hard to sit upon. No, no, I will look after your mistress." He waved a hovering Dale away. "If you would get up for just a moment, madame . . ."

I stood up again and he said: "If I place it just so . . ." in a tone that obliged me to turn in order to see what he was doing. For a moment, we were facing the settle, our backs turned to the company, my farthingale brushing his hip. With one hand, he shook the crimson cushion and set it in place, and with the other, using my wide skirt as a shield, he slid a folded piece of paper into my grasp.

"When I went out to take the air just now, madame," he said quietly, as I sat down once more, "I met the youth from the inn at St. Marc, just coming across the bridge. I know him by sight. I asked him his errand and he said he had a note for you. I said I would take it and he was too much in awe of me to argue, but he begged me to give it to you discreetly. I promised, and I have kept my word. I ask no questions." Henri gazed gravely down at me. "But I hope it is not political. If you need any help or advice from me, I will gladly give it."

I looked at it and my insides somersaulted. I felt the blood rush into my face. I tried to keep my voice steady as I said: "It is not political. It is from . . . an admirer."

"Oh, indeed! So the wind sits there! I should have guessed. Our French gallants are not backward and you are both charming and unattached. If I were not married already, I would just be sorry that someone else had got in ahead of me."

"That is a compliment. Thank you," I said. I tried to sound gracious and I smiled as I spoke, but there was turmoil within me.

For the writing on the letter was like the sweep of a sword, cutting me away from the civil war, the strange behavior of

Luke Blanchard, Queen Elizabeth's letter. I still knew that they existed, but I could no longer see them or feel them. I could see only my name, in that familiar writing.

The letter was addressed, wisely, to Madame Blanchard. But the writing was that of my estranged husband, Matthew de la Roche.

CHAPTER 7

Rendezvous

"Le Cheval d'Or, madam?" said Brockley. "You wish me to escort you there? And without Master Ryder or the Dodd brothers?"

"That dreadful place, ma'am!" said Dale fervently. "I thought we'd seen the back of it for good. What's wrong with here?"

"Well, as to that," said Brockley, "there's a fair amount wrong with here. A popish abbey is no place to be with a religious war on the point of breaking out. If Master Blanchard had said that Mistress Helene could have her way and visit her old friends at St. Marc's once more, that would have been his business. But for you to urge it, madam, when you've said over and over that we should make haste to Paris; and even to offer to bring her without Master Blanchard—well, I said at the time that I couldn't understand it!" He had, at length. "And now this!" he said. "This, on top of all else!"

"If you will let me finish, and not interrupt," I said, "you may begin to understand!"

At Douceaix, I had said that I saw no reason why Helene should not make a last visit to the Abbey of St. Marc. There was no unrest in the immediate area, and I had pointed out to Luke Blanchard that I wished to make friends with Helene and that this might help me to do so. I had also urged him to remain at Douceaix himself "to make sure you are completely recovered from your illness, dear father-in-law, before we take the road again."

So despite the religious conflict and the amount of Huguenot influence in the area, here we were in the guest house of St. Marc's Abbey: myself, the Brockleys, Helene and Jeanne, and Cecil's three men, Ryder and the Dodds.

But my wish to return to St. Marc had had nothing to do with Helene, who was merely an excuse; and my wish, now that we were here, to pay a visit to Le Cheval d'Or had nothing to do with the amenities or the safety of either hostelry or abbey. I looked exasperatedly at my two servants. They were loyal and at times very brave, but now and then I longed to seize them, in turn, by the shoulders and shake them. They were lamentably ready to conclude that I was an idiot.

True, I sometimes felt sorry for Dale. Dale should have been married early and settled into a home of her own where she could rear a family and devote herself to stillroom and linen cupboard. Brockley had given her marriage, but the life they led with me was completely unnatural to her. No wonder she sometimes found me incomprehensible.

Brockley, though, should have known better. He respected me, both as an employer and also as one of Cecil's agents, for I had proved myself in that capacity and he well knew it. But Brockley had grown up with certain attitudes about ladies. He considered, at heart, that we should be protected at all times. He deplored my insistence that both Dale and I should have our own mounts, instead of riding respectably on a man's pillion. He never forgot that he was the manservant and I paid his wages, but he also believed that as he was a man and I wasn't, I ought to attend to his advice.

He had advised me against coming back to St. Marc and

been ignored; now he was hardly prepared to listen to my explanations about Le Cheval d'Or at all.

"I don't want to speak out of turn in any way, madam . . ."

"I'm sure you don't, Brockley." He always said something like that before speaking very thoroughly out of turn. It was a reliable prelude to criticism.

". . . but have you forgotten, madam, that the landlord of that inn threatened to kill you?"

"He didn't know who I was. He was protecting Matthew de la Roche. But he won't harm me if Matthew himself is there to vouch for me. I'm going there to meet my husband."

They stared at me. Dale's jaw sagged. A frown creased Brockley's high forehead.

"To . . . meet . . . ?" Dale began.

"Yes. I've had a letter."

I didn't produce it. It was in French, anyway, and neither of them could have understood it. But if I wanted to quote it from memory, I could, for I could remember every word of the few letters Matthew had sent me.

To my wife, Ursula:
Greetings. I have heard that you are in France, in fact at St. Marc, and asking after me. If you had not asked after me, nothing would have made me write to you. But you did ask, and I know that although you abandoned me last year, you also did your best to save my life and that I might have been taken but for you. You still have some feeling for me, it seems.

And now you are here in France and inquiring after my health. I ask myself what this means. Why have you come to my country at this time of trouble? Do you wish to see me? If so, I will be at Le Cheval d'Or, using the name of Mark Lenoir, from sixth April to the morning of the tenth. Charpentier knows who I really am. It was from him that I learned of your visit to St. Marc and that you are going on to a place called Douceaix. I am sending this letter by way of Le Cheval d'Or. If you have already left, Charpentier will send a messenger after you. Do you wish to see me, my Saltspoon? If so, come.

Matthew de la Roche

"It could be a trick," said Brockley. "That's happened before."

"I know." I had once been fooled in the past, by a forged letter purporting to come from Matthew. "But this is no forgery," I said. "The writing is his. It looked odd, that other time, and this does not. Also, it uses a . . . a secret name that he has for me."

"He could have told someone else about that," said Brockley. "Master Blanchard, perhaps. Master Blanchard's been behaving very oddly."

"I doubt it," I said. "Oh, my father-in-law may know of Matthew's existence. Ryder and his men know, and Cecil may have told Master Blanchard as well. But whatever it is Master Blanchard is up to—and yes, I fear he may well be up to something—I can't see that it's connected to this."

"I don't wish to pry, but I wouldn't be surprised to learn that you two have secret, private names for each other, names whispered only in the dark. Would you tell anyone else about them?"

Dale went pink and Brockley cleared his throat. "No, madam. No. I see."

Saltspoon. Matthew had named me that because of my sharp tongue. He liked it, he said, because he liked a little salt on his dinner. That first forged letter had not used the name. Its presence this time was a seal of authenticity.

"So," I said, "I repeat. I wish to go to the inn this evening with you as escort, Brockley. We may hope to find Matthew there."

"And how," said Brockley, capitulating but with obviously bad grace, "will you explain to Mistress Helene why you aren't at supper?"

"Helene," I said, "is all taken up with her old friends and her confessor. If she asks—or if any of the men ask—Dale can say that I am tired and remaining in my room. The men will not intrude and I doubt, frankly, whether Helene will notice whether I'm here or not!"

We left at dusk to walk across the cobbled square to the inn. There was a surprisingly raucous noise from the quarters of the abbey retainers, and I waited until it had faded behind us before I said to my tight-lipped companion: "Brockley, this isn't intrigue. This is a rendezvous with my husband, that's all."

"All? It's near enough to intrigue to worry me," Brockley said. "Madam, may I speak frankly?"

"You usually do, anyway! Very well, what is it?"

"You're playing with fire. You have parted from Master de la Roche twice, but it seems that you can't make a final break. You come to France and at once you ask after him; he whistles, and you run to him. This on-and-off business can be good for neither of you. Sooner or later you must make a final choice and abide by it. He must be suffering, too. I am a man myself. Do you think we have no feelings?"

"Good God, Brockley." I stopped short in the middle of the twilit square and faced him. "Of course I don't think that. But—"

"But what, madam? Why are you going to meet him if you don't mean anything by it?"

"I don't know what I mean by it," I said helplessly. Qualms that I had been resolutely ignoring snapped at my heels. "I only know that I must go." A motive crystallized in my mind. "If only to say good-bye properly! It was hardly a proper fare-well last time, if you remember. It was a frantic decision, with a fight going on and armed men all over the place and Matthew in desperate danger. I think that's it, Brockley. I want to say good-bye properly."

"Very well, madam. But please take care. If this isn't a snare laid by someone else, it could be a trap set by Master de la Roche himself. You are in his country and you are legally his wife. What if he just means to take you home with him? Am I supposed to fight him off?" Momentarily, he rested his hand on the hilt of the sword at his side.

"No. As a matter of fact," I said, finding some relief in ad-mitting it, "I've been asking myself the same thing. I'm afraid as much as excited. But I have to take the risk. I've left the let-ter that I am to deliver in Paris, and my letter of introduction, behind at the abbey, with Dale. If anything happens to stop me from coming to Paris, then will you see that the letter to Queen Catherine reaches her? Carry it to Paris and hand it to the English ambassador Sir Nicholas Throckmorton."

"Forgive me, madam. But I think you may have taken leave of your senses."

I didn't point out that I could dismiss him for that. I wouldn't do anything of the kind, and he knew it. For one thing, I needed someone like Brockley in my service, and for another thing, annoying as he could be, he was a comfort, too. My qualms were getting worse. I even looked over my shoul-der, as though once again, someone might be following me.

There were a few people about in the darkening square, but I saw no one suspicious.

"What is it, madam?" Brockley asked, also glancing back.

"My imagination," I said.

Le Cheval d'Or had quite a welcoming air. Lamps had been lit and hung on the walls, and the door was open. Customers were going in and out. We were held up at the door as a young man emerged to join a middle-aged one, possibly his father, who was apparently waiting for him in the entrance.

The two of them blocked the door entirely for a moment while the elder man impatiently demanded to know the outcome of some errand or other. They were not locals; from their sun-browned faces and the cut of their clothes, they hailed from somewhere in the south.

I looked at them thoughtfully. I knew that the south of France, beyond the Loire and the Huguenot territory, was strongly Catholic. In these times, men were indeed on the move, as Charpentier had remarked. These two might well be on their way to join the government forces in Paris. St. Marc, a pocket of Catholicism in a district full of Huguenot influence, would be a natural place for them to stay en route.

They moved aside when they realized that we wanted to pass, and at last we got ourselves inside. There was a door to the left of the entrance lobby, leading into a public room with a log fire, and numerous trestle tables with benches. Glancing through, I saw that the place was full, mostly, I thought, with local men from St. Marc, although the ersatz Netherlands merchant, Van Weede, was there, sitting with his elbows on a table and a tankard beside him, in earnest talk with two other men; a tall, lean fellow, and a shorter, burly one.

Brockley touched my arm, and Charpentier's voice said quietly: "Madame de la Roche." I turned, and the innkeeper was beside me. "I must make my apologies, madame, for my mistake when you asked after your husband," Charpentier said. "But you were too discreet to tell me and how could I have guessed? He is here and awaits you. Will you follow me? Your man . . ."

He looked questioningly at Brockley. "Brockley comes with me," I said firmly. Charpentier said no more, but led us away to a small, paneled parlor. Here, too, there was a fire, but instead of trestles and benches, there was a table set with candles, wine, and a platter of pasties. There were chairs at the table, and a comfortable settle by the window. A man was sitting there. As we entered, he rose to his feet. He was tall and dark-haired, and wide of shoulder, with dark, narrow eyes and black, dramatic eyebrows. His chin was too long, his limbs too loose for beauty, but to me he was beautiful. I had not seen him for months, except in dreams and in imagination.

Matthew spoke first, and in businesslike fashion. "Brockley. I am glad to see you still in the service of my wife. I ask you to keep the door for us. Stand guard outside it, if you will. Charpentier, bring refreshment for Brockley, whatever he wishes. He can have it while he is on guard. Now, both of you, leave me and Madame de la Roche together."

"Madam?" said Brockley, as one who wishes to make it clear whose orders he is taking.

"Do as Matthew asks, Brockley."

"If you are sure, madam."

"I have not come here to abduct her, Brockley," Matthew said dryly. "She would only escape me again as soon as she got the chance. You can safely leave her with me."

It was one of his great charms, that underlying current of humor, which would surface at unexpected moments. Now, it broke the tension. I smiled and even Brockley briefly grinned. He went out. Charpentier had already gone. The door clicked shut behind Brockley and I was alone with Matthew.

The flicker of laughter died out. We stood there, soberly facing each other across the width of a small parlor, and the length of a year. Our last encounter had been a reunion, too, after a time of separation, and it had been stormy.

This time, somehow, was different.

We were still young. I was not yet twenty-eight and Matthew, I knew, was only about five years older than myself. But he looked more. The long chin seemed more pronounced, with lines on either side of it; and surely there was a gray hair or two at his temples. As for me, I felt as though I had aged by ten years at least in the months since last I'd seen him. Now, we neither cursed each other nor embraced. Instead, we stood in silence, each scanning the other's face, until at last he said, in French: "So you came."

"I . . . yes."

"Why?"

I could hardly say "To bid you good-bye" before I had even said hello. I hesitated and then stammered: "Y . . . you wrote to me. You said you would be here—if I wanted to see you again."

"It seems that you did."

"Yes." This dispassionate mixture of surprise and accusation confused me. For accusation was there, in the tone if not precisely in the words. I gestured toward the settle. "Shall we sit?"

"By all means." But when I took the settle, I found that he had moved to a seat at the table. Again, we faced each other across a space longer than the length of our arms. Once more, we studied each other.

"What in hell's name," said Matthew at last, "made you come to France just now? It was madness. This area is quiet, but it's an island, and the sea may pour in and drown it at any moment. The people of St. Marc and the places roundabout are Catholic but this is Huguenot territory. Full-scale war may break out any day. The prince of Condé's men could be thundering through the darkness toward us even as I speak."

"We didn't know when we landed that things were so bad," I said. "I am traveling with my first husband's father, Luke Blanchard. He has a ward at Douceaix—"

"Where or what is this place Douceaix, exactly?"

"It's a house, not far from Le Mans. I told you once that my first husband had French forebears. Some French Blanchards live there. There is a young girl . . ." I explained about Helene. "I also have to carry the queen's respects to Paris and I have a letter that declares me to be a royal messenger. There are three of Sir William Cecil's men in the party as well as Blanchard's own escort."

"And you all decided to press on and try to collect this Helene, and go on to Paris, regardless. And you came to France, just to please the queen and this Master Blanchard?"

I said slowly: "I was glad to get away from the court. I was tired of intrigue. I—work for Cecil. I find things out for him. He pays me. You know something of that."

"Yes. I grasped that last year, although what manner of man pays a young woman for such work is beyond me to understand."

"I need the money for my daughter, for Meg. But my last attempt to find something out did not go well. I lost my confidence, perhaps." Dale and Brockley knew about the man to whom I had given poison, but I did not want to speak of that to anyone else, not even Matthew.

Still less did I want to speak of my fear that what I had done might somehow contaminate my daughter. I no longer even believed that. I was beginning to think that, surely, she could not be harmed by what she did not know, and I was missing her badly. Although I could not have her with me at Elizabeth's court, I always knew that she was not far away, at Thamesbank with her foster parents, by the river just as most of Elizabeth's residences were, and within easy reach by boat. Now, the sea that lay between us was like a barrier in my mind.

I pushed all this out of my thoughts as though afraid that Matthew would read them.

"I simply wanted a rest from my work," I said. "So I agreed to travel with my father . . . my former father-in-law."

"I see. But you did ask after me."

"Yes. I was in your country, and perhaps you were not far off—I couldn't help myself. I think you were in my mind when I said I would come to France. I wanted—just to pass close to you."

Matthew poured wine, and rising to his feet, handed me a goblet and offered a pasty. I remembered, so well, the way he moved: loose-jointed, yet as coordinated as a panther.

"You put yourself at risk merely by being connected with me," he said as he sat down again and sipped his wine. "I am not popular with the Huguenot supporters, for more reasons than simply my adherence to the true faith. That's why I'm here under the name of Mark Lenoir."

"You've been spying on the Huguenots?"

"You could put it so. As a result, there are many men who would like to get their hands on me, and not to give me a friendly pat on the back, I assure you. I have also had to dodge English agents, who think that I may have useful information about Catholic adherents in England."

"And have you?"

"Perhaps. I still work for the cause of Mary Stuart as best I can from here. I am in touch with her supporters in England. I make no secret of it as far as you are concerned, Ursula. You are in Cecil's confidence, after all. No doubt you know most of what he knows, anyway."

His voice was bitter. So was mine, as I answered: "I am tired of Mary Stuart and her cause. Why can she not be content with ruling Scotland? Why can she not leave her cousin Elizabeth's throne alone? Must we talk of this? We've been all over it so many many times before. I believe that Elizabeth is legitimate: Catholics do not. We shall never agree. And from the state of France just now," I added waspishly, "it seems to me that you have work enough to defend the true faith, as you call it, here, without trying to spread it back into England!"

"Why must we talk of this, you ask? I wonder that myself. Whenever we meet, we find ourselves arguing about things that have nothing to do with our private lives. Ursula, you asked after me when you first came to this inn, and you have come to me now in answer to my letter. What do you want of me?"

"You wrote the letter. What do you want of *me*?"

"I think you know the answer to that, Ursula."

Silence fell between us again. At last, he said: "What happened, after I got away last year? You did help me to escape; I know that and I thank you for it. Tell me what you have done during the time since then."

"Tried to find things out for Cecil and failed. Lived at the court. Been a Lady of the Presence Chamber to the queen. Visited Meg when I could." I stopped, but he sensed that I was holding something back and said: "Go on."

"I lost a child," I said. "Yours."

"What? Ursula! Did I—we—?"

"Yes. But I miscarried. I was a little over two months gone."

"Did you want to miscarry?" His voice was sharp.

I shook my head. "No. Nor did I do anything to cause it. No one knew except Dale and Mattie Henderson—the Hendersons are fostering Meg, if you remember. I was staying with them at the time."

They had cared for me deftly and discreetly. Mattie had coolly ordered a bonfire to be made to "burn some rubbish" and then put two dreadfully bloodstained sheets into a sack and tossed them in. The household had been told that I was ill with a fever and a persistent sick headache. I had suffered, and wept, and recovered, and gone back to the court. But I had not forgotten.

"The last time we met, it was so briefly," he said. "We had just that one night. Were you much distressed? Yes, I see that you were. I am sorry. Ursula, if you had had the child, would it have changed anything? Would you have come to me?"

"I . . . don't think so."

"But why not? Why not? My home is yours. How many times have I told you that? The child would have had a right to its father!"

"You know why not," I said. "Because of what you want to bring back into England. And besides, when you fled, you took that man Ignatius Wilkins with you. I want no child of mine anywhere near him."

"You hate him, I know. But why so intensely?"

"Because when he was a parish priest in England, in the days of Queen Mary, he got two of his own parishioners burned for heresy. A weaver and his daughter. The daughter was nineteen. Rob Henderson, Mattie's husband, witnessed it, though not willingly."

"You know very well," said Matthew, "that I am not and never have been in favor of persecuting heretics. I am glad that the government here has given it up. People should come back to the faith because they are led, not driven. As for Wilkins, he ran into danger through working for Mary Stuart's cause and he and I were involved in that business together. I could hardly leave him behind. But he is not a favorite of mine. Hardly. In England, as you no doubt recall, he misused funds that I had gathered for Mary Stuart's cause. He is not with me at Blanchepierre. He has found employment elsewhere—here at St. Marc, actually."

"Here? Where, precisely?"

"Oh, at the abbey. He's the resident confessor to the nuns."

"He's the . . . ? Good God," I said. "That goes a long way toward explaining Helene!"

"Your father-in-law's ward? Why does she need explaining?"

"Until lately," I said, "Helene was being educated at St. Marc's Abbey. She's a tiresome girl. Frankly, she's fanatical about her religion, though I've made use of that. Her overwhelming desire to bid a further farewell to her friends at the abbey gave me my chance to come back here from Douceaix. I'm supposed to be accompanying her. Well, if she's been under the influence of Wilkins, I can understand why I find her so difficult."

"Can we put Wilkins to one side along with Mary Stuart? Let us talk of you instead. You came to France. You yielded to the temptation to ask after me. Charpentier reported it to me. He is one of the Catholics in this district on whom I rely for information. I need to know all I can about what is going on, for my own safety, as well as to help my own side. When I heard you were here, I in turn yielded to the temptation to write to you. But what now? We are here together but for how long? When you have finished your wine, will you smile and bid me farewell and go out of my life, this time forever? Or were you thinking to spend a single night with me, as you did at our last meeting, and *then* go out of my life? Or will you come with me to Blanchepierre?"

I didn't know the answer. Playing for time, I said: "Is Blanchepierre your family home? You never spoke of it when we were first married."

"No. I bought it when I came back to France. I had left sufficient funds here. I was never sure if I could settle in England, you know. I only came to please my mother. I always thought that when she was gone, I might go back to France. Blanchepierre is a little far away from the rest of my family, but it is very beautiful. You would like it."

"And you are truly asking me to come?" I said. "After— everything that has passed between us?"

"You are my wife. And as you well know, Ursula, I want—I have always wanted—you to live with me as a wife should. Blanchepierre is fairly safe, even in these days. It is not so very large, as châteaux go, but it is well defended and well found, the equivalent of a respectable fortified manor house in England. Yes, I am asking you to come."

"But . . ."

"We will bring Meg over when peace is restored, which I trust will be soon. I would not keep mother and daughter apart. In that, you may find me an improvement on Elizabeth."

"But I have promised to keep Helene company on the way back to England."

"Can't she do without you? It doesn't sound to me as though you and she are likely to get on well!"

An urgent tapping at the door, and the sound of Brockley calling my name interrupted us. Matthew scowled but strode to the door and opened it. "What is it, Brockley?"

Brockley slipped inside. "I haven't been standing guard like a statue, madam. I've been keeping my eyes and ears open. Just here, there's a window on the stableyard and when I thought I heard a voice I knew, I glanced out. I'm sorry to say, madam, that the Dodd brothers are hanging about in the yard, and so is that man Searle. In fact, I saw Searle peering in at windows. I'd know his red head anywhere. I think we've been followed here."

I remembered how I had looked over my shoulder in the square. Instinct had been keener than either sight or hearing.

"Who are you talking about?" Matthew inquired.

"The Dodd brothers are two of the three men Cecil sent with me to augment Master Blanchard's men," I said tersely. "They came back with me to St. Marc. But Searle is one of Blanchard's men and they were all supposed to have stayed in Douceaix with Blanchard himself."

"Searle must have come after us and joined forces with the Dodd brothers." Brockley's high, polished forehead creased in thought. "Madam, when you were followed in the street once, here at St. Marc, I wondered if the man who followed you was one of our own party. Now I'm sure of it."

"But—why? Where do they think I might be going? Who do they think I'm meeting?"

"Me, I imagine," said Matthew.

CHAPTER 8

Unquiet Moonlight

I lost my temper.

I had (and have) quite a fierce temper although I learned early that I would be wise to keep it on a leash. Aunt Tabitha made it clear to me that I could either suppress my rages or she would do it for me. A woman, said Aunt Tabitha, must be ever mild and gentle. "I never raise my voice," Aunt Tabitha had said.

This was quite true. She raised her hand instead, sometimes with a birch in it. My mercilessly virtuous aunt-by-marriage could terrorize her household quite easily without shouting. Mild and gentle were the last words on earth that I would have applied to her but she never seemed to notice the chasm between what she preached and what she did.

From her, I learned that if you are a powerless nobody, your anger will not be respected. Elizabeth, who had inherited old King Harry's capacity for rage, could—and frequently did—lose her temper with abandon but she was the queen. An outburst of temper is taken seriously from someone who is in a position to have you marched off to the Tower.

But eventually, after I escaped from the tutelage of my aunt and uncle, I discovered something else: that anger can be used—wielded, in fact, like a sword. I had found out, gradually, how to use that sword.

I had seen the pattern instantly. Matthew was right, of course. I had been followed in the hope that I would lead Cecil's men to him. It was possible that my father-in-law's pretense of illness, even the opportunity to go out and search for a doctor, had been designed to give me a chance to contact Matthew if I wished. Blanchard might know much more about him than I thought. He was wanted in England, both for treason committed when he was living there, and because of information in his possession that Cecil would certainly like to get out of him. And so, as a little sideshow to my journey here, Cecil had arranged for me to be watched, had possibly suborned my father-in-law, in the hope that Matthew and I might contact each other.

As we had done.

I had worked for Cecil now for a year and half. He and his wife had found Meg's foster parents for me. I had served him and trusted him. Now, in this pragmatic grab at a heaven-sent opportunity he had betrayed me. I was shuddering with fury, and a determination to slash this foul little plan to pieces.

"Let us disappoint them," I said through my teeth. "Leave this to me. I will deal with that little get-together down there in the stableyard. No, don't come with me, Brockley. And, Matthew, for God's sake stay out of sight. Is there any chance that they've seen you already?"

"No," said Matthew. "I was upstairs until a few minutes ago and no one has peered in at this window since I came down here. I would have noticed; it's the kind of thing I do notice. Besides, would they recognize me?"

"They might. You were at court when Cecil and his household were. Wait here, both of you."

I was giving orders as imperiously as though I were Elizabeth herself. Matthew, frowning, said: "Ursula . . ." in tones of protest and moved to bar my way.

I stopped short. "I said leave this to me!"

Brockley said: "What do you intend, madam?"

"If you open that window a crack and listen without show-ing yourselves, you'll hear. Don't worry! I told you: I will deal with this!"

"Mistress Blanchard can usually be relied on, sir," said Brockley tactfully.

"Just let me pass!" I snapped at Matthew, and after a sec-ond's hesitation, he did so. Heart pounding with wrath, I stepped past him and made at once for the back of the inn where there was a door out into the stableyard. I threw it open and strode out. Darkness had long fallen, but it was a clear night, with a nearly full moon, and anyway, there were three lamp poles to light the yard. I could see very well. They were there, all three of them, standing together by the stable and apparently scanning the windows of the inn. I went straight across to them.

"What in the world are you doing here? You should be at the abbey. Searle, I thought you were still in Douceaix."

"Master Blanchard felt that one at least of his men should be in your escort, ma'am. He sent me after you. But when I got to the abbey, I learned that you had gone out with your man Brockley, and that the Dodds here had gone after you."

"He followed and caught us up just as we reached here," Dick Dodd said. "Ma'am, what are you doing here? You say that we should be still at the abbey—but so should you. This is not a safe place for you."

"It is a perfectly safe place. I have cleared up all the mis-understanding between myself and Charpentier," I said in ringing tones, which I hoped would carry to the window be-hind which Brockley and Matthew must be listening. "I have taken a room here for the night and I have excellent reasons for doing so. I can't sleep at the abbey. I learned, just after we got there, that a man called Ignatius Wilkins is there. He is the resident priest. He was once in England where I came across him. I will not go into details but he is a man I loathe so much that I will not spend a night under the same roof with him."

My voice echoed passionately around the stableyard. It was easy to supply the passion because I genuinely felt it. The thought of sharing a roof with the unspeakable Wilkins really was hateful to me.

"Brockley will guard me," I informed the three of them loftily. "I have no need of you. You may go back to the abbey. I will return there myself in the morning."

They looked as though they didn't know what to do. I stared at them fixedly and after a moment, Dick Dodd, who seemed to be the one in charge, shrugged his shoulders. "If you are sure, ma'am . . ."

"I am perfectly sure. The inn is full and you will have poor accommodation here if you stay. You will be better off in the abbey."

"We will come to collect you in the morning, ma'am. At nine of the clock, say?"

"By all means," I said. "I shall see you then."

Shuffling and reluctant, murmuring among themselves and glancing back over their shoulders, they went. I watched them go out through the archway to the road before returning swiftly indoors. I found Matthew and Brockley startled and near to laughter.

"We heard every word," Matthew told me as soon as I had shut the door after me. "I never would have thought of that, I must say. You really do loathe Wilkins, don't you?"

"Yes, Matthew, I do. Brockley . . ."

Brockley gave me a thoughtful look, but accepted the hint and left the room. I turned to Matthew. "I have to stay the night now," I said frankly. "I've said I would. Have you bespoken a room here?"

"Yes. On the first floor."

I said directly: "May I share it?"

Matthew considered me thoughtfully. His amusement had faded out, to be replaced by a kind of tiredness. "You may share my room," he said, "but on what terms? Will you share my bed, too? There is a truckle bed where I can—and will—sleep if you prefer. I ask you again, Ursula: Why did you come to meet me?"

I thought of Helene, who didn't like me and wouldn't miss me if I deserted her, but to whom, nevertheless, I had a responsibility. I thought of the letter I had undertaken to deliver for Queen Elizabeth.

I thought of Cecil's betrayal (I was less concerned with Blanchard's. I had never liked him anyway).

"When I set out to come here," I said, "I had it in mind to—say farewell finally, formally. And then I meant to go home and try, once more, for an annulment that would set us both free."

I had thought of it once before, on the grounds that my marriage to Matthew had been forced. I had been advised that this might be difficult to prove.

But Elizabeth had set aside Catherine Grey's marriage on the grounds that Catherine couldn't prove it had ever taken place. My marriage had been conducted secretly, by Matthew's uncle, who was a Catholic priest, and was presumably now back here in France, where he couldn't easily be questioned by the English authorities. Also, it was doubtful whether in England he was licensed to perform weddings. Perhaps what

Elizabeth had ruthlessly forced upon Catherine, she might grant as a favor to me. If I wanted it.

"Is that what you want?" Matthew asked of me now. "I notice," he added, "that you are not wearing my wedding ring."

"In England, few people know of our marriage," I said. "Dear heaven, I don't know what I want." Then I told him what I thought Cecil had done to me. He listened without comment. At the end, I said: "Since I must spend the night here, it would be simplest if I shared your room. I will share your bed if you ask me. That's for you to say."

"And then?" His voice was tired, like his face. I thought of Brockley, asking me if I thought men had no feelings. "What of the morning?" he asked. "I ask you again, Ursula: What are your intentions? Will it be just, thank you, sweeting, for the memory of a happy night and farewell forever? Or will you come home with me to Blanchepierre, where you always should have been?"

"I can't answer that now. But in the morning I will answer it. I will only keep you waiting one more night."

"You said once before that you would come to France. You backed out at the last moment—"

"I had a reason!" I said. I thought of that reason, and shuddered.

"You say you had a reason." Matthew was relentless. "But have you any idea at all what it did to me when you refused at the last moment to come with me? What it was like, riding for my life, making for the coast and France, without you? After you had given your promise and broken it?"

No, I could not do that again. He had asked if I knew what I had done to him and I could see the answer in his drawn face.

"If I give my word tomorrow, I shall keep it. But I must

have a night to think. Matthew, I have so much to lose. A whole life, friends, people who trust me . . . I would never be able to go back. Don't hope for too much. I love you but—it's all so complicated."

"I think that if you really loved me, there would be no complications. You would come to me as a wife to her husband and make my land, my beliefs, your own. Where is the complication in that?"

We had been through it all before, and in vain. I didn't even try to go through it again. I said: "I'll sleep in the truckle bed if you wish."

"I don't wish. I was leaving it to you to decide. For my part, if I share a room with my wife, then I would most certainly prefer it if we slept together!"

"So would I."

"Very well, then. Go and tell Brockley. He and Charpentier must make sure that we can slip upstairs unnoticed. We'll have supper up there. There's a small anteroom outside the bedchamber. Brockley can sleep there and guard us through the night."

The bedchamber was comfortable, with a curtained bed and a washstand and a triple candlestick with new candles in it. Charpentier lit them for us. The three narrow windows had shutters but they were open and the moon shone in. "I like the moon," Matthew said. "If I leave the shutters and the bed curtains open tonight, will it worry you?"

"No," I said. "I like the moonlight, too."

There was a pause. Then Matthew said: "We have been married for a year and a half, and only now do we learn that we share a liking for moonlight."

"I know. I'm sorry." There was nothing else to say.

Supper was brought. We ate it and Brockley removed the tray. Then we went to bed.

It was not like any other night that we had spent together. In the past we had made love either with passion and tenderness; or else—on one occasion—with bruising, violent fury. Never before had it seemed beyond us to make love at all. But so it was.

To begin with, we turned to each other and caressed and kissed, and I sensed that what Matthew wanted was to take possession of me with such finality that in the morning I would be unable to do anything but go with him. Neither of us referred to it, but the possibility that this encounter, too, might result in a child must have been in his mind, as it was in mine. Perhaps he hoped for it. But his desire failed at the crucial moment and he turned away from me, lying down again with his back to me. And now he was the one who said: "I'm sorry."

"Let me help."

"I have never needed help in my life."

"This is different from any other time in either of our lives. Please, Matthew."

In the end, he let me do as I wished, and we came together successfully, but I did most of the work, sitting astride him in the slanting moonbeams, leaning down to him. I remember how dark his eyes were, looking up at me, and how the reflected moonlight came and went in them as my hair, swinging loose like a curtain, sent its shadow swaying back and forth.

It was not the kind of love we had known before. It was as though that had come from the heart and this came only from the body. But it brought us a release. I had not known until now how badly I needed this and although I did not ask him, I thought that his feelings mirrored mine.

At last, we lay down again side by side and our arms slid

around each other. I made some light comment about the supper Brockley had fetched. It had included a meat pie.

"They won't do so well at the abbey. The guest house is comfortable enough, but the abbey will keep to the Lenten rules. There won't be any meat. I don't think Charpentier troubles too much about Lent," I said sleepily.

"Saltspoon! Still that edge on your tongue. Charpentier keeps Lent as he should. It was beaver in that pie."

"Beaver? Well, that's meat."

"No, it isn't. Beavers have wide splayed tails like fish, and they live in water. They count as fish. Didn't you know?"

"No," I said, although it occurred to me that the taste had been familiar and that I had probably eaten it at Elizabeth's court. I didn't care, anyway. What now filled my mind was that Matthew, once more, had called me Saltspoon, and in that dear, loving tone of voice. I snuggled more closely against him. "Go to sleep, now," he said. "You must need rest, after so much traveling. Last time we spent a night together, if I remember rightly, we were interrupted in the middle of it by an uproar. Let us pray we have peace and quiet tonight."

"Yes, indeed," I said.

It was a prayer not destined to be answered. When I look back, I feel that some sportive demon was watching over the fractured marriage of Matthew de la Roche and Ursula Blanchard. I fell asleep but deep in the night, I woke abruptly. The moon still shone through the window, though it had moved from the left-most window to the far right, and cloud was coming up and drifting darkly across it. It was low cloud, swirling and thick and . . .

Then my nostrils twitched to a frightening smell and I saw the flicker of a light that was not the cool silver of the moon, but wavering and ominously red. The cloud across the face of the moon was smoke. At the same moment, a confused racket broke out. I heard shouts and running feet. Doors slammed. A horse whinnied in terror and hooves clattered wildly on the cobbles of the stableyard. Matthew and I shot upright at the same moment.

"Dear Christ, Ursula! It's a conspiracy. Someone's following us about to ruin our nights of passion! Last time, we had Dale taken ill at midnight and the whole household turned upside down. And now, the damned inn's on fire!"

We scrambled from the bed, dragging clothes on and making for the window. We gasped. Flames were leaping from somewhere at the far end of the building, but even as we looked, they sprang out of a window nearer to us.

"Wake Brockley!" Matthew shouted, half in and half out of his hose.

Brockley was awake already. As I dragged on kirtle and bodice, he began to hammer on the door. "We're coming!" I shouted. "Go on—get out of the inn!" The uproar was increasing. Somewhere below, a woman was screaming hysterically that it was the Huguenots, it must be the Huguenots. "They've fired the inn; they want to burn us all. Mother of God preserve us!" I could hear Charpentier outside, yelling orders about water from the well. Matthew, donning a shirt and snatching up his sword belt, threw my cloak around my shoulders and said: "No time for an overdress. Come on!"

We dashed out through the anteroom, where Brockley, in shirt and breeches and also gripping his sword belt, had waited for us against my orders. Together, we made for the stairs. People in various states of dress or undress were jostling past, some holding candles up to light what would otherwise have been choking darkness, for smoke was drifting up from below. People were coughing, spluttering out questions that nobody could answer; a young man was steadying a girl, who was in tears. But someone downstairs was shouting that it was all right down there as yet, come down quickly, and then someone else started to pound on a gong, presumably to make sure that no one was left still asleep. With the rest of the crowd, we stumbled down, braving the smoke and trying to hold our breath.

The public room seemed to be on fire; at least, the smoke and a waft of heat came from that direction, barring our way to the front porch. We turned the other way and blundered out through the back door, into the stableyard and into a new chaos. The fire was in the kitchens, too. The flames we had seen from our bedchamber window were coming from there. They were licking upward from its windows like the tongues of greedy cats, searching their whiskers for vestiges of cream, and finding, instead, a creeper that grew on the back wall of the inn. Fire was darting along it and catching eagerly at window frames.

Charpentier had a bucket chain going from the well and a score of men were hard at work, hurling water through the kitchen windows, and passing buckets out under the arch to attack the fire in the public room at the front, a safer means of getting at it than going through the house. The fire was nowhere near the stable, but grooms were getting the horses out as a precaution, taking them through a rear gate to a paddock. The horses were frightened, plunging against their halters, their flailing hooves endangering those who were fighting the fire.

They weren't all people from the inn; half St. Marc's seemed to have come rushing to the scene. Glancing through the arch to the street, I saw a crowd there, their faces lit with red. The hysterical woman who had been accusing the Huguenots was in their midst, still screaming out her fears and prayers and they were listening to her.

Then, beyond the roar of the flames and all the coughing and shouting immediately around me, I heard a menacing growl begin from the midst of the crowd and I saw them all turn together and surge concertedly off into the square. I heard the word *Huguenot* taken up like a chant.

"There's a couple of Lutheran families living in the square." I turned and found the so-called Netherlander, Van Weede, at my side, along with his two companions. Even in the weird mixture of moonlight and firelight, I could see that all three faces were very grim. "I know them slightly," Van Weede said. "I dined at one of their houses yesterday. The man's a master potter. I placed an order with him. I doubt I'll ever see that order now. God pity him and his, for there's nothing we can do. There's maybe fifty in that mob."

"But—what has happened? Did someone fire the inn? Was it Huguenot troops?" I couldn't see any. If Huguenot soldiers had smoked us out to massacre us, where were they now? No murderous soldiers had rushed from the shadows brandishing swords. Brockley and Matthew, who had by now got their sword belts properly on, leaving their hands free, had joined the bucket chain, and nobody was interfering with the firefighters.

"I think not," said Van Weede grimly. "But that crowd doesn't agree. They've lost their heads. That bloody screeching woman started them off. It's that black-haired bitch from the kitchens here. Their Protestant neighbors are harmless craftsfolk but . . ."

From somewhere outside the inn, but not very far away, an appalling babble broke out: a bestial roar and then a series of long, drawn-out, terrified, gibbering screams. "Oh, my God,"

I said stupidly and uselessly, and then I said it again, more loudly, because helmeted men with naked swords were erupting from the darkness after all, their intentions most certainly murderous.

A split second later, I saw that although they were Protestants, they were not Huguenots; on the contrary, they were Dick Dodd, Walter Dodd, and the redheaded Searle. Then I heard Dick Dodd shouting: "That's him! That's De la Roche!" and all three threw themselves toward Matthew, who was standing in the bucket line with his back to them. Terrified and furious, I lost my temper for the second time that night. I ran toward him screaming, and regardless of either safety or modesty, I tore off my cloak and threw it over Searle's head just as he was about to seize hold of my husband. "Leave him alone! How dare you? How dare you?"

"Orders, mistress. Out of my way!"

That was Dick Dodd. Searle's protests had been muffled by the cloak. *"Orders!* I'll give you orders!" I shouted and seizing a bucket of water from the grasp of a startled firefighter, I threw it over Dick.

"What in hell's name are you doing? Damnation on you; we're trying to put this fire out!" somebody yelled in my ear, in French, and the bucket was snatched away again. Matthew had sprung around, drawing his sword. Beside him, Brockley had done the same. Searle, struggling out from under the cloak, shouted: "Remember we've to take him alive!" and was then fiercely attacked by Brockley. The Dodds, Dick cursing and dripping, went for Matthew, apparently trying to disarm him. Van Weede ran to my side, grabbed the cloak and threw it around me again, and then, remarking in conversational tones that he loved a good fight, he, too, whisked out a sword and waded obligingly in to support Brockley.

His men came running up to join him and the burly one shouted to me to get back; they would see to all this. "Don't kill anyone! Just look after Matthew!" I shrieked, and then was flung roughly sideways as two more men with upraised blades crashed past me to join the fray. One shouted to the other in a language I didn't know, and I saw that they were the two sun-tanned individuals I had seen in the doorway of the inn earlier, the ones I had taken to be father and son. The older of the two was brandishing not a straight sword, but a scimitar.

Stumbling to a place of comparative safety on the far side of the well, I saw to my bewilderment that the two newcomers were attacking Van Weede. He fought back with fury, and so did his two companions. They had all produced swords now and they obviously knew how to use them.

The stableyard turned into a maelstrom. The struggle lurched this way and that, getting entangled with the grooms and the frightened horses, colliding with the bucket chain, attracting savage curses and yells of rage. Two horses panicked altogether, broke loose and bolted, leaving one of the grooms down on the cobbles, swearing and clutching his knee where he had been kicked. The horses bolted into the paddock where they were meant to go anyway, which was a mercy, but I heard a furious Charpentier demanding at the top of his voice that these brawlers be seized.

The fire was dying down. Everyone in the street hadn't gone to murder the Protestant neighbors and I heard someone shout that there was a second bucket chain in the front now, using somebody else's well. Then, suddenly, Brockley and Van Weede were beside me, rubbing the sweat from their faces and grinning.

"It's all right, madam. It's all over. Charpentier's got some fellows to put the Dodds and Searle under lock and key,"

Brockley informed me. "Seems he saw that they were the ones who started it or I daresay we'd be locked up, too. As it is, here we are, safe and sound."

"Just a little out of breath," Van Weede said. "But otherwise none the worse. What a night!"

"But Matthew!" I said, peering wildly around the shadowy yard. Two dark shapes lay unmoving on the cobbles. "Where's Matthew?"

"Here," said Matthew's voice behind me, and turning, I found him there, alive and strong, still with his sword in his hand. He sheathed it and put his hands on my shoulders. "I'm all right. Those two corpses over there are a couple of strangers who joined in; I don't know why. They went for this man"—he nodded toward Van Weede—"and since he was fighting on our side, I helped him deal with them. I got one of them and he got the other. One of the men who followed you here is hurt, I think, but he isn't dead."

"I didn't lead them here knowingly!" I was suddenly terrified that he might wonder if I had. "I swear it! When I saw them snooping round the inn—well, you saw how angry I was. Matthew, do you believe me?"

"Yes." He drew me apart from the others, into the deep shadow under the wall of the stableyard. "It's all right, Ursula," he said quietly. "It's all right."

"I'm bad luck for you. I belong to the other side and I can't escape from it. Oh, Matthew, I'm so sorry, so sorry!"

"Mistress Blanchard! Where's Mistress Blanchard? Is she safe? *Mistress Blanchard*!"

"That's Ryder's voice!" I said. "He must have come from the abbey!" Twisting around, I saw Ryder himself, striding about, catching people by the arm in order to question them, and accompanied, for some reason, by two men I did not know, who were also accosting people to ask after me, and doing it so roughly that several times they were brusquely shaken off.

"Who's Ryder?"

"One of the men Cecil sent with me. The abbey's only just across the square; I suppose this uproar has woken up everyone there as well."

"I daresay." Matthew pulled me deeper into the shadow. "I doubt if anyone's slept through this in the whole village."

"Matthew, listen. The Dodds knew you by sight and if they do, then Ryder probably does, too. They're Cecil's men and they could all have seen you when you were at court in England. You must get away quickly, now!"

And I could not go with him. We both knew it. It was too hasty, too quick; decisions that change lives ought not to be taken in such confusion. Nor, in any case, was it safe.

"Yes. You're right. The hunt's close behind me. Did Cecil's men fire the inn, do you think?"

"With me inside it? I hope not!"

"Well, maybe not. There really are Huguenots who would like to get their hands on me and if they didn't show themselves tonight, perhaps it was because they saw they were outnumbered. But they could have set the fire. Ursula, you promised to make your choice this morning, but I can't hold you to that. It is not only that you endanger me. I also endanger you. I dare not take you with me now."

"Mistress *Blanchard*!"

"She's safe, sir. She was here a moment ago. I'll find her for you. She's come to no harm." Brockley had pitched his voice so that I would hear him. Dawn was near. By its first faint light I saw that he was talking to Ryder and Ryder's companions, and that as he spoke, he was moving gently away toward the other side of the courtyard, taking them with him.

Matthew and I moved as one toward the paddock gate, and then, with the end of the stable block between us and those who were seeking him, we stopped and he took my face between his hands. We were looking at each other, groping for words, when Charpentier, soot-stained and angry, appeared beside us. "Someone's asking for you, madame."

"In a moment. Please keep everyone away from us meanwhile," said Matthew.

"It's another of the men you had with you before, madame. He has two of the abbey riffraff with him." Charpentier's voice conveyed distaste. "An abbey, even a women's abbey, can't do without retainers but many of St. Marc's best men have rallied to the call for Catholics to take up arms in Paris, and the abbess has had to fill the gaps with whatever she can get. Riffraff, as I said. They bully the town shopkeepers for special terms. They are detested. They and your man, madame," he added accusingly, "are also asking for the three I've got shut in my cellar for attacking the Seigneur de la Roche."

"My wife did not lead them here." Matthew answered the accusing tone rather than the words. "They came here to seize me but not with her knowledge. She is innocent of all offense against me. I must go now, Charpentier. I must get away before I am recognized and I must leave my wife here. I charge you to treat her with the utmost respect. Go and make sure those men don't come near us. Say Madame is helping someone who is hurt and will come presently. And tell someone to fetch my saddle and bridle and catch my horse."

Charpentier muttered under his breath, but went. Matthew held me closer, and I held him in return. "Ursula," he said softly, "since you cannot come with me now, finish what you came to France to do. Pray for peace, so that France may grow safe again. And then—make your choice. This way, you will have time to think." His voice grew rough with the intensity of his feelings. "Only, let it be the right decision, and the last. When you know your mind, let me know, somehow."

"But where will you be?" I didn't want to let him go. "How will any message from me find you?"

"I shall be at home in Blanchepierre, or else in Paris or wherever the royal forces are. If war breaks out in full, I may join them in the field. Letters sent through the court at Paris will find me. Ursula . . . don't leave me waiting and hoping and wondering for too long."

"I promise," I said.

We clung to each other for a moment, but there was no more time. Day was broadening every moment. A groom came through the gate with a pile of saddlery and a sieve of oats. "The bay gelding, over there in the corner," Matthew said brusquely, and while the groom went to entice the horse, Matthew and I kissed farewell. Then we stepped apart. Standing there by the gate, my mouth still imprinted with the memory of his, my body still aglow from his hands, his warmth, I saw him cross the paddock to where the groom had now bridled his mount and was putting the saddle on its back.

Once more, we had been forced to part, and I must not linger here for fear that Ryder should evade Brockley and Charpentier, come in search of me, and find Matthew as well. I was crying as I turned away. Fortunately, it didn't matter. After escaping from a burning inn, nearly being caught in the midst of a fight, and having to listen to murder taking place nearby, any woman might shed tears. When I joined John Ryder in the courtyard, he greeted me with fatherly concern but the white streaks on my grimy face didn't surprise him in the least. He willingly accepted my statement that Matthew had fled two hours ago.

CHAPTER 9

Levantine Lions

The full dawn revealed that although one-half of the inn was still more or less intact, much of the other half had been reduced to a smoking shell. The two swarthy men who had attacked Van Weede lay dead in the yard, where they had fallen. They were very dead indeed, the older one half sliced through; the younger nearly decapitated. They lay amid their own blood, a dark, congealing pool on the cobbles.

Most of the kitchen was lost in the ruin but Charpentier had a stout stone-built larder with a massive door, which had repelled the flames. Van Weede, who seemed to be a resourceful individual, had taken it upon himself to organize an impromptu breakfast for helpers, in the harness room. Charpentier had given it the nod. It left him free to deal with other matters, such as us.

Charpentier's private rooms were at the unharmed end of the building. It was here that the innkeeper, his face bloodless with exhaustion under stubble and soot, confronted us: myself, Brockley, and John Ryder. He sent Ryder's tough-looking companions to eat with the helpers, but the rest of us were herded into his sanctum.

"We will speak in private," he said grimly, and added, to my horror: "Then we will find out just what you Anglaises have done to my inn and why!"

The black-haired woman who had whipped the crowd up into hysteria during the night had reappeared, her broad face full of an ineffable and horrible smugness. She brought us bread and cheese and informed us that there were no stinking Huguenots left alive in the town. "But for these Anglaises," she added, giving me a glance of sheer hatred.

"We didn't start the fire," I snapped at her. "And I don't suppose your unfortunate neighbors did, either!"

"There, madame, I agree with you," said Charpentier. He pushed the bread and cheese across the table toward us. "You may eat. I keep an inn, after all. Listen. I detest my Huguenot neighbors. I hate all of the Lutheran persuasion. But like you, I do not believe they started the fire. They are—or were—humble and quiet enough; I grant them that. That, however, leaves your men, who it seems came here to seize the Seigneur de la Roche if they could. Your husband said you did not lead them here, but still, they came. Perhaps they set fire to the inn so as to drive him out of it and into their arms. Who else is there?" He stared accusingly at Ryder.

Turning to Ryder and Brockley, who had not followed this, I told them what had been said. Brockley exclaimed indignantly and Ryder burst out into a wrathful denial.

"Of course my men didn't start it! We would never have put you in such danger, Mistress Blanchard. We had orders to take Master de la Roche if he put in an appearance, but most certainly not to put you at risk. Just explain that to this innkeeper here, if you please, mistress."

I did so. The black-haired woman, marching in again with a flagon of wine that she put in front of us with a resentful bang, paused to listen to me and then walked out again with a loud snort. Charpentier didn't look much more convinced than she did.

"I have to take the word of Seigneur de la Roche that you did not lead your English retainers here on purpose," he said, though it was clear that to believe in my innocence pained him considerably. "But I still believe that they fired the inn. The blaze was obviously started on purpose."

"Where *are* my English retainers?" I interrupted.

"In my cellars. At this end of the inn, quite safe and well away from where the fire was. Permit me to finish. In the middle of the public room I have found the remains of logs that someone dragged out of the hearth, still alight, no doubt, and pushed among the furniture. The same was done with the kitchen fire; at least there is ash in a pile on the floor. My servants have quarters of their own to sleep in; I do not have them sleeping in the kitchen. I think someone got in. There is a window frame in the front of the house that is splintered as though it has been forced. It is blackened, but one can tell."

"That is very shocking, madam," Brockley said to me, when I had dutifully translated. "But I can't believe it of the Dodds, or even of Searle."

"Fetch my men up here," barked Ryder. "Let us hear what they have to say!"

Once more, I translated, this time for Charpentier's benefit. "I can guess what they will have to say, and it will all be lies!" Charpentier seized a goblet in his soot-stained hand, poured himself a hefty draft of wine, and gulped at it. "Those men will stay in my keeping until I can bring them before the mayor. Do not expect considerate treatment because you are foreigners. The seigneur your husband may vouch for you, madam, and that I will accept, but why should I believe the protestations of this man Ryder? Or Brockley? It is my opinion that those miscreants in my cellar—"

There was a tap on the door and then, without waiting for

permission, Van Weede walked in. Considering that he had been up most of the night, sword-fighting and firefighting, he looked astonishingly spruce. His shirt and hose might be dirty, but he had combed his hair and beard and washed his cheerful, rosy-brown face. His dark eyes were as bright and his step as springy as though he had just risen from eight hours on a down mattress.

"Excuse me for interrupting," he said in French. "But the woman who has been serving you came to where I was eating breakfast, and repeated something of what is being said here. I have come to say that I think I know who fired the inn and why, and to assure you that it had nothing to do with Madame Blanchard's men, or with the unhappy disputes that are now disturbing the peace of France. The offenders were trying to smoke me out of my room in order to kill me. They—or colleagues of theirs—have tried to kill me before. But it's too late to take reprisals against them because they're the two who are lying dead in the stableyard."

We all stared. I muttered a hurried translation for Ryder and Brockley.

"I ask your pardon, Charpentier," said Van Weede seriously. "I thought I had shaken off the pursuit. But I have looked closely at those bodies out there and I recognize one of them. Besides, they attacked me last night. There really is no doubt that they were responsible for all the mayhem. I am really *very* sorry, Charpentier, and I shall offer you compensation."

Charpentier had risen indignantly to his feet. "What is all this? You stride in here uninvited and begin talking nonsense! I tell you that my inn was set alight by the men attached to Madame here, who sought to seize or kill her husband, a prominent supporter of our good Catholic cause."

Van Weede, unimpressed, shook his head. "I think not. The

perpetrators were almost certainly men in the employ of a consortium of merchants who object to the idea of England trading directly with Persia and bypassing tolls and middlemen of Turkey and Venice. I'm traveling under a false name. I am not really called Van Weede, and I'm not from the Netherlands. I'm another of the Anglaises who are so unpopular here just now, although believe me, I have no interest in the civil wars of France, one way or another. I am a man of business, pure and simple. I am an English merchant in the employ of the Muscovy Company and my name is Anthony Jenkinson."

"The trouble began soon after I left Persia and started for home," Jenkinson told us, over the wine. He had declined the bread and cheese, saying that he had eaten already and now would rather talk. He did so bilingually, speaking every sentence first in French and then repeating it in English, bridging the language gap with what was evidently practiced ease. "I meant," he said, "to go back by the route I'd used on the outward journey, and travel north up the Caspian Sea, then by river to Moscow, and then north again to Archangel, and westward round the Norwegian coast, before next winter begins to freeze the seas. I don't know if you recognize any of these names, but . . ."

"I've heard most of them. Merchants come to this inn," Charpentier said briefly. He seemed prepared to listen, though he had obvious reservations.

"When my first husband was alive," I said, "we lived in Antwerp, where my husband was employed by Sir Thomas Gresham. The voyages of merchants and explorers were often discussed. Since then, I have been at the court of Queen Elizabeth, who also takes an interest in such things. I understand very well."

Ryder nodded agreement and so did Brockley. Brockley was always well informed. Jenkinson looked pleased.

"Good. It makes it easier to explain. I had had a successful audience with the Shah in Persia and I found him willing to enter into a trade agreement with England, although there were protests from Turkish and Venetian representatives then at his court. They appeared to yield gracefully when the agreement with me was made and signed. But then they left Persia rather suddenly and that made me uneasy. I thought they might well have gone to consult with their superiors in Istanbul or Venice. Istanbul probably; it would be nearer. I should have heeded that feeling and taken myself off at once, but I wanted to purchase a first consignment of goods to carry home, and I wanted to inspect the workshops where fabrics were woven and jewelry made. Unwisely, I lingered, though I planned to set out north before Christmas, intending to reach Russia in spring—you don't make rapid headway with a merchant caravan—and travel round the Norwegian coast in summer.

"But I left it too late after all. We chartered two vessels to take us across the Caspian Sea but halfway across, we were attacked by what we at first thought were pirates. We fought them off and we took a prisoner, and from him we got some interesting information. He was no pirate, or not in the usual sense. It seems," said Jenkinson, "that the merchants of Venice and Turkey were very upset indeed at the prospect of losing so much valuable trade through me. In particular, there is a consortium of merchants who call themselves the Levantine Lions. I've heard of them before. They have a ruthless reputation and they had decided not to let me get back to England with my treaty. According to our captive, I had a whole pride of lions on my spoor. He and his piratical friends were in their pay."

No one asked what had finally happened to the captive. It would have been a silly question. Jenkinson had natural charm, but it was a velvet covering over a chain-mail gauntlet.

He also had a resonant, flexible speaking voice, and that curious thing known as presence. He was capable of holding even a reluctant audience.

"And so?" Charpentier, however weary, dirty, and furious about the disaster to his inn, was growing interested in spite of himself.

"I talked with my men," Jenkinson said, "and we decided to make it more difficult for the enemy by dividing our forces. I was carrying two signed copies of the treaty. We changed course, reached a small port, and hired some extra men as additional protection for the main party and the goods caravan, which I sent off on our planned route, in charge of a man I could trust. One copy of the treaty went with him. The other copy I kept on my person. With three companions I then set off home but by a very different route."

Here he paused and smiled. It was a wicked and engaging smile. I had a feeling—an awed feeling, I may say—that I knew what was coming next.

"I decided," he said, "that the safest thing to do was the most unexpected. The Levantine Lions represent the interests of Turkey and Venice. They wouldn't expect me to appear, therefore, in either place. So I arranged passages for us to Istanbul."

We gazed, fascinated, at this insouciant adventurer whose idea of avoiding dangerous and well-organized enemies was to saunter into the heart of their territory.

"You say your name's Anthony," I said. "Shouldn't it be Daniel?"

Jenkinson smiled again. "Maybe it should, because after all, I think somebody did recognize me. Merchants go everywhere. Every great fair brings them together from far-flung places. I daresay that in every city of Europe or the Levant, there's someone who knows me by sight. Though God knows, I was careful. I did have an idea of revealing myself and complaining to the authorities, because I doubt if the Levantine Lions are official in any way. English relations with both countries are good and I don't see the rulers of either Turkey or Venice wanting to wreck them by assassinating respectable merchants. But I decided not to risk it. It wouldn't be the first time a government's right hand hasn't been quite clear about what its left hand was doing.

"I took the name of Van Weede and melted into the scenery—or so I thought—as a Netherlands merchant interested in luxury goods. Most ships were laid up for the winter but there's always coastal and short-haul traffic. I managed to get us to Rome—changing ships at Athens—and I thought I'd escaped. I lost a man on the voyage to Rome, but that was through some sickness or other that he'd picked up in Turkey. That left me with the two you saw last night. They're still having breakfast."

"Remarkable swordsmen," Brockley observed.

"Are they not? Stephen Longman and Richard Deacon, their names are. Deacon fights like a leopard, and though Longman isn't so very tall, he has shoulders like a bear and can kill a man by picking him up and hugging him. I took them on as lads and I trained them myself," said Jenkinson smugly, "and though I say it myself, they're a credit to me. Well, we got to Rome, and then we were attacked in the street after dark. I was glad of Longman and Deacon then, I can tell you. We fought them off and we didn't take any prisoners to question this time, but I think they were Lions. There were six of them and they all looked to me like Venetians or Turks. Unfortunately," he added, "we only killed three. The rest ran away."

"And then?" Ryder asked.

"We found another ship as fast as possible. It was bound for Marseilles. Well, France was on the way to England, so to speak. I decided that we would cross France overland and get a ship to England maybe from Calais. It saved trying to get a passage out round Spain. You may not know about this," he explained, "but the Atlantic tides pour into the Mediterranean and one needs not only a favorable wind to get out against it, but a strong wind, as well. Sometimes ships have to wait weeks for the right conditions. It's such a waste of time. Marseilles would do very well, I thought.

"I had no idea, of course, that France was on the edge of a civil war. I'd got out-of-date with the news, what with all my wanderings round the Caspian Sea and the Mediterranean.

"We reached Marseilles and the moment we landed, Deacon said to me that he was sure he'd recognized a man on the quay as one of those who had attacked us in Rome. He said you tend to remember a face when the last time you saw its owner, he was trying to stick a sword into you."

It was probably Master Jenkinson's airy, almost amused tone that accounted for the strangled voice in which Brockley said: "Quite so."

"There were a couple of fast vessels in port," Jenkinson said. "Someone could have got to Marseilles ahead of us, once they learned which ship we were on and where it was bound. I fancy we were chased all the way from Istanbul. We were three days changing vessels at Athens. Our pursuers could have caught up with us easily enough.

"Well, we got off that quay as quick as we could, and put up at an inn. The three of us shared a room and slept with our swords beside us, which was just as well because that night two men crept into the room with daggers.

"Luckily, I'm a light sleeper and I woke up in time and so did my companions. We made a quick job of things and there wasn't much noise. It was all very awkward, though, because it meant we had two corpses on our hands."

"Yes. That would be very awkward indeed," Ryder agreed, with a straight face. Even Charpentier was now staring at Jenkinson with the bemused expression of a child being shown around a menagerie of exotic animals.

"But this time," Jenkinson said, "once again, I got some information out of one of them before I dispatched him to his maker. Or rather, he spat it at me. He said I need not think that he and his companion were all I had to worry about. There were others, he said, and more still following.

"I knew there was at least one other—three got away in Rome. But this sounded as though we still had quite a pack on our heels. It worried me. I thought," said Master Jenkinson, "that our trail would be all too obvious if we were kept in Marseilles to answer questions in an inquiry about the said corpses. We had to do something."

"Such as?" Charpentier inquired.

"Escape, of course," said Master Jenkinson, like a tutor deploring a pupil's inability to perform simple addition. Two and two make four, boy, not five. And if you're staying at an inn and you happen to have killed a couple of midnight intruders and don't want to answer questions, you flit by moonlight, fast and quietly. What else?

"We got dressed," continued Jenkinson. "We put the bodies in our bed—it was big; we'd all been sharing it—and on a table we left enough money to pay for our night's lodging. Then we took our packs and climbed out of a window and slithered down a most useful vine on the wall. We hid in the town until daybreak, and then we hired horses and got out of Marseilles. We soon found that we were in a very disturbed country. Maybe that's why there was no hue and cry after us, or not one that ever caught up with us, anyway."

"And since then?" inquired Ryder.

"Since then, we've been traveling through France but on a wandering path and not just because of the war. We wanted to confuse our trail. But we didn't confuse it quite enough because a couple of Lions caught up with us last night. I recognized the older one. His name is Silvius Portinari. He's a well-known Venetian merchant, dealing mainly in Persian carpets, and I'm frankly surprised to find him pursuing me in person. I think the other was the third man who got away from us in Rome—he's Turkish by the look of him."

"Well, they're dead. They can't harm anyone now," said Brockley.

Jenkinson glanced at him. "The fellow in Marseilles spoke of others following and my captive on the Caspian Sea told me—albeit reluctantly—something of how the Lions work. The wealthy merchants who are the Levantine Lions all have a few willing cutthroats in their employ, to send out after nuisances like me. I would guess that Portinari came along to point me out to them because he knows me by sight, just as I knew him. He wouldn't have intended to help personally with murdering me. He probably came last night because I and my men had wiped out all but one of his killers and he didn't think one was enough on his own and didn't want to wait for reinforcements either, in case I gave him the slip. But I think the reinforcements are on their way.

"I am known as a formidable man." Jenkinson said this without conceit, as though remarking that he was known to like quinces or to perform competently on the spinet. It was to him a fact, no more. "A second wave is very likely following, to make sure of me, in case I dealt with the first wave—as I did. I daresay they needed time to assemble the extra men. With luck," he added, with that so-engaging grin, "I have drawn the pursuit away from the merchant train I sent through Russia. It may not have occurred to them that there is a second copy of the treaty, and they would want my blood, anyway. I'm the offender who arranged the treaty in the first place. But I am determined to survive and hand my copy of that treaty to Her Majesty in person."

I believed him.

Charpentier scratched his head and still seemed only half convinced. But when he had the Dodds and Searle fetched upstairs, their outrage at the suggestion that they might have fired the inn was almost enough on its own to persuade him that they spoke the truth and that Jenkinson's explanation was the right one. Dick Dodd had a cut on his left forearm with a length of torn shirt wrapped around it. Jenkinson produced salves and bandages from his luggage and I dressed the wound. While I worked, Dick Dodd expressed his opinion of the arson accusation in language so forceful that I was obliged to tell Charpentier that I couldn't translate it literally. "But he doesn't usually swear like that," I said.

In addition, Jenkinson was apparently carrying a fair amount of money and was willing to pay the innkeeper substantial compensation then and there, including a sum for the burial of the two bodies that still adorned the cobbles in the stableyard.

Money, it is said, can talk. It certainly talked to Charpentier, who looked at the gold coins Jenkinson was offering, and yielded after only the briefest attempt at haggling. Jenkinson good-humoredly increased his bribe by a modest amount and Charpentier agreed to accept that the fire had probably been raised by Jenkinson's enemies and not by my men or by Huguenots, and to let us all go. Though I think most of St. Marc's believed it was Huguenots and probably they still do.

I saw, afterward, what had happened to the Lutheran families who lived nearby. It was when we had at last finished at the inn, and were all going back to the abbey: myself, Ryder, Brockley, the Dodds, Searle, the abbey retainers, and also Jenkinson and his men. Charpentier was closing his inn for the time being and all the other guests had gone already.

As we walked back across the square, we passed the houses where the Huguenots had lived. They were adjacent to each other. Their doors were half off their hinges, their windows smashed, and they were being looted. A pair of laughing youths were carrying a carved cupboard out of one and some women—respectable-seeming women—were bringing out rugs and cooking pots from the others.

Much to my annoyance, the two scruffy retainers from the abbey dashed into one of the houses. We walked on but presently they caught us up, grinning, and informed us that they'd found a sliding panel upstairs, which everyone else had missed, and look what they'd got—a rope of pearls in a little velvet bag, and a pearl and garnet pendant in a pretty sandalwood box. It looked as though they had some experience of looting. They were obviously better at it than the townsfolk were.

I ordered them to put the things back but they ignored me, and when Ryder and Jenkinson added their voices to mine, one of them, a particularly unpleasant type with a three-day stubble, merely retorted: "Why? Them as owned them don't need them now."

It was true. The rightful owners would never need their belongings again. Their bodies hung in a row from their own upper windows, the ropes knotted around the mullions. I had hurried past, trying not to look but I had already seen more than I wanted to see.

There were children among them.

I could only thank heaven that Meg was safe in England.

CHAPTER 10

Stained Glass

At the abbey, we found Dale in a state of great anxiety, although Walter Dodd had run on ahead to announce our safe return. She was waiting on the porch and rushed at me and Brockley, ricocheting between us as though she hardly knew which one she had worried about most.

"Oh, ma'am, thank God you're all right. Roger, what happened? Oh, my God, you're all over soot! We saw the flames going up, right from the windows here, and then Master Ryder came out and shouted up to us that he was going to find out what was going on . . . and then he went and didn't come back either . . ."

"Madame Blanchard! We are all most relieved and we will give thanks for your safety." The abbess appeared, black-gowned and calm. She was a tall woman, probably in her forties, with one of those brown southern European faces that look as though they have been carved from teak. She had a beautiful smile when she did smile, but it wasn't often.

Helene reverenced her, but I found her unnerving. It was Ryder, not I, who said to her candidly: "A Huguenot family has been massacred and the two abbey retainers who were with me looted their house. I doubt if they're the type you require to serve an abbey."

The two concerned had already taken themselves off to their

quarters. The abbess did not, however, pretend she didn't know who was meant. She inclined her head politely toward Ryder. "I know their shortcomings. I do not approve the Lutheran faith but I do not condone either murder or looting. In these difficult days, I employ what men I can find but I agree that the two of whom you speak are deadwood and I shall soon, I trust, cut them away. I have three others but last night I kept them back to defend the abbey and my nuns, if the fire should mean a Huguenot attack." She glanced around, hearing footsteps. "Here is Helene."

Helene hurried to meet me, with Jeanne behind her.

"I am so glad that you are safe, madame." She bobbed me a conventional curtsy.

"We will send word to Douceaix," the abbess said. "Rumors fly fast these days and we must make sure that your relatives know, as soon as possible, that you have come to no harm. A messenger will leave at once."

"Thank you," I said. "Helene, I will come to you and tell you all about it very soon. For the moment, if you will excuse me, I wish to go to my chamber and tidy myself."

"Of course. Come, child." The abbess led Helene and Jeanne away. I made haste to my room with Dale, telling Brockley to wash and change quickly and then join us.

While we waited for him, I, too, seized the chance to wash and Dale helped me into the one spare gown I had brought with me to St. Marc. "Did you see your husband, ma'am?" she asked as she got it out of the press where she had hung it.

"Yes, and spent the night with him—until the fire started! But he's gone again now." I told her the whole story, briefly, while she buttoned me into my sleeves and did my hair, making horrified exclamations at intervals during my story. Presently, Brockley arrived, pale from his night's exertions, but clean and tidy once again. We sat down together. The guest quarters of the abbey were plain, in the sense that they had no wall hangings or carpets, but they were quite adequately furnished. My room had a tester bed for me, a truckle bed for Dale, a settle-cum-chest, and a window seat. I was sitting on my bed. Dale had the chest and Brockley perched sideways on the window seat.

They gazed at me and I said furiously: "I am so angry that I could burst. I've been used in the most shameful way! And now I don't know what to do!"

"Madam, what are you talking about?" Brockley asked.

"I mean that Cecil planted three men on me with orders to see if Matthew contacted me and arrest him if he did—in his own country. Master Blanchard's men also seem to be involved. Searle is one of them, and he was with the Dodds when they followed me to the inn last night. I daresay that Master Blanchard is perfectly well aware of the whole scheme and probably cooperated with it."

They burst into exclamations of consternation and outrage on my behalf, which were comforting to hear.

"I suspect," I said, "that Master Blanchard even pretended to be ill so as to keep me not too far away from the Loire for a while! So do I now go on and help him bring Helene back to England, or do I simply refuse to go a step farther with him?"

"But, ma'am," said Dale anxiously, "what about Paris and the queen's letter?"

"I can go to Paris without either Master Blanchard or Helene," I said. "Brockley has already said so much."

"Mistress Helene is quite innocent in all this." Brockley, after his first outburst, had begun to think. His gold-freckled brow was creased with thought. "Even Master Blanchard probably had little choice. I have no wish to defend him, but that's very likely true."

I sighed. "Yes, it is. I know myself that it is very difficult to say a blunt no to Cecil. And why should he, anyway? Gerald's father has never liked me. The scheme failed, at least. Matthew escaped—again! I suppose it would be best to go on and finish my errands."

"Madam—I don't mean to be inquisitive—but when you parted from Master de la Roche, did you make any arrangements to meet again?" Brockley inquired.

"Not exactly." I had already told Dale on what terms Matthew and I had parted. I repeated them to Brockley. He nodded.

"He was talking good sense, madam. With France in such a turmoil, this isn't the moment for you to join him, even if that's what you want to do. I'd say it was in your interest to get that letter safely delivered to the queen mother. You told us it was an offer from Queen Elizabeth to help in mediation, between her Catholic government and the Huguenots. What's their leader's name? The prince of Condé? Well, a peaceful France would let you make your mind up freely, and meanwhile, you will, I suppose, have to go on living at the court of Queen Elizabeth. Best to please her, wouldn't you say?"

I found myself reluctantly smiling. "You've a good brain under that high forehead of yours, Brockley. You're right, of course. Until there is peace in this country again, my whole life is like a pot left simmering on the edge of the fire, until someone has time to attend to it. And yes, in the meantime I suppose I must go back to England."

"And we oughtn't to fall out with Master Blanchard." Dale, too, had been thinking. "We're all traveling together in this dangerous country. Travelers in perilous places ought to stick together. If you ask me, he's more frightened of France even than we are!"

"Yes, I daresay. I'm more angry with Cecil than with Master Blanchard," I said. "Sir William Cecil saw a chance and seized it, I fancy! He's a servant of the queen first of all and laying hands on my husband could benefit England, in their eyes. But to use me as bait!"

I choked on the words, thinking of my last glimpse of Matthew, as he took the bay gelding's bridle from the groom. Where was my husband now?

"Very well," I said at last. "We will go on as before. And the sooner the better, I feel. We'll start for Douceaix later today. I must take some rest first, but we will leave after dinner. Brockley, you had better let Ryder know."

"I'll tell Master Jenkinson, too, madam. He was talking, on the way here, of riding with us to Douceaix and even on to Paris, given that you and Master Blanchard agree. It would be a good disguise, he says, to blend into someone else's escort as just one more retainer."

"I can hardly imagine Mr. Jenkinson as just one more retainer. He'd stand out of any crowd," I said. "And what if these Levantine rivals of his are still on his scent? Haven't I got trouble enough? I'm getting very tired indeed of mysteries and alarms." I paused to think. "But if he wants to come with us to Douceaix, I can hardly refuse him. He has done well by us and I owe him something. I must find Helene. She'll want to know what happened last night and I must tell her to make ready to leave. She should have had time enough by now to say goodbye to all the nuns and confessors in the province. Go and see Ryder, and then get a little sleep, Brockley. Dale, attend me."

Brockley withdrew. Dale and I went in search of Helene.

She was not in her room, but a lay sister who was sweeping the stairs near her door said that she thought Helene had gone into the church. "Perhaps to give thanks for your safety, madame."

I had doubts about that, but with Dale, I went out of the guest house and across the courtyard to the church. It was a big place, ornamental on the outside, with gargoyles and elaborate carvings on the stone walls. Inside, it was cool and dim, fragrant with incense, and the shadows were touched here and there by the gentle flames of votive candles, and by shafts of light through stained glass.

The day had turned sunny and on the eastern side of the church, a window depicting the Last Supper blazed with azure and ruby and deep amber and cast jewel-colored patches onto the stone of pillars and floor, and on the golden candlesticks of the altar candles. One glowing ray lit up a niche in which stood a golden statue of the Virgin and Child. But above all, there was quietness here. I could see no sign of Helene, but the atmosphere of prayer and worship was like a calming hand on me. Even Dale, whose prejudices were stronger than mine, responded to it. Benches were set in rows on either side of a central aisle and I sat down. Quietly, Dale sat down beside me.

I let Helene slip out of my mind and once again, I thought of Matthew. I had believed, when I left England, that the way back to him was closed; that I had closed it myself a year ago when I refused to flee to France with him. But now, once more, there was a possibility . . . a chance . . .

Presently, I slid forward to my knees and silently prayed, to whichever version of God might be listening, that one day the warring sects might be reconciled and I might at last find Matthew again and live in peace with him, and that Meg should be with us, so that we could live as a family.

I prayed, too, for the souls of the Huguenots who had been murdered last night. Anglicans aren't supposed to pray for the dead but no one would know except God and I hoped he would understand.

Then Dale, who was still sitting upright on the bench at my side, whispered: "Ma'am!" and nudged me and at the same moment I heard footsteps approaching. Opening my eyes, I shifted back onto the bench and turned to find myself looking up at a thickset priest with a silver-gray tonsure. I gazed into watchful brown eyes and into a well-remembered fleshy face, scored with lines of ruthless authority.

"I saw you come into the church. I want to speak to you, Mistress de la Roche," said the phlegm-filled voice of Helene's confessor, Dr. Ignatius Wilkins.

I had used him as an excuse for staying at Le Cheval d'Or, but in all the uproar of the night, I had completely forgotten him. I came to my feet. "Dr. Wilkins!"

"So you remember me," he said. "Why are you here?"

He was speaking English. He was, of course, English by birth. He had once been a parish priest in Sussex, not far from my old home. They had been Sussex people, the father and daughter he had committed to death in the flames.

They had died together. How hideous to know, in that last agony, that the parent, the child, you have loved is sharing the same torment. If I were to die so, it would double my anguish to know that Meg was suffering the same thing, and her pain would be doubled by mine. Wilkins might want to speak to me but I didn't want to speak to him. I had to say something, but I kept it brief.

"I am acting as companion to Helene Blanchard. You know her, I think. Her guardian is taking her home to England."

"Yes, poor child. She has come to ask my blessing and such

comfort and advice as I can give her, before she sails for her exile in a heretic country."

His tone was almost sentimental. But his voice issued from a relentless mouth with a strong upthrusting lower lip and down-turned corners. I was instinctively afraid of him, but I wouldn't show it. "It's your own country, Dr. Wilkins," I said.

"No longer," Wilkins said. "Not until such time as it returns to the true faith." He was barring my way out to the aisle. "I have heard," he said, "of the events of last night at the inn. Your men have talked freely. They are full of regret that their quarry, your husband, got away. They seem hardly aware that they are in a Catholic abbey. For myself, I rejoice that the Seigneur de la Roche has once more escaped from your coils. You say you are here as a companion to Helene Blanchard. Indeed? I think otherwise. It is not well done, madam, when a wife betrays her husband and brings the emissaries of a foreign land to seize him."

The attack took me by surprise. I was too startled to answer. Not that it mattered, for Wilkins's thick voice was still speaking. "A wife should be subject to her husband, should follow him wherever he leads, keep his counsel, and avoid speech with his enemies. But *you*! You have betrayed him three times over."

"Last year," I said, recovering myself, "I saved his life and yours as well. I kept the door barred while you and Matthew escaped out of the window!"

I had raised my voice and it echoed in the wide spaces of the church. Wilkins raised a quelling hand.

"Do not raise that shrill voice of yours in the house of God. Women should be silent in church."

"I will not be silent when unjust accusations are hurled at me, in church or out of it!"

"Unjust? Oh no, I think not. You refused to come with us," Wilkins said. "You chose between your husband and your false faith, and you did not choose your husband. I have warned him since never to trust you again and now see how right I was."

"How wrong you were!" Dale leapt to my defense like a fighting cock going into battle, all spurs and beak. "My mistress did not know she would be followed to the inn! She came here to bear Mistress Helene company, and then her husband wrote to her. So she went to see him. How dare you say she betrayed him?"

"All right, Dale!" I didn't want her to attract Wilkins's ire. But I patted her arm by way of thanks for her support before I said to him: "Why did you follow me in here to throw accusations at me? What is the point?"

"The point," said Wilkins, "is to warn you to keep away from Matthew de la Roche in future. All women are a snare to men, that I know very well." He gave Dale a single brief glance, acknowledging her existence for the first time. Then his unfriendly brown gaze shifted back to me.

"But you," he said, "are a particular snare to this man. He is a noble defender of our faith, one of the sharpest spearheads in the great offensive of God that we shall one day launch against your Lutheran island and against that apostate queen of yours. Matthew de la Roche is not to be seduced in your soft coils or endangered by your foul plans. For I have no doubt at all that you came here as an agent of your queen with his harm in mind. If the chance should present itself," said that thick, odious voice, lowered now but in menace rather than respect for sanctified surroundings, "I will save your heretic soul for you. But you will not enjoy the process."

As he spoke, he took a single step back, drawing himself

up, as though distancing himself from me before pronouncing judgment. The light from Judas's crimson robe in *The Last Supper* turned his face to the color of flame. For a moment, he looked so demonic that superstitious dread engulfed me. My knees trembled and I could not speak. It was Dale, far too furious to be afraid of him, who cried out: "How dare you threaten my mistress!" Once more, I put out a hand to her, resting it on her shoulder.

"Dale, don't." We were in France, after all, not England.

"You seem to have a devoted servant, Mistress de la Roche," Wilkins said. "And you seem as protective of her as she is of you. A touching spectacle. But I would advise you both to watch your tongues and take care. I have faith in the mills of God. And in my own long memory."

He turned on his heel and strode away. He wore sandals, like a monk, but his tread was heavy, all the same. Shaken, I sat down again on the bench. I knew what his threat meant. I thought of his two burned parishioners.

"That man is wicked!" said Dale vehemently. "Evil!"

"Yes, he is." I made myself stand up. "And I want to get away from him, and from here. Where in the world is Helene? We'll go back to our chamber. Perhaps she's waiting there."

Which turned out to be a more or less prophetic statement, for Helene was indeed in our room, although she couldn't be precisely described as waiting for us. She was going through our baggage.

We halted in the doorway, hardly able to believe our eyes. I almost forgot Dr. Wilkins in my indignation. Our baggage for the visit to St. Marc was not large; a pair of saddlebags each and one modest pannier. Helene had them all out on my bed, and she was rifling one of Dale's saddlebags. When we interrupted her, she was just removing a small phial of dark liquid from the bag. She did not see us at once, and while we stood staring, she drew out the stopper and sniffed at the contents. Outraged, I opened my mouth to ask her what she thought she was doing, but Helene saw us at the same instant and spoke first. As though she had a perfect right to search our belongings and ask questions about them, she demanded: "What is this?"

"Put that down at once!" gasped Dale. "What are you doing? Mistress Blanchard, she's been pawing through our things!"

"But what is it?" Helene persisted. She held the phial up to the light. It seemed to be made of blue-green glass. She tipped a few drops of the contents into her palm and I saw that they were a murky brownish-green. Helene put out her tongue and made as if to taste the liquid.

"Don't do that! Don't taste it!" Dale shrieked. "It's yew-tree poison!"

There was a frozen silence before I said: "Yew-tree poison? You're carrying yew venom, Dale?"

She had been with me that night when I cut yew twigs and brewed the deadly potion over my bedroom fire during the hours of darkness. In fact, I had asked her advice. Dale was fairly knowledgeable about extracting essences from plants. She knew how to make the poison. What I couldn't understand was why on earth she should want to. I gazed at her in bewilderment.

Dale seemed unable to answer. "Sit down," I said. "Both of you. I want to know why there is poison in your baggage, Dale. And, Helene, I want to know what in the name of all the saints you think you're doing poking into our things. Helene, you first!"

I tried to sound authoritative, though I didn't feel it. What I really felt was exhausted and miserable. I had had enough of this fraught journey. In that moment, I even forgot Matthew in my longing to go home, to be safe again. I wanted to be in England, walking or riding in Windsor Park with Elizabeth; sitting in a sunlit arbor with the other ladies, embroidering myself a new pair of sleeves; or—above all—at Thamesbank, playing with Meg. I had but to close my eyes to see my dark-haired daughter, who was so like her father, running toward me across the lawn of Thamesbank, where the greensward sloped down from the house to the landing stage and the Thames.

Corrupt her? No, I had been wrong to fear that. On the contrary, she would be health and salvation for me. I certainly didn't want to be here where inns caught fire, and assassins sprang from the shadows; where innocent families were slaughtered and wars came between man and wife; where fathers-in-law pretended to be ill when they weren't; and people searched your baggage the moment your back was turned.

I was still waiting for Helene to show some sign of embarrassment. But she neither stammered nor offered excuses. She just looked smug.

"I thought it might be poison," she said. "So I pretended I wanted to taste it, to frighten the truth from you."

"You impertinent girl!" squealed Dale. "Who do you think you are? The Grand Inquisitor?"

"I know all that happened last night," said Helene, ignoring Dale and continuing to address me. "You said you would come to tell me, but there was no need, for the whole abbey is humming with it, madame. I know how you led your men to capture your husband. He is your husband, is he not? The famous Seigneur de la Roche, who is so great a supporter of our Catholic cause, both here and in England?"

"Is that any of your business, Helene?"

"It is the business, madame, of anyone who holds to the true faith."

"I said from the first that she would be trouble, ma'am! The wretched Papist creature! I can't abide them!" Dale was furious and I couldn't blame her. The high and righteous pitch of Helene's voice was one of the most irritating sounds I had ever heard. Controlling a strong desire to box her ears, I said grimly: "You are under a misapprehension. I did not lead anyone to the inn. I was followed. And I still want to know why you were going through our baggage."

The fact that I was furious seemed to have penetrated at last. Helene, for the first time, eyed me with some uncertainty. "I was only looking for some white thread, madame. The hem of my shift is coming down and Jeanne was careless and did not bring white thread with her. And then I grew interested in what kind of person you are, madame. I looked at the book of poems you have with you." Here, she seemed to retain some confidence, apparently through contempt. "They seem mostly to concern the lusts of the flesh," she said disdainfully.

"They're poems of love," I said coldly. "They contain the works of Sir Thomas Wyatt and Henry Howard, Earl of Surrey. Yes, they wrote of passion. Rather than despising them, I advise you to study them before you enter into the married state. You could learn something useful."

The spurt of confidence faded. She threw back her head, however, visibly bracing herself, and I was oddly reminded of my own efforts not to show my fear of Wilkins. "Did you bring that poison with you in the hope of giving it to your husband?" Helene inquired.

"What?" I reeled. The sheer horror of the suggestion made me refute it, even though Helene had not a shadow of a right to question me. "I'd have taken it with me last night if that was its purpose! Don't be so silly!"

"Then what is it for?"

I turned to Dale. "It's your turn now. Why were you carrying it, Dale? What *is* it for?"

"It's for our safety," said Dale. "Because this is a land where decent Protestants are called heretics and what if persecution were to start again and we were seized? The poison is so that we can escape the flames. It's for you as well as us, ma'am, if the need arises, which God forbid. Brockley and I made it, the night before we left Greenwich. When you let us spend the night together."

"When you . . . ? Brockley knows about this?"

"Roger thought of it, ma'am. We stole what we needed from the queen's topiary garden at Greenwich, after dark. I was frightened," said Dale candidly. "Oh, ma'am, all those dark yew bushes, cut to look like horses and huge birds! At night, you almost think they're coming alive! But we got what we wanted easily enough and went back to Roger's lodgings and made the brew over his brazier."

I held out a commanding hand for the phial and Helene let me take it. I looked at it. There was probably enough there to kill three people. I twisted the stopper back into place. "So now you know," I said to Helene. "Dale has brought along a potion that will let us quickly out of the world if we are threatened with death as heretics. It's not for anyone else; just for ourselves. In future, keep your fingers out of other people's belongings, and don't hurl silly accusations about. Do you understand?"

Helene stared at us, eyes wide. It was as though we had flung open a window that showed her a completely unexpected view of her own world. But she could not make sense of it. She had been too carefully taught. She could only repeat the religious platitudes on which she had been nurtured.

"How can I believe you? The true faith is there for everyone and it is wicked to deny it! You have only to accept it and you would have no need to carry poison. The stake is only there to save the souls of those who abandon God and warn souls who are in danger back to the true path."

"Helene," I said, handing the phial back to Dale, "it is my duty to look after you and be a companion to you, but I think if I have to hear that superior, languid drawl of yours for many more minutes, I shall lose my temper. I'm on the verge of losing it now. Leave this room. Go to your own, and tell Jeanne to pack. We are setting out for Douceaix immediately after dinner. And, Helene, never touch our things again without our permission. You will be sorry if you do."

I meant it. She saw it in my face and fairly fled from the room. I sat down on the edge of my bed, shaking.

"Much more of this, Dale, and I think I shall go mad."

Dale, putting the phial away in her saddlebag, said: "It can't have been her that searched our baggage the first time, madam. She wasn't there. What's going on?"

"You mean, was she lying about the white thread, and are the two searches connected? Helene couldn't have carried out the first one but the same person could have ordered both—is that what you're trying to say?"

"I think so, ma'am . . . I'm not sure. It's all so muddling."

"You're right about that. Well, you might find out from Jeanne whether or not she brought any white thread with her. But even if . . . oh, for God's sake. I can't work it out. For

God's sake, let's get out of this place, on our way to Paris and then, as soon as possible, let's go home!"

We set out after dinner, though not as promptly as I had hoped, because Helene made a great to-do about her final farewells to her friends in the abbey and kept us waiting for half an hour in the courtyard. The farewells culminated in a last emotional embrace with the abbess on the porch. Wilkins didn't appear, though, which was a relief.

Dick Dodd had been tended in the abbey infirmary and had his arm in a sling but said he could ride well enough with one hand. Walter placed himself protectively at his brother's side. They maintained their normal courtesy toward me, but Searle kept giving me sullen looks as though last night's defeat and the hours he had spent shut in Charpentier's cellar were due to an act of spite on my part.

Our little cavalcade was augmented by three, for Anthony Jenkinson had duly asked if I would let him and his two men, Stephen Longman and Richard Deacon, ride to Douceaix with us, and I had agreed.

He had dressed plainly, in a well-worn buff jacket and hose and a creased collar. None of it fitted too well; I think he had borrowed an outfit from the burly Longman. Jenkinson was himself quite thickset, but the clothes seemed loose on him. The slightly untidy effect, though, was probably what he wanted. It made him look surprisingly commonplace. He might pass as an ordinary retainer after all.

Halfway to Douceaix, we met Luke and Henri Blanchard, accompanied by a whole crowd of men including William Harvey and Mark Sweetapple, riding hard in the opposite direction, intending to fetch us from St. Marc.

I greeted my father-in-law coolly. After some further talk

with Brockley, whose common sense I trusted, I had definitely made up my mind that I would do best not to take up with him the matter of his pretended illness and the part it had played in Cecil's schemes against my husband. Matthew was safe, and Blanchard's extraordinary behavior was a solved mystery over which I need not any longer puzzle.

It was quite possible, Brockley had said, that the two searches of my baggage were not connected; that whatever Helene's motives had been, the earlier search had been merely Cecil's men looking for signs that I was in touch with Matthew. Well, no matter. Let me just perform my errand for the queen and get home again and after that I need have nothing more to do with either Blanchard or Helene. I would let them pass out of my life and that would be that. No doubt Blanchard had been put under pressure by Cecil. I knew what that was like! I need not pretend to warm friendliness. I need only be polite and distant and leave it at that.

It was fortunate that we had other matters to discuss. Blanchard had had the message from the abbess, but it had been lacking in detail and both I and Jenkinson had to do a good deal of explaining. After hearing us out, which he did patiently enough, Blanchard pulled a solemn face and said in his portentous bass voice that yes, he had in fact known of my marriage to Matthew de la Roche because Cecil had told him; and no doubt it was natural for me to wish to see him, but Matthew was a wanted man, after all, and he hoped I would do nothing of the kind again.

I made one single reference to my new knowledge. "I realized last night that you knew of my marriage to Matthew," I said in an even voice. "I understand many things now. He is safe away, I'm glad to say."

My father-in-law looked chagrined, but he did not pursue

the matter. Instead, he turned to Jenkinson to ask him for more details of his own part in the night's events. He had heard of him, apparently, and now turned out to be an admirer.

He expressed horror concerning the Levantine Lions and also clicked his tongue a little when he understood that Jenkinson had entered the fray on Matthew's side. However, he then declared magnanimously, Master Jenkinson could not have known that in defending Matthew, he was defending a traitor.

"I am sorry if I offend you, Ursula," he added, "but that is what De la Roche is, and well you know it."

I was silent. From his point of view, of course, it was true. I knew that. But he should not have said it to me. I stared at him coldly. "I am sure," he observed, "that Master Jenkinson here fought bravely in what he imagined was an admirable cause. He appears to be a very brave man. I can only hope, sir, that you have now finally put paid to these miscreants who have been trying to hunt you down and that they will trouble you no more."

Or anyone in your company was the unspoken rider to that last sentence.

Jenkinson, picking up the nuance, studied Blanchard thoughtfully for a moment and then said gravely that if he had any further pursuers, they were assuredly far behind. "I think the danger now is very slight," he said. "May I, however, ask if I and my men can travel on with you to Douceaix? Mistress Ursula has consented already but we did not then know that we would meet you on the way. Just as a precaution, we wish to fade out of sight and what better way than to journey as someone else's retainers?"

Blanchard's expression was doubtful, but Jenkinson's reputation had visibly awed him, and Jenkinson's personality wasn't easily gainsaid. "You will be most welcome," said my father-in-law politely, turning his horse to face back toward Douceaix.

Blanchard fell in beside me as we rode on, and began to talk to me of the night just gone by. He actually asked if I knew where Matthew had gone. "I have no idea," I said icily. I didn't, however, trouble to add: "And I wouldn't tell you if I did."

I didn't want to discuss Matthew with him anymore. I only wanted to reach Paris, deliver my letter, and then go home.

Except that . . .

Talking about Matthew had made me think of him again, made me think of the night just behind me, and our united bodies in the warm darkness of the bed, before the fire disturbed us.

I was no longer sure where my home might be.

CHAPTER 11

The Serpent Queen

We reached Douceaix that evening. Henri and Marguerite were duly appalled by our story, impressed (and slightly alarmed) by Jenkinson, who admitted his identity and his plight to them, and astonished to hear of my marriage to Matthew.

"You have a hard choice to make," Marguerite said to me. "I will pray that you may choose with wisdom." Henri said little but regarded me with grave sympathy. They were good people; I appreciated them even if Helene didn't.

We waited a day at Douceaix, hoping that Dick's arm, which was giving him trouble, would improve quickly, but although it was not infected, Marguerite said firmly that he should rest it, for safety's sake. We decided, therefore, that on the following day we must set out without him. It meant leaving both the Dodds behind, since his brother wished to stay with him.

Of Cecil's men, I would still have John Ryder. Probably they thought it was no longer necessary for them all to keep close to me. They had missed Matthew once and he was unlikely to risk coming near me again. There should be enough sword arms in the party for simple protection against the normal hazards of the road, for Jenkinson and his men were to come to Paris with us, though, they would part from us there, and take a ship down the Seine.

"I don't believe that even if there are still any Lions following me through France, they're likely to find me before I get to Paris. I fancy I have covered my tracks," Jenkinson said to my father-in-law, who once more gave in, though as before, his face was dubious.

John Ryder was present and listened with noticeable amusement. After we set out, he said to me privately that Master Blanchard wouldn't want to look churlish or timid before a bold fellow like Jenkinson. "But if you ask me, he's shaking in his riding boots for fear of the Lions."

"Is he right, I wonder?" I said. "I'm grateful to Master Jenkinson and glad to help him, but the Lions make me nervous, as well."

"The whole of bloody France makes me nervous," said Ryder candidly. "The Lions are the least of our worries, if you ask me! We'll have three men fewer coming back from Paris. I have recommended to Master Blanchard that unless the country is much calmer by the time Master Jenkinson leaves us, which isn't likely, we should consider sailing home from Paris ourselves and abandoning the *Chaffinch*. If you want to know, mistress, I've already told the Dodds to make for Nantes as soon as Dick's fit enough and not worry about us. We ought to leave France by the shortest route."

Brockley, who was riding just behind us, at this point expressed vigorous agreement. "The sooner we all get safe home the better."

I agreed with them, and my agreement grew stronger with every hour. The ride to Paris, which took several days, was one of the most unpleasant journeys I have ever taken.

It was so disagreeable that Easter came and went while we were on the road and we didn't even notice it. To start with, there were crosscurrents in the party. It soon became clear that because Jenkinson and his two men had fought on Matthew's behalf at the inn, the other men regarded them as intruders. Searle in particular refused to speak to them, and would hardly speak to me either. On my side, although no one could help liking the acute and fatherly John Ryder and the cheerful, ever-hungry Mark Sweetapple, I distrusted my escort and although I accepted that a truce with my father-in-law was necessary, I could barely tolerate his company.

As for Helene, whose companion I was supposed to be, she loathed me and I loathed her back, though I did now and then remind myself of Helene's youth and her bereavement and I was glad that her woman Jeanne had agreed to come with her as far as Paris. Jeanne was a sensible woman with a genuine attachment to Helene, and a real concern for her.

Before we left the abbey, Dale had casually asked Jeanne for some white thread, to see what transpired. Jeanne at once produced a sizable quantity of it and offered a needle to go with it. This was interesting enough, but during the journey toward Paris, Jeanne made an opportunity to ride beside me, and said that she wished to apologize to me for her young mistress's bad behavior in looking through our baggage.

"She came and told me what she had done, and that she had made an excuse about wanting thread. She tells me most things, my little Helene. I have been with her for many years; I even went to the abbey with her. I have been like a mother to her. This I cannot approve of, and so I told her." Jeanne's lined face was worried. "She did it from youthful curiosity, wanting to know more about you, madam, and I fear she has invented foolish explanations for the things she found. My young mistress is passionate for her faith. She wished to be a nun, or if not a nun," said Jeanne, with a glint of humor, "then a martyr. I tell her I would rather she was a married woman—and a lady."

Jeanne, in fact, did what she could to smooth our quarrel

over. But it went too deep for that. I would do my duty by Helene, but I would be glad when it was finished.

Anthony Jenkinson talked to me a good deal on that journey and was pleasanter company than most of the others, although somewhat inquisitive. He had gathered from Luke Blanchard some of the details about my marriage to Matthew and understood that a trap had been set for him, but a few things still puzzled him.

"Master Blanchard says De la Roche is wanted in England for treachery. But you were with him that night as his wife, were you not? Yet here you are now, riding off without your husband, and still using the name of Mistress Blanchard."

As ever, I kept silent about my work for Cecil, but I explained that as a young widow, I had married Matthew "in some haste" in England, and then parted from him when I found that he was involved in a plot to replace our queen with Mary Stuart. "But I still have feelings for him," I said.

I also explained my relationship with Master Blanchard and how I had come to France to help him with Helene and present our queen's compliments to Queen Catherine. "But I couldn't resist Matthew's approach when his letter reached me at Douceaix. I wish now that I had."

His response was much like that of Henri and Marguerite.

"You have a difficult life, Mistress Blanchard," Jenkinson said. "I can only pray that the future holds more happiness than the past. I won't try to advise you. You know your own business best." I was glad of both his sympathy and his detachment. He had struck me at first as a more than slightly crazy adventurer, but there was something solid beneath all that blithe courting of danger.

We were rid of Searle before we got to Paris, although the circumstances were horrible. Our own private squabbles would have been quite enough to cope with, but we had those of France, as well. Ryder had been right to worry about them.

We soon came across more signs of trouble: refugees from a village where Catholics had been attacked, and then the village itself, burned out, with bodies lying in the street, and three times we were stopped at roadblocks.

The first two were manned by officers of the government's Catholic army. The officers were impressed by my letter of introduction from Queen Elizabeth and let us pass. But it was a different story at the third block, which was unofficial, made of a couple of tree trunks thrown down across a woodland track, and manned by six unshaven and extremely aggressive Huguenot mercenaries.

Although most of us were English and, therefore, should have been regarded as friends, we came near to being hanged then and there as "spies," although it wasn't at all clear what we were supposed to be spying on. But although the six were armed and murderous, we outnumbered them by almost two to one and when the situation began to look dangerous, our escort drew their swords and attacked.

It was fortunate that all the women were riding their own mounts, and, therefore, not encumbering any of the men. We hung back out of the way as the fight raged till Ryder suddenly emerged from the melee, caught my eye, jerked his head toward the trees and mouthed: "Now!" I saw what he meant and swiftly herded Helene, Dale, and Jeanne into the woods, past the block, and back to the track on the other side.

Presently, breathless and bloodstained, the men rejoined us. Three of the enemy were dead and the others had run for it. But we had had two casualties of our own. One was Jenkinson's man Deacon, the one Jenkinson had said could fight like a leopard. His feline agility had not saved him this time.

The other was Searle. Deacon had been killed outright. Searle was still alive, and we tried to help him, but he had been run through, and he died while Jenkinson and Ryder were trying to examine the extent of his wound.

We did not want to linger there, but we took a few moments to lay the enemy bodies out with some semblance of decency. No doubt they would have been relieved at their post before long; their own comrades would see to them. We all helped. Helene was coolheaded about it. Jeanne said to her that this was not work for a young girl, but Helene merely replied that they were only Lutherans, after all. I turned away before I said something unfitting in the presence of the dead. Our own two casualties we placed across their horses and led them on, intending to get well away and then find a secluded place where we could bury them.

Two miles farther along the road we came on another burned-out hamlet, but one in which there were a few survivors who had got away and hidden in the woods during the attack. One was the village priest. His church had been fired along with the houses—"but consecrated ground is still consecrated," he said, when we asked him if we could use his churchyard.

He was not young, but for all his gray hairs and the white cataract over one eye, he was tough. We had found him organizing the other survivors into putting roofs back onto a couple of houses to provide shelter. We said we had been the victims of Huguenots and Helene was wearing a silver crucifix that was visible when her cloak swung open. I suppose he took it for granted that all of us were Catholic. At least, he didn't ask, and we didn't enlarge. The men of our party dug a single big grave in the churchyard and there Deacon and Searle were laid together.

The priest recited a burial service for them. I found it moving. I hardly knew Deacon and I hadn't liked Searle, but they were human beings, with lives and no doubt with loves. I cried for them, and when I saw that Blanchard, too, was weeping, I felt more kindly toward my father-in-law. He had his human side, it seemed. There were tears in the eyes even of hefty Stephen Longman. Longman, who could kill a man by hugging him, was actually an amiable soul and his heavy-boned face was attractive in its way. I had gathered that he and Deacon had been friends as well as comrades.

No, a hateful journey altogether though Blanchard and I were on better terms by the end of it. But the innkeepers were suspicious of foreigners and we were often inadequately fed and tired from restless nights on thin pallets. The only good thing was that we saw no sign of Jenkinson's pursuers. I was more thankful than I can say when we arrived in Paris at last.

If anyone had asked me, I would have said the court of Queen Elizabeth was a place of formality and protocol, and that Elizabeth was the most regal of queens.

Compared to Catherine de Médicis, queen mother of France and regent, until the young King Charles, who was still only a boy of eleven, should reach years of discretion, Elizabeth was as easy to approach as a stallholder on market day.

We began by going straight to the English ambassador, Nicholas Throckmorton. He was thin of face, with sharp blue eyes and a fair, pointed little beard, which reminded me somewhat of Cecil's, and a tired air. We found that he knew the proper procedures and was willing to put them into operation for us, but he thought there might be some delay.

"I am a Huguenot sympathizer," he said frankly. "I do my best but I am not popular with Queen Catherine."

With such a person as the ambassador, I had been frank about the real nature of my message. This, too, made him doubtful. "I'm not sure how welcome an offer of mediation from Elizabeth will be. Still, you have your orders. Though you are a Lady of the Presence Chamber, you say? An unusual choice for a royal messenger, surely?"

A Lady of the Presence Chamber is nothing much in the court hierarchy, and isn't usually chosen even to transmit conventional messages. I explained, however, that Elizabeth particularly wanted an unobtrusive messenger, and he accepted this with a nod of understanding.

"Queen Elizabeth knows the value of making contact with other rulers. She never misses an opportunity," he said in tones halfway between respect and indulgence. "You were coming to France, and represented such an opportunity, no doubt."

He found us lodgings in an official residence, sent word through the official channels that he wished to present us to Her Majesty Queen Catherine, and told us next day that we had been lucky. The queen was at the palace of St. Germain, to the west of Paris, and we could be received in two days' time. However, there were things that we must know . . .

He then explained the details of the ceremony surrounding presentations such as ours. They were incredible. We were rehearsed beforehand as though learning the steps of an intricate dance. We would be greeted by such and such officials. We must speak here, be silent there, curtsy or bow to such an extent in one place, to another extent in another, and not at all somewhere else; do this, avoid that . . .

I remembered my first presentation to Elizabeth, and how I was overwhelmed by what now seemed like very simple instructions. I wondered what would happen at the French court if one made a mistake. Would the culprit be instantly conducted to the royal menagerie and thrown to the lions?

Jenkinson was still calling himself Van Weede and keeping out of the light so those who were to be presented numbered only three: myself, Helene, and Luke Blanchard. Accompanied by Throckmorton, and escorted by the ambassador's retainers, we set off on the appointed day, traveling by hired boat down the Seine, all of us dressed in our best. My overgown had the usual hidden pocket but all I had in it was my purse. Lock picks and dagger I had of course left in my discarded traveling gown. I was going into the presence of royalty. Queen Elizabeth's letters I now carried openly, in a little embroidered pochette.

The Seine is a winding river. It meanders so much on its westward journey from Paris to the sea that there are places where it flows directly north. St. Germain stands beside it at such a point, on a plateau on the western bank, with a little town below. To the north lies a deep forest, which occupies all of a great loop of the river.

The residence was beautiful, and interesting, too: a modernized fortress. The lower story of St. Germain, with its thick walls and small windows and the tough-looking towers at the corners, had obviously been built to withstand a medieval siege. But between the towers, from the first floor upward, was a modern palace with airy windows and handsome balconies, obviously built for times of peace and gracious living. The effect, combined with the sheer size of the place, was one of immense power and great sophistication. Used though I was to Elizabeth's palaces, this made me nervous. My father-in-law clearly felt the same. "What a place," he said uneasily.

The procedure went smoothly, however, though it was tedious. We were admitted, handed over to an usher, guided across a courtyard and in at another door, and then received by a new official. After that, we went through a series of marvelously decorated galleries and anterooms, changing escorts several times on the way and often having to wait for the new escort to appear. Throckmorton reminded us when to do this or say that in accordance with protocol. After an hour or so, we arrived at Queen Catherine.

She was seated regally at the far end of a long room adorned with the most remarkable tapestries I had ever seen. Their themes were mostly biblical, but they pulsed with color and some of the figures were extremely voluptuous. The room was lit by windows but also by lamps and candles and there were dozens of gilded lamp stands and wall sconces in convoluted, sensual designs. Smooth golden curves pleaded with you to brush a palm over them, fluted patterns begged to be explored with the fingertips, and everything glittered as though freshly burnished.

The room was full of people, including about forty court ladies, most elaborately dressed. The restrained good taste of Douceaix and Marguerite Blanchard was not the fashion here. I had brought a special gown for the occasion, all blue damask and silver embroidery, with a moderate farthingale and a silver-edged ruff. I had thought it fine enough and tasteful enough to turn heads anywhere. Amid the spreading farthingales and swishing trains of the Paris ladies, and their bouffant sleeves and the shoulder puffs that rose up to their ears, I felt like a maidservant. Even Helene fitted in better than I did, since she was young. For her, the maidenly white and silver chosen by Marguerite had an appropriate air.

Well, it was too late now to do anything about it. With Throckmorton, we walked along a carpeted aisle through the midst of the crowd, to make our obeisance at the foot of Catherine's dais, and then to rise and kiss the fleshy hand that she held out to each of us in turn.

It was oddly reminiscent of my first introduction to Elizabeth and yet very different. Catherine de Médicis was utterly unlike her English counterpart, and not only because she was in her forties and was married with children, whereas Elizabeth was in her twenties and still unwed. They were women of completely different types. There was something faerie about Elizabeth but there was nothing at all magical about Catherine de Médicis.

Elizabeth needed full formal skirts in order to fill a throne up; Catherine's skirts were bunched at the sides because Catherine herself occupied almost every inch of the wide seat. Elizabeth was pale, her features fine. Catherine was swarthy, her greasy skin dotted with huge pores, her nose and lips thick, and her eyes bulgy.

She wore purple, much adorned with gold embroidery, and here, too, there was a curious contrast with Elizabeth. For formal audiences, Elizabeth had a very ornamental wardrobe, but with her, they resembled the defenses of a citadel, and that was as it should be, for those who knew Elizabeth also knew how aware she was of her youth and delicacy, how conscious of being vulnerable.

Catherine's splendor, on the other hand, was aggressive. It said: *I am the ruler of France. Beware.*

I did beware. Catherine de Médicis had a reputation for being both subtle and unsentimental. She was known in some quarters as the serpent queen. I was here as Elizabeth's representative, and as I looked into Catherine's prominent eyes, I felt inadequate.

I also felt a little unwell, although the reason was actually a relief. I had woken that morning to find that this last encounter with Matthew had left no aftermath. There would be no child, or miscarriage, this time. But now I was out of sorts and there was a dragging pain in my stomach.

We had been announced, but Nicholas Throckmorton was now enlarging on the introductions. He was being obsequious. I saw that it was true that Catherine de Médicis didn't greatly care for our Protestant ambassador. Helene was curtsying again and Catherine, glancing pointedly away from Throckmorton and looking at Helene's silver crucifix, was saying what a pleasure it was to welcome such a lovely and obviously pious young girl to her court. The courtiers ranged on either side of her throne murmured in agreement. None of them knew Helene, I thought sourly. I wondered whose taste was reflected in the voluptuous tapestries and the opulent gold wall sconces and would have wagered that it wasn't Catherine's. They probably represented the influence of her husband's famous mistress, Diane de Poitiers.

I was wearing, deliberately, Elizabeth's ring. When it was my turn to take the royal fingertips in mine and touch my lips to them, I made sure that Catherine had a chance to see it.

"That is a fine ring, Madame," she said. I could not tell whether she knew its significance or not. Between physical discomfort and intense nervousness, I must have looked ill at ease, for suddenly she smiled at me. "No need to be afraid. All guests are safe in our court, and we honor all messages from our dear sister of England." Her eyes met mine steadily, and I saw suddenly she was telling me without words that she had recognized the ring. "You are bringing a message to us, are you not?" she said.

Her voice, speaking French with a strong Italian accent, was a melodious contralto, and although her teeth were in a sorry condition, her smile had unbelievable charm. I smiled back, and would have opened my pochette, except that a young courtier was instantly beside me, holding out his hand for it. "If that is a letter, you must give it first to me. I will give it to

Queen Catherine when I am sure it is harmless. That is the rule."

The voice was vaguely familiar. I looked up and found myself gazing into the odd-colored eyes and the sharp, cold face of Seigneur Gaston de Clairpont, whom I had last seen at Le Cheval d'Or in St. Marc.

He made no reference to our previous meeting, however. Instead, he added coolly: "I am responsible for the safety of Her Majesty's person. I must examine anything you wish to present to her."

I drew my two letters out, and selected the privy message from Elizabeth. "Here it is. But my instructions were to present it personally," I said.

I could feel Nicholas Throckmorton bristling with indignation at what, after all, was an implied insult to Queen Elizabeth. But he held his tongue and Catherine remarked that De Clairpont was doing his duty most admirably, but that Madame Blanchard did not seem to be afraid to touch the letter with ungloved hands.

"That being so, we are sure that we can do the same. We do not suspect our sister of England of wishing us ill; in any case there is no need to quarantine the letter until you are sure it has not poisoned you." De Clairpont bowed gracefully and Catherine once more gave me that astonishing smile. "We will receive the letter," Catherine said. "He will hand it straight to us, madam. You may give it to him."

De Clairpont, bowing again, and positioning his feet as precisely as a dancer, took the letter from me. I handed it over willingly enough, glad to be rid of the responsibility.

Catherine broke the seal at once, remarking that she could recognize her royal sister Elizabeth's elegant hand. She read, frowning. "Strange. Normal diplomatic channels would have sufficed, I would have thought. But no matter. We will peruse this at length, later."

It seemed a careless answer to something that Elizabeth had thought so important. But perhaps Catherine did not wish to reveal its importance in public. I studied that ugly, intelligent, curiously vital face and realized just how well earned was that serpentine reputation. She had used subtlety when conveying to me that she knew the significance of my ring; now she might well be employing it again.

Power and subtlety: an intimidating combination. But then, it must take guile to wield power in this disturbed land and keep the court so orderly.

"I am also," I said nervously, "to present the compliments of Queen Elizabeth and her hopes that you are in good health, and that France may soon know peace once more."

Yet again, she smiled. "We thank our royal sister for her good wishes. Her hopes reflect our own. You are welcome to Paris, Madame Blanchard. And so are you, Seigneur Blanchard, and you, Demoiselle Helene. While you are here, we must show you that despite the troubled times, life here still goes on and there are happy events to celebrate.

"The day after tomorrow, one of our ladies is to be married in the chapel here and a banquet will be held for her. You shall attend. You shall send for your belongings and servants, and lodgings will be found for you at St. Germain. Then, we trust, you will have joyful memories to take away with you and a good report of France to carry back to your home."

It was an order, not an invitation. And the audience was at an end.

We were guided back through the galleries and anterooms and shown to a chamber where refreshments were offered to us.

A number of court dignitaries accompanied us, and we found ourselves engaged in polite conversation. Throckmorton busied himself with pointing out the tastiest delicacies to Helene and answering her questions about the court. Helene seemed to be impressed with it. She had also been impressed with the Seigneur de Clairpont.

"Who was the young man who passed the letter to the queen mother? He was very handsome."

Good God, I thought. The girl is human after all. I didn't think highly of her taste, but although De Clairpont was too cold-featured to be what I would call handsome, he was certainly elegant. I wondered if Cousin Edward had turned out to be elegant but doubted it. He had my uncle's lumbering build. Helene might well be in for a disappointment.

Throckmorton obviously knew a good deal about De Clairpont, and his position at court. He began to explain it to Helene. My stomachache had faded away now but I still felt tired. I moved away to sit in a window embrasure and found my father-in-law beside me.

"I have just heard Helene asking about De Clairpont," he said. "She should not be taking any interest in any young man other than her betrothed. All the same . . ."

During the journey to Paris, I had regained the trick of normal conversation with Blanchard. "She'll soon forget De Clairpont when she's home in England and preparing for her own wedding," I said. "At least we know now that she notices young men."

"You may be right," Blanchard said. "I admit I had begun to fear that all she ever thought about was religion."

"I know. Perhaps the wedding we are to attend will help to turn her mind toward her marriage."

"Perhaps, though I wish we could set out for England tomorrow," said Blanchard restlessly. "I am not interested in delaying to attend a stranger's marriage party. Well, we can make our plans, anyway. I think if we can get a ship down the Seine, we should do so, and forget about the *Chaffinch*. Ryder advises it and says he has already told the Dodds to make for Nantes independently as soon as they can."

"I'm sure that would be wise," I agreed.

"The weather's good," said my father-in-law. He sighed, and gave me a wry look. "My visit to France hasn't been all I hoped. I didn't bargain for so much disturbance. Well, well. With luck, we'll be home within a week."

CHAPTER **12**

The Marriage Party

Throckmorton sent word back to Paris to summon the rest of our party. Jenkinson and Longman came, too. My father-in-law, observing several ships anchored at St. Germain, had quickly made inquiries and found one which was shortly sailing for England and could give us passages. We agreed to tell Jenkinson that he was welcome to travel with us and should join us at St. Germain with the others.

He arrived looking pleased. "Another move will help to cover my trail," he said. "I must not let myself become complacent, just because of my success at St. Marc. Poor Silvius Portinari," he added thoughtfully. Head on one side, dark eyes gleaming, Jenkinson really did look just like a cock robin who had just swallowed a juicy worm. "What a situation for him! Either to wait for reinforcements, without being sure they would come, which would give me a chance to slide out of sight and cover my tracks; or else be prepared to get his own hands dirty—or bloodstained. How hard it must have been for him to decide what to do!"

He sounded almost sympathetic, as though for a suitable consideration he might have tried to help his frustrated fellow-creature to overcome his troubles.

"Well, he tried taking part himself," Jenkinson said, "and lost his life for it. But the reinforcements remain a possibility.

That fellow in Marseilles seemed sure that they were coming. I hope to keep ahead of them but I had better remain vigilant." His expression now became rueful. "I've been thinking it over," he said, "and I fear that I have indeed been guilty of complacency. If Portinari hoped that reinforcements would follow him, he presumably did what he could to make that possible. Very likely, he left a trail of messages behind him to help any further pursuers keep on the scent. If he found me, then they can. They may also augment their numbers with local help. They probably have contacts in major cities, and may be able to lay their hands on local assassins, though that isn't always so easy. One can't just go out and hire a killer as though he were a saddle horse."

John Ryder, who was with us, let out a snort of laughter and my father-in-law agreed in a staggered voice that yes, the two things were a little different.

Jenkinson, however, was shaking his head quite gravely. "I disapprove of carelessness, including my own," he said, "and I may have made some errors. If I am traced to St. Marc, my pursuers will soon learn what befell Portinari and his companion, and Portinari's message trail—I'll be surprised if there isn't one—may have told them that I'm using the name of Van Weede. If they then learn that a man called Van Weede went to the abbey guest house after the fire and left for Douceaix next day, the danger could be close on my heels. Well, Henri Blanchard knows the situation and won't help any inquirers, but servants and villagers can be pumped or bribed to talk. I should have changed my name again. Why didn't I? I curse myself."

"I'm relieved to hear that you're fallible!" said Blanchard, quite sardonically.

"But I can't afford to be fallible," Jenkinson said. "It's too

expensive a luxury. It could cost me my life! I am very glad of
the chance to come to St. Germain and I thank you for it. You
have found a ship, you say? When does she sail?"

"Two days after the wedding," I said. "And the wedding's
tomorrow. It isn't long to wait."

Throckmorton had a rented house in the town below the
castle, and was able to give advice about finding good lodgings. Jenkinson and most of the men took rooms in the town
accordingly. Harvey, though, stayed with Blanchard, sharing
his master's room in the suite we had been lent in one of the
towers at the palace. It was empty because the court official
who had occupied it had gone to join the marshal of France
and the Catholic army, and sent his family out of the country
until peace was restored.

With the suite went the right to eat in a dining hall reserved
for guests or else to send our servants to fetch food from the
kitchens, and it provided us with three good-sized rooms: two
bedchambers, one for my father-in-law and Harvey; one for
the women to share, and in between them, a sitting room with
a writing desk in it as well. Most of the windows overlooked
the river, but the women's chamber also looked north, over
the forest.

I wanted Brockley to remain at hand and he found a bed in
a stable loft among other grooms. When he discovered that
there was a great to-do among the palace servants because the
preparations for the wedding banquet were behindhand, he
offered his help, and later on, he came to me with a highly
entertaining report on the preparations.

"Quite astonishing, madam. The bride is only a lady-in-
waiting. I can't think what they'd do for a princess. There are
satin ribbons and silk banners all over the place and the cooks
are going mad in the kitchen, because there's to be a giant

pie with live singing birds in it that'll fly out, tweet-tweeting, when the crust is lifted, and the first try at making a crust big enough all fell into a heap of crumbs. There will be garlands of spring flowers, too; the maidservants will be out at dawn on the great day to fetch them in."

"It all sounds very pretty and charming," said Dale, going misty-eyed. "Jeanne and I must peep in if we can."

"If you do, there's something I'd best warn you about," said Brockley in a prim voice. "Up on the top table where the bride and groom will sit, there's a clockwork toy."

From his tone, he might have been saying giant slug or pile of manure. I raised my eyebrows at him.

"It's clever in its fashion," said Brockley. "It's two bronze horses, a couple of feet high, and when they're wound up, I'm sorry to say that they do what horses have to do if there are ever to be any more horses, but as a table decoration at a wedding party—or anywhere else for that matter—I don't call it respectable."

"I'm glad you told us, Brockley," I said, strangling a desire to laugh. "I'll try not to be too shocked."

"Shocked is what you ought to be, madam. You'd never see a thing like that at Queen Elizabeth's court. I'll be glad to see the back of this place."

"We'll be sailing in two days' time," I said. "Even if the winds turn contrary, we should be home in a week."

Jenkinson wasn't going to the wedding, but he supplied us with a gift for the bride. It was a golden brooch, in the shape of a bird, with a spray of turquoise for a tail, and a ruby eye. "I got it from a Persian jeweler," he said. "I buy such things whenever I get the chance. On long journeys in foreign lands a few small valuables can be as useful as money, or more so.

If my voice isn't sweet enough to talk me past border guards or into houses I want to visit, maybe a little golden bird with a ruby eye and a jeweled tail will do the talking for me, and I don't even have to worry about local coinage."

Brockley was right to be impressed by the splendor of the occasion. The chapel ceremony the following morning was lengthy, dignified, and crammed with guests in such a magnificence of silks and velvets and jewels, ruffs and farthingales, billowing sleeves and flowing mantles, that the congregation seemed to consist more of clothes than of people. The bride and groom were if anything the most simply dressed of all; the groom in red velvet and the bride in blue and cream brocade.

The service was followed by a long parade to the banqueting chamber, and an interminable reception, before at last trumpeters announced the arrival of Queen Catherine, who came in accompanied by the young King Charles, to take her place at her own separate table. When the food was served, I was not surprised that the cooks had, in Brockley's words, been going mad. They had been required to work miracles. And they had succeeded. There were astounding subtleties of spun sugar; a complete model of St. Germain in marchpane; and the promised pie full of singing birds had been made successfully at last. The birds duly flew out, piping and twittering, to perch on lamp stands and banners and the tops of the exquisitely molded and gilded pilasters around the walls of the chamber.

There were a few untoward moments. The clockwork horses that had scandalized Brockley jammed at a point in their performance that drew whoops and whistles from a gathering by this time more than a little flown with the excellent wine, and some of the singing birds, probably frightened, misbehaved.

And although it looked as though the entire court had been

wedged into the banqueting hall, this was not the case. I saw messages brought now and then to guests, including Nicholas Throckmorton, who was seated near the dais. At one point, too, a party of drunken young gentlemen tried to gate-crash, and I saw the Seigneur de Clairpont, who was also among the guests, leave his seat and go to help the guards deal with them. He came back presently but within five minutes had been summoned out a second time. The man in charge of the royal security was never off duty, it seemed.

A second variety of wine came around, and at the top table, someone began to make a speech. We were not at Throckmorton's table, but farther back, so that I couldn't quite make out what was being said, or who was speaking, but thought it was the bride's father. I didn't mind, however. I sipped appreciatively at my wine, thinking that this was the first time I could say I had enjoyed myself since I had set foot in France.

I felt so mellow that I turned to Helene, who was beside me, and asked if she was enjoying herself, too.

"Yes, madam. But naturally," said Helene primly, without smiling. Oh well. Very soon now, we would all be in England and she and I could part company.

"We won't be able to manage quite such an elaborate affair for you on your wedding day, but we'll do our best." Luke Blanchard, on the other side of her, was in a jovial mood, too. "It will be summer, and if it's fine, we can have lanterns outside. We could time it for full moon and hope for clear skies. How does that strike you?"

Helene said something in reply, but I didn't hear what it was because at that moment, there was a commotion at the door, and suddenly, I saw Brockley there, arguing with the guards. I came to my feet and he saw me. I signaled to the guards to let him through. They did so, and he came striding, and then running, between the tables to reach me. I went to meet him.

"Brockley?"

His face was shockingly white, and his eyes held a blank look that horrified me because I had never seen him like that before.

"Madam—Mistress Blanchard—come quickly!"

"What is it? Brockley, what's happened?"

He seemed unable to speak further. He caught my elbow and almost dragged me toward the door. Heads turned and people stared. There was a little laughter and a hum of gossip. Behind me, I was aware that Helene and my father-in-law had got to their feet and were following us out. I kept on saying: "Brockley, what is it?" but until he had hustled me past the guards at the door and out into the wide antechamber beyond, he made no answer. Then he said frantically: "Madam, it's Fran! Oh, God, something terrible has happened to Fran!"

"What do you mean?" Blanchard had caught up by now, with Helene close behind him.

"Men came to search your rooms," Brockley said, still hurrying us along through the linking chambers, the corridors and staircases that led to our suite. "Fran was there, and Jeanne. Fran tried to say they should fetch you, that you should be there, too, but it was no use. They wouldn't let her go, to tell either you or me. But they did let Jeanne go, and she came straight to me. But by the time I got there . . . oh, I couldn't believe it!"

He was almost crying. "Yes, Brockley?" I said. "And by the time you got there?"

"They'd searched all your things. They'd found that phial— with the yew-leaf brew in it—in Fran's saddlebag. I arrived to find them in the very act of arresting her on suspicion of trying to procure the death of the queen mother or the young king or both. And it was me that thought of bringing the venom. Oh, my God, madam, they've taken Fran away!"

"Yew-leaf brew? What is all this?" Blanchard demanded. As we raced up the last staircase toward our rooms, I gave him a rapid explanation. "Helene has seen the phial, too," I said.

We reached our door. We had returned there, I think, instinctively, wanting privacy; somewhere to talk and decide what to do. But the door, which should have been locked, was open, and there was no question of privacy. The room was quite full. Jeanne was there, trembling on a settle. Two helmeted guards were also there, standing side by side behind the writing table, and seated at the table, looking at us across the room, was the Seigneur Gaston de Clairpont.

We all burst into speech at once but De Clairpont raised a hand for silence and we stopped, intimidated by his cold stillness and the presence of his guards. Only Brockley said: "My wife . . . my wife . . . !" But even his voice tailed away.

"I will speak English," De Clairpont said, "so that you may all understand. I gather that even the serving woman Jeanne can follow it." I had not somehow thought he would have English, he was so much a Frenchman, but he turned out to be fluent. "I waited," he said, "because the suspected person is in your employ, Madame Blanchard, and you may be able to answer some questions about her. You may all be seated."

"This entire charge is nonsense!" I found my voice again. "I have heard what it is. Something about a suspected attempt on someone in the royal family. Why should anyone suppose such a thing?"

"Why," said De Clairpont, "should anyone enter a royal residence carrying poison in their baggage? A somewhat perilous thing to do, I would have said, above all in these disrupted times when anyone in a position of power could be a target. But do, please, be seated. I have sent for wine."

"Sent for wine?" My father-in-law was ashen, as though he feared that the arrest of one of our party presaged the arrest of us all. The same thought had occurred to me. But he was trying to put a bold face on it, and for that I admired him. "Is this a social call, sir?" Luke Blanchard demanded.

"No. But one should be civilized, should one not? Ah. Here it is."

And there it was, indeed. A page boy had arrived with a tray laden with goblets and a flagon. In bemused silence, disposing ourselves on various stools and settles, we let him bring it in and serve it. When the boy had gone, I said: "The reason why my servant had poison in her baggage was in case of any danger to herself—or to her husband or to me. She was frightened of coming to France. She is a most pious Protestant and there has been persecution of such people here quite recently."

"And it was my idea, not hers!" Brockley burst out. "I was afraid for her, and for us all, if you want to know."

"Really?" De Clairpont's voice was coolly questioning. "But the persecution, as you call it, has been ended, by royal decree."

"How can one tell what will happen in a land at war? I tell you, it was my idea!" Brockley said furiously. "Arrest me and let Fran go. It was my idea, I tell you!"

"Your chivalry does you credit, Master Brockley, but you are not under suspicion. A certain amount is known about you. You are of good repute, you will be glad to hear."

"What I can't understand," I said quickly, "is why we are not all under arrest." It needed to be said. It was frightening me and Blanchard alike and it was better aired than hidden.

"You, madame, are an emissary of Her Majesty Queen Elizabeth. Such rulers as your Queen Elizabeth and our Queen Mother Catherine do not poison each other. Also they are careful in the messengers they choose. You and the Seigneur Blanchard are not under suspicion either."

It is a wicked world, full of deceit, and even queens can be misled about the nature of their employees. Our immunity from suspicion struck me as being based on thin evidence and Brockley's apparent immunity on no evidence at all. Furthermore, the sophisticated De Clairpont must know that perfectly well. Once again, I had the sensation of being surrounded by mystery, of standing on ground that might disintegrate beneath my feet at any moment and plunge me into a pit. Or a dungeon. I suddenly saw that it was dangerous to delve into this particular mystery because if De Clairpont were encouraged to think about it too much, he might yet change his mind and clap us all into prison. I kept silent. So, wisely, did my father-in-law.

De Clairpont smiled. "We have, however, no information about Mistress Brockley, or Dale as she is sometimes called, beyond the fact that she is ardent in her faith. She could perhaps have been persuaded to cooperate. Or bribed or threatened, even. She could have been approached by an enemy of our royal house either in England or after arriving in France."

"My wife is a decent, simple woman!" Brockley shouted. "I keep on telling you! It was I who—!"

"Again I say your sentiments do you honor."

Brockley swore.

"Oh, this is all absurd!" Blanchard ran frantic fingers through his gray hair. "How could a mere tiring woman such as Dale possibly put poison in the food or drink of a member of the royal house? How could she get near such things?"

"Believe me," said De Clairpont, "the simple serving man

or woman is often best placed of all for such a task. Such people can go into the kitchen on errands for their employers,
may even lend a hand here and there at busy times. I believe
that Brockley here helped to prepare the banqueting chamber today. Such a person might perhaps find out which dishes
are being prepared for the royal table. May seize a chance to
doctor something. The royal family have tasters, of course,
but poison does not always show itself at once. A taster is not
complete protection."

"This is fantasy!" I said in despair.

"Of course it is. Complete nonsense!" My father-in-law
backed me up valiantly.

"Perhaps, Madame Blanchard," said De Clairpont, unper-
turbed, "you would answer some questions."

He questioned me for half an hour. He spoke only to me;
the others were ordered to be silent. Helene and Jeanne sat
together, round-eyed, listening. Blanchard quietly seethed. In
the midst of it all, William Harvey, who had been off duty, came
back, beheld the scene with amazement, was briefly explained
to, and also sat down to listen in bemusement. Brockley, who
had sunk onto the window seat in misery and dejection, tried
several times to break in, but in vain. "The husband's testi-
mony cannot be taken into account."

"But it was my idea; I keep on telling you—"

"Hold your tongue, man. You may know less than you
think. We are aware that you and the woman Frances Dale
have not been man and wife for very long. Now then, Madame
Blanchard . . ."

On and on. How much did I know about Dale? How long
had she been in my employ? Who were her friends? What, at
home, was our pattern of worship?

I did my best, but it was difficult. De Clairpont had a disagreeable knack of assuming that whatever I didn't know about Dale must of necessity be dubious.

So I didn't know very much about her family? I knew little about her acquaintances? I need not give my opinion on whether or not she was rabidly anti-Catholic, for she had expressed such views openly in Le Cheval d'Or. Silently, I cursed Dale's outspokenness. I had tried to warn her, but she hadn't heeded me. De Clairpont was still persisting. Could she, either in England or since reaching France, have met anyone who was a secret representative of the Huguenots? Could I swear on the rood that she had not? Oh, I thought it was most unlikely? But could I swear . . . ? No, he thought not. Perhaps I could tell him . . . ?

I did my best, fighting for Dale as best I could, with words, and knew I was losing.

At the end, I said: "I want to see Dale. Where is she?"

"That I cannot allow, madame."

"And her husband? Can Brockley see her?"

"Not until she has been questioned, madame."

I shuddered. Dale was under arrest. It would not be the kind of questioning I had just gone through.

"Seigneur," said Blanchard suddenly, "do you regard yourself as a man of honor?"

"Naturally." De Clairpont looked mildly surprised.

"And do you, as a man of honor, consider that you have a responsibility toward those whom you employ?"

De Clairpont's odd-colored eyes narrowed. "I do."

"In that case," said my father-in-law, "it is natural that Madame Blanchard should wish to see her servant and offer what comfort she can. I cannot see that your case would be harmed by it and it would be an honorable way for Madame Blanchard to behave toward her tirewoman."

"And for a husband to behave toward his wife," I said. "Seigneur, please!"

"The Catholic cause in Paris," said De Clairpont, "is troubled at the moment by the need to arm and feed the soldiers we are mustering. I might," he said, with a frankness that I think was meant to be disarming but was actually chilling, "look favorably on a reasonable request from anyone who offered a contribution . . ."

I fetched money from my room and counted out as much as I dared spare. Blanchard hemmed and hawed and then sent Harvey for his own locked money chest. Two lots of gold coins changed hands. Fifteen minutes later, we were in the bowels of the castle, in the dungeons. Where Dale was.

I had seen dungeons before, but this was worse. The cell to which we were escorted by De Clairpont, the two guards, and a turnkey, was behind a door in a fetid passage lit only by a tiny grating and, just now, by the jailer's streaming torch. We weren't allowed into the cell but could see Dale only through a little barred opening in the door. She clung to the bars and thrust her hands toward us and both she and Brockley wept because the guards wouldn't let them touch each other. She told us, sobbing, that the cell was tiny and that she had no bed, only some straw and a dirty rug, and that the walls were damp. "I'll die if I'm left in here! Oh, Roger! Ma'am! I'm so frightened!"

"We'll get you out!" I promised. "We will get you out. It's all right, Dale. It will be all right."

"They say I wanted to poison someone! And they say that even if they can't prove it, they can still try me for . . . for . . . you know . . ."

"Heresy," said De Clairpont.

Dale screamed aloud and shook the bars in desperation. "We'll pray for you!" my father-in-law promised. "We're all on your side. I feel as though I'm surrounded by madness," he added to me. "This can't be real."

Helene said eagerly, in English: "But, Dale, if you were to embrace the true faith, I'm sure . . ."

"Yes, do that! Say anything, Fran, anything to save yourself!" Brockley begged her.

"I've said I'd do that, but they'll kill me just the same, I know they will!" Dale wailed.

And how would they kill her? I dared not imagine that.

I turned on De Clairpont. "Why are you doing this? You can't believe there's any truth in this absurd accusation!"

"We shall arrive at the truth, I trust."

"Do you mean what I think you mean? If so, then you are going to force poor Dale to say whatever you want her to say. But that won't be the truth!"

De Clairpont shrugged. I felt that if I put my hand on his bare skin, it would be like touching ice. "I am a loyal servant of Her Majesty Catherine, the queen mother, and of the Catholic cause that we both serve. I will root out their enemies wherever I find them. It may be that the innocent sometimes suffer with the guilty. But then, innocent Catholics have been murdered by the Huguenots, have they not? That is what happens in war."

He spoke French this time and Dale, her face pressed to the bars, could hear him but not understand him. I saw her terrified eyes, asking me what we were saying, begging me to tell her that I had made him see it was all a mistake.

But I couldn't. We had to go away and leave her there. I felt as one feels at funerals, when the moment comes to turn one's back and leave a loved one alone in the cold earth. As we went, we heard her weeping slowly fade behind us.

But I had one more weapon in my hands, or rather, on my hand. De Clairpont left us at the door to our suite, saying that we must hold ourselves in readiness to answer more questions. He then took himself off. To the others, I said: "I must see Sir Nicholas at once. I'm going back to the banqueting hall."

Blanchard and Brockley came with me. Our timing was good. The banquet had just finished, and people were leaving. I saw Throckmorton crossing the anteroom with a group of gentlemen, and led the way quickly toward him.

"Sir Nicholas!"

He stopped, courteously. "Mistress Blanchard? I saw you being fetched out of the banquet. What has happened?"

"Can we speak apart?" said Blanchard.

"By all means." He excused himself to his companions and drew me to the side of the room, out of the stream of people. "What is it?"

We told him between us, and then I held out my hand with the ring on it. "Do you recognize this?"

"What's this about?" Blanchard demanded, taken by surprise.

"It's all right, Master Blanchard. This is a little device that Queen Elizabeth sometimes provides to help those in her service." Throckmorton's eyes met mine gravely. "You wish to use it to speak to Queen Catherine?"

"Yes. I have had one audience and perhaps might have to wait for another. But this is urgent. I think," I added, "that Queen Catherine recognized the ring when I was presented to her."

"I understand. Return to your suite and wait. I will do my best."

CHAPTER 13

Golden Conversation

The wait was dreadful. Brockley was in despair. I had never seen him like this. Ever since I had known him, he had been a rock of dependability but now, he was the one who must depend on others for strength. He alternated between pacing about, muttering, and striking the furniture with his fist, and sitting down to stare into space as though at a nightmare visible only to himself. William Harvey had sensibly sent for food and drink, but Brockley would touch nothing.

For my part, I used some of that weary wait to ask Helene a few questions. She, after all, had searched our baggage at St. Marc.

"You found that phial in Dale's saddlebag, Helene. Since we've been here, you've shown an interest in De Clairpont. Have you met him without any of us knowing?"

"I hope not!" My father-in-law broke off in the middle of trying to persuade Brockley to eat. "Clandestine meetings with a man, Helene? If you have dared to do such a thing . . ."

Old grudges die hard. He couldn't forbear giving me a sharp look as he said it. I had met his son behind his back, and those of my own guardians, which was why I now called him father-in-law.

"No, I didn't!" said Helene resentfully.

"Please!" I said. "I just want to know what induced De

Clairpont to order that search. It might not have been an assignation, Master Blanchard—it could have been a chance encounter. But, Helene, we need to know. Did you—even by chance—talk to De Clairpont and if so, did you mention that phial?"

"No!" She was, as usual, wearing her silver crucifix. She held it up. "I swear on the cross. I have never had private speech with the Seigneur de Clairpont or any of his men either, and I did not tell him about the phial of poison."

I believed her, because I did not think she would lie when swearing on the cross, and anyway, since we came to St. Germain, she had hardly been out of my sight. Others besides Helene might have seen that phial when our luggage was searched at Le Cheval d'Or. After hemming and hawing in my mind, I had decided that Cecil's men were responsible for that, hoping to find a letter from Matthew. But what if I were wrong, if that rummaging were part of some plot which I didn't understand, quite unconnected with Cecil's trap for Matthew? *Something* was going on below the surface of things. I was somehow enmeshed, but I couldn't see the web that held me.

I stood by the window, staring out as dusk fell. The banquet hadn't been the end of the wedding festivities, of course. The guests would have gone to another room for dancing and by this time, they were probably getting raucous. In which case, Queen Catherine would surely withdraw. By now, Throckmorton might have been able to send word to her.

Harvey said: "Someone's at the door. This'll be your summons, maybe."

It was.

Throckmorton was there to escort me. Elizabeth's ring, it transpired, had near-magical properties. Someone of my standing would normally get no nearer to Queen Catherine than a public audience chamber and that only after a delay. The ring brought me to her private apartment that same day.

Though not for a tête-à-tête. In a handsome room with a vaulted ceiling and wall tapestries depicting more biblical scenes, Catherine de Médicis was seated amid a crowd of ladies and courtiers, eating sweetmeats as though she didn't know what a banquet was and feared no one would give her any supper.

She was also watching a play enacted by dwarfs. She signed to me to stand and wait until the scene in progress should finish. It was not easy to follow because the French was very rapid and there was a great deal of shouting and exclaiming in absurd voices that I realized were meant to be funny. A male dwarf with a humpback, but a very broad chest, swaggered and bellowed and knocked several other dwarfs flat. Another dwarf, slightly taller than the rest and dignified in mien, was marched before the humpbacked one, and apparently tried for the crime of being a Catholic. This seemed to be a peculiar drama for the head of the Catholic faction to be watching but Catherine appeared to be enjoying it. The swaggering hunchback knocked the prisoner down, too, and shrieked that he must hang for the crime of patriotism and supporting his lawful rulers. The prisoner was taken away and the hunchback, exclaiming at the top of a falsetto voice that he was the savior of his people and inspired by God, was then overcome by his own wondrousness, rolled his eyes heavenward, and collapsed backward into the arms of some diminutive henchmen.

They laid him tenderly on a settle, calling him mighty prince. The surrounding ladies and courtiers burst into cheers and clapping and it dawned on me that Catherine's dwarfs were making fun of the prince of Condé, the leader of the

Huguenot faction, who was reputed to be both hunchbacked and aggressive. It was likely, I thought, that Elizabeth's offer of mediation was quite pointless.

As if she had heard me thinking, Catherine beckoned me to her and under cover of the applause, she said: "If a land is divided, one may compromise to restore peace. We have done so already. But we may still have our own private opinions of those who would destroy us and our beliefs, and in private, may express them. That is our privilege. You are making use of a privilege, too. At this moment, you are yourself claiming one; that of speaking with us as a matter of urgency, Madame Blanchard. Well, you may speak."

Throckmorton had brought me to her side and then stepped back, but he had told me what to do. Kneeling before her, I put my case as succinctly as I could.

"My tirewoman, Frances Brockley, also known by her maiden name of Frances Dale, has been arrested on a false charge. For some reason, our baggage was examined while I was at the banquet today. A phial of poison was found among Dale's belongings. She was carrying it because she was afraid of coming to France, of being accused of heresy. Such things have happened here recently, after all."

"Until we softened our principles in the hope of placating the enemy and called the hounds off the heretics," Catherine remarked. "But we did call them off. This is a very strange story. However, you may proceed."

"Dale has been accused of seeking the life of . . . yourself or the young king She did not. It is not true. Your Majesty, I plead for the release of my tirewoman. A tirewoman is all she is. She would never harm anyone. I represent Queen Elizabeth and I would never have brought with me anyone who was not absolutely trustworthy."

Succinct, but not succinct enough. Catherine's attention was wandering. She beckoned the hunchbacked dwarf to her, and presented him with a dish of sweetmeats coated with gold leaf. "You have made us laugh. A fine performance." She snapped thick, swarthy fingers at a hovering attendant and a purse was placed in her hand. She gave it to the dwarf. "For you and all your troupe."

The hunchback retired backward, bowing. I said, as though I had not noticed the interruption: "Your Majesty, can you, will you, help me and help Dale?"

"Music!" said Catherine. "We will have music!" She spoke loudly, and as if conjured by sorcery, a group of musicians emerged from the crowd, carrying instruments, took up positions in front of Catherine, bowed to her, and set to without delay, on the rebec, harp, and drum. But as the throng shifted out of their way, a heavily built cleric, who up to then had been concealed at the back, came into view. Across the room, his eyes met mine. He showed no surprise at seeing me there. He merely bent his head in polite recognition. But on his fleshy face, there was a smile.

A triumphant smile.

And then I understood. This was why only Dale had been arrested—not myself, or Blanchard, or Brockley.

The argument that Dale would have little chance to poison anyone in the royal house was actually quite sound. No one in their senses would choose a visiting tirewoman for such an errand. I wondered how De Clairpont, who was surely intelligent enough to know that, had been persuaded into pretending otherwise. But I knew who had done the persuading. He was there, smiling across the room at me, and he had guessed why I was here and on my knees.

"How dare you threaten my mistress?" Dale had said to him.

And what had he said in answer? You seem to have a devoted servant, Mistress de la Roche. And you seem as protective of her as she is of you. A touching spectacle. But I would advise you both to watch your tongues and take care. I have faith in the mills of God.

That earlier search of my baggage, I thought, must have been somehow or other connected with him. Charpentier had told Matthew that I was in France and asking for him. Had he told anybody else? Told, for instance, another ardent anti-Huguenot who chanced to be at hand? Someone who had later brooded over what he saw as my attempt to betray Matthew yet again, and conceived this as an act of vengeance?

A cruel vengeance, but what else could one expect of that subtle, obsessed, pitiless so-called man of God, Dr. Ignatius Wilkins?

He had chosen not to attack me directly. He had threatened to save my heretic soul for me but he had decided on this oblique onslaught instead. My heart should be broken for the sake of the servant for whom I cared: my poor, innocent, terrified Dale.

I stared fixedly across the room at him, and once again, he smiled back. In the folds of my skirts, I clenched my fists.

But Catherine was speaking to me again. "We understand your concern for your servant." I dragged my eyes away from Wilkins and turned eagerly toward her.

"Ma'am . . ."

She raised a hand to silence me. "But do you know how often the friends, the families of condemned men—and women, too—bring petitions to us to intervene? We cannot take upon ourselves the control of our entire judicial system. We have officials to do it for us and they must be allowed to work unhindered. Your woman—and you also—will have a chance to speak in her defense. Be content with that."

"But, ma'am, she is innocent!"

"We are sure that you believe that, Madame Blanchard."

There was a silence. The rebec wailed drowsily, like a drugged cat. "We have made it a rule," said Catherine, "only to intervene in very extreme circumstances. One of them is the likelihood of innocence, naturally. But rulers, whether regents or those who reign in their own right, cannot be sentimental. If we are to overturn the judgment of our own officials, thereby incurring their indignation and perhaps damaging their loyalty, then there must be some advantage to us or to our realm. A greater advantage, my dear Madame Blanchard, than that of a purified conscience. That is something we cannot afford. That is for cookmaids, not for queens."

The words came out of me slowly, as I dredged my mind to fetch them up. But they came out accurately. They were the words De Clairpont had spoken earlier that day: "The Catholic cause in Paris is troubled at the moment by the need to arm and feed its soldiers." It struck me that this was probably the means by which De Clairpont had been induced to arrest Dale. Perhaps Catherine was susceptible to the same inducement. "Ma'am," I said, "would you look favorably on my plea if I offered a—substantial contribution to . . . to your cause?"

For the first time, Catherine looked at me with real interest. "You speak, in effect, of a ransom?"

"Yes, ma'am."

"Money has a golden voice, of course," she said. "You are right; our coffers are always hungry, above all at present. If the offered contribution were sufficiently substantial, we would delay the trial until it was produced, and have the woman released the moment the ransom was in our hands. But what kind of substantial ransom, Madame Blanchard, can you possibly offer?"

I paused again, frowning, as once more I delved in my mind to recall the words aright. Then I recited them, as I had done in the treasury at the Tower of London, the day Elizabeth gave me the letter that had brought me, and Dale, to this place.

"Item, one full set of gold plate, value approximately ten thousand pounds, including twenty-four drinking goblets, marked with the badge of a noble Spanish house, set in cabochon rubies and emeralds.

"Item, a golden salt, two feet high, shaped as a square castle tower, with a salt container under each turret and spice drawers below. Decorated with the same badge, set in rubies. Value approximately twelve thousand pounds.

"Item, a silver salt, with a fluted pattern and a chased pattern of birds and leaves around the rim. There is a hinged lid in the likeness of a scallop shell, beneath which are four salt containers that may be lifted out. Value approximately three thousand pounds . . ."

On the verge of adding the last item, concerning the sundry small costly ornaments, total value approximately seven hundred pounds, I checked myself. Fetching all this would involve considerable expense. The small costly ornaments could be useful and any that happened to be leftover could be offered when the time came, as an extra sweetener, like a drift of sugar over a cake.

"Allowing for the approximations . . ." I had a rough and ready knowledge of the equivalents between pounds and crowns ". . . it could be a total value of over between eighty-seven and eighty-eight thousand crowns."

Royal personages are very good at keeping their faces blank, no matter what their thoughts may be, but Catherine's eyes widened as soon as I embarked on the discription of that golden salt. "This is golden conversation indeed," she said, and her voice was impressed. "And the items are obviously most beautiful. Exquisite. Surely we would like to see them, and if we were to sell them, we would hope that their new owners would cherish them and not melt them down. But can you, Madame Ursula Blanchard, truly lay your hands on this treasure?"

"I think so, ma'am, although I would have to make a journey to fetch it."

"Where is it?"

Silently, I blessed Sir Robin Dudley, whose perfidious antics had caused Elizabeth to display her treasure to the Spanish ambassador. Without that, I would never have remembered what resources Gerald had left hidden, their whereabouts known only to me.

"Under the floor of a warehouse in Antwerp," I said.

"You are insane," said my father-in-law. He looked completely panic-stricken. "You can't go to Antwerp and dig up treasure, just like that! What does it consist of, anyway?"

"Gold and silver plate, of various kinds," I said evasively. Catherine de Médicis's expression when I started reciting the details of that golden salt had warned me to be careful what I said. Gold inspires quite enough lust on its own, and gold in the shape of exquisite artifacts arouses lust in an extra dimension. Gerald had told me that once and now I saw that he was right. "I never actually saw it," I said mendaciously. "But Gerald read me the inventory. There were plates and goblets, I think. But it was valuable enough to interest Queen Catherine."

"But you can't just—just pick it up and transport it back

here!" Poor Master Blanchard, six feet tall with an intimidating eagle profile, was clucking like a hen. "It will be heavy, bulky! Besides, it ought either to go back to the Netherlands treasury or onward to the Tower. It isn't yours! You're stealing—either from Antwerp or Elizabeth, I'm not sure which—but stealing all the same. Whatever this treasure consists of, it's obviously worth a great deal. A queen's ransom for a tirewoman!" snorted Master Blanchard. "Hah! Very appropriate, since Elizabeth would no doubt say that she, the queen, was paying it! You could end up in the Tower for this!"

I had maintained the truce with Blanchard very successfully so far, especially since I saw him weep for Searle, but now I blazed at him. "And where will Dale end up if someone doesn't pay it?" I demanded. Brockley had waited in the suite for me to come back and I saw his face blanch. "I have no alternative," I said harshly. "I have to use that treasure. Dear heaven, do you think I *want* any of this?" Outside, the wind was getting up. It whined round the fortress like someone weeping. Like Dale. "I'd far rather go home and see my daughter," I said, and at that moment I was in no doubt that home meant England. "The last thing I want to do is go all the way to Antwerp and all the way back. But I must. I shall use the treasure in the service of the queen, as Sir Thomas Gresham and Gerald intended, and if saving one of Her Majesty's subjects from an unjust and horrible death doesn't count as that, then it's time it did! I will tell Queen Elizabeth afterward what I've done, but not until I've done it!"

"But how can you get there? This is absurd!"

"You and Helene can take a ship to England. Helene must do without female company."

"No, madame. I will go with her." From the corner of our sitting room, Jeanne spoke quietly. "On the journey from

Douceaix, I saw and heard such things . . . I am prepared now
to leave France. I will go with my young mistress."

"Will you? Thank you, Jeanne," I said. "Very well. You will
all go to England. I will find a ship to take me to Antwerp."
I quietened my manner and spoke persuasively to Blanchard.
"Perhaps, Father-in-law, you would let a couple of your men
come with me? I suggest Mark Sweetapple and Hugh Arnold."

The quiet Hugh Arnold and Blanchard's other man, Tom
Clarkson, had somewhat mellowed toward me in the last few
days, perhaps because they saw I was genuinely shocked by
Searle's death. Arnold, though, struck me as the more able of
the two, which was why I asked for him.

"I want to leave Ryder here if he'll agree to that," I said,
"because Brockley, of course, must stay behind, to be near his
wife, and he should have someone with him, another man, for
moral support. He and Ryder are friends."

Brockley nodded speechlessly. "Brockley," I said, "we will
get her out. We will! The queen mother has said she shall be
moved to a better cell and you will be allowed to see her each
day."

"Thank you, madam. I know you're doing all you can," he
said listlessly.

I had been bold in asking for those extra stipulations but
Queen Catherine, thoughtfully picking fragments of sweet-
meat out of her teeth, had suddenly given me that engaging
smile of hers and said that driving bargains amused her and
yes, she would agree.

"How long will it take to bring the treasure from Antwerp?"
Brockley asked.

"I don't know. But I shall move as fast as I can."

"I should come with you," he said. "I know that. But
Fran . . ."

"Needs you to be near her. You will stay, Brockley. That's an order."

"Can the rest of us not go to Antwerp?" said Helene. "Should not Madame Blanchard have moral support, too?" I glanced at her in surprise and she turned faintly pink. "It would be only right," she said defensively.

"No," said my father-in-law in alarm. "It is my duty to take you home to England as soon as possible, and out of all this . . . all this danger. This is a mad enterprise; I say it again. I couldn't possibly agree to come to Antwerp. I will send Sweetapple and Arnold with you if you wish, Ursula. I have no power to constrain you, and I certainly want you to be safe. We will go down to the town at daybreak tomorrow to explain matters to the men. Helene, you will stay here with Jeanne tomorrow and wait for us. You may as well begin packing."

I had a bad night. I lay awake until just before dawn, listening to the wind. It was growing worse. I got up once, and went to the window. Opening it, I heard the forest to the north creaking and swishing as the gale raced over it. There was another sound, too, faint, far off, but still enough to make the goose-flesh rise on my forearms. Somewhere in that forest, wolves were howling. There were no wolves now in England, but here in France, the deer were still hunted by creatures other than man. Compared to France, England was small and tame. Once more, I longed with all my heart to be back there.

I returned to my bed and lay thinking of Dale, wondering if she had yet been moved, and whether she was asleep, or lying wakeful and crying with fear and loneliness.

That night, Brockley shared the second bedchamber with my father-in-law and Harvey, but from the look of him the next morning, he hadn't slept either. We broke our fast to the sound of rain squalls being driven against the window, and as soon as we had eaten, he went to see if he could visit Dale again. The rest of us left Jeanne and Helene folding clothes and filling hampers, put on cloaks and stout footwear, and made our way to the town below the fortress to talk to the others of our party. They were already aware of the crisis, because William Harvey had visited them the previous evening and told them. We found them all at Anthony Jenkinson's lodging. A further crisis had broken.

"Two men have been inquiring for me," Jenkinson said. "I actually saw them, coming out of an inn down the road. One was of Turkish appearance and the other, from the cut of his cloak, was Venetian. Astronomers," he added, "are interested in unusual conjunctions of planets, and just now, I'm interested in that particular conjunction of nationalities."

He was, of course, grinning cheerfully. The idea of being pursued across continents by homicidal commercial rivals really did seem to stimulate him. "When they were out of sight," he said, "I went into the inn, adopted a harmless manner, gave a false name—another false name, I mean; I called myself Drury, after a friend of mine in England—and said I was trying to trace a couple of contacts. My arrangements to meet them had gone amiss, I said. Were the well-dressed gentlemen I had glimpsed from a distance looking for me? The innkeeper said no, they were seeking news of a man called Van Weede. I don't think they'd described me, because he didn't seem to connect me with Van Weede at all. But I think I've been traced, as I feared I would be. The second set of Lions have caught up."

"Then you'll be glad to sail as soon as possible," Luke Blanchard said. "So will we all. Well, we have our passages to England and no one has threatened to hinder us, thank God. We now have to find a ship to take Mistress Blanchard here to Antwerp."

"Ships?" said Jenkinson. "You'll be very, very fortunate."

"But we already have passages for England. You know that. We do have to find a vessel for Antwerp, but—"

"You landlubber!" said Jenkinson. "Haven't you noticed the weather?"

CHAPTER 14

Hard Riding

Most sailors claim that they can foretell the weather and most are no better at it than anyone else. However, some older seamen do have a way of being right. A lifetime of seeing the patterns of weather, of being dependent on them, has its effect. When four experienced sailors out of six all say the same thing, you may as well listen.

Harvey and Sweetapple, heavily cloaked against the wind and rain, which was growing worse, went down to the quay to ask questions. They came back to report that no ships were leaving their moorings today. They also reported that the consensus among the sailors to whom they had spoken was that the weather wouldn't improve much for at least two days and possibly not then. If the wind eased a little, we might get a vessel down to the mouth of the Seine, but it would have to ease a lot before we could hope to travel a yard farther.

"Oh no!" My father-in-law was ready to bang his head on the wall. "I have never wanted to get away from anywhere as much as I want to get away from France! How long will we be marooned here?"

"Who can say?" Jenkinson was philosophical. "Even if it improves tomorrow, we must still travel all the way down the Seine to the sea, with no guarantee of fair winds when we do get there. The journey either to England or to Antwerp could be slow. That's sea travel for you. The same trip can take two days or two weeks, or more, depending on wind and weather."

"I once said you ought to be called Daniel," I remarked. "I begin to think that Jeremiah would be better!"

"I'm not a Jeremiah," said Jenkinson firmly. "Just a realist. I have a further suggestion. Crossing to England means a sea trip, of course. There's no avoiding that. But one can go overland to Antwerp. Now, Mistress Blanchard here wants to get to Antwerp; Master Blanchard clearly has a distaste for France, and just now, so have I. I certainly don't wish to be kept here with Lions sniffing round in the very same town! Overland, it's a good two hundred miles to Antwerp, maybe a bit more, but it can be done in a week, by someone willing to ride hard and change mounts often. Going by land, you can reasonably rely on getting there within a certain time. And by the time we get to Antwerp," he added, "the weather might be better and those of us who want to go to England at once might find it easy enough. Plenty of shipping in Antwerp."

"Are you suggesting," demanded Blanchard, "that we all go to Antwerp, and sail from there? Except for Mistress Blanchard, who will of course have to come back to France?"

"I am suggesting just that," said Jenkinson. "I have been to Paris and St. Germain before, and I know who will hire us good horses. We could set out today."

So that, in the end, was what we did. Jenkinson set about arranging for the horses, while those of us who had belongings in the palace went back to collect them, and to collect Helene and Jeanne as well. Jeanne was waiting for us, passing the time in embroidery, but Helene, she said, had gone to the palace chapel to pray for Dale. "I escorted her there and said I would return for her in an hour. The hour wants only ten minutes. I will fetch her now."

I remember muttering crossly at the delay but Jeanne was back with Helene in a very short time and Helene apologized nicely for holding us up, though she rather spoiled the effect a moment later by pulling a face when I told her that the hampers and most of their contents would have to be left with Brockley and Ryder, to be brought on to England by ship after I had got back from Antwerp.

"We can't take packhorses," I said. "We can only carry what will go into our saddlebags or into satchels slung on our shoulders. We bought some satchels on the way here. Here's yours. It's no use looking sulky. Now, sort out the things you really need and make haste."

Helene obeyed me, but with obvious disgust. As I stuffed my own satchel with clothes and linen, I wondered where Brockley was, but he appeared before I had finished, and said that he had seen Dale and that she was in her new cell.

"Ground level, madam, with some daylight, and they've given her a proper pallet to sleep on. She's calmer."

We gave him the news that we were setting out on horseback forthwith. "I hope we won't take too long over it," I said. "My husband had a lease on that warehouse that is still in force—at least, he paid for five years in advance, so I suppose it is. At any rate, he had a key to it that is on my key ring now. I can get us into the place, and I'll get those floorboards up somehow. Coming back will be slower. It's true that the treasure will be bulky to carry. It'll mean a ship or else pack mules. But we'll make all the haste we can. Keep your heart up, Brockley, and try to keep Dale's up, as well. I would visit her again, but there's no time. You'd rather I set out quickly, I imagine."

"Yes, madame. I would. Will you be safe?"

"We're all going together as far as Antwerp, and I shall have Sweetapple and Arnold on the way back."

"God be with you, madam," Brockley said. He paused and then added: "I've never told you much about my early life, madam, have I? Except that you know I went to war with King Henry in 1544."

"That's so. Why?" I asked him.

"I was married as a young man," Brockley said. "The daughter of an innkeeper in London. Joan, her name was. I had to leave her behind when I went to fight, in the train of the gentleman I served. When I came back, she'd gone off with a group of traveling players." He saw my startled face and added hastily: "Oh, I'm married to Fran, right enough. Joan died long ago. I found her again, but it took me a couple of years, which was a poor joke on the part of fate, because though I didn't know it, for most of that time, she'd been living half a mile from my employer's town house. She quarreled with her lover and left the troupe, and came back to London and she'd been supporting herself—well, you can guess how." Brockley's face expressed distaste.

"She'd got with child and got rid of it," he said, "but whatever it was she did to herself, it killed her. She was dying when I found her. Well, she died and I buried her and I didn't expect to wed again. The thing with Joan was that she had something mysterious about her. I never knew quite what she really felt or thought; there was always something withheld, just glimmering in her eyes or her little half-smile. I fell in love with her because of that; it was—as if she was always beckoning. But after she was gone, I didn't want to follow any more beckoning women. And then I met Fran.

"With Fran, there are no mysteries. What you see is what there is. No pretenses, no secrets. And if anything happens to her, because I was a fool and tried to protect her with that damned phial of yew poison. . . . I shall do what the old Romans did, madam. I shall fall on my sword."

"We are going to save her," I said. I wished I felt more certain of it, but I put all the conviction into my voice that I could. "You are to take your things down to John Ryder's lodgings in the town," I said. "He has agreed to stay with you."

I had had quite an argument with John Ryder about that.

"I am here to guard you, mistress, under orders from Sir William Cecil. I have to remain with you, not with your manservant." He was kindly, fatherly, and firm. I looked him in the eye.

"Master Ryder, you are under orders to shadow me in the hope that I will lead you to Matthew. I know quite well that guarding me was just a pretext and that hunting Matthew down is the real reason why Sir William Cecil sent you with me. Well, now that I know this, you can rest assured that I shall take great care not to lead you to Matthew. Also, he is in any case in France, and I'm going to Antwerp, more than adequately escorted. If necessary, I will hire extra men for the return journey. There is no need at all for you to come, too."

Ryder flushed. "Mistress Blanchard, I can assure you that Sir William was most concerned for your safety and . . ."

"Brockley needs a friend beside him. Sir William never foresaw any of this."

He thought it over, frowning. It was obvious, of course, that if he had orders both to guard me and to hunt for Matthew, then these two purposes must now part company. He could not seek Matthew while traveling to Antwerp, nor guard me and still remain in France. Nor had he any mandate to stop me from going to Antwerp.

At length, after much hesitation, he said he would respect my wishes and stay with Brockley. By which I knew that I was right, and that he was principally here to find and arrest Matthew. Well, Brockley would be glad of him. I could only pray that Matthew would evade him.

"You can do something for me," I said to Brockley now. "Keep John Ryder occupied. Keep him beside you. But no more talk, if you please, of falling on your sword!"

We set out, therefore, in terrible weather, saddlebags bulging and satchels bouncing on our backs. Jenkinson (who was now calling himself Simon Drury, which was confusing because we had to get used to calling him that) was carrying the most. His saddlebags would hardly fasten and instead of a proper satchel, he had on his shoulders an overstuffed thing like a leather sack with buckles. We rode like demons, our mounts' coats often as dark with sweat as with rain. Few inns kept enough horses for us all to change mounts at once, but we took what we could find, in turns.

I drove us onward, keeping pauses for food and drink as short as I could; bullying everyone to make them rise early and get into their saddles with their mouths still full of breakfast; urging us, every evening, to do those last few miles that might in the end add up to one day less on the road.

The men could stand up to it and so could I, for I had been accustomed to an energetic life, but although Helene and Jeanne both rode quite well, neither was used to long hours of riding. By the end of the first full day, Jeanne looked worn-out and Helene was complaining that she was sore. I told her brusquely to pad herself with saddle-dusters.

When at the inn we had found for our third night's lodging, Jeanne had to be helped off her horse and almost carried inside, Jenkinson came to speak to me. "You're overdoing things. If you kill yourself—or us—with exhaustion, will that help Dale?"

He was right, of course, and I should have listened. Traveling together, we had become friends. I had by now told him a good deal about not only Matthew but also my runaway match with Gerald, and I had told him as much as I could of my reasons for detesting Dr. Wilkins, and why I believed that he might have something to do with our present emergency. I was careful not to speak of my work for Cecil but I could say I had been one of the queen's ladies, and complain that Cecil had used me as bait to catch my husband without mentioning that I had ever been a spy myself.

"I notice," he said, "that you are not on very friendly terms with Helene. What is wrong between the two of you?"

"Helene went through our baggage once and found that phial," I said. "Though it wasn't Helene who told De Clairpont about it; I challenged her with that and she denied it and I think she spoke the truth. She swore on the cross and I don't think she would have done that if she were lying. Anyway, she hasn't had much chance to go tattling. I suspect that the phial was found by someone else—I don't know who—much earlier." I told him about the mysterious search of our luggage in Le Cheval d'Or. "That was probably nothing to do with Helene. Cecil's men might have been looking for signs that I had been in touch with Matthew . . . but on the other hand . . . perhaps it was someone else. Oh, I am so tired of mysteries. I just want to get to Antwerp and get back with Dale's ransom and then get out of France forever and say farewell to Helene forever, too. I don't suspect her of harming Dale, but I still can't forgive her for poking into my bags, or for her insufferable sanctimoniousness."

"She's an aggravating girl, I agree," Jenkinson said comfortingly. "And I don't like Dr. Wilkins any more than you do. I met him briefly at St. Marc's Abbey."

But although he was now a friend I trusted, I didn't trust him to be right when he said we were riding too hard. I made us press on at the same pace. The continent of Europe, when one is in a hurry, seems unending. In England, even the topography seems to know that it is on an island and that each landscape, each area of chalk hills, forest, upland plain, fen, or moorland, must be confined within a reasonable space if all are to be fitted in. On the Continent, everything has much more elbow room and uses it. Deer grow bigger antlers, wolves continue to thrive, and landscapes go on apparently forever.

The bad weather seemed determined to go on forever, as well. The wind and rain did not abate and although we all had stout leather cloaks, the end of the day always found us soaking wet as well as exhausted.

On the afternoon of the fourth day, Jeanne virtually collapsed again and had to be shifted onto Sweetapple's horse and held there with his arm around her. We were obliged to slow our pace, and then, just to add to my exasperation, Blanchard's mount went lame. We could do nothing but halt at a most uncomfortable hostelry attached to a hamlet in the middle of nowhere. There were allegedly a couple of horses there for hire, but they were out and not expected back for two days, and Jeanne, in any case, needed to rest.

We were at least over the French border by then, though not by much. This had cheered my father-in-law up a good deal, but it did little for me. We were still a long way from Antwerp.

I cried that night, thinking of Dale in her prison and Brockley, waiting in anguish for my return. At breakfast the next day I knew my eyes were red. Jenkinson noticed, and later on, came to the damp little parlor where I was listlessly sitting with Helene while Jeanne lay in bed.

"We shall get there. Don't be afraid. We can pass the time," said Jenkinson firmly, "by laying a few sensible plans. I intend sailing for England, as you know, but I'm unlikely to find a ship at once and meanwhile, if I can help you, I will. Now, exactly what do you intend to do when we arrive? I do know Antwerp a little." I wondered if there was anywhere that Jenkinson didn't know. Cathay possibly, although I wouldn't have gambled even on that. "Where precisely is the warehouse?" Jenkinson asked. "Near the river Schelde? Most of the warehouses are by the river or close to it."

"It's close to it," I said, "maybe a couple of miles north of the cathedral. There's a kind of network of waterways and docks leading off from the river and it's beside one of the waterways. It has a landing stage. There's a land entrance, too, onto a street on the other side. The street's called Hoekstraat— Hook Street, that is. When Gerald took me to see the warehouse, we walked through Hoekstraat first. It's shaped like a hook, with a straight stretch and then a curve. The straight part runs parallel with the waterway and the warehouse is one of a row in between them. But the best way to get there is by boat. After he'd shown me Hoekstraat, Gerald hired a rowing boat and we went along the waterway and entered the place by way of the landing stage." I frowned, remembering. "I rather think that the easiest way to transport the treasure would be by water. There are dwellings beside some of those waterways. If we could arrange to stay somewhere from which we can go by boat all the way to the warehouse . . ."

"But surely, madam," Helene said, "the owner will long since have learned that your former husband is dead and that you have gone away. What if he's let it to someone else by now?"

"I have a key," I said.

"So we are to—burgle it?"

"Yes," I said bluntly.

"We shall need to find a hostelry at first," Jenkinson said thoughtfully. "But we could look round then for a rented house on a suitable waterway. A house would give us more privacy, anyway. You've said that you and your first husband were in the household of Sir Thomas Gresham. Will you call on him?"

I had been thinking about that. If one has something to hide, it is well to behave as normally as possible.

When I reached Antwerp, to visit Sir Thomas would be the normal thing to do. If I didn't, and he learned of my presence by accident, he might wonder why.

"I might," I said, "but I must be careful what I say to him. He would want that treasure sent to England. The plight of one tirewoman in France might not seem to him so very important."

"Yes, I see." Jenkinson stroked his brown beard thoughtfully. "I have met him," he said. "I would like to call on him. There are some matters of commerce I might fruitfully discuss with him, and he could help us obtain passages for England. We could all visit together. You can simply say you and Master Blanchard wished to get out of France quickly. I see no difficulty about that."

"I wish we weren't having so much difficulty in getting to Antwerp in the first place," I said.

But for all my impatience, I was tired, and secretly glad to rest from the hard riding for a while. I was sleeping badly, too, and when I did sleep, I had nightmares. Twice, the following night, I woke from terrifying dreams. Once, I sat up with heart pounding, sure that someone had set fire to the inn. I sat bolt upright in the darkness for several moments before the quietness and the complete lack of any smell of smoke convinced me that all was safe.

I lay down again and drifted off to sleep once more, and this time dreamed that Dr. Wilkins had come into the room and was telling me that I would never bring the treasure back from Antwerp. He sat on the end of my bed and laughed at me, making the bed shake.

I shot upright again, to find that it was morning and that the rain had stopped. The wind still plagued the trees that grew at the back of the hostelry, but it was less boisterous and there were traces of blue between the racing clouds. Helene was already up; indeed, it was she who had been shaking my bed, although gently.

"It is time for breakfast, madame. See, I am dressed already and I have been out into the open air. The weather is much better."

"But Master Blanchard's horse is still lame and the horses belonging to this place are still out. And how is Jeanne? Is she much better as well?"

"Yes, madame, she is. She can go on tomorrow, she says, if only we need not ride for quite such long hours."

"The horses should be back today," I said. "But they will need a night's rest . . . tomorrow will have to do, I suppose," I said grudgingly.

Tiredness and worry were making me bad-tempered. I was angry with Jeanne for falling ill, even angry with Blanchard's horse for going lame. We could have been much farther on our way but for these maddening mishaps.

Hoping that fresh air would help me, I took a walk myself after breakfast. I went through the small village, looking at the farmland, listening to the local patois, which was a curious mixture of French and Low German. I was glad to get out of the inn. True, it wasn't quite as primitive as the one before, which had the last-century system of dormitories for men and

women and no private rooms at all. This one, despite its re-
moteness, did at least have some separate rooms for hire. But
the beds had bugs, the tables were inadequately scrubbed, and
the wooden platters carried the encrusted remains of previous
guests' meals. The place was run by a father and a middle-aged
daughter who snapped and shouted at each other all the time.
Le Cheval d'Or was a haven of comfort and good cheer by
comparison.

The walk did help. My mood grew less stormy, though my
spirits stayed low. I missed both Dale and Brockley. I had long
leaned on Brockley's common sense and reliability. Jenkinson
was a good companion, but his interests were his own and not
mine. Brockley was like a sturdy windbreak, and without him,
I felt the draft.

I went back to the inn to eat an indifferent dinner of dumplings in a thin stew, indigestible barley bread, and an allegedly
sweet omelet that was sloppy in the middle and not properly
sweetened either. Jeanne, who had got up for dinner, said,
though wanly, that she would sit in the parlor with Helene,
and I decided to go upstairs, take off my shoes, and lie on my
bed for a while. I fell asleep, awakening suddenly, much later,
to realize that it was already nearly evening, and that in my
father-in-law's bedchamber next door somebody was shouting
and somebody else was in tears.

Hurriedly, I put on my shoes and went to investigate. I
knocked at the door and called, but no one took any notice, so
I turned the handle and stepped inside. Helene, red in the face
and weeping copiously, was backed against the window and re-
iterating, over and over: "No, it isn't true; I didn't; I haven't!"
She was leaning back as if to get away from my father-in-law,
who was shaking his fist in her face.

"Master Blanchard!" I shouted.

Blanchard swung round. "Ah, Mistress Ursula. And where have you been all afternoon? Jeanne is resting again; but you are supposed to be Helene's companion. You should have been with her, watching over her, instead of letting her run about unsupervised. What have you to say for yourself?"

"I was asleep myself," I said. "I left Helene with Jeanne. But what has Helene done?" I found it hard to imagine what a model of piety like Helene could possibly have done, especially in a lonely place like this. The opportunities for mischief seemed so very limited.

Blanchard promptly confounded me. "She's been meeting a man, that's what she's been doing! I saw her myself, from the window. She was out there with him, under the trees, and what's more, I think I know who it was. I knew the shape of him. It was that thickset fellow Longman. She crept out of the inn on her own this afternoon, because you weren't keeping an eye on her—"

"I didn't, I didn't!" Helene wailed.

"I saw you with my own eyes," bellowed Blanchard. "I saw you leave him and come back into the inn yard; I watched you all the way till you came indoors. Don't whine to me that you didn't, you didn't! You did, madam, you did! You're betrothed, let me remind you! Betrothed to a young man from a good Sussex family, a good *Catholic* family; and what'll they say if he finds out on your wedding night that you're damaged goods? Answer me that, slut!" He grabbed Helene's shoulders and shook her. "Has he had you? Has he?"

"No, I'm not a slut, I'm not!" bawled Helene.

"But you met him! I saw you." Blanchard shook her again.

"Yes, all right, but it was only to talk, just to talk. He's nice. He's kind. He's good company. But we didn't do anything wrong, we did not!"

"If you're lying," said Blanchard menacingly, "if I find out that you're lying—if you lose your virtue before you get to the altar with your lawful bridegroom, you'll wish you were dead. You'll cry tears enough to float a merchantman and you'll sleep on your stomach for a week. I'll have to compensate your groom for taking you secondhand. If he takes you at all, that is! Most likely, he won't and I'll lose all the profit I ought to have made!"

He had begun this speech in a moderate tone but ended it in a shout because, by then, Helene was not so much crying as screaming. She jerked about in his grasp, turning her head from side to side. Finally, he stepped back and let her go, and Helene's screams subsided into sobs. I found a handkerchief and handed it to her.

"Perhaps," I said to Blanchard, "we ought to have a word with Longman."

"It won't be any use," said Helene in muffled tones from behind the handkerchief. "He'll deny it all. We . . . agreed that he should. If any questions were asked. He values his employment. It'll be his word against yours."

"I saw the two of you together!"

"But we were only talking!"

"Were they?" I asked Blanchard. "Did you see more than that?"

Unwillingly, my father-in-law admitted that he had not. "Go into our chamber," I said to Helene. I saw her through our door myself and as I did so, I whispered: "If all you did was meet and talk, there's no harm done. That is all it was, I hope."

"He kissed me," Helene whispered back. "But that was all. Truly, that was all."

"Still no harm done. But don't do it again," I said, and turned the key on her before going back to Blanchard.

"I think she's telling the truth," I said. "She hasn't had much opportunity for assignations, with Longman or anyone else, and these things take time to develop. Especially with good, pious girls like Helene. Can you imagine anyone seducing Helene without having to work at it?"

"I had no idea . . . no idea," said my father-in-law, "what a responsibility a girl of sixteen can be." He wiped a hand across his brow. He was actually perspiring with rage.

"It could even," I said, "be a good thing."

"*A good thing?*"

"You were quite glad when she showed an interest in De Clairpont," I said, "because it meant that she was human. So does this. What sort of wife would an alabaster saint make? A wife needs a few natural urges."

"She's not entitled to natural urges until she *is* a wife. You *would* say a thing like that," said Blanchard, quite pettishly. "You and Gerald eloped, after all. You let your natural urges get the better of you, both of you. Oh, never mind. All that water flowed under the bridge and down to the sea a long time ago now. But I shall speak to Jenkinson. I shall tell him to keep his man in order. The horses attached to this inn have come back—they came in this afternoon. We'll be on our way in the morning. Oh, how far is it to Antwerp? Will we never get there?"

CHAPTER 15

Leaping Fish

Altogether, it took ten days to reach Antwerp. Blanchard continued to be annoyed. In his opinion, Jenkinson had not been shocked enough by Longman's assignation with Helene.

"Stephen's no fool. He wouldn't try to seduce your ward, Master Blanchard. But a little flirtation—well, why not? It might do that girl good," said Jenkinson, and added: "I've never known him to be attracted by pious airs and a lanky figure before. He likes them plump and giggly as a rule. But I'll have a word with him if you like."

"I've no confidence in what he calls having a word," my father-in-law confided to me. "He doesn't take it seriously."

Whether Jenkinson did or did not speak to Longman, I didn't know. But Helene showed no further inclination to creep out to clandestine meetings. We traveled more slowly on the last part of the journey, but both she and Jeanne were exhausted at the end of each day and Helene was content to remain in her room in whatever inns we found, and even to take meals there rather than join us downstairs.

The final day was easy riding, since the road was well maintained and the land was flat. Antwerp, like most trade centers, was surrounded by villages as a prince is surrounded by courtiers or, as Anthony Jenkinson more cynically remarked, a mouse hole is guarded by cats. As we passed through the last village, we saw the tall pinnacles of the Cathedral of the Holy Virgin coming nearer, and soon we were in Antwerp itself, in the winding streets among the tall, narrow houses that I remembered so well. By dinnertime, we were unsaddling in the courtyard of an inn called, if translated into English, the Sign of the Leaping Fish.

Both Jenkinson and I had been there before, though at different times. Although Gerald was a member of Sir Thomas Gresham's household, we had not lived under Sir Thomas's roof. Before we left England, Gresham had noted Gerald's talent for getting to know people and persuading them to talk to him, and had decided that this young man would be good at finding people who could be bribed or blackmailed into helping to steal the city's treasures.

If so, his prospective victims would trust him more easily if his address was not the same as Gresham's, and we spent our first few days in Antwerp at the Sign of the Leaping Fish, while we looked for lodgings. Jenkinson, it now transpired, had stayed there two years before us. We both remembered it well, however, and agreed that it would be a good choice if it hadn't changed hands.

It hadn't. The landlord we had both known, Meister Piedersen, was still there. He was big and ginger-bearded, one of those highly professional hosts with a memory for names and faces, and he spoke English. "Mistress Blanchard! Master Jenkinson! But of course, of course, I remember you both. And this is your father-in-law, Mistress Blanchard? You are most welcome, sir. And where is Master Gerald? Dead? I had no idea. What a tragedy. I am desolated to learn of it. And this is your ward, sir? Welcome, Mistress Helene. You have had a long journey, it seems. You must be thankful to be out of France. The stories we are hearing . . . ! You wish to be known as Master Drury, sir? By all means. You can trust my discretion. Yes, we have rooms. A merchant and his train have just left . . ."

The inn reminded me of Gerald. As we took our late dinner, I found myself constantly remembering meals I had eaten here with him. Afterward, most of the others went gratefully to rest. But another of Piedersen's professional skills was that of recognizing the needs of his guests, sometimes even before the guests themselves. "Do you wish to be alone, mistress?" he asked me quietly, as I paused hesitantly just outside the dining room. "You will have memories to think about, perhaps. My other guests are mostly out and the inn is quiet. There is a parlor here where you can be private for an hour or so."

"Thank you," I said.

I did want to be alone, but until that moment, I hadn't known how much. The parlor was small and gloomy, paneled in some dark wood, but the moment Piedersen gently closed the door after me, I felt as though I were in a haven. The solitude was like a long drink of cool water after hours of thirst. I sat down on the window seat, turning to look out into the narrow alley at the side of the inn. In one direction, I could glimpse a waterway. Waterways were as much a part of Antwerp as roads. I wondered, but could not quite remember, how far we were from Hoekstraat.

But if I couldn't recall where Hoekstraat was, I remembered every detail of this room. Gerald and I had played chess together here. Closing my eyes, I pictured him. He had been dead just over two years and much had happened in between, but in two years, memory does not fade so very much.

I loved Matthew. I had married him less than a year after Gerald's passing. But the marriage had been forced on me. Matthew had attracted me, yes, but I would never of my own free will have gone to him so soon. Here in this place where Matthew had never been, where Gerald and I had been happy, I sought out my first love, Meg's father, once again.

What if the door of the room were to open, and Gerald were to come through it? What would I feel then?

Memory may not dim much in two years, but the pattern of life can change irrevocably. I had gone on from Gerald, formed a new link and almost broken free of that as well—accepted new tasks and faced new conflicts. Gerald was buried here in Antwerp, but I had already decided that I did not want to visit his grave. And yet . . . if Gerald were to walk in . . . would I run to him crying his name? Or sit in dumb distress, realizing that the man I had once loved wildly enough to run away with him was no longer important to me—was now an embarrassing irrelevance?

But he was dead. Never again would he open a door and walk into the room where I sat. When he first died, the fact that he was gone and would not come back was all but unbearable. I couldn't believe it or endure it. I longed so much for the impossible to happen. Now, I saw that the finality of death was a blessing, for it had set me free to journey on. How would bereaved people repair their lives if they were never sure whether or not the bereavement was permanent; if there was always a risk that a door would open and the lost one would return? The finality was anguish, but at least you knew where you were.

For a moment, thinking it out, I closed my eyes. Only to open them again in terror because the door *was* opening. Someone—a man—was coming in. Then I let out my breath in a sigh of relief. "Master Jenkinson!"

"The landlord said you were here. He said you wished to be alone, but when I explained I had something important to discuss with you and that you would want to hear it, he showed me to this room. I'm sorry if I've disturbed you."

"No . . . no, it's all right. It's just . . ."

"What is it?" He came quickly forward. "Mistress Blanchard, what is the matter? You look ill!"

"I'm not ill. I've been remembering Gerald, and being here with him. And . . ."

For other anxieties had now shot to the surface of my mind, awakened by the memory of my warm, safe life with Gerald. Those memories had shown me how far from warm and safe was my present situation.

"I'm afraid," I said. "All the way here, I've buoyed myself up, telling myself that I have only to collect the treasure and then take it back to Paris, and set Dale free. But what if it's gone? Or we can't get into the warehouse in Hoekstraat at all? Suppose it's been demolished, or swept away in some unexpected flood tide? What if—?"

"Hush, hush. You're panicking," said Jenkinson. "Wait!" He stepped to the door, put his head out, and shouted. Someone answered and Jenkinson snapped: "Wine for two, and something to eat as well. Bring it all to this parlor, quickly!" He came back and placed himself on an oak settle. "I noticed that you took very little dinner. You need something to revive you. You'll feel better then."

"I'll feel better when I've got my hands on that treasure. Because if I don't get my hands on it—oh, God, what will happen to Dale? She's living through day after day, not knowing if I'll be able to save her, terrified of what will happen to her if I don't. Brockley gave her that phial to save her from just this danger, but now it's thrown her into it instead. The potion has been taken from her and even if we made a fresh one we might not be able to smuggle it to her. I can't bear it for her,

230 230

or for Brockley. If I don't bring the treasure back . . . what will I do?"

"If you fail to find the treasure, there are still other things that may be done," Jenkinson said firmly. "The queen mother might have a change of heart. The political situation may alter so that it becomes wise and politic for her to be merciful to an English captive. Or we may think of another way to raise the ransom. There's no need for such despair yet."

"I want to get to that warehouse. I daren't ask questions about it so I'll have to reconnoiter. I wanted to be here before this but with Helene and Jeanne wilting like flowers that haven't been watered, and—"

There was a tap on the door and Piedersen came in with a tray containing pewter goblets, a flagon, fresh bread, and a platter of sausages in a dark sauce. The spicy smell caught at my nostrils and told me how very hungry I still was.

"Your refreshments, Meister Jenkinson. Sir, two gentlemen—very well dressed, very well spoken—have just called to inquire whether a party accompanying a Meister Blanchard was staying here, and if so, whether anyone by the name of Jenkinson or Van Weede was among them."

"Indeed!" Jenkinson spoke sharply. "Did they give any names themselves?"

"One gave his name as Signor Bruni," said Piedersen. "He was Venetian, I think. The other called himself Signor Morelli, but we see people from every part of the known world here in Antwerp and I do not think he comes from anywhere in Italy. I think he was Turkish. In accordance with your instructions, I denied all knowledge of people called Blanchard, Jenkinson, or Van Weede. No mention was made of Drury."

"While you were unpacking," Jenkinson said to me, "I explained my situation fully to Meister Piedersen. He can be trusted."

"But we traveled so fast! How could they catch up? Did they fly?"

"Two men can travel faster than a party with Helene and Jeanne in it, and besides, we had that two-day delay halfway. Yes, they could have caught up. Exactly what did they say, Piedersen? And did they have a description of me?"

"No, sir, they gave no description. Apart from asking if you or the Blanchard party were here, they said very little. I denied all knowledge of any of you, and suggested other inns and lodgings they might try," said Piedersen.

"Thank you, Piedersen. And here is something for your trouble." A coin changed hands. Piedersen accepted it with a polite nod, but no obsequiousness, and took himself off: a man in control of his business and his life, and in no way belittled by a gratuity from a satisfied customer.

"I told him nothing of your affairs," Jenkinson said as the door closed. "I let him think you are just a group to which I have attached myself. It seems plain now that I was too careless after the business at Le Cheval d'Or. I am sorry." He tore off a piece of bread, put a sausage on it, handed it to me, and began to pour the wine. "Mistress Blanchard, I want to help you get your hands on that treasure. I think you may need help and that your father-in-law is none too willing to give it. If only I can evade my pursuers for long enough! Have you given any thought to the best way of getting it back to France?"

I took a heartening mouthful of sausage. It made me feel better at once. "The weather seems to be settling. Could we consider going by sea for the return journey?"

"I think we well might. Your wine, Mistress Blanchard. We spoke, did we not, of visiting Sir Thomas Gresham and asking his help in arranging passages to England for Master Blanchard and Helene? He might be able to help with getting a ship to Paris, too, if we can think of a good excuse for wanting to go back there. A sea journey could be safer than an overland one, though we must pray for luck with the wind and weather. Pack mules laden with treasure need a very strong guard. I could send a messenger overland on horseback to announce that we're on our way, and put some heart into Dale and Brockley."

"We?" I queried. "But you're going to England."

"The treaty I carry is," Jenkinson corrected. "It can go with Blanchard. Another copy went with my own goods caravan, if you remember, and I hope it got through but if not, Blanchard will be as safe a courier as any. He may as well be of *some* use! Because the reason why I may not go with him is I think you need more support. In my opinion, your father-in-law is letting you down. If you succeed in getting hold of the valuables, you need more of an escort than just Sweetapple and Arnold and maybe a few hirelings who are strangers to you. Longman and I represent two more sword arms and good ones, though I say it myself."

I was grateful but also alarmed. "But what if you can't keep ahead of the hunt? Those two Levantine bloodhounds have been to this very inn! What if they find out that you are here? They might! They might easily find some innocent soul who will tell them that a party answering to our description were seen entering Meister Piedersen's premises!" I gulped most of my wine in one swallow.

Jenkinson refilled my goblet. His dark eyes had begun to sparkle. Imminent danger was having its usual effect on him. "Trust Uncle Anthony. I've told Piedersen that we want to shift to lodgings—I suggested that before, if you remember.

He has supplied a map of the city and the names of several landlords. I've already sent Longman out to look for somewhere, preferably on a waterway, with a landing stage, and not too far from Hoekstraat, which is marked on the map. Go on, drink up."

I did as I was told. The wine was red, deep in color and velvety. It put some heart into me but nothing was going to move this burden of anxiety. It grew heavier, as the moment came nearer when we must set out for that warehouse and—so I hoped—come face-to-face with over twenty-five thousand pounds' worth of treasure, and then get it back to Paris.

"In the matter of Hoekstraat," Jenkinson said, "can you recall exactly where the warehouse is?"

"I hope so." The wine was strong so I took another sausage to soak up the fumes, and pushed the platter toward Jenkinson. "The straight part of Hoekstraat is about half a mile long and then it curves away from the water, almost back on itself. The warehouse is on the straight section, fairly close to where the curve begins. There are warehouses on both banks, with wharves and landing stages, and there's a path on each bank, too—a narrow one between the buildings and the water. What I want to do is first of all make sure I know which warehouse is the right one, and then decide exactly how and when to enter it."

Chewing thoughtfully, Jenkinson nodded. "Very well. We will find somewhere to rent, and move there as soon as we can, and then we'll hire a rowing boat and take a look round. I recommend you to make sure you can recognize the warehouse after dark. We would do well to fetch the treasure at night."

I said: "When should we visit Sir Thomas Gresham?"

"I told Longman to call there as well, and ask for an appointment. We still have to think of a reason for going back to

Paris, but I think I can deal with that. I have ideas about other things, as well. Mistress Blanchard . . ."

"Yes?"

"This is a time of great anxiety for you and I am loath to add to it but . . ."

He talked earnestly for some time. I listened with horror. Even if we fetched the treasure without difficulty, I thought, the chances of getting safely back to France with it seemed terrifyingly slender.

"I just hope you're wrong," I said. "You must be wrong."

"I would like to think so. Of course, I have no certainty," Jenkinson said. "But I think we would be wise to take what precautions we can. Do you not agree?"

There was another tap on the door, and Piedersen was there again. "A man has come from Sir Thomas Gresham's house, Meister Jenkinson. You will be welcome there, with your party, from eleven of the clock onward, tomorrow morning."

"Thank you," said Jenkinson.

Yes, a visit to Sir Thomas must come first. I was longing to get to the warehouse and all delay added to the length of poor Dale's misery, but this delay was essential. If Jenkinson was right . . .

The wine was indeed making me sleepy but my intelligence was still working. I didn't want him to be right and I thought his evidence tenuous, but all the same, it held together. His theory was possible and therefore precautions had to be taken. In my mind, an idea was taking shape regarding those precautions. For reasons connected with that as well as for other purposes, I must see Sir Thomas Gresham, quickly.

On the strength of the wine and the sausages, I slept all afternoon, waking early in the evening to find that Longman had discovered lodgings for us and that we could move at once. "I doubt if they're anything marvelous," Jenkinson said. "Too cheap and too quickly available. But they're well placed for what we want. We shan't need them for long, I trust."

Jenkinson said that we should go after dark, and should therefore take supper first. Luke Blanchard groaned at the prospect of packing up again, but when he heard that the Lions were on our heels again, he changed his mind. We waited out the evening in the parlor and the card room. Jeanne and I passed the time with a little stitching: a loose hem on my night rail and a split seam in Helene's spare kirtle. Helene still looked wan and I sent her upstairs again to rest a little more before we set off.

Piedersen, entering into the spirit of the thing (we had paid him as though we were staying the night, plus a generous reward for being so cooperative), said that we should leave candles burning in our rooms as though we were still in occupation. He would extinguish them later. We collected our belongings and made our stealthy way out of a rear entrance. The horses could stay in the Leaping Fish stables, Piedersen said, and he would send them back to their home stables tomorrow. We were all glad that we had kept our luggage to a minimum.

The back entrance led into an alley, along which we crept nervously, hoping we were not being watched. Piedersen had lent us lanterns, for we needed to see where we were putting our feet, but we kept them turned down as low as we could.

When the alley joined a wider one, Jenkinson conferred with Longman and then led us through a tangle of lanes, every now and then stopping to check for movement behind us. "I've a good head for mazes," he said, when Blanchard asked him anxiously if we were lost. "I know where we are and where we're going."

It was half an hour or more before we at last arrived at a tall, forbidding house, where Jenkinson brought out a key and led us up the steps. "We've got the whole place," he said quietly over his shoulder, "except for the landlady in the basement. Come on."

The front door led into a dark entrance hall that smelled of mildew. Jenkinson called, and a quavering voice answered. A bobbing light appeared at floor level, showing us a basement stair. The light turned into a candle, and an aged crone, wrapped in a mass of shawls, came up to greet us. She said something in her own tongue. Jenkinson replied, and then turned to us. "This is Klara van den Bergh and she hopes we will be comfortable with her."

We gazed around us. What little the candlelight showed us was discouraging. There was a moldering tapestry on one wall of the hall, stains of damp on the rest, and the two heavy doors that led off the hallway were both dragging on their hinges.

"We've got to stay here?" said Helene. She used English but her tone was unmistakable, and I saw Klara van den Bergh flinch. "All because of these people who are following Master Jenkinson? I would not wish to be rude, Master Jenkinson, but would it not be better if you parted company with us? We were well off at the inn, but this . . . !"

"Yes, indeed. What a place!" said Jeanne in distaste.

"It smells of the river," said Blanchard.

Mark Sweetapple said it was enough to put him off his food and no one laughed. Arnold and Harvey grunted in assent. Only Longman said staunchly that it wasn't as bad as all that. Our landlady shrank into her shawls and looked appealingly at us as though afraid we were all going to turn around and run away. I realized, with pity, that this house was her only asset; she was widowed, probably, and trying to earn a living by let-

QUEEN'S RANSOM   237

ting rooms, but had no money for servants or constant roaring fires and no strength for cleaning.

Jenkinson took control. "We're staying." He spoke to the landlady, and she indicated with a gesture that we should follow her, and she would show us around.

In fact, Longman was right. The hall was dreadful but the rooms were not so bad. They too had damp patches, but not serious ones, and the wall hangings and furniture that they contained had once been costly and were still in reasonable condition, though dusty. Upstairs, we were agreeably surprised to find small fires lit in the bedchamber hearths, and clean, dry bedding.

"She keeps it aired," Jenkinson said. "Longman went into all that. I told you the place wouldn't be anything special but it's not intolerable, either.

"And besides," he added to me as we began to sort out who was to sleep where, "it is beside a waterway that leads into the one alongside Hoekstraat and the kitchen door is also a river entrance. There's a jetty and a rowing boat for the use of tenants. What more could we want?"

CHAPTER 16

Net of Gold

I dreamed that night of Thamesbank, and Meg.

It was commonplace enough for parents to send their children to be trained in other households; even if Gerald had lived, I might have had to part from my daughter. I knew that she was safe with her foster parents, the Hendersons, and I had taught myself to accept our separation.

But I had always minded it, at Elizabeth's court as much as now. Every day, I wondered what she was doing and whether she was well. I knew now that whatever I had done in the course of my work, I was still her mother and she was still my child. I woke feeling restless and depressed. I wanted to collect that treasure, rescue Dale, and go home. The visit to Sir Thomas Gresham, however necessary, felt like an obstacle between both Dale's safety and my reunion with my daughter. Once I was with Meg again, then I could decide about Matthew . . .

Oh no. Not now. I couldn't—I mustn't—think about Matthew now. I pushed my coverlet off. The sooner to work, the sooner to rest. In her truckle bed, Jeanne was still curled up and fast asleep, and at my side, Helene, who was sharing my bed, was lying on her back and snoring. I roused them both. "Time to get up and get on with things," I said.

It was barely after dawn but there was already an appetizing smell in the house. Dressed in wrappers, we went downstairs to find that Jenkinson and Longman had got there first, discovered Klara in the kitchen cooking breakfast, and taken the job away from her. She was enthroned in a basket chair with her shawls tucked around her while Longman, already dressed for the day, unpacked the fresh loaf and the warm rolls he had just fetched from a nearby baker and set down the pail of clean water he had brought from a well.

Jenkinson, in the brown doublet and hose that he used when impersonating a retainer, was deftly wielding a long-handled pan while he fried chops and bacon at the fire, all the while talking flirtatiously over his shoulder to Klara, using her own language. He exuded charm as a rose breathes perfume, and Klara, who must have been seventy at least, was as pink and giggly as a girl.

I watched him with misgiving, liking him very much and wondering if I was right to do so. The other men came down to join us, and Jenkinson had us all fed and the dishes washed with astounding ease and speed. Then he said that he must get ready for his visit to Sir Thomas Gresham and at this point we discovered what had been in the sack-cum-satchel that he had carried on his back all the way from Paris.

He sent Longman to fetch it down and opened it there and then, in the kitchen. It contained one unutterably beautiful cherry-colored satin doublet embroidered with little silver stars; matching puffed breeches and a pair of plain cherry-colored hose; a pair of elegant tawny kidskin shoes with small heels and slender straps across the instep; a white linen shirt and ruff; a high-collared tawny velvet cloak that almost matched the shoes; and a tawny velvet cap.

And finally, while we gazed round-eyed, came a large plain linen square that might have been cut from a sheet, a flatiron, and a goffering iron.

The clothes were more than a little creased from their long journey in the sack. I said: "I'm sure Jeanne would . . ." but Jenkinson waved the notion of Jeanne away.

"I'm a traveling merchant and we learn to look after ourselves, the same as old campaigners do. Now, if somebody could clear the kitchen table for me while the iron gets hot on the fire . . . ?"

Before our eyes, he heated the iron, spread the cloak tenderly out on the table, damped the linen square, and laid it over the cloak and set about removing the creases. I looked at the pile of other garments awaiting attention, and at the ruff and the goffering iron, and wondered how and when the rest of us would be able to get our own clothes ready.

Luke Blanchard said that a pair of fresh hose and his traveling doublet, properly brushed, would do for him, but Helene and I both had things in need of pressing. Jeanne had a small iron with her, but the kitchen table was the only one in the house that could be used for such a purpose (the dining table was big, but it was also a good one, and Klara begged us not to take a hot iron near it).

In the end, we all became nearly frantic with impatience because Jenkinson was so meticulous and took so long. I think we would have set out for Gresham's in our wrinkles, like last year's apples, except that I had an inspiration. Fetching a blanket and sheet from my bed, I put them on the kitchen floor and since Jeanne's middle-aged knees found squatting difficult, Helene and I crouched down and did the work, taking turns and using a damp cloth supplied by Klara, while Jenkinson, unchivalrous for once, continued to hog the table.

The results were satisfactory, though. Helene and I had each brought one respectable dress. We had had to abandon our farthingales, but we did very well without. Helene had the white and silver damask she had worn when she was presented to Queen Catherine, with the same white pearl-edged cap on the back of her head, and her mouse-colored hair crimped in front of it, while I had mustard-colored satin, embroidered with red and blue flowers. Jeanne brushed my hair until it shone like a blackbird's plumage, packed it into a gold net, and added a very small mustard satin cap, which didn't hide too much of the rather expensive net. We each had earrings and a match-ing pendant (pearls for Helene; gold and turquoise for me), a small ruff, and a pair of carefully cleaned shoes.

We set out on foot: a cluster of fashionable visions (Blanchard's black velvet doublet was very well cut and once brushed, looked elegant), followed by Jeanne and all the men, who, if not visions, were at least clean, tidy, and workmanlike. Twenty minutes' walking brought us to the expensive quarter, where Gresham had his house, a magnificent place, with steps up to a majestic porch, and a tiled roof all tall narrow gables and ornate chim-neys. It stood beside the river Schelde, up which came ships from every corner of the world, bearing exotic fabrics, silk thread, and wool yarn ready to be turned into cloths and tapestries; sugar-cane from the Western Indies; furs and leather from the Nordic countries; spices and precious stones, iron and gold and silver from a score of sources. From his dining hall, Gresham could see the tall masts gliding past.

For me, it was like going back in time. So often, I had climbed these steps, passed through this porch, with Gerald. The black and white tiles of the entrance hall, the blaze of color from the wall hangings, were just as I recalled. So was the pervasive murmur of voices and the sound, somewhere, of music, and the aroma of splendid cooking.

Sir Thomas himself came to greet us, and I felt as though I had last seen him only yesterday. There he was, Gerald's employer, whom I liked, but also feared a little. He was so overwhelming. He possessed power, wealth, and influence in enormous quantities and if, when I first met him, I didn't fully understand that such things are always accompanied by ruthlessness, I soon learned it.

For the work he demanded from Gerald had littered Antwerp with people who had been forced, one way or another, to help Gresham steal from the city. A number had lost their livelihoods because of it, and most had lost their self-respect. Some could have paid even more dearly, with liberty or life. I didn't know for sure, but it was possible.

Clad dashingly in crimson slashed with yellow, Gresham was even tall enough to look down at my father-in-law over his long nose with the distinctive bump in the middle of it, but he greeted us with a friendliness in his shrewd light brown eyes and a smile in the midst of the ginger beard, which his barber had carefully trimmed and combed into points.

"Mistress Ursula Blanchard! This is such a surprise and such a pleasure. And Master Jenkinson. Now what brings you to Antwerp? I wonder. And this is . . . ?"

I presented Luke Blanchard and Helene to him, and watched him assessing them even as he welcomed them to his house. Then he swept us into a wide paneled room where there was already a crowd of people, drifting in and out through a farther door that led into a courtyard with a pond. A group of musicians were playing in a little gallery and servants went hither and thither with trays, while in various corners, well-dressed men, all velvet doublets and fur trimmings, were in seemingly casual huddles, doing business or exchanging information.

"Open house, open house. You know my custom," said Gresham blithely. Our escort had disappeared, magically absorbed by a household that was used to the arrival of guests with

army-sized escorts. There were whole suites set aside for the refreshment of retainers and personal maids. "You had no need to
send your man to make an appointment to see me, Jenkinson,
you should know that," Gresham was saying. "You should just
have come! My hospitality is yours at any time. And the same
goes for you, Mistress Blanchard. You will dine, of course."

"Of course," said Jenkinson. "But I made the appointment
to make sure of seeing you in person. If we had called on the
off chance, you might have been elsewhere. We have need of a
little advice from you."

"But by all means. How can I help you? Are you looking
for a loan?"

"No," said Jenkinson. "We want passages on ships—two lots
of them. Five to England and five on a ship going to Paris—
well, St. Germain. It's urgent . . ."

Taking our august host by the elbow as though he were a
mere brother-man, Jenkinson led him aside. I was left with
Helene and Blanchard, to find a seat, listen to the music, and
be offered drinks from a tray carried by a page. The drinks
were in tiny goblets and these, too, were familiar; not wine but
a northern liquor, transparent as water and lethal as a spiked
cudgel if you took too much. I murmured a quiet warning to
my companions.

Gresham and Jenkinson reappeared after a while, both smiling broadly. "The *Leopard* leaves for England in a few days'
time," said Jenkinson. "Her captain owes Sir Thomas a favor.
There is also a Captain Ericksen who can probably be induced
to sail round to the Seine and call at St. Germain, if suitably
rewarded."

His eyes met mine with a question. "Master Blanchard
and I have sufficient funds," I said. "Both for passages and
sweeteners." But the idea that had come to me in the parlor

of the Leaping Fish would need extra finance and we didn't have enough for that. I wanted to speak to Gresham alone. I opened my mouth to ask if he could spare me a few moments in private, but he spoke first.

"Mistress Blanchard," Gresham said, "I'm truly very glad to see you again. I have been stricken in my conscience about you. When your husband died, I did what I thought was best for you. I did not think you would want to go either to your own family or his, even if they invited you, and so I asked Sir William Cecil to see if he could find you a post at court. I was relieved when he was able to help, and pleased to hear that you were prospering. But I should have done more. I think I should have offered you a place in my own household, out of respect for Gerald's memory."

I shook my head. "You are kind. But there was no need. I am well placed at Elizabeth's court." I noticed that Blanchard, who was in conversation nearby, had ignored my warning and was gulping down the contents of another thimble-sized goblet.

Gresham saw it, too, and within his beard, his smile glinted. Then he horrified me by saying: "Will you grant me a few words in private? Concerning your deceased husband, there is something I have long wished to ask you."

I had wanted a private interview but it was alarming to find that he wanted one, too, for his own purposes. I murmured agreement and then followed him nervously to an adjoining study. This, too, had a view of the river and the reflections of its ripples played over oak paneling and a set of bookshelves that occupied one whole wall. He motioned me politely to a settle and I sat down, terrified in case the question he wanted to ask had something to do with treasure under the floorboards of a warehouse in Hoekstraat.

It had not. "I don't really wish to discuss Gerald," he said. "The subject may well be painful for you, even now. But he was a good excuse for speaking to you where no one else could hear. Mistress Blanchard, I gathered from Master Jenkinson's original message that you all left France in haste, because of the war. But now, it seems that you and Jenkinson for some reason wish urgently to return to St. Germain. He would not tell me why, but he did say that it concerned some private business of yours. I sensed anxiety in him and it has left me wondering. Are you in any kind of trouble? I should have helped you more when Gerald died. Can I help you now?"

I have never wanted to trust anyone as much as I wanted to trust Gresham then. I wanted nothing more than to unload my burden of worry onto shoulders so strong, resourceful, and wealthy. But although neither I nor Gerald had ever had anything from him but considerate treatment, I knew that in this case I dared not confide in him. He was first and foremost Queen Elizabeth's financier, and I knew what he had done in her service. He was generous in matters that did not cut across his business interests, but his business came first. In some ways, he was not unlike a Levantine Lion. He might well consider that twenty-five thousand pounds was too high a ransom for a tire-woman, especially when it had been earmarked for Elizabeth.

I remained silent, and he said: "Will you not tell me why you want to go back to Paris?"

I took a deep breath. "Sir Thomas, I am so sorry. It must seem discourteous of me not to answer you. I can only say that I have an honest and sufficient reason for wishing to return. I was intending to ask your help, and if you can give it, without pressing me for details, I would be so very grateful."

Gresham sat down behind his desk. "Is this something to do with an errand for Sir William Cecil?" he asked.

I jumped, and he laughed. "Cecil makes me privy to certain things. I know that you work for him. You can speak freely to me."

"I wish I could," I said. I thought frantically and found an excuse for discretion. "Some secrets are not one's own," I said. "I have promised silence on certain matters." It sounded quite convincing. "Will you forgive me, and hold me excused?"

Slowly, Gresham nodded. "Well, I trust you," he said. "You would not be in partnership with Anthony Jenkinson if you were not to be trusted. . . . What is it? Your face has lit up."

"Today I meant to ask you for your assurance that *Jenkinson* is to be trusted," I said. "He has offered to help with . . . with the handling of the affair I am engaged on. He learned of it by chance—the fact that he knows of it doesn't release me from my promise of secrecy. I have been very worried. I want to be certain . . ."

"You need have no fear of Jenkinson. He is a man of integrity."

A vast relief surged through me. I had not known until then just how lonely and overburdened I had felt. I missed Brockley so much. At least, now, I could turn freely to Jenkinson. "There is no difficulty about paying the passages to England and St. Germain," I said, "but I do have need of some other ready money." I was wearing, as usual, an open-fronted skirt, with the usual hidden pocket. From this I now took a couple of trinkets that I had dropped into it while dressing, on top of my purse and the lock picks and my dagger. They were my most expensive rope of pearls, and a brooch with a ruby in it. "If I offer these as surety," I said, "could I possibly borrow five hundred pounds?"

Having finished with Sir Thomas, I then needed another private discussion, this time with Jenkinson. "I must talk to you," I said to him quietly when I rejoined him. I looked about me. Blanchard was now sitting in a corner, very flushed over the cheekbones and nodding as if about to fall asleep. Helene was listening to the music. A part-song was in progress, performed by a bass, a tenor, and a boy soprano. "But we need to talk alone," I said.

"The tenor sings flat," said Jenkinson with aplomb, and loudly enough to be heard by anyone nearby who might be listening. "Will you take my arm, mistress, for a stroll into the courtyard? The sun is out and there are some pleasant seats out there."

We sat down on a bench beside a lily pond and I told him my idea. "I've borrowed enough money," I said, showing him the purse that Gresham had given me. Gresham had accepted my surety, with loan, interest, and collateral recorded in a ledger and no chivalrous protestations about not taking collateral from a lady. As I said, he was a businessman. "All going well," I explained to Jenkinson, "I will recoup with the help of what's under those floorboards. I hope so."

Jenkinson had been listening to me with interest and dawning enthusiasm. "Is this a trap or merely a safeguard?" he inquired.

"A safeguard," I said. "We can hardly take prisoners. The deception will soon be discovered but that won't matter if it seems that we are the ones who were deceived."

"You may well be right. You intrigue me, Mistress Blanchard. You are not quite like the average lady of my acquaintance. My wife, who is very dear to me and a woman of some learning, too, would still never think in the convoluted way that you do. We will try this. We must take care, though, that . . ."

We sat on by the pond for another half hour, discussing details, until a trumpet sounded, calling us to dinner.

Jenkinson had to give my father-in-law a shoulder to

steady him as we went in to dine. We sat one on either side of Blanchard during the meal, nudging him every now and then to encourage him to stay awake and eat. But there was wine with the meal and before the end of it, he had fallen into a deep sleep, and we had to lift his nose out of his platter.

On the way home, the men literally carried him, and once in our lodgings, Harvey put him to bed. He slept until the following morning when he woke with a shocking headache.

That meant that when Jenkinson and I took the house rowing boat and set out on an exploratory trip to the canal alongside Hoekstraat, Blanchard couldn't come with us. Since he regarded the expedition to collect the treasure as my business and not his, I'm not sure if he would have done so anyway, but I was glad that there was now no question of it, because it enabled me to avoid Helene's never very exhilarating company as well.

"I know Harvey will look after your guardian," I said solemnly, "but it would be a pretty attention if you stayed with him, too. You could make him a posset later on."

"But I'd like to come!"

"Remember," Jenkinson told her, "that I have dangerous men on my trail. Mistress Blanchard is obliged to take part. But you can stay safely at home, and still be useful."

"I wish I were at home," Helene said miserably. "St. Marc's Abbey is home to me. I think of it all the time. I may never see it again. Very well. I will stay and make possets and pray for your success."

"I truly pity Helene sometimes," I said as Jenkinson and I set off. "I knew her prospective husband when I was a child; he's my cousin, as it happens. I didn't like him."

"Helene and you," said Jenkinson, "are two quite different people."

CHAPTER 17

Laying the Bait

As Jenkinson rowed us along, I felt increasingly anxious. What if after such a lapse of time I couldn't identify the place? I had only seen it once, when Gerald showed it to me after he first rented it. He had shown me the hiding place under the floorboards, and I had watched him mark them, so that he could easily retrieve anything concealed there. I thought I could remember where on the floor to look for the mark. But suppose there had been changes since then?

I hadn't seen the treasure hidden, although I knew that it had definitely been hidden; Gerald had told me so. But he was already feeling unwell that evening, and he hadn't gone into details. Alarming possibilities now haunted me. Suppose the building was in use with huge heavy crates right over the floorboards we wanted? Or suppose the space under the floor hadn't been big enough for those hefty salts?

I knew that, at first, Gerald had considered just packing the things into crates and leaving them on the floor surrounded by other crates, empty or with unimportant contents. He had finally decided that this wouldn't be safe enough, especially if they had to stay there for some time. But what if he had been forced to leave them out on the floor because they wouldn't fit under it? In two years, anything could have happened to them. Even if no one else had taken the place over, unvisited warehouses attract attention sooner or later. The treasure could have been stolen long since.

Oh, God, I said fervently, if silently. Let me know the building when I see it, and let the treasure be there. Please!

In other circumstances, I would have enjoyed the water journey, if nostalgically. The April sun was flashing on the water, and busy, lively Antwerp was just as I remembered. Vessels were on the waterways, bringing cargoes to and from warehouses; moving in and out of repair docks: stout, tublike Netherlands traders; merchantmen from half a dozen countries; and hordes of small craft, the private transport and the ferryboats that carried people about the waterways and across the river. A glimpse of the river itself revealed a stately galleon with towering masts being rowed upstream.

All the smells and sounds were familiar: the tang of water; the calls of the gulls that had followed the ships inland in search of scraps; the scents of leather and spices from the warehouses; the splash of ripples breaking on the banks as moving vessels sent their wakes outward; the shouts of the men winching the cranes that heaved goods on and off the decks and wharves. Once I smelled strong cheese, which reminded me of the *Chaffinch*.

But I was here on business. Longman had chosen our lodgings well and we were soon into the waterway that, according to the map, ran beside Hoekstraat. I scanned the scene intently. Quays and landing stages, some with moored craft alongside; warehouses, mostly adjoining but with occasional alleyways between. The buildings were generally three or four stories high, with rows of tall, narrow windows. They were dreadfully alike. I was noting this with increasing unease, just as Jenkinson observed cheerfully that all we had to do now was find the right building, because it wouldn't do to burgle the wrong one. I stared at him without answering, and he read my face.

"It's all right. Give yourself a fair chance. Think back. Can you recall any landmarks or identifying features?"

"No. I've been trying! We're going the right way," I said, trying to steady myself. "We aren't there yet. It's on the right-hand bank. But . . ."

"You said it had a landing stage. Wood or stone?"

"Wooden," I said. "And—yes—there were double doors painted blue—though that could have changed, I suppose." I thought again and to my relief, some more details surfaced. "Just beyond the warehouse we want," I said, "was a bigger one, with a stone jetty and steps, very weedy. Green with weed and slippery. When Gerald brought me, a ship was unloading there and a man slipped on the steps and fell in, along with the box he was balancing on his head. There was another man at the top of the steps, cursing enough to make the heavens fall, and shouting at the sailors on the ship to get the box out before it sank . . . and they weren't to mind the fool who fell in; if he couldn't swim, let him drown. He actually shouted those words. I'll always remember that."

"And did he drown?" inquired Jenkinson with interest.

"No," I said. "He scrambled out onto the steps, cursing even louder than the other fellow."

Jenkinson laughed. "We should be able to find it! In fact— are those the blue doors, just ahead? Is that the place?"

"Yes. Yes! I can see the wooden stage and there's the stone jetty just beyond!"

Excited, I half rose and Jenkinson yelped at me to sit down again before I capsized us. "We'll go on a little farther and take a good look. Just keep calm."

Slowly, we slid level with the blue doors. I recognized the

faded blue paint at once, and the yellowish stone of the walls. The ground-floor windows were barred and the doors looked as though they were still securely shut.

But gaining entrance was not a difficulty. "We could go in at once," I said. "I have a key. I have the right. My husband paid the rent for five years in advance."

"We've no tools for lifting floorboards and no sacks for putting the treasure in. We might get in without causing comment but imagine coming out in broad daylight with gold and silver plate all flashing in the sun! It is mostly plate, isn't it?"

I had given the full description only to Queen Catherine. Now, I said: "There are salts as well, two very fine ones. I keep thinking that someone else may be using the place and perhaps they've put racks or piles of boxes all over the floorboards we want."

"We will come back tonight," said Jenkinson soothingly. "We will come under cover of darkness, with tools, and plenty of time to move or dismantle anything that's in our way, and put it all back afterward. And since we have to do all that, and the treasure may well be heavy, we may need extra hands and even an extra boat. We'll bring Longman and young Sweetapple. Even Blanchard could lend a hand if he's willing."

At the lodging, we found Blanchard out of bed and eating. He was interested to learn that we had found the warehouse but declined to join us that night, or to allow any of his men to do so.

"It's not my enterprise," he said candidly. "Helene and I are leaving for England as soon as possible, and I don't wish to get arrested for robbing a warehouse, or to allow any of my men to get arrested either. I am sending Sweetapple and Arnold back to France with you out of care for your safety, Ursula, but that's as far as I'll go. Our passages have been confirmed, by the way, both to England and to St. Germain. A message came from Sir Thomas Gresham while you were out. This is Thursday. The *Leopard,* under Captain Drayton, sails for England on Monday; Captain Ericksen and the *Britta* sail for France the day after that. Both captains advise us to be aboard the previous night."

It was only what I expected from my father-in-law. I shrugged and said nothing. Jenkinson, however, merely said that the news about our passages was excellent and then asked what everyone's plans were for the afternoon. "I have things to buy, including tools for getting floorboards up, and some food." Klara's larder was well provided with shelves but there wasn't very much on them. "Will you come and help me, Mistress Blanchard?"

"If you wish," I said smoothly. "Do you want to come, Helene? We could buy you some wedding clothes. You and I could do that while Master Jenkinson buys the other things."

"I'm tired. I'd rather rest," Helene said.

"You tire too quickly for a girl of your age," said Blanchard disapprovingly.

"Well, you and I will go together, Mistress Blanchard," Jenkinson said. "There's a lot to do. As I said on the way back this morning, I think we should hire a second boat, a bigger one, in case the treasure is very heavy. Longman could do that, and row it back here, ready for tonight."

I was tired myself by the end of the afternoon, for the shopping expedition was intensive, and it was a good thing that Helene and her trousseau hadn't formed part of it. Jenkinson needed my help. Longman, who I now realized had quite a good command of the local language, went to find a boat, while Jenkinson and I set about spending Gresham's five hundred pounds as wisely as we could.

"If this evening's effort fails," Jenkinson said, as we returned home, heavy-laden, "I'll dispose of some of the costly little gewgaws in my baggage, and buy some of these items off you, Mistress Blanchard. Then you can redeem your jewelry from Gresham. I daresay I'll turn a profit on these goods once I get them to England."

He was a businessman, too.

We had not neglected the matter of food. In the lodging once more, I helped Jenkinson to fill Klara's larder shelves, while Klara watched us, her watery eyes full with gratitude, as she realized that when we sailed away, quantities of cheese, dried fruit, dried fish, rice, and bacon would be left for her, plus a good supply of wine. She even managed to thank us in English, of which it seemed she had a few words. Longman had obtained a suitable second boat, and everything that we would need was piled into it. All was ready and we had only to wait for nightfall.

Until then, I could rest. But the time dragged, and also, it was disturbed. Helene was nowhere to be seen when we returned and Sweetapple told us that she had gone out after all, with Jeanne, to the cathedral, to pray for us "in what she calls the right atmosphere," he said. She woke me up on her return, just as I had fallen into a doze. After that, I got up. The evening found me in such a state of nervous tension that my teeth kept wanting to chatter.

"You need not come, any more than Helene," Jenkinson said quietly, as he entered Klara's somewhat gloomy parlor, where I was sitting with my book of poems in my hands. "There may be danger. If there is an attempt to seize the treasure, it could be made here but it's more likely to come, I think, on the canal, which is full of very cold water and where there is nowhere to take shelter. Longman and I can take your key and fetch the treasure if you can tell us exactly where to search for it."

I shook my head. "I can't. Gerald left a mark but it was very tiny and I need to be there myself to find it. It won't be easy to see by lantern light. Besides, it's my responsibility."

"No one in the world would blame you, a young woman, for sending men on your behalf."

"You might still have trouble finding the right part of the floor. No," I said. "I have to come."

"And I might take off into the blue with the booty and use it to trade with the Shah of Persia," said Jenkinson, nodding wisely. "I quite understand."

"Of course I don't think that! Sir Thomas assured me—"

"So you took up my references? Quite right," said Jenkinson bluntly. "You'd have been a fool not to. Gresham spoke the truth," he said candidly. "I'm trustworthy, as it happens, but where gold is concerned, it's wise to trust as few people as possible."

"It has nothing to do with not trusting you, but I must come. You need me, and anyway, if I don't come, I shall go frantic with worry, waiting for you to return."

"Very well. I will say no more. We shall take all the care that we can. You may as well go and get dressed. But do make sure," added Master Jenkinson, "that you put your breeches on the right way round. I mention it, because you seem to be trying to study the works of Thomas Wyatt and Henry Howard upside down."

I laughed shakily, and realized that it was true. For half an hour, I had been staring at a page of print without even noticing that I couldn't read it. I had been too busy thinking.

We had decided that I would be more comfortable in men's

clothes and our shopping had also included a shirt, a pair of dark brown breeches, and a matching doublet, in sizes to fit me. Dale, who always rode astride, wore breeches when traveling as a matter of course and more than once, during my adventures on behalf of Sir William Cecil, I had thought that they would serve me better than skirts. I had never tried them before, however. I was surprised at the sense of freedom they gave me. Movement was suddenly easy. Dressed like this, I could climb a fence or swarm up a tree, leap up and down steps or in and out of boats with no fear of catching a heel in a hem. I had already stitched a pocket quickly into the doublet and transferred the contents of my hidden skirt pocket to it. My key ring was among them.

We set out at last. Klara had gone to bed, but the others all gathered at the river entrance to wish us luck. "Have we got everything?" I asked, finding myself inclined to whisper. "Cloaks? Lanterns? Bag of tools?"

"It's all aboard, mistress," Longman assured me. "Master Jenkinson doesn't forget things," he added reprovingly.

"There's another testimonial for you," said Jenkinson gallantly, and handed me into my boat.

It was a cool night. There was light from a waxing moon and from flambeaux mounted on poles, though the buildings on the bank cast deep shadows. There were a number of dwellings on the banks of this particular stream. Now and then, we saw candlelit windows and sometimes music and laughter drifted out across the water. A number of small boats were about. Our two boats blended into this world. Rowing along, Jenkinson and myself ahead and Longman following, we were neither hindered nor remarkable.

I wondered if the warehouse doors would still look blue after dark, but as we drew near, I saw that one of the flambeaux

on poles was just beside our destination and the flame, streaming in a light breeze, showed the blue paint clearly. "There it
is," I said.

Jenkinson peered back over his shoulder. "There's a craft
coming toward us. When it's gone past, the oarsmen will be
facing our way. We'd better get into the shadow on the opposite side and wait until it's out of sight."

My stomach was churning with impatience and fright. It
was anguish to be so near, yet still have to linger. The other
boat was crammed with people who must have been to a party.
They were singing. They broke off to call raucous good nights
to us as they went by and we shouted cordial good nights back.
Then Jenkinson steered us into a patch of deep darkness opposite the warehouse. Longman, glancing back for guidance,
followed. We found a landing stage, and looped both painters
around a bollard while we waited for the partygoers to recede
far enough for safety.

They seemed to take forever, and of course, as soon as they
had gone, two more craft appeared, going the other way. As
they passed through the pool of light under the flambeau, I
read the name of one of them, *Anna,* painted on its side. We
had to wait for what seemed like a further century, until they,
too, were out of sight.

After that, we still didn't move. "What are we waiting for?"
I whispered.

"The watch," said Jenkinson. "I can see his lantern coming
along the walkway. The authorities keep an eye on the warehouses after dark. He'll have dogs."

Another century or two went past before the man with the
lantern and the two leashed mastiffs had paced steadily along
the walkway from the farther end and gone past us. "He'll go
the length of the walkway, and then come back by way of the

street on the other side of the warehouses," Jenkinson said. "Let him get a little farther." Again, we waited. The lantern receded. "Now!" said Jenkinson, unlooping our painter.

We pulled out into the stream. Longman came after us with the second boat. We crossed the waterway and bumped gently into the wooden landing stage attached to the warehouse we wanted. "Best move round to the side of the stage away from the light," Jenkinson said softly, and hauled us hand over hand into the shadow that lay between our wooden platform and the stone jetty of the next-door warehouse, only a few feet away.

With both boats safely moored in the gap and virtually invisible to any passing craft, we climbed out onto the stage. "The key," whispered Jenkinson.

I brought out the key ring. I could scarcely see it, but the key of the warehouse was a massive iron object with decorative wards, and bigger than any of the other keys on my ring. I found it by feel. Advancing on the warehouse door brought me into the light again. I made doubly sure that the key was the right one, and then pushed it into the lock.

The gleam of fresh new metal around the keyhole should have warned me. The key refused to turn.

Somebody had changed the lock.

I let out a sigh. I had kept the secret of my unlikely profession so long and so carefully, but now I could keep it no longer. While Jenkinson was saying: "We'll either have to break the lock or get the door off its hinges and either way, I'm afraid it'll make a noise," I was fishing again in my pocket and bringing out the lock picks that had traveled all the way from England with me and had come on this expedition in my doublet's pocket.

"Just a moment," I said, and slid the wires into the keyhole.

It was a long time since I had had occasion to use this particular skill, but it came back to me at once. Closing my eyes, I tried to see with my fingers, as I had been taught to do by the unkempt locksmith, gambler, and probably petty criminal who had been hired by Cecil to instruct me. I moved, pressed, jiggled, pressed again, and felt the lock yield. I slid a second wire in and then came a satisfying click and the door was open.

"There we are," I said.

Jenkinson said: "I can't believe what I've just seen. Mistress Blanchard, who or what are you? Where did you learn how to . . . ?"

"This is not the time to discuss my life history," I said. "I was hard up and hard put to it to support life at court and also support my little daughter. Sir William Cecil offered to employ me to—make inquiries for him. I accepted. Gresham knows. He will vouch for me, just as he vouched for you."

"Sir William Cecil . . . ?"

"Yes! Look, we can't stand here on the landing stage all night, or until someone sees us and warns the watch. Come on!"

"Lead the way, Mistress Blanchard! Longman, stay and guard the boats. Dear God. I never thought to see such a thing in my whole life! Do you carry lock picks with you all the time—a respectable young woman like you?"

"Yes. And a dagger as well. Brockley lives in a constant state of scandalized amazement." I pushed the door open. Beyond it was impenetrable darkness. Professional agent or not, I found it frightening. I was glad that Jenkinson was with me. "My work enables me to pay Brockley's wages," I said airily, forcing myself to a pretense of sangfroid, "but he doesn't approve of the way I earn my living, not in the least. Where are the things we need? The lanterns, the tool bag, and the rest?"

"Pass them up, Longman. But be careful. Keep in the shadows."

Stealthily, Longman handed up what we required. One of the lanterns had been lit before we started and carried in the bottom of Longman's boat. Arming himself with this, Jenkinson moved boldly ahead of me into that terrifying blackness. Nervously, I followed him, closing the door after us. There were bolts on the inside. I shot them before we set about lighting the rest of the lanterns from the candle in the first.

The light was a relief, driving back the shadows. It showed us that the ground level of the warehouse was big and open, supported by a few timber pillars, with stone walls all around. There was a door on the opposite side. "That gives on the street," I whispered.

Jenkinson crossed to look at it. Here, too, there were heavy bolts on the inside, and these had been shot home. "All secure," he said, coming back to me. "We've been lucky. The last person to leave here must have gone out through the landing-stage door. We'd have been in trouble if whoever it was had used the street door and bolted the one we've just come in by. All the lock picks on earth wouldn't have got us through it then. Ah. The place *is* in use, but there isn't much here, all the same, which is fortunate."

He was right. There were racks of shelving along one wall, and some of the shelves held bales of cloth. But not many, and there were no racks or bales out on the floor.

The owner must have rented the place out again when he learned that Gerald was dead, but whoever had taken it on was either doing poor business, or going through a lull between consignments.

"We've been very lucky indeed," I said, shaken by new and awful possibilities. "If those shelves were full of eastern brocades or unpolished diamonds, we might have had a welcome from a private army of watchmen, with a whole pack of guard dogs!"

"Where now?" Jenkinson asked.

"Here," I said. "It's on this level, under these very floorboards. I need to find Gerald's mark."

Jenkinson used his lantern to scan the floor. "What sort of mark was it?"

I managed a tremulous jest. "Well, he didn't chalk *Here Be Treasure* on the floor! It was very small, and not quite in the middle of the room. Let me look."

Taking a lantern, I moved to and fro, stooping. I had watched Gerald make the mark, and he had told me what he was doing. "I'm drawing a triangle with the tip of a knife. A very small one, only an inch across. It won't cause any comment if anyone notices it. Boards in timber yards get marked for all sorts of reasons—to identify the buyer, if he's leaving the wood there to season, or even to set a trap if there's been pilfering and someone is suspected. If the board is stolen, the suspect's premises will be searched and a marked board can be recognized."

But what if the mark was gone? What if some of the boards had gone rotten and been replaced? What if . . . ?

No. None of the floorboards were new and all the nailheads were brown with rust. Holding up the lantern, I saw that I had moved too far toward the rear wall. I came forward again, bumped into a timber support, and remembered that wherever the hiding place was, it hadn't been close to a support. I moved away, lowering the lantern again to scan the floor. Then I saw it. It was dark now with ground-in dust; it had been easier to see when it was new. But it was there; a triangle, an inch across.

"Got it," I said.

Jenkinson came over and squatted down. Opening the tool bag, he attacked the nails of the marked board, digging at the wood around the nailheads with a sharp awl, and then wrenching the nails out with a clawhead hammer, shuffling along the length of the board in order to deal with them all. Then he produced chisels, and kneeling beside him, I helped him lever the board up. As we laid it aside, we paused. We could hear the ring of nailed boots approaching along the street. The watch was on his way back, along the street side of the warehouses. We lowered our lanterns out of sight into the cavity, in case a gleam of light should show through any crevice, and waited, motionless, until the footsteps had gone past.

Then we looked into the cavity to see what our lanterns had to show us.

I had been right to think that it was too shallow for such bulky items as two-foot-high salts, but Gerald hadn't let that worry him. Beneath the floorboards were joists, and below the joists was an older floor of cobbles. It must have been hard work, but Gerald and his servant, John Wilton, had dug some of the cobbles up to make a square hole with sufficient depth, and into this, several bulging sacks had been stuffed. To get at them, we had to shift two more floorboards. Then we hauled out the first sack. It was very heavy. Jenkinson cut the cord that tied its neck and we pulled out a linen-swathed object that we carefully unwrapped. A gold dish, elegantly chased around the rim and with a crested bird engraved in the middle, lay gleaming warmly in the lantern light.

Jenkinson yanked out a second sack. This proved to contain what Gerald's inventory had described as sundry small costly ornaments, total value approximately seven hundred pounds. I whispered this information to Jenkinson and we examined them together, concluding that they had been undervalued and were probably worth nearer to a thousand pounds than seven hundred. I had seen them before, once, but I had never handled them and had not remembered what they were like. They were in linen bags, some of which contained sets of pieces, all wrapped individually to keep them from abrading one another. The sets included several little gold figurines of pilgrims, and a lady's toilet set of silver, crystal, and white jade, complete with silver manicure tools and three tortoiseshell combs.

Other bags held a pretty gold box with an enameled pattern on the lid, a ruby pendant on a gold chain, a silver cup, small but exquisitely chased, and last of all, a chess set, the board made of polished woods, the chessmen of ivory, so intricately carved that when I picked one up to examine it closely, I gasped.

"They're so delicate!" I touched the chessmen gently, half afraid of damaging them.

"Come on," Jenkinson muttered, urging me on as earlier I had been urging him. "The watch will come back along the walkway eventually. Besides, Longman's guarding the boats on his own."

From the direction of the bolted street door, there came a very faint sound. It just might have been someone stealthily testing the door. Crouched beside our lanterns, we froze, heads up like startled deer. From the other direction, from the waterway, came a splash of oars. "That's just another rowing boat," whispered Jenkinson. "But I think we should hurry."

We hurried, dragging out the last two sacks. Undoing the first of them, I saw the miniature turrets of the golden salt in the shape of a castle tower. I removed another fold of sacking and revealed the crested bird set in rubies. Jenkinson whistled softly, impressed. A swift look into the last sack showed us the scallop shell lid of the silver salt, slightly tarnished.

"I think it's all here," I said. "Oh, how I wish we could just, simply—"

"We'll keep to our plan," said Jenkinson. "It may be a needless precaution, but we should make certain. It isn't far to the lodging, Ursula. We shall be back here and away again before daylight."

"If only we knew for sure if there was going to be an attempt. And how and when!"

"If we knew all that, taking precautions would be easy," Jenkinson pointed out. "As it is, we can only guess and hope for the best. Come on, now. Which of the small items shall we risk losing?"

I made myself be businesslike. "We'll hazard the toilet set and two of the figurines." I set them aside, and began to put the other items back inside their sacks. Then I noticed that Jenkinson was watching me in a curious, covert fashion. "What's the matter, Master Jenkinson? What's wrong?"

"Is it true—that you work for Cecil as . . . an agent?"

"Yes." I folded sacking tenderly around a golden turret. "But please, please treat it as a secret."

"That goes without saying. But—it's not right. Not for someone like yourself." Jenkinson was much in earnest. "You're beautiful, you know." He paused, sitting back on his heels and looking at me with frank appreciation. "Not in a voluptuous way like a tavern wench but . . . I have heard it said," said Jenkinson, "that Queen Elizabeth has a spirit full of incantation. I had an audience with her once, and I know what was meant. I think there is incantation in you, too. Midnight hair and eyes that shift from green to dark and back again; there's something magical about you."

"I have no magic," I said. "I do what I do to support myself and my child. That's all."

"But how many other young women in your position would do what you do? You're so unexpected. You're like a small, neat black cat, all softness and purrs one moment; but the next, it's steel springs under the fur, needle claws, and glittering eyes. I was there when you hurled that pail of water over your henchman at Le Cheval d'Or, remember! And now you produce a set of lock picks! In a way, they add to your enchantment, but it is a dark enchantment. My very dear Ursula—for you have become dear to me, even though I am a married man and I have a wife I care for deeply, and have been parted from, perhaps, too long—my sweet Ursula, claws are natural to a cat, but are lock picks and fights in inn yards natural to you? So far they haven't dimmed your beauty but one day they might. Do you realize that?"

"Yes," I said bleakly. I thought again of the man to whom I had given yew poison. But for that, Brockley would never have thought of bringing yew poison with us to France; and if he hadn't, then Dale would not have been arrested and I would not now be crouching in an Antwerp warehouse, wrapping up treasure and shivering with dread. "I think," I said, "that it has already dimmed my soul."

"Then change your way of life," said Jenkinson. "You have a husband. Go to him. Or if you can't do that, if you can't live with him, then find a way to release yourself and take another husband. I am a man of the world, Mistress Blanchard—or De la Roche. My advice is worth having."

"Brockley has said much the same things."

"Brockley is no fool. He is probably," said Jenkinson unexpectedly, "the type of man you should be married to."

"Oh, really!"

"I know, he's your manservant. But men of his stamp are to be found in other stations of life. I'll say no more. For the moment, we've got to get out of here. Let's set about it."

Rapidly, we finished our preparations and then went out to the landing stage, each of us carrying a sack. "Longman?" Jenkinson kept his voice low, but clear. "We've got it. Be ready to . . ."

He stopped short. Longman was sitting in the boat. He was sitting very still indeed. This was because, on the stone jetty of the adjacent warehouse, only ten feet or so away, stood two men with crossbows, the bolts trained steadily on his heart.

We could see all this quite easily, because the crossbowmen were not alone. Beside them, holding up a blazing flambeau, stood a bulky and authoritative figure. The light threw all the planes of his fleshy face into relief. Dr. Ignatius Wilkins. Of course.

"Ah. Mistress de la Roche and Master Jenkinson." Wilkins's thick voice greeted us as sociably as though we had met at a reception. "Yes, I thought you would use the water entrance, though I do have a man watching the street door. Let me present my companions. They are retainers of the Abbey of St. Marc, graciously lent to me by the abbess to assist the cause of the true faith. They will be joining the Catholic army as soon as this little assignment is over."

The flambeau gave us a good view of the crossbowmen's faces. I recognized them at once. So did Jenkinson. "Ah. The abbey riffraff we met at St. Marc's. They looted the homes of some murdered citizens, Dr. Wilkins. Did you know?"

"The fate of heretics, or their goods, is no concern of mine," said Wilkins. "I have no complaint of my retainers."

I recalled that the abbess of St. Marc's had said she intended to get rid of her deadwood. Wilkins, presumably, had given her the opportunity and she had taken it.

I was too afraid to speak, but Jenkinson, still cool, said: "What is all this about? What do you want with us?"

"The treasure you have come to collect, of course," said Wilkins. "I have no intention of allowing that wicked woman, Frances Dale, to be ransomed. The treasure will go straight to the Catholic cause, and the woman Dale will burn. I have just heard you announce that you've found it—and those bags you have there are part of it, presumably. Thank you for retrieving it for me."

His voice was thickly pleased. We said nothing. Wilkins ordered Longman to get up to the landing stage and join us, and then spoke to one of the crossbowmen, who handed his weapon to Wilkins and then, unexpectedly, whistled a little tune. This must have been a signal, for a third man appeared from an alley between the two warehouses.

"He's the fellow who was keeping watch in the street," Jenkinson said in my ear. "We heard him trying the street door."

"Attend to me!" Wilkins's voice was pitched low but it was menacing. "Put those sacks down and step back from them. Then stand still, all three of you. The crossbows are now trained on you, Mistress de la Roche, but I hope we won't have to shoot you. Even though you are disporting yourself in men's clothes, which is deplorable. I suppose it is what one might expect of such a one as yourself."

We did as he bade us, and then stood there, facing the crossbows. Jenkinson spoke for the first time. "Don't concern yourself, Dr. Wilkins. We shall give you no trouble. Frankly, the treasure's not all that we hoped for."

"Indeed?" said Wilkins. He sounded faintly disconcerted. There was a question in his voice, which we didn't choose to answer. "Well," he said grimly, "we shall see."

The man who had whistled and the man he had summoned came around by the bank to our landing stage, collected our sacks, and loaded them into one of our boats. Then they went into the warehouse and emerged with the remaining sacks. They leered triumphantly at us as they passed us. "There's a nice gold figurine at the top of this bag here!" one of them called to Wilkins. "The treasure's not so poor as all that!"

"I thought it might not be," Wilkins said. "Well, get on with it. We've no time to waste."

"I'd like to kill that man Wilkins," I muttered. "I'd like to see him lying dead at my feet, in a pool of blood."

"Don't be so vindictive," said Jenkinson. "They'd better hurry. They certainly don't have time to waste. The watchman will be back very soon."

They did hurry. In a very few minutes, the last sack had been loaded. Then, while we watched in silent outrage, Wilkins's men took both our boats and rowed them out to the middle of the canal, while Wilkins and the crossbowman beside him, taking turns to cover us, went down into a boat that was moored by their own landing stage. As Wilkins passed his flambeau to the other man, it lit up the name of their craft. The *Anna*.

"When we return to France," I said in a choked voice, directing my words across the few yards of water between the two jetties, "I shall report this to Queen Catherine."

"I shall do so myself," said Wilkins. "I shall donate the treasure to the Catholic cause, without strings. I doubt if Queen Catherine will raise any objection. It is a cause dear to her heart, whereas the death of a heretic servant is of no great moment to her. I do not fear you, which is why I am happy to let you live—to see the fate of Frances Dale—or perhaps I should call her Mistress Brockley. You will have to walk home, I fear." He pointed back along the walkway. In the distance, we could see a bobbing light. "The watchman is coming back. He has taken his time. But I believe he sometimes stops at a house in Hoekstraat for a tankard of mulled ale. There's a lady who makes him welcome, even in the middle of the night. Since Eve tempted Adam, woman has been a temptation and a peril unto men. I do not pity you, or your servant. Good night to you all."

The three of us watched him go, part of a small fleet that included our two boats. We would have to compensate Klara now, and the yard that had hired us the second craft.

"Well, well. He'll look so sweet with those tortoiseshell combs in his tonsure," said Jenkinson cheerfully. He added: "There are plenty of small craft moored along the waterside. When the watch has gone past again, I'll see if we can borrow a couple. But for the moment, we had better get out of sight. Come on. Back into the warehouse."

He led us in. For the second time that night, we waited silently in the dark, shielding our lanterns with our bodies. I think one of the dogs scented us, for as the watchman's footsteps reached our landing stage, we heard a low growl, and there was a snuffling and scrabbling at the door. But we had once more bolted it on the inside. The watchman tried it, found it secure, and hauled the dog away. We heard him accusing it of trying to run riot after rats.

When we were sure that the watch was sufficiently far away, we crept out to search for vulnerable boats. We found what we wanted quite quickly, and rowed them softly back to the warehouse.

"Well, they took the bait. I'm glad the attack came at once. It would have been unpleasant, waiting for it and wondering. Let's make haste," Jenkinson said.

I yawned, suddenly conscious that I was very tired. He shook his head at me.

"Brace up, Mistress Blanchard. You can't go to sleep yet. The night's not over!"

CHAPTER 18

Dawn Catch

It was nearly dawn when we reached the lodging again. When we dragged our burdens in at the back door, we found the kitchen full of candlelight, and the entire household, except for Klara, waiting anxiously for us and more or less fully dressed, although Helene and Jeanne were in slippers and shawls.

Everyone gathered around us, exclaiming, as we piled the sacks on the table. Even the distant William Harvey looked quite thrilled, while Clarkson and Arnold actually jostled each other in their eagerness to look. At Jenkinson's request, Sweetapple helped me bring in a second load, while Jenkinson and Longman slipped back to the boats, untied them, and pushed off. Blanchard felt the hard and knobbly outlines of one of the sacks, picked it up, raised his eyebrows at the weight, and would have peered inside, except that I put my hand out and stopped him. He looked at me in surprise. "What's the matter? And where, may I ask, have Jenkinson and his man gone to?"

"They'll soon be back," I said grimly. I wasn't looking forward to what lay ahead. But Jenkinson and I had talked as we rowed back and arrived at a decision. It was not pleasant but it was necessary. "It's best that the treasure remains in its sacks until we're all here."

Helene exclaimed with disappointment, which was echoed by murmurs from the others. My father-in-law said crossly:

"But why? You were the one who brought us all to Antwerp to fetch it. You want it to ransom Dale. Why must Jenkinson be here before we can inspect it? And where is he?"

"He and Longman are returning a couple of borrowed boats," I said. "Our own boats met with—an accident, shall we say?"

Horrified exclamations broke out. "But, mistress, were you hurt? Was anyone?" Mark Sweetapple sounded appalled.

"Mistress Blanchard isn't wet. She's not been in the river." Harvey sounded almost regretful. Unlike the others, he had never mellowed toward me.

"No," I agreed, "I didn't have to swim for my life. It wasn't that sort of accident."

"Then what kind was it?" My father-in-law, if anything, was indignant. "What is all this? Why so mysterious, Ursula? I don't like mysteries."

The memory of his imitation illness at the inn rose up in my mind and before I could stop myself, I had said acidly: "No. Neither do I." He heard the edge in my voice and stared at me in surprise. I think he was going to ask what I meant by it but Helene broke in first, pleading to look into the sacks. "Why can't we look? Where is the harm?"

"Please humor me," I said. "We shall have full explanations soon, but I want to wait for the others. It's cold. I'll mull some wine."

"Mull some wine?" Harvey stared at me. "Well, I'll be . . . !" For once, it seemed, I had impressed him. "Hot drinks because the air's chilly? Now?" He pointed at the sacks on the table and then threw himself into the basket chair and for the first time since I had known him abandoned himself to laughter.

"Mistress Blanchard," said Hugh Arnold solemnly, "if I had three hundred pounds a year and a farm, and you didn't have a husband living, I'd ask you to marry me. Not one young woman in fifty thousand would stand beside a table piled with sackloads of treasure, and talk about the weather!"

"Mulled wine!" I said determinedly.

Blanchard growled and Helene pulled a face, but I had my way and so we waited in the kitchen for Jenkinson and Longman, stoking the fire and warming the wine, in an atmosphere of mixed-up amusement, antagonism, and perplexity, until, at last, we heard a tap on the street door, and Jenkinson's voice calling softly to be admitted. He and Longman came into the kitchen, rubbing cold hands.

"There's an east wind getting up," Jenkinson declared. "That means a fair wind for England, if it holds, but it strikes cold, I must say. What's that you're all drinking? It smells very pleasant. What a good thought!"

"There have been a lot of thoughts while we've been waiting," said my father-in-law, as I poured out two goblets and handed them over. "Good ones, and some that were less good. We've had little to do but think, since Ursula here refuses to open her mouth and explain what has happened or how the boats met with an accident, as she puts it. Are you going to explain? And can we now see what's in those sacks? So far, Ursula hasn't let us do that either."

Jenkinson and I exchanged glances. I nodded. He took a sip of his hot wine and then put the goblet down, as though it were business he couldn't yet attend to. He moved to a seat at the table, alongside the treasure. "Yes," he said. "We can examine everything and have all the explanations. I'm sure of my ground now."

There was an odd silence, during which I noticed that Jenkinson had very much the air of a judge presiding over a court. Others noticed, too. "What is all this?" demanded Harvey.

"I'll show you the treasure in a moment," said Jenkinson. "But first, I want to tell you, briefly, what happened tonight. We found the warehouse. We found the treasure. We had left Longman watching the boats. When Mistress Blanchard and I went outside with the first of the sacks, we found Longman sitting very quietly in one of the boats while two unpleasant characters pointed crossbows at him from the neighboring jetty. In charge of the two unpleasant characters was a man of whom you may have heard, Master Blanchard—if you have talked very much to your ward Helene. He is or was her confessor at the Abbey of St. Marc. Ursula has also met him in the past, in England. His name is Dr. Ignatius Wilkins. He demanded the treasure."

There was a blank silence, until William Harvey said: "But you've got it there," and pointed to the sacks.

"Yes, we have. Show them, Ursula."

The worst of this business was yet to come, but there is pleasure to be had from seeing and handling beautiful things. I had never described the treasure to any of them beforehand, beyond saying that it included gold and silver plate, and at the sight of those spectacular salts, everyone gasped and reached inquisitive fingers to touch. "You just said *plate*! I didn't expect *this*!" Blanchard exclaimed, awed, as I unwrapped the glittering turrets of the gold salt.

Out it all came: the scallop-pattern silver salt next ("tarnished, but it can be cleaned," Jenkinson said), gold plate, ivory chessmen, ruby pendant, silver cup, and the remaining gold figurines, and I enjoyed seeing them in a good light, and listening while they were admired. We let the others all look thoroughly before Jenkinson asked everyone to sit down again, and with Longman's help, I once more veiled the lovely artifacts in their wrappings.

"But if Dr. Wilkins demanded that all this be given to him, and he had crossbowmen . . . ?" said Helene.

"We were a step ahead," Jenkinson told her. "Fortunately for us, and for Ursula's woman Fran Dale, who is lying in prison waiting—praying—to be ransomed, we suspected that an attempt might be made to seize the treasure. We didn't know when the attack might come. We made sure we were ready, whenever it happened. The sacks that we carried openly out of the warehouse to the landing stage—and the second load we had left lying about on the floor—were a false treasure, prepared in advance."

"We bought our imitation valuables yesterday," I said. "Longman stowed them in the hired boat. We took it all into the warehouse with us. When we found the real thing, we donated a few genuine valuables to it—we felt that a few really good items would make it all seem more convincing. But most of what Wilkins took away consisted of dishes and goblets of base metal, gilded or silver-plated."

"Not rubbish exactly, but not very valuable either," Jenkinson said. "The kind of goods people buy who want to make a show but can't afford real quality. There's more gold in just one of the figurines you've just seen than in all the thinly gilded plate that was stolen from us. Mistress Blanchard borrowed money to buy our pretend treasure. We told Wilkins we ourselves were disappointed with what we'd found. With a little luck, he will go on believing that his useless booty really is what we found in the warehouse." He gave me a mildly reproving glance. "You should have cried, mistress. You really should have wept with rage at the poverty of the find. It would have helped the deception."

"The crossbows paralyzed me," I said candidly. "But the plan worked anyway."

"You were most courageous." Jenkinson's face had become judicial again. "And now you must take up the tale. Would you tell those present about your dispute with Dr. Wilkins and what you believe lies behind all this."

It was time for me to bear witness. I had prepared my words. "As most of you already know," I said, "I have an estranged husband here in France. He heard I was in his country and sent word asking to see me. I agreed. But I was followed to the meeting by two of the men who were sent with me by Sir William Cecil, and by one of your men, Master Blanchard. The one called Searle, who has since been killed fighting. It wasn't the first time I had been followed, but it was only on that night that I understood why. My husband is wanted in England, for . . . for knowledge that he possesses and now I have learned that Cecil hoped my presence in France would draw him into the light, as it were. The men Cecil sent with me had orders to follow me in the hope that I would lead them to him, and to take him if they could. I am thankful to say that Matthew escaped. However, since Searle joined them, I suspect you were a party to the scheme, Master Blanchard. Your apparent illness at Le Cheval d'Or was I fancy meant to keep me within range of Matthew's home in the Loire valley for a while. Not that I am blaming you. No doubt you had to accept Cecil's orders."

"Yes," said my father-in-law shortly. "I did."

"Later," I said, "at the Abbey of St. Marc, I met Dr. Wilkins, whom I first came across last year in England. He doesn't like me. He accused me of having led Cecil's men to Matthew deliberately. I most certainly did not, but he refused to believe me. He threatened me. And he also noticed that Dale and I are attached to each other.

"I think he somehow arranged for Dale to be arrested on a false charge, as a way of being revenged on me. She had a phial of poison with her, because she and her husband feared being taken up as heretics while they were in France. They feared it for me, too. The poison was to be our escape road from the fire, but it brought on her the very danger it was meant to hold at bay. Her baggage was searched and the poison was found and now the authorities are claiming that she meant harm to one of the royal family. If, as I believe, Wilkins engineered both the search and the arrest, then, it seems likely that he knew in advance that the poison would be found among Dale's things. But if so, how did he know?"

There was a silence. I could feel the uneasiness, growing into fear, within one person in this room. But I could not afford pity. I thought of the horror that menaced my dear Fran Dale, and I cleared my throat and went on.

"I've been assuming that it was seen when our luggage was searched on an earlier occasion. Someone went through it at the inn, Le Cheval d'Or, when we first came to St. Marc." I paused for a moment, but no one moved or spoke. "I thought," I said, "that whoever did that must have been associated somehow with Wilkins and told him about the phial. Now, I think that perhaps that wasn't so. I believed originally, Father-in-law, that Cecil's men had done it. Then I began to doubt that but now I think that perhaps I was right after all. Perhaps you can tell me?"

"I made that search," said Harvey shortly. "In case your husband had corresponded with you."

I nodded. "But Wilkins still learned that the phial was in the baggage. Isn't that strange?"

"And how did Wilkins track us down?" demanded Harvey. "How did he know when and where to seize the treasure?"

"I rather think," said Jenkinson, "that one of us has been in close touch with him throughout our journey, and before it."

There was a breathless, chilly silence. I saw people glancing uneasily at one another. Jenkinson turned to Longman.

"Stephen, I've asked you this before, but now I wish to ask you again, before witnesses: Did you, during the journey here from Paris, have a little flirtation with Mistress Helene? Did you meet her outside the inn where we stayed when Jeanne was ill, and steal a kiss from her?"

"No, Master Jenkinson, I didn't." Longman turned a dispassionate gaze on Helene. "I wouldn't do that, sir. I don't flirt with innocent maidens, or betrothed ones, either."

Helene gasped. "Oh, Stephen, how can you tell such cruel lies? You know you asked me to meet you and—"

"I saw her myself," Blanchard shouted. "I saw her out there with him!"

"No," said Longman. "If you saw her with a man, it wasn't me. You mistook someone else for me, maybe. I'd say so if it had been me. Why not? It's no crime to kiss a young woman. But I didn't kiss Mistress Helene."

"I believe you," Jenkinson said. "But in that case, who did Helene meet outside that inn? A thickset man who might at a distance be mistaken for you, Longman—could it perhaps have been Dr. Wilkins instead?"

"No," Helene shrieked. "It was Stephen!"

"Mistress Blanchard?" said Jenkinson. "Could it have been Helene who told Dr. Wilkins about Dale's phial?"

"Yes," I said. "Our luggage has been searched three times altogether. Once at the inn, again at St. Germain, when Dale was arrested—and in between, by Helene, in the guest house at St. Marc's Abbey. Dale and I caught her at it. She had the phial in her hand when we walked in on her. She asked us what it was. And Wilkins, of course, was her confessor at the abbey."

"But I swore to you that I didn't tell anyone about the

phial!" Helene cried. She had gone white and there were tears in her eyes. "I swore on the cross." She pulled out the silver crucifix, which was as usual on its chain around her neck. "I wouldn't swear a lie on this!"

"No more you did," I said heavily. "For what you swore was that you had not told the Seigneur de Clairpont. No one mentioned Dr. Wilkins. You never said on oath that you had not told *him*."

"And you have had several chances to meet him and talk to him since then," Jenkinson said. "Have you not? Mistress Blanchard knows of some of them."

"That is true," I said. "For instance, Helene, you have twice been to church unaccompanied except for Jeanne. Once you went to the chapel at St. Germain and once to the cathedral here, yesterday. Jeanne, what happened on those occasions? Did you see your mistress meet anyone?"

"No, Mistress Blanchard," said Jeanne firmly. "I did not."

She sounded honest and convincing, but I saw Helene's round shoulders sag with relief. Jenkinson saw it, too.

"Loyalty between maid and mistress is admirable, but this is too important for that, Jeanne. I ask you again—"

"Sir, my mistress is little more than a child and she is not strong. She has been up all night. I ask leave to take her to her room and—"

"And I ask *you*," barked Jenkinson, "to describe to us exactly what happened when you went to church with Helene on those two occasions."

"By God, yes. And you'd better answer!" Blanchard was enraged. "The truth, mind. You may be Helene's maid, but the one who pays your wages these days is me. I'll throw you out into the night as you are, in slippers and shawl, unless you speak up."

"You can't do that!" Helene shrieked. "You've no right!"

"Haven't I, my lady? You may be surprised at the things that I, as your guardian, have a right to do!"

Jeanne was a brave woman. With immense dignity she said: "If I am cast out, then I am cast out. There is nothing I can do about it."

"You can tell the truth!" shouted Blanchard.

"I think, sir, that you mean tell you what you want to hear," said Jeanne steadily. "But what if the truth is that at neither chapel nor cathedral did I see my mistress speak to anyone?"

"Harvey," said my father-in-law, "and Arnold. Put this woman out into the street."

They rose obediently and advanced on Jeanne. I started up, exclaiming in protest, but Jenkinson caught my eye and mouthed: "No!" at me, so commandingly that I stopped. I already knew that Anthony Jenkinson's amiable rosy-brown face and dark bright eyes represented velvet over steel; now I felt the nature of that steel—the razor edge of it. Slowly, I sat down again.

Harvey and Arnold jerked Jeanne to her feet and hustled her out. She did not resist, or look at Helene. We heard the bolts of the street door being drawn back.

"Don't!" screamed Helene.

"Stop," shouted Jenkinson. "Bring Jeanne back. That's right. But keep hold of her and be ready to march her out again if necessary. You wish to tell us something, Helene?"

"Wish to tell you something?" Helene's face had turned from white to an angry crimson. Her eyes were blazing. "Yes, I wish to tell you something! I wish even more to do something, except that you would prevent me!" She pointed at me. "I would like to scratch her eyes out! Watching me, catching me out, and all the time she's a pawn of that heretic queen in England, and . . ."

The company was suddenly augmented by one, as Klara, wearing a wrapper and with a woolen scarf twined around her head, appeared in the doorway. She spoke angrily in her own language. I couldn't understand the words but I followed the meaning well enough. She was complaining about the noise, which I suppose had woken her up. Helene screamed at her to go away. Klara glared at her, shuffled over to the water pail that stood always by the hearth, scooped out a beaker of water, and would have thrown it over Helene except that Jeanne caught at her arm and stopped her. Helene, gasping in outrage, fell silent.

Klara said something. "She says the girl is hysterical," said Jenkinson. "That she is. No more screeching, Helene, or I'll empty that beaker over you myself." He spoke to Klara in her own language, and Klara, after muttering some further angry remarks, gave Helene a bitter look and once more withdrew.

"I repeat," said Jenkinson, "have you something to tell us, Helene? If you have, do so. But in calm and reasonable words, please."

Helene regarded us all with hatred. She clasped her hands on her lap and raised her chin.

"If I am called to be a martyr, then so be it. I am alone here in the midst of heretics and can do nothing to defend myself but I will not let you harm Jeanne. She has done nothing wrong."

"Neither has Fran Dale!" I snapped.

"The woman Dale is a heretic like the rest of you." Helene's high voice had never sounded more exasperating. "I'm not ashamed of anything that I have done. I'm proud of it! As for Jeanne, whatever she may have guessed, she knows very little. She spoke the truth when she said she did not see me meet anyone in the churches."

"That is so," said Jeanne. "Once, I thought I heard you speak to someone, but I did not see who it was."

"I made her leave me at the chapel and come back for me," said Helene, "and at the cathedral, I asked her to wait outside. That way she would see nothing and need never be burdened either with knowledge or with lies. Thank you for your faithfulness, Jeanne." She stared at me. "Dr. Wilkins told me what you are, madame; how you have twice betrayed your husband because of his adherence to our Catholic cause, and how you led men here to capture him—"

"That is a slander," I told her. "You have already heard me say that it is not true. Never would I do such a thing."

"Dr. Wilkins says otherwise. When we went to St. Marc, and I saw him there, he said he was sorry to see me in your company, but that I could help him and the Catholic cause if I would. He told me that when you married Matthew de la Roche, you were offered salvation, but you threw it back in the teeth of God and deserted your husband. Dr. Wilkins said that this time you were trying to have him seized by English agents."

"You know nothing about it!" I told her angrily.

Helene's chin went up still higher. "I trust what my confessor told me. He asked me to search your things, yours and Dale's, and see if I could find proof of your plans—something in writing, perhaps; orders that you were carrying out. He wanted to convince your husband that you were worthless! He said that while Matthew de la Roche was still besotted with you, he would never be safe from you."

"What is between me and my husband," I said through my teeth, "is nothing to do with you, or with Dr. Wilkins."

"It is to do with God, however," said Helene. The knuckles of her clasped hands were white. She was frightened of us. But she kept her head high. "I found no useful writings," she said. "But I did find the poison. I told him and he was pleased. At least, you could be made to suffer for your intransigence. He said he knew how to arrange that, but that you were clever, madame, more than a woman should be. He said you had the cunning of a snake, and that he wished to know of any schemes you laid to outwit him. He wished me to tell him everything that you were doing or planning to do."

"I can't believe my ears," said Blanchard, flabbergasted.

Helene ignored him. "Dr. Wilkins told me I would hear from him again, and at St. Germain I received a note saying that at certain times each day, he would be at the chapel if I had anything to tell him. I met him there. I told him of the treasure and how you meant to go to Antwerp. I said at first that you were going by ship, but when Jeanne came for me and called me from the chapel door, she told me that we were all to go to Antwerp, and by land. I asked her to wait a moment, that I had a last prayer to make, and I went back into the chapel. Dr. Wilkins was still there, though Jeanne did not see him. I told him of the altered plans."

"And you set him on our tracks!" Blanchard said angrily. He looked ready to burst.

"Yes, of course! When Dale was arrested," said Helene, "I guessed at once that he was behind it, but when I met him in the chapel, he told me himself. And he told me that she was on no account to be ransomed and that he meant to follow us to Antwerp and make sure that you did not bring the treasure back."

I felt too sickened to speak. Helene, however, was going on with her appalling narrative. "When we set out," she said, "you made us go so fast, madame, that I feared we would outdistance him. I tried to slow us down—"

"Oh, *did* you!" I said, finding my tongue after all. "So your weakness was all pretense!"

"Jeanne's wasn't pretense. You were making her ill. Tell them, Jeanne!"

"Yes. I am past the age for such fast riding," Jeanne said wearily.

"During that delay," Jenkinson remarked, "the Levantine Lions caught up as well. They were in Antwerp almost as soon as we were. They can only have been a few miles behind us. You may have done more harm than you know, Helene."

"I did what I thought was right," Helene said defiantly. "Dr. Wilkins told me that I was greatly privileged to be in a position to serve my faith so well. He told me to look out for him everywhere. I used to slip out when I could, and that day when Jeanne had to rest, I went out early and found him walking round the inn. He'd arrived late the night before and lodged with the village priest."

"I heard his voice," I said suddenly. "I thought it was a dream, but—"

"I met him again, later, by appointment," Helene said. "Whatever I could glean of your plans, I told him. There were trees near the inn and we tried to keep in their shadow but Master Blanchard saw us. By good fortune, he thought Dr. Wilkins was Longman, because it seems they are not unalike, at a distance. I thought it best to pretend he was right. As if," said Helene shrilly, "I would have anything to do with a retainer!"

"Thank you, mistress," said Longman, undisturbed.

"And you have seen Dr. Wilkins since? Communicated with him here?" I said. "In the cathedral?"

"Yes, I have. When I met him under the trees, he told me that in Antwerp I could leave notes at the cathedral deanery,

but that he would often be in the cathedral himself. And so
he was, for when I went there, I found him. I kept him informed of what you were doing as best I could, although I
never learned quite enough, it seems," said Helene bitterly,
and with no sign of contrition.

"You told him more than enough!" said Jenkinson. "Where
we were lodging, presumably, and precisely when we intended
to fetch the treasure. You must have been very disappointed
that we wouldn't let you come with us to find out exactly
where the warehouse was! But no doubt the information that
it was in Hoekstraat, overlooking the water, was good enough.
Wilkins and his unpleasant friends were hovering about in a
boat when we got there, watching to see which building we
went into. Luckily, they kept back a little, so that they didn't
see us taking the false treasure inside. We were fortunate, Mistress Blanchard!"

"I knew nothing of your imitation treasure," Helene said.
"You kept it a secret." She actually sounded aggrieved.

"We did," I told her. "If you had come shopping with us
yesterday, Master Jenkinson would have bought it alone while
I took you elsewhere to look at clothes and materials."

"Let me understand this clearly." Blanchard was seething. "My ward—my own ward—my own niece—has tried
to prevent my daughter-in-law from carrying out her errand
of mercy? Ursula, whatever has happened between us in the
past—and despite the task that I reluctantly—most reluctantly,
I assure you—undertook for Cecil while we were in France,
concerning your husband—despite all this, I respect your very
proper care for your maidservant. That this girl—this chit—
should attempt to ruin your efforts—I can't believe it. Tell me
I'm dreaming!"

"You're not dreaming, Father-in-law," I said. I turned to

Helene. "Dale is in a cell at St. Germain," I said. "She is there because of a false accusation. Wilkins somehow induced De Clairpont to bring that charge. De Clairpont knows it's false; if he really believed it, he would surely have arrested me and Brockley, too, and perhaps Master Blanchard here—"

"Dr. Wilkins told De Clairpont he would persuade the abbess of St. Marc to contribute some of the gold ornaments from the church to the Catholic cause," Helene said. "They are valuable."

And De Clairpont would probably sell his own mother, let alone someone else's heretic tirewoman, to support the cause. Another case, I thought savagely, of money talking with a golden voice. Aloud, I said: "Dale has no chance of a fair trial, no chance of acquittal. Only the ransom can save her. If we fail to get it to France, she will die a horrible death. You know Dale, Helene. And yet you are willing to destroy her one chance of escape!"

"Fran Dale is a *heretic*. And so are you, madame. That means that you are damned. Only the fire on earth can save the souls of heretics in the hereafter. And you are damned again for betraying your husband and for refusing the chance he offered you to turn from your unbelieving ways—"

"You self-righteous bitch!" I shouted. "How dare you sit there preaching? How dare you regret that Dale, who never harmed you or anyone else, may be saved from dying in terror and agony! Have you any *idea* what she is facing? Have you ever seen it? Do you *know?*"

"Dr. Wilkins says that whatever the suffering at the stake, it is better than suffering throughout eternity."

"I'm tired of hearing about Dr. Wilkins," remarked Blanchard.

"So am I," I said. "But Helene is now going to hear about

something else. With your leave, Master Jenkinson, I intend to tell her about reality."

"By all means," said Jenkinson. "I am not actually in charge here, even if I've given that impression. Proceed, Mistress Blanchard."

Uncle Herbert and Aunt Tabitha, who largely brought me up, were still adherents of the old religion. My mother, who had died when I was sixteen, had preferred Lutheran beliefs and taught them to me. I was twenty when Queen Mary of England, Elizabeth's elder sister, began her policy of burning heretics. My aunt and uncle witnessed one of the earliest. That was the execution that they described to me so graphically, forcing me to listen.

I had never forgotten. I never would. My uncle had stood with his back to the door to keep me from running out of the room, and when I put my hands over my ears, Aunt Tabitha seized my wrists and dragged them down. Then, turn by turn, they described what they had seen. One of the worst things had been the fierce pleasure in their faces. I had recoiled from it although I was then too young to know what it meant. Later, recalling those eager, glittering eyes and bared teeth, I knew it for the sexual excitement that it was.

I had never thought I would repeat their words to anyone, least of all another young girl. But now, for Helene's benefit, I repeated every hideous detail and when Helene, lips quivering, also tried to put her hands over her ears, I did to her what Aunt Tabitha had done to me, seized her wrists and dragged her hands down so that she would be forced to hear.

She struggled against me and tried to drown me by praying aloud that she might not have to listen to the deceits of the enemy but suddenly, Longman was there, taking her thin wrists in one hand and putting the other over her mouth, pressing her head against the high back of the settle on which she was sitting. "Go on, mistress," he said to me.

I went on. My uncle and aunt had spared me nothing and I spared Helene nothing. I spewed it all out: sight, sound, stench. Her eyes beseeched me to stop but I wouldn't. Not until I had quite finished did I nod to Longman to let her go. She at once burst into frantic weeping. Through the tears and the hiccups, she wailed that Dr. Wilkins said she would be blessed in heaven; that she had done right, she had done right, and she hated the sight of me and I would burn in hell for this.

Klara, poppy-red with rage, reappeared in the doorway. "Master Jenkinson," said my father-in-law, "you can talk to Klara. Please apologize to her and tell her that the noise will now stop, and ask her for linen and rugs to make up a bed in an empty room for Mistress Blanchard here. She has been sharing with Helene and Jeanne but I propose to lock them up in their bedchamber and move Ursula elsewhere.

"Helene, stop that bawling or by God I'll knock you on the head. Listen to me. I am appalled at what you have done. I can hardly bear the sight of you; I feel ill at the thought of sleeping under the same roof with you. I shall not now come with you to England. Jeanne will go with you, and Clarkson here will escort you both. He will carry a letter to my son Ambrose, saying that you are to be married as quickly as possible, for I don't want to find you in my house when I finally come home. I shall return to France with Ursula. I trust we shall be safe. We shall go up the Seine to St. Germain and as soon as possible, return down it. There will be no traveling within France."

Listening to that, I almost smiled. My dear father-in law; ever mindful of his safety! Not that I blamed him. I wasn't myself eager to go back to France. But Dale and Brockley were waiting for me. I had no choice.

Jenkinson was speaking quietly to Klara, who was nodding approval. "Harvey," said Blanchard, "accompany Helene and her tirewoman upstairs and keep them under guard. Ursula, you can go and remove your things from their room. Then Harvey can lock their door and bring me the key."

Jeanne led her mistress away, followed by Harvey and Klara. I watched them go, feeling, just for a moment, too exhausted to get up and follow them. Jenkinson echoed my thoughts.

"What a night!" he said. "Well, daylight's broken, but I think we had all better go to bed. Ursula, will you have the treasure stowed under your bed? You should be its custodian."

"I want to say something to Ursula," said my father-in-law. To my surprise, he was looking at me quite shyly. "On this journey, Ursula, I have got to know you for the first time. I think you already understand that my opinion of you has changed. Once, I thought that you did harm to Gerald when you ran off with him but for quite a long time now, I have thought that he chose better than I at first believed. I just want to say that now—I think he chose very well. And I am glad that, after all, your husband has escaped Cecil's pursuit. And now, Master Jenkinson is right. We had better all retire. Thank heaven we still have three days to rest before our ship sails for St. Germain on Tuesday."

Before I went upstairs, I said to Jenkinson: "I would have gone after Jeanne, you know. I wouldn't have left her out in the street."

"I'd have gone after her myself," he said. "But I wanted to see first if it brought Helene into the open. Well, we know our enemy now. But we must still beware. On no account must she get in touch with Wilkins again, and the Lions are still prowling."

CHAPTER 19

Misdirection

I woke late in the morning, surprised at first to find myself in a different room. As I sat up, still groggy with tiredness, my four hours of oblivion having been nowhere near enough, I realized that what had woken me was the sound, in the adjoining room, where Helene and Jeanne had been locked up, of my father-in-law thrashing Helene. I almost put the pillow over my head and left them to it. Even now, Dale was still not out of her cell; things might still go wrong, and in that case, Dale would scream more loudly than this.

Then in the midst of Helene's crying came a brief babble of words. "I was trying to do right! I was trying to do right! . . . oh! . . . oh!" At this, I scrambled out of bed and grabbed a wrapper. As I did so, the sound of blows ceased. Luke Blanchard said something, harshly, and I heard him slam out of the room, locking it after him.

After a moment's thought, I stepped out to see if he had left the key in the lock. He had. Quickly, I fetched a pot of salve from my little array of remedies against illness or injury on the journey. I had included them when packing for the ride to Antwerp. I had used some of the salve to help Dick Dodd when he was hurt but half the pot was still left. I took it in to Helene.

She was lying on the bed, sobbing bitterly, while Jeanne

tried to comfort her. One side of Jeanne's face was reddened, as though Blanchard had struck her, too, perhaps for trying to defend her mistress. At the sight of me, Helene snatched up her own pillow and hurled it at me.

"I hate you. I hate you. And I hate all men. The only men I've ever known who were kind to me were my father and Dr. Wilkins!"

"Wilkins? Kind?" A more unlikely description of the odious doctor would be hard to imagine. It completely took me aback.

"Yes, kind!" Helene wept. "He was always good to me. He said I was truly pious, an example to other women. He approved of me. Now I'm told that everything I thought was right is wrong. And I have a guardian and look what he's done to me! And last night that hateful Stephen Longman held me while you . . . you . . . and Master Jenkinson accused me . . . and I don't want to be married. I want to be a nun and never have to be mauled about by any man. That's what the nuns say husbands do. They maul you and push themselves into you. I wish I were dead!" wailed Helene.

"Madame," said Jeanne. "Please go."

"I've brought some salve," I said. "It will help. Here."

I handed it to Jeanne, and then took myself off. I did indeed pity Helene. But for all that, I pitied Dale much more.

Helene and Jeanne remained locked up—"and will do so until it's time to get them to their ship on Sunday evening," Blanchard said when I joined him in the kitchen, for a curious meal that was half breakfast and half dinner. The men were there as well, and Blanchard jerked his head at Clarkson. "He'll take them to the *Leopard*. I don't want to set eyes on Helene again."

I said diffidently: "I suppose she was only behaving as she had been taught."

"Aye. That Wilkins has a lot to answer for," Arnold said, and Mark Sweetapple, his mouth being full at the time, nodded agreement.

"She said she wanted to be a martyr," said her guardian brusquely. "She longed to die for the faith—she told us that at Douceaix, remember? Sanctimonious nonsense. We'll hear less about that from now on."

He sounded grimly satisfied. I made no comment. I was still too tired and too anxious about Dale. "Where's Jenkinson?" I asked.

"He and Longman went out while you were still abed. They've gone to see if there's room on the *Britta* for myself and Harvey here. I meant it when I said I would come to St. Germain."

Jenkinson and Longman reappeared an hour or so later, looking weary but pleased with themselves.

"We found the captain of the *Britta,*" Jenkinson said. Our meal had trailed on and we were all still lounging about in the kitchen and nibbling desultorily. Jenkinson helped himself to cold meat pie and a glass of wine. "We'd have needed to talk to him anyway. One or two things have occurred to me. One was that our friends the Levantine Lions, who turned up at the Leaping Fish, may think of making inquiries among sea captains in case I've booked a passage to anywhere. I wanted to make sure that Captain Ericksen wouldn't tell them anything. They were ahead of me. They'd spoken to him already."

I had been sitting in relaxed fashion on a settle. I shot upright. "What?"

"It's all right. Ericksen is one of Gresham's captains and he akes good care of those Gresham recommends as passengers. He is discreet. He told them he'd never heard of anyone called Jenkinson, Van Weede, or Blanchard and if I hadn't gone to see him this morning, he would have been in touch with me to know who they were and what he should say if they came to him again. I explained them to him. He has heard of the Lions. He will continue to deny all knowledge of us. But there's more. It struck me last night or rather this morning, as I was dropping off to sleep, that our friend Wilkins will presumably be making his way back to France, just like us, and how embarrassed we would all be if we found that he was traveling on the *Britta*, too."

We all stared at him, appalled. Mark Sweetapple swallowed a piece of cheese the wrong way and started to cough. Longman banged him on the back.

"But we couldn't!" I said. "We couldn't sail on the same ship as Wilkins! Even if I stayed in my cabin the whole time to avoid him—I can't bear him—the real treasure would be there on the ship as well!"

"Quite," Jenkinson agreed. "But you need have no fear. I asked Ericksen outright if Wilkins had approached him. I said we knew Wilkins and that there was a dispute between us and that it wouldn't do for us to travel together. I added that we needed passages for two extra people, which might, as it were, make up for any loss of business if he turned Wilkins down. He said we needn't worry. Wilkins was ahead of us, too. He approached Ericksen this morning, apparently, and asked about passages—"

"Oh, God!" said Blanchard.

"—but Captain Ericksen didn't care for the trio of cutthroats who were with him. Captain Ericksen is very respectable as well as very discreet."

I burst out laughing. "Riffraff!"

"Quite. That's what our good captain thought. He told Wilkins that he had no room for any more passengers, and recommended him to try a ship called the *St. Margaret,* which is sailing two days after us. She's not a very sea-worthy vessel, I understand." He gulped some wine. "Maybe," he added dispassionately, "she'll sink."

Jenkinson had had a further errand while he was out. He had found a buyer for two of his little gold bird brooches. Though so small, they were valuable, sufficiently so to provide us with some spare money as well as the wherewithal to repay Gresham. If we had not found the real treasure, I would have given Jenkinson the imitation one in return. Since we did have the genuine treasure, I settled with him by handing over the ruby pendant and a gold figurine, which we reckoned came to roughly the same value. We had not dared to try selling those in Antwerp, because they had presumably been stolen from someone or somewhere there in the first place.

"It doesn't matter," Jenkinson said when we discussed these fiscal adjustments. "I can take them to England and I'll certainly make a good profit on them there. Meanwhile, you'll have your collateral back by tomorrow. I'll enjoy selling these far more than I would have enjoyed selling cheap gilded plate. It's truly a pleasure to do business with you, Mistress Blanchard."

When all this was over, everyone went off to rest a little more, although we got up again for supper. The daylight was fading and Klara had lit candles. We were all still tired and did not talk much as we ate the soup and dumplings she provided. Harvey took a tray up to Helene and Jeanne. Afterward, we all wandered into the kitchen where Longman and I helped Klara to scrape platters and put them in hot water to soak.

"I think," I said as we were drying our hands, "that I must go upstairs soon and have some more sleep. I shan't feel myself again before tomorrow morning."

"We all need a good night's rest," Jenkinson agreed. "And we've earned it, what's more. But I don't think we can go to bed just now. I can hear oars outside. I think we have callers at the back door."

We all cocked our heads. He was right. There were low voices just outside, and boots were scraping on our landing stage. Someone tapped on the door. "Klara van den Bergh? Are you within?"

Klara, grumbling under her breath, went to the back door and opened it. Then, in violent contrast to the gentle tap and the quiet call, a crowd of men crashed through into the room. Klara shouted indignantly and tried to bar their way but one of them picked her up bodily and threw her aside. She struck her head on the handle of the open door, and slid moaning to the floor. The rest of us sprang up, tiredness forgotten. Jenkinson, Sweetapple, and Harvey all instantly produced daggers. Blanchard shouted: "Who are you? What do you want?" and groped for a sword hilt that wasn't there because he wasn't wearing it.

Then he desisted and so did the others, because the foremost of the intruders made straight for me, jerked me in front of him, and held me there with a knife blade against my jugular. Just, I thought crazily, as Charpentier had done, back in Le Cheval d'Or.

"Back against the wall!" said my captor. "All of you. And sheathe your weapons if you value this woman's life."

They all obeyed at once, but as they angrily sheathed their

daggers, Sweetapple said in furious tones: "And would these gentlemen, by any chance, be calling themselves the Levantine Lions?"

There had seemed at first to be at least a dozen intruders but there were actually six. Four looked like local hired bullies. One of these was holding me and from the smell of him, his more regular employment was gutting fish. The other two were different, however. They were well dressed and well armed, with velvet caps and sword hilts tooled with gold, and the big man with the heavily handsome face and the dark curling hair was surely an Italian, while the lean brown fellow whose eyes were brown, too, but not, somehow, the European shade of it, and whose beard was not clipped in the European fashion either, was just as surely a Turk.

I was not, therefore, unduly surprised when the Italian, in heavily accented but fluent English, said to Sweetapple: "You are right, my friend. But to reach that conclusion, you must have heard of us and most likely were expecting us. In which case, you have had dealings with one Anthony Jenkinson."

No one answered. The hand gripping my chin jerked my head back a little farther. I considered scraping my heel down his shin but there are degrees of ruthlessness and one can sense them. This man was more dangerous than Charpentier had been.

Klara moaned again and the lean brown Turk noticed her. He went to her and helped her quite gently to her feet, saying something in what sounded like an awkward version of her own language. He seemed to be apologizing. He examined her bruised head, added a few words in a comforting voice, guided her to the basket chair, and put her into it.

The Italian, meanwhile, was addressing me with what could

almost have passed for genuine sorrow. "We regret the need for this, signora. But alas, you are the only means by which we can keep this meeting from turning into a brawl. It will not please us to cut your throat, and I pray that God and Mother Mary will keep you and all your companions wise and quiet, so that we do not have to."

Blanchard made a peculiar noise, halfway between a snarl and a snort. Mark Sweetapple shot me an anguished look and ground his teeth loudly enough to be heard. Harvey muttered a swear word. The others remained quite still. We waited.

The Turk said: "We waste time. I, too, regret the disrespect to the young woman, although in my country, a woman who wishes to be respected is not found thus in the company of men. If it comes to the point, Signor Bruni, I will give the order if you wish."

"Thank you, Morelli." So these were indeed the two who had inquired for Anthony at the Leaping Fish. The Turk had masqueraded as a Venetian. "But let us trust," said Bruni, "in the chivalry of Signor Antonio Jenkinson. He has set out to endanger the prosperity of our countries, and he has killed some of my friends, but perhaps he would not care to kill one of his own, and a lady at that." He gazed inquiringly at the row of men against the wall. "Well? Which of you is he? Speak out, Signor Jenkinson!" He could not keep the hatred out of his voice. The *signor* was a sarcastic courtesy.

My sleepiness had been banished but I was still tired. There are, however, times when tiredness is almost an advantage. When the brain is too weary to be its usual busy and officious self, deeper knowledge and sounder instincts sometimes rise to the surface and take charge. In that brief quiet moment, I recognized and saw how to use the fact that had just been vouchsafed to us all.

Jenkinson, talking of the Lions, had described how he and his men had disposed of many of his pursuers, on the Caspian Sea, in Rome, and in Marseilles. In the stableyard of Le Cheval d'Or, the leader, Portinari, whose proper business was to point Jenkinson out and leave the rest to his underlings, had taken a hand himself, presumably because he had run out of underlings. Jenkinson believed that a second set of hunters had followed the first, and it looked as though he was right. Here they were, Bruni and Morelli. Jenkinson thought that Portinari had left messages for them, to help them follow quickly, and no doubt he had. They apparently knew he had been using the name of Van Weede. But a few important details had been missing.

These were surely the two who had inquired after Jenkinson in St. Germain, and certainly the two who had asked for him at the Leaping Fish. In neither place had they given a description of him, and no wonder. They did not know what he looked like. He was here in front of them now, and they had not recognized him.

"Jenkinson?" I said in tones of loathing. *"Him!"*

"Him?" Bruni echoed my tone precisely, with a query in it. "You sound less than loving, signora. Well, which is he?" He waved an arm, indicating the silent row of candidates.

I saw from the gleam in Jenkinson's eyes that he had guessed the tack on which I was steering. But I did not let my glance linger on him, or on any of them. I looked instead at Bruni.

"If you want him, you can have him and welcome but you won't find him here. By God, you won't!"

"Really?" Bruni's voice was disbelieving and my captor's grip tightened.

"Tell this man to let go of me!" It was easy to let it out as a pathetic wail. "Of course Jenkinson isn't here! That . . . that bastard has made off with goods that I own, worth several hundred pounds—and I meant them to ransom a servant of mine who is a prisoner in France! I can't rescue her now. My poor Dale!" The frightened shake in my voice was real. Fear for Dale was ever-present in me. I had only to give it utterance. "And if you've been asking for him under the name of Jenkinson or Van Weede," I said, "then it's no wonder you've not found him. He's calling himself Ignatius Wilkins and making out that he's a doctor of theology or something of that sort. God knows where he is now!"

They had all understood by now. "The lady is right," said Harvey forcefully. "He is no better than a thief and we've been after him ourselves. He's probably going to make off by sea, but we haven't found out yet which ship he's going on."

Klara, sitting in the basket chair, still with a hand pressed to the side of her head, asked a question in her own tongue. Sickening terror went through my stomach. Klara might not have followed the conversation. She might not understand what we were about. And she was old and frail and could easily be frightened. If they distrusted us and asked Klara if she could point Jenkinson out; if they threatened her . . .

Longman started to answer her, in short, rough tones, but before he had spoken three words, Bruni snapped at him to be silent, quelling any attempt by Longman to transmit information to Klara. The Italian then addressed Klara himself. He spoke her language very haltingly, but she could follow; she was answering. She nodded once but then clutched at her head as though the movement had hurt her. I heard her speak the name of Jenkinson. I dared not look at him.

It was my father-in-law who cleared his throat and asked: "What's she saying?"

Bruni turned to him and shrugged. "She bears you out,

more or less. She says he was here—well, that we guessed. We
knew he was traveling with a Master Blanchard, and we knew
this house was taken in Master Blanchard's name. We have inquired among landlords, who often know one another's business. But Klara says she has not seen Jenkinson since yesterday.
She says she thinks there was some dispute between him and
you."

I breathed a silent, thankful sigh. Klara, bless her heart, was
no fool. She had heard the hatred with which Bruni spoke the
name of Jenkinson and she had heard me reply, uttering the
same name in tones of loathing and rejection and she had a
little English, too. She had grasped the essentials: that these
men were after him but didn't know him when they saw him,
and we didn't mean to give him away.

"She may be lying." The Turk considered Klara thoughtfully. "How can we be sure how much English she knows?"

"There's an easy answer to that." Signor Bruni was capable
of gallantry but not apparently of humanity. He gave an order
to one of his henchman. I didn't understand what he said, but
I understood well enough when I saw the man put a poker
into the fire. I gulped in horror. Bruni actually smiled at me.
"Jenkinson is reputed to have a gentleman's manners. If so, he
will not let me hurt her. Now will he?"

My inside churned again with nausea. I pressed a hand to
my stomach and felt, through my skirt, the dagger that was
hidden as usual in the pocket just inside my overskirt. I could
grip the sheath from the outside and slide the other hand in,
and draw . . .

It would be a terrible risk. My throat might be cut before I
could get my blade out and stab backward. But either way, I
would no longer be any use as a hostage and the men might
have a chance to get their own daggers out and attack the

enemy. I could see Jenkinson bracing himself to surrender. Heart pounding, I closed my fingers on the sheath.

Klara heeded none of this. She had been sitting propped in the corner of her chair, leaning her head on her hand. Now she sighed, so that all eyes turned to her. Then she slumped forward and slithered untidily to the floor. Bruni uttered a startled exclamation and the Turk, moving quickly, knelt down beside her and lifted her head. Blood ran from her ear, and I saw to my distress that one side of her face was distorted, as though a hand were pressing on the flesh and dragging it downward.

The man holding me was leaning forward to see. For a moment, his attention was not on me and his grip slackened. I caught the eye of Longman, who was nearest to me. He understood and in the same moment, he leapt at us and seized my captor's wrist. With the knife gone from my throat, I twisted free and threw myself aside as the scene dissolved into pandemonium. Daggers appeared as if by magic. In a moment, the two sides would be killing each other.

That wasn't at all what I wanted. I knew what I wanted. I knew how to get it, too. I'd found that out in the stableyard of Le Cheval d'Or on the night of the fire. It had worked on Dick Dodd. Last night, Klara had threatened the hysterical Helene with it. The pail of water was in its usual place by the hearth. I picked it up and threw the contents over the fight.

"Stop that!" I screamed. "I hate the very name of Jenkinson! I want him dead! He isn't here! We can't find him! If you can, Signor Bruni, then for God's sake go and do it and kill him for me!"

They all stood there, a lot of very wet men, gazing at me in astonishment. My father-in-law's jaw had dropped so far that he actually looked funny. Jenkinson was grinning broadly. "Go, Signor Bruni," I said, "and find the man who is calling himself

Dr. Ignatius Wilkins, and let him out of this world before he does any more damage to decent, innocent people! Go!"

Signor Bruni removed the velvet cap that throughout all this had sat firmly on his head. Holding it in his hand, he bowed to me. "There is great passion in your voice, signora. I almost believe you."

"You would do well to believe her!" barked Blanchard. "Jenkinson would steal a rattle from a baby if it happened to be gold!"

"And he's as slippery as an oiled eel," I added. "We know he hasn't taken a passage on any boat for England. We think he might set off for somewhere else, to throw us off the scent. Go after him and save us the trouble! *Please!*"

There was a short, tense pause, during which Bruni and the unsuitably named Morelli conferred. We waited. My father-in-law, using his imagination, said roughly to Jenkinson: "I told you to keep watch at the back door. Why do you never do as you're bid?" and Jenkinson said: "I'm sorry, sir," in tones of humble apology.

Then Bruni bowed to me again. "Very well. We think, signora, that you are speaking the truth. We will be your good hounds. We will hunt down your quarry and dispatch him. Our apologies for troubling you. And"—he looked toward Klara—"we regret that. Do what you can for her."

With that, Bruni gathered his men with a gesture, and they were gone, like shadows, out of the back door. We heard them rowing away.

"They regretted that she was hurt!" I said hysterically, yanking the poker out of the fire. "They . . . I could hardly believe my ears!" I was soaked in sweat, shaking with reaction. "Of all the . . ."

"You didn't mention the *St. Margaret*," said Jenkinson.

"He may not be on it; we can't be sure." I tried to pull myself together. "Besides, naming the ship would have sounded too pat." I stumbled across the room to Klara and knelt at her side. "Oh, never mind about Wilkins! Come here, all of you. Klara is in a very bad way."

Klara's condition was alarming. She was breathing, but in a stertorous fashion. One eye was wide open but did not seem to see us and the other was closed. Jenkinson spoke her name. Slowly, the closed eyelid opened. He said something to her in her own language and in a slurred fashion, she answered.

He looked at me across her. "She didn't want to give me away," he said. "She says we bought food for her and that I cooked breakfast on that first morning, after we had kept her up so late the previous night. No one ever did that for her before, she says."

We fetched neighbors to help her, and they called a physician. But by morning, she was gone; one more casualty, I thought, of this bitter journey. It was highly likely that her seizure resulted from the bang on the head when she was thrown against the wall. But we did not mention that, or refer to our violent visitors at all and neither did Klara, although for the first hours of her illness, she was still able, in a slurred fashion, to speak. It transpired that Jenkinson had told her about Dale; and although she didn't know about the treasure, she understood that we were in Antwerp to arrange a ransom, and that our errand was urgent. She told her neighbors and the physician that she had been taken suddenly ill after supper and when the physician noticed the bump on her head, she said she had done it when she fell out of her chair.

It troubled our consciences but we accepted her charity. If we had told the truth, we could have been kept in Antwerp for weeks while the authorities investigated. Klara was beyond our help by daybreak, but Dale lay in desperate need of rescue.

Klara van den Bergh was a good woman and we did what we could. She had no living relatives, so we organized the funeral and paid for it. She was buried on Monday, with all the dignity we could arrange at short notice and we were all there except for Helene and Jeanne, who together with Clarkson, had sailed for England that morning. On Tuesday, as intended, the rest of us left Antwerp aboard the *Britta*.

We saw the *St. Margaret,* a scruffy vessel if ever there was one, lying at the quayside with stores being carried on board, probably preparing to leave as well. I wondered, very much, whether Dr. Wilkins would travel aboard her, and where Bruni and Morelli were, but I preferred not to make inquiries. I didn't even speculate out loud.

CHAPTER 20

Betrayal

Catherine de Médicis was no longer young and I doubt if she was ever beautiful, or had any of Elizabeth's spirit of incantation. But she was royal; she had style. When we paid over the ransom for Dale, the business was performed with ceremony and panache.

It also took nearly a week to arrange, which exasperated us all. Brockley was thankful to see us, but became taciturn with frustration and impatience; and my father-in-law, his nerves already undermined by the Levantine Lions and ten days of seasickness on the voyage to St. Germain, turned into a bundle of ill-temper and jitters.

His state of mind was not improved either by the alarming news that greeted us in France. The civil war was now in full flower. The prince of Condé and his Huguenots had seized Orléans, despite an order from Queen Catherine to lay down their arms, and although St. Germain was still quiet, violence stalked the rest of the land. The glimpses we had caught of it on the way to Paris had been nothing by comparison. "I won't be happy till I see Dover's white cliffs again," Blanchard said to me fervently.

But the day for which we had striven and waited came at last. Queen Catherine presided, dressed in blue velvet and seated with dignity in a great carved chair halfway along a gallery in

St. Germain. A trestle table, spread with a blue cloth, stood before her in the midst of the gallery; ladies and courtiers, all in blue and silver, stood behind her and to either side. Sunlight streamed through the tall windows. It was the seventeenth of May, and the days had grown warm.

At the exact hour of nine in the morning, the two parties came in from opposite ends of the gallery. Through the east door came the Seigneur de Clairpont, followed by a clerk carrying two scrolls, and finally by Dale, between two helmeted guards, each grasping an elbow.

I entered through the west door, walking between Brockley and Blanchard, and behind Sir Nicholas Throckmorton, who was leading the way. Behind us came Jenkinson, and after him, Harvey, Ryder, Arnold, and Sweetapple, carrying the ransom between them in two chests. I had been lent the same apartment as before and the chests were part of the furnishings. They made an impressive way to bring in the treasure.

The parties advanced toward each other and halted, a few yards apart. There was a pause. But De Clairpont and his clerk had moved a little aside, and we had a clear view of Dale. I had been allowed to send her fresh clothes and a comb, and she was in a clean gray gown and a white cap, with good shoes on her feet. But her hollowed, bloodless face was dirty and the hair straggling from under the cap, though combed, was in rats' tails from lack of washing, and even from where I stood I could see how sunken and haunted were her eyes. Beside me, I knew that Brockley had seen all these things, too. I felt him jerk forward, and gently I placed a hand upon his arm.

We waited. Queen Catherine smiled, enjoying herself, enjoying the little impromptu ceremony that she had created to enliven a morning that would no doubt, otherwise, have been full of more portentous business. "Proceed," she said.

"You know what to do." Throckmorton had briefed us carefully. "Go on."

Our men stepped forward with their burdens and placed them in the center of the table in front of the queen, opening the lids. "Show us," said Catherine.

One by one, the items were lifted out and ranged on the table, on either side of the chest. Dishes, bowls, goblets of chased gold; the crenellated golden salt; the scalloped silver salt; and the remaining smaller items.

The clerk undid one of his scrolls and came to lay it on the table, trapping the corners under some of the ornaments to keep it flat. Edging forward and craning my neck, I saw that it was headed *Inventory*. Throckmorton and De Clairpont both went to examine the objects. They handled them, conferred together, referred to the list, nodded. My father-in-law, beside me, quietly seethed. "The goods have been inspected. Clairpont sent assessors three days ago! What's all this?"

"Formalities," I whispered, and added, in anguish in case he gave offense and we lost Dale even now: "Hush!"

But Blanchard had at least had the sense to mutter into my ear, and no one had noticed. De Clairpont turned to the queen. "The treasure would seem to be correct according to the inventory made by the assessors, and the quality of the items meets the descriptions given. The value is in fact greater than that originally offered by Mistress Blanchard."

Queen Catherine asked to examine the salts more closely. More formalities: a way of giving the ceremony strength through length, as it were. I understood that, but the delay was torment. Brockley's face was rigid with strain and Dale seemed to shrink and grow more sunken-eyed than ever.

But it ended at last. Queen Catherine was satisfied. "Let the business be completed," she said.

De Clairpont's clerk stepped forth, importantly unrolling his scroll. He read out a declaration to the effect that inasmuch as a ransom consisting of (he went painstakingly through the list), approximate value ninety thousand crowns, had been paid over for the release of the English prisoner, tirewoman Frances Brockley, otherwise known as Frances Dale, the charges against her had been withdrawn and she was free to return to her husband and her employer, who would, however, be held responsible for her good behavior as long as she remained in France.

Then Dale's guards, at last, let her go and she ran to us. Brockley's arms went around her, tight and hard. I was glad to see it, and I was thankful to feel such gladness—to know that it was not diluted because I was alone without either Gerald or Matthew and might never feel loving arms around me again. It always is a blessing when one feels the right emotions without having to strain after them.

There were a few more courtesies. Throckmorton gave a short speech of thanks. I curtsied to the queen and spoke my own thanks. But Catherine was already tired of her little drama, and besides, she had business waiting. Every day now she had reports to hear; councils of war to attend. De Clairpont's men came and packed up the chests again, and we were dismissed.

With Throckmorton, we left with Dale, by the west door. "It's over," I said with relief as we made our way back toward my apartments. "Oh, Dale, we are so very happy to have you safe, and with us again."

"I'm grateful, ma'am. All you've done . . ." But Dale, half-carried in the crook of Brockley's arm, was too overcome to say very much and her eyes were brimming. Brockley murmured something soothing, and hurried her along a little faster.

"I doubt if any of us will be able to call ourselves safe until we're out of this country," he said to me bluntly. "We'll be leaving for England soon, I trust, madam."

"Yes," I said. There was, for the moment, no other course to take, but I still had the future to think about. I had had so little opportunity to make any decision about Matthew, but soon I must. Where was he now? I could hardly seek him out across this war-torn country; nor would he expect that. But the war must end one day and if he survived it . . . oh, Matthew, what if you don't . . . ? but if, God willing, he did . . .

What had he said, when we parted at Le Cheval d'Or?

Ursula, since you cannot come with me now, finish what you came to France to do. Pray for peace, so that France may grow safe again. And then—make your choice. This way, you will have time to think. Only, let it be the right decision, and the last. When you know your mind, let me know, somehow. . . . Ursula, don't leave me waiting and hoping and wondering for too long.

I would have to take shelter in England until the turmoil in France had subsided. Besides, Meg was there. For the time being, I would have to go back to the court. But when France was at peace once more . . . then what would I do? I didn't know. I couldn't see that far ahead.

Throckmorton was saying something, telling us that our journey home would be easy to arrange. "You'll be able to travel under safe conduct. You've returned at the right moment."

"How do you mean, Sir Nicholas?" I asked him.

"Ah," he said, amused. "Wait and see."

He would say no more. He left us at the door of my apartments and Harvey also took the men off, saying that they were going to celebrate in a tavern by the quay.

"The one we have in mind is hosting a cockfight after dinner," Ryder added.

The rest of us went inside. I had set food and wine in readiness, and now I left Blanchard pouring wine for himself and Jenkinson, while Brockley and I took Dale into my bedchamber. I had myself laid a fire in the hearth and put a kettle of water beside it. I lit the fire and started heating the water so that Dale could wash, and then went to fetch a tray of food.

After that, I left them alone together and went back to the sitting room. My father-in-law handed me a glass of wine and observed acidly: "You are waiting on your servants, I see. An odd reversal of the usual state of things."

"It seems right, at the moment," I said mildly.

"I've looked after my men when they've been hurt or ill, on journeys," Jenkinson said. He was at ease on the window seat, one knee drawn up and a dish of meat pasties in his hand. "Once when Longman had a fever, I sat beside him three times a day for six days, spooning milk into his mouth as if he were a baby. That was last year, on the way south to Persia. Longman couldn't travel; we had to pitch camp and stay put for nearly a fortnight."

"The other men should have looked after him," Blanchard said fastidiously. "Such menial tasks were not your business."

My father-in-law was in one of his irritable moods and was determined to bicker. Jenkinson always seemed to find it amusing but I did not. I was relieved when we were interrupted by a tap on the door. I opened it to find a page on the threshold. He bowed deferentially and said, with a creditably correct English pronunciation: "Sir Henry Sidney, madam."

Dudley's brother-in-law looked exactly as he had looked the last time I saw him, which was in the Tower of London, when Elizabeth inspected her treasury. He was as lissome in his movements as ever, his auburn beard as precisely trimmed; and

I thought he was wearing exactly the same russet velvet doublet and breeches. His shoes matched; so did the hat he was politely carrying in his left hand. He came in, bowed courteously to us all, and then gave me a friendly hug.

"My dear Mistress Blanchard! I am most relieved to find you here, safe and well and all your household with you. I have heard from Sir Nicholas about your troubles. I am so very sorry and so glad that you have your tirewoman back unharmed. Sir Nicholas said you had Anthony Jenkinson with you, too . . . ah, Master Jenkinson! He and I have met before, in England, Mistress Blanchard. Master Jenkinson has attended council meetings to report on matters to do with trade. And this is . . . ?"

"I am Luke Blanchard, the father of Ursula's late husband Gerald." Blanchard, putting bad temper aside and obviously impressed by this exalted visitor, bowed politely and gestured to the wine.

"I arrived the day before yesterday," Sir Henry told us, taking a seat and accepting the offered refreshment. "When Sir Nicholas told me your news, I said I must see you as soon as possible, but he said, better wait until this morning's ceremony was over and your woman was safely back with you. As soon as Sir Nicholas sent me word that all went well this morning, I set out to see you. Did Sir Nicholas tell you that I was here, by the way? Because I said to him that of course, you could travel home with me."

"He didn't mention you by name," I said. "But he hinted something about our journey home being made easy."

"Very easy," said Sir Henry. "I sailed over—and will sail back—on a most comfortable ship; modern vessels really do take the misery out of sea journeys."

"Can anything?" asked Blanchard.

"Oh yes, to some degree. Deeper keels, more stable construction altogether; these things make such a difference. When we arrived," said Sir Henry cheerfully, "we berthed next to a ship that I would hate to sail in. Built, by the look of her, for maximum wobble, and not even well maintained. The *St. Margaret*, she was called. I only hope her saint is watching over her; she must need supernatural help to stay afloat."

At the name of the *St. Margaret* there was a momentary pause, which I quickly covered by saying: "But what brings you here, Sir Henry? How do you come to be in France?"

"Ah. As to that . . . now, there's an interesting thing, and another reason why I wanted to see you, Mistress Blanchard. If I might . . . ?"

He glanced politely but meaningly at Jenkinson and Blanchard. Taking the hint, they picked up their wineglasses and retired into the second bedchamber. I took Jenkinson's vacated perch on the window seat and looked inquiringly at Sir Henry.

"Really," he said, "it's most odd. Most odd. I can't account for it at all. I am here to present to the queen regent a letter from our Queen Elizabeth, offering to act as a mediator between the Catholic government and the Huguenots, in the hope of bringing about a peace. It would save many lives and might well save the Huguenot cause. Elizabeth fears they will be crushed if the war continues unchecked and she does not want that. Wherever there is a country where Protestants thrive, she feels England has friends. England completely surrounded by solidly Catholic countries is England under threat." Sidney sighed. "I myself would see no harm in it if England reverted to the old religion but few would agree with me, I know. Queen Mary Tudor saw to that."

"Yes. She did."

"I see that you hold that view. Well, well, never mind. The point is that the prince of Condé has sent appeals for help to all countries where there are Protestant communities, and one of them, of course, is England. The letter I brought to Queen Catherine is Elizabeth's response. But when I delivered the letter, I learned that Queen Catherine had already received one. Mine had various proposals for the ways in which mediation might be carried out and I learned that the earlier letter was much less detailed. What I cannot understand is why there was an earlier letter at all. Queen Elizabeth is good at being one step ahead of everyone else, but there seemed no point in this. At the time when she wrote the letter, war had not yet begun. There had only been a few isolated acts of violence, and no one had appealed for foreign help."

"Indeed?" I said cautiously.

"Yes. There is normally a protocol in these matters. One does not intrude in foreign affairs unless asked. In fact, that earlier letter has done harm. Queen Catherine seems to feel that our own queen is much too anxious to help; she suspects ulterior motives and I fear that she will reject the offer I brought. But she spoke to me with some frankness; she knows I have sympathy for the Catholic faith. I learned, Mistress Blanchard, that the bearer of the earlier letter was yourself. Can you throw any light on this oddity?"

I looked away from him, out of the window, at the river. I could not, from here, read the names on the vessels down there but one of them was presumably the *St. Margaret*. I wondered again who had journeyed on her.

But it was not Wilkins who now filled my mind. Elizabeth had made such a point of sending me to France with that letter. That needless, unasked, ill-timed letter. Why?

And then, cruelly, as though the words were being written

in my soul by a cold, cold pen—by an icicle—I saw what the answer to Sidney's question might be.

"I don't know," I said to Sir Henry. "Believe me, I am not in Her Majesty's confidence to a sufficient extent. I imagine she thought she was, as you suggest, keeping one step ahead of everyone else. Perhaps it was a mistake. I did as I was told, but I am only a Lady of the Presence Chamber. I am not a council member."

Sir Henry sighed. "I suppose that is true. But I did want to ask you."

He was a likable man, was Sir Henry Sidney: competent, intelligent, far far kinder than his sister's husband, Robin Dudley, but for that very reason, in some ways an innocent. If I had guessed right, then that letter had had a very definite purpose, though not one to be discussed with Sir Henry. It was my private business.

"I need to speak to you," I said to my father-in-law. "Privately, if you will."

He gazed down at me, frowning, but saw that I was very serious, and said mildly enough: "The sun is warm. Let us go to the courtyard garden."

The courtyard garden was a good place for private conversation. The box hedges that surrounded it and edged the little gravel paths between the regimented beds of flowers were only two feet high. No one could lurk behind them and overhear us. The flowers were familiar, blooms I had known in England: golden and purple heartsease, little blue forget-me-nots. In the center of the garden there was a flowering tree and beneath it was a bench, where we sat down. Then I came to the point without wasting time for I was by now extremely tired of mystery and evasion.

"I already know," I said, "that when you brought me to France you knew a trap was being set for my husband, Matthew de la Roche. To keep me close to his home for a while, you feigned illness at Le Cheval d'Or. You knew that Cecil's men were watching me. One of your own men, Harvey, searched my baggage in case Matthew had written to me. All this, I have already discovered. But was there more? I thought that Cecil was just seizing the opportunity given by my journey to France. Now, I think that my entire journey was planned for that purpose."

"What?" Blanchard stared at me.

"I think," I said, "that Cecil asked you to seek my help in bringing Helene over; so that I would not suspect that it was his idea and that of the queen; so that I would not suspect I was to be used as bait! I think, too, that the queen gave me a pointless letter to deliver to Paris in order to keep me in France longer, to take me to the court, where Matthew might well be if he were not at home in the Loire. All to increase the chances that Matthew and I would contact each other."

I thought back bitterly to that summons after the visit to the Tower, to that apparent last-minute request to carry a letter to Queen Catherine. It had been clever. Elizabeth had made use of the massacre at Vassy to give color to it, to make it seem extra important.

"I remember," I said, "how you always shouted out my name very loudly whenever we reached an inn. Almost as if you wanted to tell the whole of France that Mistress Ursula Blanchard had arrived. Am I right?"

"Of course not!" But he had gone crimson and when I stared at him fixedly, he would not meet my eyes.

"I am quite wrong?" I asked him. I added: "I do not blame you for obeying the queen and Cecil. I have said as much before. Everyone obeys them. We have been over all that. Matthew is safe away and I can afford, Father-in-law, to understand your position. But just what was that position? When you asked me to come with you to France, did you really do so as a private family matter? Or because the queen and Cecil had ordered you to ask me?"

Blanchard's dignified face was full of resentful misery. "Very well! Since you will have it, madam! Cecil knows—a great deal. He must keep himself informed about a good many things that one might think are none of his business. He knows who all your relatives or relatives by marriage are; he knew about Helene and he knew that I wished to bring her to England."

I wasn't surprised. Cecil, no doubt, had an informant in the Blanchard household. He had them in all sorts of places.

"He sent for me," said Blanchard shortly, "and, yes, proposed that I should ask you to go with me, and told me why. Well, what was I to do? Cecil is the Secretary of State and he was acting on behalf of Queen Elizabeth. She did all she could to ensure that we would be safe in France, you know." He sounded querulous. "And it was mostly for your safety, not for mine. For God's sake, what difference does it make whether Cecil and the queen made use of my journey to France—or arranged it from the beginning? It's not much of a distinction!"

"Is it not? If the trap for Matthew was a mere sideshow, tacked on to the side of a journey for another, private purpose, that is one thing. But if the entire enterprise was a trap, with me as the cheese . . . yes, I think there is a distinction! I wonder what would have happened if I had refused to go at all. But I suppose I know the answer to that." I sighed. "I would have been ordered to go, to carry the letter. And I would have obeyed orders, just as you did."

"Yes. One does—obey orders. Even when I pretended to be ill, I was obeying Cecil's bidding. That was his idea. He told me to make it seem convincing—even to sending for a physician. When you offered to fetch one," he added, "I wondered if you were seizing on a chance to escape from the inn to make contact with your husband. I had you followed."

"I know," I said.

"When I had your luggage searched," said Blanchard, "it was because the doctor's errand boy had just brought my medicine. Harvey told me that a messenger had come asking for you. We didn't then realize it was the doctor's lad. Harvey and I both thought it might be someone with word from De la Roche. My men," he added, "are of course fully in my confidence. Sweetapple did not care for the deception and once even had the impertinence to say so, but when I reminded him that it was being done on the queen's orders, for the purpose of apprehending a traitor—"

"Sweetapple, too, obeyed orders," I finished for him. "Yes, I see. I can accept all that, though if Matthew had been caught I might feel differently. I know about orders from Queen Elizabeth and Sir William Cecil. So, I have it right?"

"You have it right. Ursula, I had to do as I was bid. Things can happen to men who refuse orders from the court. They can find themselves losing their lands, their positions, or their sons can. And besides . . ."

"Yes?"

"I was not altogether unwilling. Your husband," said Blanchard, "*is* a traitor to England. I have said that to you before. And you know it as well as I do."

"He is still my husband."

"I once said to you that, after all, Gerald chose well. One might say that Matthew de la Roche chose well, too. But do you choose well, Ursula? Your choices seem to make a good deal of trouble, every time."

"Thank you," I said. "I understand everything now."

There was no more to be said. I walked out of the garden by myself, leaving my father-in-law to stare after me. I had forgotten him almost before I reached the gate, for he, after all, was not the one who mattered. I felt as though I were looking into hell.

CHAPTER 21

White Night

I endured the rest of the day as best I could. I went to see Dale, who was sleeping in my bed, with Brockley watching beside her, and I was glad for them. I returned to the sitting room. Blanchard had not yet come back and Jenkinson was out, too. I read my book of poems for a while, and then tried to do some embroidery, which is usually a soothing occupation. It did nothing to soothe me now. I gave up, and took to pacing the floor.

I was pulled up short by Jenkinson, who suddenly burst in with Ryder. They began talking animatedly to me before they were well through the door. "News, Mistress Blanchard! Such news! Ryder came to my lodging to tell me and now we're bringing it to you!" Jenkinson was incandescent with it.

"We found out at the cockfight." Ryder was grinning broadly through his brindled beard. "You did well, Mistress Blanchard, very well indeed."

"Did well? What do you mean, Ryder?" I could make no sense of this.

"I've been told everything that happened in Antwerp," Ryder said. "I know almost as much as though I'd been there. Mistress Blanchard, a ship called the *St. Margaret* is in port here! Is that name familiar to you? I'm sure it must be."

"Yes. I knew she was here and I've been wondering about her."

"Wonder no more!" said Jenkinson. "Tell her, Ryder!"

"The tavern where we saw the cockfight was full of it, mistress," said Ryder. "The skipper of the *St. Margaret* was in there. He brought his ship in yesterday, he said, and according to him, he'd never had a voyage like it. He was enjoying himself, I can tell you. He had his audience in his palm. Most actors would sell their teeth or their souls to get such attention. And by the time he'd finished, he had half the clientele vying to buy him drinks."

He paused, teasingly, and I said: "Well, go on."

"It seems," said Jenkinson, "that he'd sailed from Antwerp with some passengers, a learned doctor named Ignatius Wilkins with three servants, and also two respectable Venetian merchants . . ."

"Really?" I said.

"Really. But although he started off with six passengers, he ended up with only three. Go on, Ryder. It's your story. I only know it secondhand, from you."

"It seems, mistress," said Ryder, "that one morning, the learned doctor and the two merchants didn't come to the dining cabin to eat breakfast, so he sent sailors to see if they were ill and they came back saying that all three were gone. The cabin the merchants had shared was empty, of belongings as well as people. The doctor had a cabin to himself—his men shared a different one—and the doctor's quarters were in confusion as if there had been a struggle. There was no blood, but everything was thrown about and the bedding was all anyhow. And that wasn't all. One of the small boats that the *St. Margaret* carries in case they have to abandon ship was also gone. They were quite near Ostend, not far offshore, and the captain put in to make inquiries. He didn't learn much, but he did discover that two men resembling the Venetian merchants had had breakfast at a hostelry in the town. There were only the two of them. But from the state of the doctor's cabin, he didn't leave willingly. It looks as if only two men reached the shore, not three. The captain of the *St. Margaret* himself thinks that."

"And so do we," said Jenkinson. "It appears that the captain of the *St. Margaret* mentioned the names of the two merchants. They were Signor Bruni and Signor Morelli."

"I take your meaning," I said. "Excuse me one moment."

I went quietly through to the room where Dale was asleep. Brockley smiled at me from the other side of the bed. "She'll mend, madam," he said. "A few days of food and rest. They did feed her, and they did give her a better cell, but she's been so frightened she could scarcely sleep or eat."

She had had much to fear. Ignatius Wilkins would have consigned Dale, living, to the flames. I would not pity him.

But I knew what had happened, as clearly as though I had witnessed it. Bruni and Morelli had crept into Wilkins's cabin at night. He must have resisted, or the cabin wouldn't have been in confusion, but they had made sure that he made no noise. If they had told him they believed that his name was really Jenkinson, they hadn't let him shout out his denials. They must have stopped his mouth, and if he was lucky, they had stopped his breath as well before they dragged him out. But they had cruelty in them, those two. It was likely; it was all too likely . . .

That they had not killed him but merely gagged him before they carried him out and threw him overboard.

Death by drowning is easier than death by fire, much easier. But it was not pleasant to think of him, struggling and choking in the bitter water as the ship drew away against the stars; perhaps swimming—if he could swim—frantically after it, knowing all the time that he could never catch it up and that no one could hear his cries for help. Knowing that his prayers would be ignored by his God; that he was going to sink under the waves, alone, in the night, that this was the end of the world for him.

Once again, I had brought about a man's death. I knew that in the same circumstances, I would do the same again, for it was my innocent Dale who mattered, and the other honest, frightened people who might now live because Wilkins was dead. But it was hard, all the same, to take it in and accept it finally as a part of myself.

Although I knew I must, and knowing it, I made a beginning then and there.

"Dale?" I said, my voice determinedly hearty. "Could you take a little more food? It's nearly suppertime."

Wilkins had been a greater barrier between me and Matthew than I knew, until I learned that he was dead. Now that I knew I would never see him again except in bad dreams, it became possible to think of staying in France. Why not?

There was a war on, but I was married to a Frenchman and France should be my country now. I could not send for Meg until peace returned; no of course not. But to go back to England meant returning to the court of Elizabeth, who had used me in a fashion I did not think I could ever forgive.

But . . . but . . . there were so many *buts*. And with that, I fell prey to a welter of emotions so violent and conflicting that I felt they might kill me.

I had loved Elizabeth for many reasons. One bond was that of sympathy for we shared a tendency to white nights and sick headaches. Both of these horrors now descended on me. I lay awake throughout almost all of the following night, only falling into a heavy doze when dawn was near, and waking, little more than an hour later, to blinding pain.

It was as though a vise were clamped around my brows, and all the bones of my skull were being ground together. Later in the day I threw up, but the pain only eased for a little while, before returning with renewed violence to start the cycle again.

Dale, shaky though she was, got up and ministered to me, bringing me the chamomile potion that sometimes helped. This time I couldn't even keep it down and so great was the pain that I hardly slept the next night, either. By the following morning I was desperate, my stomach muscles sore from repeated vomiting, and my head a ringing gong. People came to see me: my father-in-law, Jenkinson, Sidney, all of them worried and none of them with anything useful to suggest. They went away shaking their heads anxiously.

"Oh, ma'am, what am I to do for you?" Dale was in despair. "Who can help you? Shall I get a physician?"

"Don't you dare. A physician would bleed me and probably offer me something disgusting like a mouse coated in honey," I said, trying to be humorous, and then grabbed for the basin again because the mere image of a honey-coated mouse was enough to launch disaster.

I did need help, most certainly, but not in the form of potions or medicines. I needed advice, from someone solid and sensible, on whom I could rely.

"Dale," I said, "bring Brockley here. I want to talk to him."

Brockley had been nearby although he had stayed tactfully out of the sickroom. Now he came in quickly, glad to be of service. "Madame, I am so very sorry. You wanted to see me? Is there something I can do?"

"Yes. Dale, will you guard the door? I want no one to come

in, or hear what I'm going to say. Brockley can tell you all about it afterward; it's not a secret from you. But it has to be a secret from everyone else." Dale bobbed a conspiratorial curtsy and went out, shutting the door firmly after her. "Sit down, Brockley," I said, "there, on the edge of the bed, and listen."

"I'm all ears, madame." It was one of Brockley's rare jokes, an attempt to amuse the invalid. I was grateful to him. As he sat down, his outline was slightly blurred because my eyes could not focus properly. But in all creation, if anyone could tell me what to do, it was Roger Brockley.

"I've been betrayed, Brockley, by the queen and by Cecil, and in a way that I can hardly believe, except that my father-in-law has confirmed it. You know of course that Cecil sent three men with me, hoping that while I was in France, my husband would contact me?"

"Yes, madame. You told us that in the abbey at St. Marc."

"Quite. And it was with Master Blanchard's connivance. Well, I have been talking to him and it seems that things were worse even than I thought. The fact is that Matthew is badly wanted in England. He has information that Cecil wants, concerning those in England who would like to see Mary Stuart in Elizabeth's place. I knew all that, and I even understand it—but Matthew is my husband. In this respect, the queen and Cecil should have been willing to do without me. But instead . . . I just didn't know how *much* Cecil—and Queen Elizabeth—want that information, and I didn't know how far they were willing to go to get their hands on Matthew.

"I thought Cecil was just taking advantage of the fact that I was coming to France. It wasn't so. My *whole journey,* from the beginning, was planned so that I should be the bait. I was given a letter to carry secretly to Queen Catherine, but there was no need for that letter, no need for any secret messenger. The letter was nothing but a devious Tudor plot in a fine Tudor hand!"

Bitterly, I told him the whole story of the invented errand.

"Matthew knew he was in danger," I said. "He'd been taking care. Cecil and the queen hoped that if I passed close by, it would bring him into the open and so it did, and I helped it to happen because I couldn't forbear to ask after him. I played their game, Brockley, but unknowingly. And so we all came into peril, Fran most of all. I am so very sorry, Brockley."

"You were hardly to know, madame."

"No. I didn't know. I never thought Elizabeth would use me so. Never! Cecil, perhaps—but not Elizabeth."

"She is the queen, madame. To her, perhaps, England must always come first."

"I know. I understand that; at least I think I do. But all the same, to use what is between man and wife; to exploit that!— shouldn't some things be sacrosanct; even if a realm requires them?"

"I don't know, madame. You see it one way and Elizabeth sees it another, perhaps."

"All right." I closed my eyes. I was coming to the point now and in my head the pain crescendoed. "Brockley, I have to decide what to do. When I parted from Matthew, he said that when the war was over, when France was safe again, then I must decide finally whether I wished to come to him or part with him for good. Until I learned the full story of how I had been used as bait on this journey, I was going to go home to England and wait, and think. By the time peace was restored here, I thought I would have made up my mind. But now, I don't want to go home at all. I want to stay in France, to let Matthew know, and let him decide where I should live until the war ends and I can join him at his home. At least," I added, "it won't now bring me into contact with Wilkins."

"I see," said Brockley. He hesitated and then said: "You have been caught up in a dirty business, madame. I for one would be glad to see you out of it."

"I'd be glad to be out of it, too, but . . . oh, Brockley, what am I to do? I am not compelling you and Dale to stay with me; you are free to do whatever you wish to do. But if I stay in France, what of Meg? What of my daughter? She's in England. I can't abandon her! But I can't bring her here in the middle of a war either, and what if I can't get her out of England even when it's over? What if Cecil won't allow it? What shall I do? I can't look Cecil in the face; I can't go back to Elizabeth, not after what they've done to me! I want to stay with Matthew. I want to be with Meg. And I worry about you and Fran. Brockley, I think I'm losing my mind."

In speechless sympathy, Brockley handed me the basin. I lay back afterward, empty and exhausted but with the pain, at last, beginning to recede. "I can't go back to my old life," I whispered. "But Meg is with foster parents arranged by Cecil. What if he goes back on that?"

Sickness makes the voice husky. There was well water in a jug by the bed, and a cup next to it. Brockley poured me some water and held it for me. "Just sip a little, enough to cool your throat. Why shouldn't you stay with your husband, madame? That's where a wife should be. Whether Fran and I stay with you or go home will be up to Fran, I think. I shall ask her. She has been through a terrible time here, but we owe you much and we shan't forget it. Your only real worry is Meg. Isn't that the truth of it?"

I nodded and at once wished I hadn't, but the bolt of pain through my skull was a little muted this time. I looked at

Brockley, screwing up my eyes to make them focus on him, but at least, this time, managing to focus.

"Sir Henry Sidney is a decent man," Brockley said. "And he seems friendly toward you. Would he not carry your message back to England and safeguard Meg's interests for you if necessary? It may not be. I wouldn't think, madame, that Cecil would want to harm a small child. He is not a fool; he must know why you feel ill-used and in the past, has he not himself told you that your proper place is with your husband?"

"Yes, he has."

"Then try Sir Henry as your emissary, to explain that you are staying here, and to watch over Meg. Tell him that you want Meg to stay with the Hendersons. I'll go with him if you wish, and report back to you. The Hendersons are fond of her; they will have her interests at heart. If you will let me advise you . . ."

"Please do. It's why I called you in."

"Don't tell Sir Henry that you want to bring Meg over when the war ends. Say that you wish her to stay in England and be brought up there. That should please Cecil and when the time comes, it will be easier to spirit her away. You can't be refused permission if you never ask it!"

"Just in case Cecil chooses to use her as bait, to get me back?" I said.

"Something like that, madam. Madam, how do you mean to get in touch with Matthew de la Roche? Do you know where he is?"

"No," I said. I leaned back on my pillows. My headache was receding, receding, like a tide ebbing down a beach. Brockley had done his office. He had cleared my muddled thoughts. I could release myself from a way of life that was harming me. No more men should take poison or drown or face the gallows because of me. Instead, I would be with Matthew; in time, I would have Meg as well. It would be all right. And I would make the Seigneur de Clairpont help.

The Seigneur de Clairpont, unlike Dr. Wilkins, had not actually tried to stop me from rescuing Dale. But in return for the treasure of St. Marc's Abbey, he had connived at her destruction. I remembered the golden candlesticks in the abbey, and the golden Virgin and Child. Pretty things, precious things, and perhaps other treasures had gone with them, but they were not worth Dale's life. If De Clairpont thought they were, then I didn't want to set eyes on him ever again. The mere idea of it made my head throb anew. But I could use an intermediary.

"The Seigneur de Clairpont is in St. Germain," I said. "I think he may know where Matthew is and if he doesn't, I'm fairly sure he can find out. I don't wish to talk to him—but Nicholas Throckmorton could make the inquiry for me. I shall be better by tomorrow. Here's a task for you, Brockley. Get word to Sir Nicholas, and ask if he will come to see me, on an urgent private matter."

CHAPTER 22

Château Blanchepierre

It was winter when I first saw my husband's home, the Château Blanchepierre, the January, in fact, of *1564*. In the spring, it would be two years since that white night in St. Germain. War had raged across France. Catherine had refused Elizabeth's offers of mediation; Elizabeth had sent a force to help the Huguenots and been driven back by losses and bad weather and disease. Peace did come in the end, an uneasy peace that was more like a truce, but still, it was calm of a kind. And Matthew, who had been in the fighting while I waited and worried in lodgings in Paris, thankful that I still had Dale and Brockley for company, came at last to take me home to the valley of the Loire, and Château Blanchepierre.

There were many greater houses in France, but Blanchepierre was beautiful. Though its crenellations and turrets and towers were meant for practical use, they were designed with such artistry that they were decorative rather than stern. The name of the house meant White Rock and it was apt, for like Douceaix, it was built of pale Caen stone and it changed color with the sky. When I first saw it, standing on its bluff above the river, under steely winter clouds, it was as white as frost, but a week after we arrived there, the weather grew mild and there came a glorious sunset that turned the whole building to rose and gold.

The small dining chamber, where breakfast and supper were usually served, had a door out on to the wall overlooking the river. I stood there, looking over the battlements at buttresses below, and the cliff below that, and then the narrow riverbank and the river itself, where the château was reflected. The tinted walls and turrets wavered as the current rippled, lovely and insubstantial as the palace of a fairy princess.

"Are you looking at the reflection?" Matthew came out on the walls to join me. "I know, it's magical. I've brought you a cloak. You must not take cold. This is warm for January, but there's still a chill in the wind. Have you given orders for supper?"

"Yes. Soup, rolls, fish in the herb sauce that you like. The herbs are only dried, of course, at this time of year, but I inspected the herb garden today and we shall have good fresh flavorings as soon as spring arrives."

"Excellent. I gather you have also been making yourself familiar with the account books. That is as it should be. Are Dale and Brockley learning to be at home?"

"Gradually. Madam Montaigle is not fond of any of us, but she has not been difficult, only distant."

Madam Montaigle, who was the housekeeper, looked on me as someone who had once failed Matthew to the point of endangering him, and I knew it would be years before she softened, if she ever did.

"She is growing older," Matthew said. "Next year, I shall invite her to retire to one of those cottages beside the vineyard. She has served me well, but you will be more comfortable without her, my Saltspoon. In the spring, I will show you the vineyards. You must learn how wine is made."

"I would like that," I said.

Practical matters, because Matthew, who harbored such unrealistic dreams of leading the benighted English back to the true faith, was in domestic life an entirely practical man. Here in his home, I had been given a new view of him.

I had known him, on and off, for years. We had been lovers, and enemies. I had seen him as a leader of men, as a conspirator, as a fugitive. But never before had I seen him clearly, for never before had I seen him in his proper context. I had glimpsed the complete Matthew, perhaps, at Withy-sham, the house he had briefly owned in England, but it was no more than a glimpse for his heart had not been there. It was here, in France.

Here, he was himself: a Frenchman of means under his own roof; concerned about his vineyard and the retirement cottage for his loyal but cantankerous housekeeper. This was the life that from now on, I would share. I would organize meals, welcome guests, get to know his relatives, make sure the herb garden was all it should be. I would rear the children. We would be a happy French family, just as Henri and Marguerite were at Douceaix. We had stayed with them on the journey from Paris to Blanchepierre. Matthew had said that one day they must come to stay with us.

"Tomorrow is Sunday," Matthew said. "Do you feel well enough to come to early Mass? It would look well in the eyes of my household; that is, if it won't be too much for you. The welfare of my child comes first, most decidedly!"

"The journey was no trouble," I said. "I was a little tired afterward, but that's all. You took such care of me. A litter all the way and only a few miles each day. I scarcely noticed I was traveling."

"I'm glad. I wanted to get home but I did wonder if it was wise. You have only three months to go, after all."

"I'm sure no harm was done," I said with a smile.

"Saltspoon, is anything wrong? You are being so polite to me. It isn't like you."

"I am getting used to my new home, that's all. This is where I have to put down roots. But it's so very different from anything I've known before and even you seem—different—here. It will pass," I said.

Below us, the broad river flowed westward, toward the distant sea. If one were to travel to that sea and then sail northeast, the ship would come at last to the English Channel and then to Southampton. To England.

Somewhere in England, Helene was making her life, happily or miserably (I wondered which) with my cousin Edward Faldene. Somewhere in England, Sweetapple was eating like a gannet and Ryder and the Dodds (Brockley had reported that the Dodd brothers were safely home) were serving in Cecil's household. Somewhere in England, Elizabeth was strolling in a garden or dancing or sitting in council with Cecil and her other lords, inventing Machiavellian schemes for the protection of her realm.

And at Thamesbank, a little way up the River Thames from Kingston, Meg was studying and playing in the company of the Henderson children, being cared for by Bridget, her nurse, and wondering, perhaps, why her mother had gone away to France and had never, in two years, once come back to see her.

For all my rage against Cecil and Elizabeth, they had treated Meg fairly. Sir Henry Sidney had taken my message home and Brockley had duly gone with him, and brought a satisfactory answer back. I would be much missed at court but it was accepted that my place was with my husband. They would all pray for my safety in war-racked France. The Hendersons would gladly go on fostering my daughter, and would send me news of her growth and progress.

Both the queen and Cecil had to realize that I knew what they had done. Luke Blanchard would have made a report to Cecil and he had surely told them. But they did not mention it. My message had not mentioned it, either. I sighed, a little, faint sigh, but Matthew heard.

"Are you thinking of your daughter?"

At times, he read my mind. "Yes, I am. I was wondering how she was. I get letters, of course." Meg wrote to me herself sometimes; with dutiful reports of her studies, and formal expressions of affection. If she had ever included wistful inquiries about when I was coming to see her, then the Hendersons had made her leave them out on the fair copy, no doubt meaning not to worry me. I wished I knew. The Hendersons themselves had written that she was well and happy and so had Jenkinson, who had promised, when I said good-bye to him, to watch over her when he could, and keep me informed. But I longed to see for myself. "It's so long," I said, "since I last saw her."

"The war is over now. Do you want to bring her here? She would be very welcome. She would be the eldest child of the house. I would treat her as my own, you know."

I thought of Meg with such powerful longing that I felt it must go out of me like an arrow, or a bird released from a cage, to fly over all the miles between the Loire and the Thames, to descend in Thamesbank and bear my love to my little one.

It was growing cold. I ought to go indoors. I should go to bed early, too, if I were to be up in good time for Mass in the morning.

And with that, my longing for Meg came up against a solid rock. She was Gerald's child, not Matthew's, and she was growing up now where Gerald would have wished her to grow up, in England. It was her proper home, just as Blanchepierre was Matthew's. She was safe with the Hendersons. I could go to Mass, and it did not matter because I knew very well what I believed and what I did not believe; I could go through the motions to please Matthew and still remain myself. But Meg was young and if she came here, she would be changed.

She would be taught, as Helene had been taught, to believe that monstrous cruelty toward those the Church condemned as heretics was the will of a loving God. Wilkins was dead but she would meet those beliefs, all the same. The chaplain here was Matthew's uncle Armand. He was not by nature a cruel man but even he believed those things. He said he had to; that they were enjoined on him. Could I counter that teaching?

"Not yet," I said. "I think she should not come yet." Within me, Matthew's baby, due to be born in March, kicked restlessly. The child seemed vigorous, for which I was glad. I had had a long struggle to bring Meg into the world and could only hope that Matthew's child would enter it more easily. "Not until her brother or sister is safely here and I've got over the birth. Then we'll see."

I wanted Meg so much, so much. But I was not sure that Blanchepierre was the right place for her.

I had not yet brought myself to face the further question: whether Blanchepierre was, after all, the right place for her mother.

Bibliography

Among numerous works consulted while preparing this book, were:

All the Queen's Men by Neville Williams (London: Weidenfeld & Nicolson, 1972).

A Concise History of France by Roger Price (Cambridge University Press, 1993).

Elements of Herbalism by David Hoffmann (Shaftesbury, Dorset: Element Books, 1990).

Elizabeth I by Wallace MacCaffrey (London: Edward Arnold Division of Hodder Headline PLC, 1993).

Elizabeth I by Anne Somerset (London: Weidenfeld & Nicolson, 1991).

Elizabeth and Leicester by Elizabeth Jenkins (London: Panther, 1972).

Elizabethan England by Alison Plowden (London: Reader's Digest Association, 1982).

The Elizabethan World by Lacey Baldwin Smith (New York: Houghton Mifflin Company, 1991).

Elizabeth the Great by Elizabeth Jenkins (London: Victor Gollancz, 1968).

Mary Queen of Scots by Antonia Fraser (London: Weidenfeld & Nicholson, Mandarin Paperbacks, 1989).

Paris and the Ile de France, Phaidon Cultural Guide (London: Phaidon Press, 1987).

The Reign of Elizabeth by J. W. Black (Oxford History of England, edited by Sir George Clark, Oxford University Press, 1988).

The Tower of London—900 Years of English History by Kenneth Mears (London: Phaidon Press, 1988).

The Tudor Age by Jasper Ridley (London: Guild Publishing by arrangement with Constable & Co., 1988).

The Tudor Age by James A. Williamson (London and New York: Longman, 1979).